THE LAND OF STORIES

BEYOND THE KINGDOMS

CHRIS COLFER

ILLUSTRATED BY BRANDON DORMAN

(L)(B)

LITTLE, BROWN BOOKS FOR YOUNG READERS
www.lbkids.co.uk

By Chris Colfer

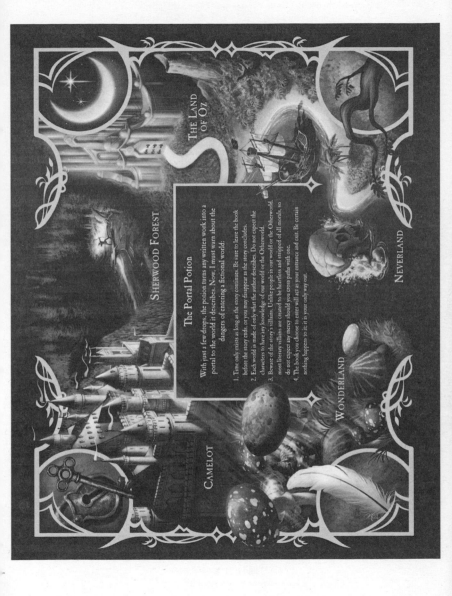

THE LAND OF OZ

SHERWOOD FOREST

NEVERLAND

WONDERLAND

CAMELOT

The Portal Potion

With just a few drops, the potion turns any written work into a portal to the world it describes. Now, I must warn about the dangers of entering a fictional world:

1. Time only exists as long as the story continues. Be sure to leave the book before the story ends, or you may disappear as the story concludes.
2. Each world is made of only what the author describes. Do not expect the characters to have any knowledge of our world or the Otherworld.
3. Beware of the story's villains. Unlike people in our world or the Otherworld, most literary villains are created to be heartless and stripped of all morals, so do not expect any mercy should you cross paths with one.
4. The book you choose to enter will act as your entrance and exit. Be certain nothing happens to it; it is your only way out.

LITTLE, BROWN BOOKS FOR YOUNG READERS

First published in the United States in 2015 by Little, Brown and Company
First published in Great Britain in 2015 by Hodder and Stoughton
This paperback edition published in 2016 by Hodder and Stoughton

7 9 10 8 6

Text copyright © Christopher Colfer, 2015
Cover and interior art copyright © Brandon Dorman, 2015
Excerpt from *The Land of Stories: An Author's Odyssey* copyright © 2016
by Christopher Colfer

The moral rights of the author and illustrator have been asserted.

A CIP catalogue record for this book is available from the British Library.

ISBN 978-0-34912-440-7

Printed and bound in Great Britain by Clays Ltd, St Ives plc

The paper and board used in this book are
made from wood from responsible sources.

Little, Brown Books for Young Readers
An imprint of
Hachette Children's Group
Part of Hodder and Stoughton
Carmelite House
50 Victoria Embankment
London EC4Y 0DZ

An Hachette UK Company
www.hachette.co.uk

www.hachettechildrens.co.uk

To my parents,
for always loving and supporting me.
There wasn't a parenting book in the world
that could have prepared you for my eccentricity.
I'm sorry for denting the coffee table with
my ninja swords. Yes, it was me.

"BOOKS ARE A UNIQUELY PORTABLE MAGIC."

—STEPHEN KING

THE OTHER SON

1845 Copenhagen, Denmark

I n the cozy study of his home, Hans Christian Andersen was busy writing at his desk.

"High up on a tree, taller than all the steeples in all the land, a lonely little bird awoke in her nest," he read aloud as he wrote the first sentence of his newest story. The soft scratches of his quill came to a halt and the author scratched his head.

"Wait, *why* is the bird asleep?" he asked himself. "Wouldn't she wake at dawn with the other birds? She may appear lazy and unrespectable if not. I want the readers to like her."

Hans crumpled up the piece of parchment and tossed it into the pile of previous drafts on the floor. He retrieved a new quill, hoping a darker and longer feather would rejuvenate his storytelling.

"High up on a tree, taller than all the steeples in all the land, a lonely little bird was building herself a nest..." He stopped himself again. "No, if she's building a nest, the readers will wonder if she's about to lay eggs, and then they'll think the story is about an unwed mother. The church will accuse me of alluding to something unholy... *again*."

He crumpled it up and tossed it with the other attempts.

"High up on a tree, taller than all the steeples in all the land, a lonely little bird searched the ground for worms..." Hans covered his eyes and groaned. "No, no, no! What am I thinking? I can't start the story like this. If I say the tree is taller than the steeples, some imbecile will think I'm comparing the tree to God himself, and make an unnecessary fuss."

The author sighed and tossed his latest effort aside. Being a writer in a nineteenth-century society could get frustrating at times.

The grandfather clock near his desk chimed as it struck six o'clock. Hans stood for the first time in a few hours. "I think it's time for a walk," he said.

Hans took his coat and top hat off the rack by the front

door and left his home. He was easily recognizable to the other pedestrians as he walked down the street. After a quick glance of his prominent nose and thin stature, there was no denying the famed author was among them. Hans politely tipped his hat to those who gawked at him and then hurried away before they bothered him.

Eventually, Hans arrived at the Langelinie promenade and had a seat on his favorite bench. The Øresund water ahead sparkled in the remaining daylight. He took a deep breath of salty air and his mind relaxed for the first time all day.

This was Hans's favorite spot to decompress. Whenever his head was filled with too many ideas to concentrate, or empty of all imagination, a simple walk to the promenade always took the edge off. If he was lucky, he would find inspiration in the land and waters to take home. And occasionally, if he was *really* lucky, the inspiration would find *him*.

"Hello, Mr. Andersen," said a soft voice behind him.

He looked over his shoulder and was delighted to see an old friend. She wore light blue robes that sparkled like the night sky. She was very warm and welcoming, but a stranger to everyone in Denmark except for Hans.

"My dear Fairy Godmother, it's good to see you," Hans said with a large grin.

The Fairy Godmother sat beside him. "You as well," she said. "You weren't at home, so I figured I would find you here. Are you having trouble writing this evening?"

"Unfortunately so," Hans said. "Some days words flow through me like the Nile, and other days I'm as dry as the Sahara. I'm afraid you've caught me in the middle of a drought, but I'm confident rain shall fall again."

"I have no doubt," the Fairy Godmother said. "I've actually come to congratulate you. We've just heard the news that your fairy tales are being published in other countries. The other fairies and I couldn't be happier. You've been very successful in helping us spread the tales of our world. We're very grateful."

"I'm the grateful one," Hans said. "When you found me as a young man, at that terrible school in Elsinore, I was ready to give up writing for good. The stories you gave me to craft as my own inspired me as much as the children they were intended for. I wouldn't have found my way back to storytelling if it weren't for you."

"You give us too much credit," she said. "You knew exactly how to adapt our stories for the current times by adding elements of religion. Otherwise, the societies of today may not have embraced them. 'The Ugly Duckling,' 'The Snow Queen,' 'The Little Mermaid,' and the other tales would have been forgotten, but you've immortalized them."

"Speaking of, how are things in the fairy-tale world?" Hans asked.

"Very well," the Fairy Godmother said. "We've entered quite the golden age. My darling Cinderella married Prince Chance of the Charming Kingdom. Princess Sleeping

Beauty was finally awoken from the awful sleeping curse. Snow White replaced her evil stepmother as queen of the Northern Kingdom. Not since the dragons went extinct has there been such cause for celebration."

"But, my dear, I asked you the same question almost a decade ago and that was your exact answer then," Hans said. "Even as a child I was being told the same stories. The fairy-tale world must be frozen in time."

"If only," she said with a laugh. "This world moves so much faster than ours, but one day, I'm confident the worlds will move as one. I don't know how or why, I just have faith they will."

They enjoyed the soothing sights and sounds of the promenade. An elderly couple leisurely strolled close to the water. A small dog chased seagulls twice its size. A father and his sons flew a kite in the field nearby, while the mother cradled their newborn daughter. The boys giggled as the breeze blew the kite higher and higher into the air.

"Hans?" the Fairy Godmother said. "Can you remember what made you happy when you were a young boy?"

It didn't take him long to remember. "Places like this promenade," he said.

"Why?" she asked.

"It's a place of unlimited possibility," he said. "At any moment, anyone or anything could appear. A parade could march through the field, a flock of birds from a tropical land could fly across the skies, or a king from a distant country could sail through the waters on a massive ship.

I suppose any child is happiest wherever his imagination is stimulated."

"Interesting," she said.

Hans could tell from the look in her eyes that something was weighing heavily on her mind. And if her question was any indication, it was about a child.

"Forgive me," Hans said. "I've known you for so long, I'm embarrassed to ask, but do you have children?"

"I do," she said, and smiled at the thought. "I have two sons. Both are the spitting image of my late husband. John is the oldest—he's a very happy and adventurous child. He's constantly making new friends and finding new places to explore. Everyone is very fond of him back home."

The Fairy Godmother went quiet suddenly. "And your other son?" Hans asked.

As if she had suddenly sprung an emotional leak, all the happiness drained from the Fairy Godmother's face. Her smile faded and she looked down at her hands. "His name is Lloyd. He's a few years younger than John, and very . . . *different*."

"I see," Hans said. It was obviously a very sore topic.

"You must forgive me," she said with a long sigh. "I can't hide the frustration anymore. My life's work is about providing people with keys to happiness, but no matter what I do, I can't seem to unlock my son's."

"He's having a difficult time, I take it?" Hans didn't mean to pry, but he had never seen the Fairy Godmother so visibly helpless.

"Yes—although I don't think it's a phase," she said.

Once she started on the subject it was hard to stop, but Hans was eager to hear about it. He put a comforting hand on her shoulder and the floodgates opened.

"This may be an awful thing to say about my own child, but when my husband died I think something broke inside of Lloyd," the Fairy Godmother confessed. "It's as if his ability to be happy died with my husband—I haven't seen him smile since he was a baby. He likes to be alone and hates socializing. He barely speaks, and when he does, it's never more than a word or so. He couldn't be more different from John. He just seems so miserable and I'm afraid it may last forever."

A single tear rolled down the Fairy Godmother's face. She retrieved a handkerchief from the pocket of her robes and dabbed her eyes.

"There must be something he enjoys," Hans said. "Does he have any interests?"

The Fairy Godmother had to think about it. "Reading," she said with a nod. "He reads constantly, especially literature from this world. It's the only thing that appeals to him, but I'm not altogether sure he actually *enjoys* it."

Hans thought it over. Entertaining children had always been his strong suit, not fixing them. He imagined himself in Lloyd's shoes and thought of something that might get a rise out of him.

"Perhaps *reading* isn't enough," he said, and his face lit

up with a grin. "If books are what he's interested in, maybe there's a way to expand the passion."

"What do you mean?"

Hans explained. "When I was an up-and-coming writer, I was given a grant by the Danish king to travel across Europe. I traveled all over Scandinavia, through Italy and Switzerland, to England, and back again. I cannot describe in words how exhilarating it was to see with my own eyes all the places I had only read about. Words never did justice to the wonders I saw. It left a smile on my heart."

The Fairy Godmother wasn't sure what he was getting at. "John loves this world, too, but Lloyd refuses to leave his room whenever I invite him to come along."

Hans raised a finger. "Then try inviting him into a world that *does* appeal to him," he suggested. "What if you took him into the story of one of his books? He may only be mildly interested in what he reads, but if he actually *saw* the places he spends so much time reading about, I'm sure you'd get his smile back."

The Fairy Godmother looked out at the sea as if the answer to a long-standing mystery had sailed in. "But am I capable of such magic?" she asked, almost in a trance. "I can travel between realms that already exist, but how could I *create* them? How could I bring the written word to life?"

Hans looked around the promenade to make sure only the Fairy Godmother could hear what he was about to say. "Maybe you won't have to *create* anything," he said. "What if every story ever told was just a realm waiting to be discovered? Perhaps happiness isn't the only thing you were meant to provide keys for."

The thought was so enticing and so exciting, the Fairy Godmother was almost afraid of its potential. What if she could travel into any story as easily as the fairy-tale world and the Otherworld? What if she had the power to turn any book into a portal?

"It's getting late," Hans said about the ever darkening skies around them. "Would you like to join me for a cup of tea? This conversation reminds me so much of another story I've been working on called 'The Story of a Mother—'"

He looked back at the Fairy Godmother, but she had vanished into thin air. Hans couldn't help but laugh at her sudden departure. His idea must have been good if she couldn't wait another moment to explore it.

The following weeks were the busiest of the Fairy Godmother's life. She locked herself inside her chambers at the Fairy Palace and worked around the clock. As if she were inventing a new recipe, she searched for components to carefully combine that would make Hans's idea a reality. She read all the books of spells, books of potions, and books of enchantments in her possession. She studied dark magic, white magic, and the history of magic.

She slowly patched her creation together, one element at

a time, like sewing a quilt. She kept a journal of her progress, frequently referencing it so she didn't make the same mistake twice. Finally, after she discovered the correct ingredients and stirred them together and let the mixture sit under moonlight for a fortnight, her concoction was complete. She poured the potion into a small blue bottle.

As with any experiment, the Fairy Godmother needed a good test subject. She retrieved Mary Shelley's *Frankenstein* from the bookshelf and placed it on the floor. She opened it to the first page and cautiously poured three drops of the potion onto it, one drop at a time.

As soon as the third drop made contact, the book illuminated like a gigantic spotlight. A bright beam of white light shined out of the book, and since there was no ceiling, it shined directly into the night sky. It could be seen miles away from the palace.

The Fairy Godmother was so eager to see if the potion had worked, she lost all sense of caution. She clutched her wand and stepped straight into the beam of light. She was no longer standing in her chambers at the Fairy Palace, but in a world of *words*.

Everywhere she looked, she saw written text spinning, bouncing, and hovering around her. The Fairy Godmother thought she recognized some of the words from familiar passages in the book. She watched in amazement as the words spread out into a vast space surrounding her. They morphed into the shapes of the objects they described, gained texture, and soon created a world around her.

She was now standing in a dark forest of spindly trees. The *Frankenstein* book and the beam of light emitting from it were the only things that had traveled with her into the peculiar forest. She leaned back through the light and saw her chambers on the other side—*the beam was a portal!* She only hoped it had taken her to where she intended.

A flash of lightning across the dark sky made her jump. She could make out the silhouette of a massive gothic structure with several towers on the top of a nearby hill. Her heart raced at the sight of it.

"My word," the Fairy Godmother gasped. "It's Frankenstein's castle! The potion worked! I've traveled into the book!"

She left the world of *Frankenstein* and returned to her chambers through the beam. She closed the illuminating book on the floor with her foot and the light vanished, restoring the book to its normal state.

The Fairy Godmother could barely contain her excitement. She scooped up the potion bottle and ran down the hall to Lloyd's room, certain the news of her latest invention would excite him. She knocked a happy beat on his door.

"Lloyd, sweetheart?" she said, and stepped into her son's bedroom.

The room was darker than any other room in the Fairy Palace, especially at night. The palace was a very open place, but Lloyd had hung sheets and blankets around his room in lieu of walls for privacy, making it feel like an isolated tent.

The Fairy Godmother's son had a shelf of jars full of small rodents, reptiles, and insects. However, they seemed more like prisoners than pets by the way they desperately struggled to find a way out of their containers. His mother picked up a jar and was sad to see a moth had died—the same moth her son had promised to free just a few days before.

Lloyd was sitting in his bed reading *The Man in the Iron Mask* by candlelight. He was a small and thin child, with a plump face and dark hair. He never looked up from reading, even as his mother had a seat at the foot of his bed.

"I've made you something very special, darling," the Fairy Godmother said. "I've worked really hard on it, and I think it's going to make you quite happy."

Lloyd continued reading and acted like his mother was invisible. She took the book out of his hands, forcing him to pay attention to her.

"What if I told you there was a way to travel into your favorite stories?" the Fairy Godmother teased, and showed him the potion bottle. "This is a very powerful potion I've just created. With a few drops, we can transform any of your books into a portal! Wouldn't that be wonderful? Wouldn't you love to see all your favorite places and characters in person?"

Lloyd was silent as he processed the information. For a brief moment, the Fairy Godmother could see the intrigue form in his eyes as he looked over the bottle. Her heart soared as she thought a smile would surface on his face at any second. To her dismay, Lloyd only sighed.

"Traveling can be so tiring, Mother," Lloyd said, and took his book back. "I'd much rather stay here and read."

His mother's hopes had flown so high only to plummet back to earth. If *this* couldn't get a reaction out of him, she feared nothing ever would.

"Never mind, then," she said, and stood to leave his room. "But please let me know if you change your mind."

Too heartbroken to sleep, the Fairy Godmother wandered the halls of the Fairy Palace until she came to the Hall of Dreams. She pushed open the double doors and stepped into the boundless space and watched the thousands of orbs floating around. Each orb represented someone's dream, and she hoped she could make *someone's* dream come true before going to bed.

An intriguing thought came to her as she looked around: She had spent too much time *guessing* how to make her son happy. What if her son's biggest dream was floating around the Hall of Dreams? If she peered into it, maybe she would discover how to help him.

The Fairy Godmother raised her wand and waved it in a quick circle. All the orbs in the Hall of Dreams instantly froze. Only one large orb in the distance kept moving. It floated toward her and landed in her hands. She peered inside it, anxious to know what her son's dream looked like.

Everything was hazy inside, like it was full of steam or

smoke. As the haze cleared, the Fairy Godmother let out a small scream from what she saw. There was destruction everywhere she looked. Castles and palaces were crumbling to the ground and villages were on fire. The ground was covered in carcasses of every creature imaginable. It was as if she were looking at the end of the world.

In the center of all the chaos, on top of a pile of debris, Lloyd was perched on a throne. He wore a large golden crown on his head. A chilling smile grew across his face as he observed the obliteration around him. In the distance, the Fairy Godmother saw something that made her skin crawl, and shivers went up and down her spine. It was a freshly dug grave, and her name was engraved on the tombstone.

The Fairy Godmother was sick to her stomach. Now it was clear why she could never make her son happy; his biggest dream was her greatest nightmare. Frankenstein wasn't the only one responsible for creating a monster....

CHAPTER ONE

THE WITCHES' BREW

The creatures of the Dwarf Forests knew to avoid Dead Man's Creek tonight if they valued their lives. At midnight of every full moon, witches from the forests and neighboring kingdoms gathered at the creek. The meetings were strictly for witches only, and they enjoyed making gruesome examples out of those who disturbed them.

Dead Man's Creek was shrouded in mystery, making it an ideal place for the witches to assemble. Every so often, without any warning or explanation, the creek redirected itself to flow *uphill* into the forest. And every time the rerouting occurred, coffins floated in from an unknown location.

The dead bodies in the coffins were never identified, nor was who or what had sent them—not that any time was given for an investigation. When corpses were found, the witches picked them apart like vultures, taking home what they needed in jars to stock their potion supplies.

The midnight gatherings were held at the Witches' Brew, an old tavern made entirely of twigs and mulch that sat in the middle of the creek like a giant beaver dam. Smoke rose from the tavern's single chimney, filling the air with a foul odor and signaling to the witches traveling to the creek that the meeting was about to begin.

The gatherings were usually uneventful and low in attendance. However, due to a recent crisis that had taken the kingdoms by storm, tonight's attendance was expected to be much higher than usual.

Some witches traveled to the creek on foot or by mule. Flocks of witches flew toward the tavern's smoky signal on broomsticks. A few sailed down the creek by boat or on makeshift rafts. Some even slithered through the water like serpents.

At half past midnight, the tavern was fuller than it had ever been. A hundred or so witches were seated around an enormous cauldron in the center of the tavern, while the latecomers stood in the back.

Dark magic was known for leaving a mark on those

who partook of it, and each woman's appearance had been affected differently. Some witches had warts, enlarged noses, decaying flesh, or eyeballs that hung out of their sockets. Others had been transformed past the point of appearing human and resembled other species. They had hooves and horns, tails and feathers; some even had snouts and beaks.

A short and stout witch with skin made of stone approached the cauldron. She threw a handful of rocks inside and the liquid glowed, illuminating the room in a menacing green light: The meeting had begun.

"Welcome, sisters," the stone witch said in a gruff voice. "I am Gargoylia, the Stone Mistress of the Dwarf Forests. I assume we've all come tonight to discuss the same matter, so let's not waste any time."

The witches looked around the tavern and nodded to one another. They may have been a diverse group, but they were united in paranoia.

Serpentina, a witch with scaly green skin and a long forked tongue, took the floor.

"We're here to *dissscuss* the *missssing* children," she hissed. "*Ssso* let me be the *firssst* to *sssay*, whichever witch *isss* taking them *needsss* to *ssstop* at once before *ssshe getsss usss* all killed!"

Most of the tavern was outraged by her remarks. Charcoaline, a witch made of ash and soot, hit the side of her seat so hard that part of her fist crumbled off.

"How dare you blame us!" she hollered at Serpentina.

Embers flew out of her mouth as she spoke. As her temper rose, a lava-like glow filled the cracks of her skin. "We're always the first ones accused whenever there's a crisis! I expect better from someone of our own kind!"

Arboris, a witch whose hair was made of sticks and whose body was covered in tree bark, stood by Serpentina's side.

"Twelve children from the Corner Kingdom and twelve children from the Charming Kingdom have disappeared without a trace," Arboris said. "Only a witch would be stealthy and brave enough to commit such a crime, and she's probably among us in this tavern!"

Tarantulene, a large witch with fangs, four hairy arms, and four hairy legs, descended from the ceiling on a web produced from her abdomen. "If you two are so certain a witch kidnapped the children, perhaps it was one of you!" she growled, pointing with all four of her hands.

The tavern grew increasingly loud as each witch voiced her opinions on the matter. Gargoylia threw another handful of rocks into the cauldron, and a blinding flash of green light hushed them.

"*Silence!*" Gargoylia yelled. "It doesn't matter which witch is responsible—the kingdoms will hold *all of us* responsible when they're caught! I've heard rumors that a witch hunt is being organized throughout the villages. We must prepare ourselves!"

A witch wearing scarlet robes stepped forward. "May I offer a suggestion?" she asked calmly. She lowered her hood and a few witches gasped. She was a completely normal-looking middle-aged woman—and a pretty one at that.

"Hagetta!" Gargoylia said with a dirty gaze. "After all this time, you've finally graced us with your presence."

"Ssshe doesn't belong here!" Serpentina hissed.

"She's an embarrassment to all *real* witches," Charcoaline said.

Chastising Hagetta was the only thing all the witches could agree on, but Hagetta had come to the tavern expecting to cause a fuss.

"Practicing white magic doesn't make me any less of a witch than you," Hagetta said. "And I guarantee you, no one outside this tavern will care what kind of witchcraft I practice if more children disappear. Angry mobs will sweep through the woods until every last witch is found. We'll *all* be rounded up and burned at the stake. So, unlike the rest of you, I've come to present a *solution* that will hopefully prevent a witch hunt from happening."

The witches mumbled and grunted insults at her. Gargoylia tossed another handful of rocks into the cauldron to quiet them.

"None of us want a witch hunt, so if Hagetta thinks she can save us from one, let her speak," she said. "But make it quick—I'm out of rocks."

Hagetta looked around the tavern, making eye contact with as many witches as possible. She knew it would be a challenging audience, but she wasn't going to leave until she convinced them.

"I say we stop assigning blame and put our efforts into finding the perpetrator," she said. "The world has always blamed all of us for individual witches' mistakes. None of you would have come tonight if you were responsible, so let's work together and turn over the one who *is* responsible. We'll prove our innocence if we decide to *help* the kingdoms solve the mystery of the missing children."

"We can't turn in one of our own! This is a sisterhood!" Charcoaline yelled.

"It won't be much of a *sssissterhood* if we're all dead," Serpentina said.

"The last thing the humans want is help from witches!" Arboris argued.

A witch standing in the back with a large stomach and a carrot-like nose burst into tears, and the entire tavern turned to her.

"I'm sorry," the emotional witch said. "I just relate to what Hagetta is saying. I'm not a saint, but I've been blamed my entire life for things that I'm innocent of."

She blew her nose into the cloak of the witch standing next to her.

"THERE'S NO SUCH THING AS AN INNOCENT WITCH!" shouted a deep voice no one was expecting to hear.

Suddenly, the front doors of the tavern burst open, causing all the witches to jolt. A man wearing a sack over his head strolled into the tavern as if he owned it. A dozen soldiers in red and white uniforms followed behind him. All the witches jumped to their feet, outraged by the intrusion.

"Forgive us for interrupting, *ladies*—and I use that term loosely," the Masked Man said with a cocky laugh. "I've been listening to your discussion all night, and I'm afraid I can't keep quiet any longer."

"How dare you disturb us!" Gargoylia shouted. "No one disrupts us and lives to tell—"

He raised a hand to silence her.

"Before you turn us into mice for your familiars to feast on, please allow me to introduce myself," he said. "They call me the Masked Man—for obvious reasons. The men behind me are what's left of the Grande Armée that nearly conquered the world five months ago. Perhaps you've heard of us?"

Although none of them had been directly involved with the recent war, the witches knew very well about the pandemonium the Grande Armée had caused.

"This man is a joke," Hagetta said, knowing she had to intervene somehow before the witches' curiosities grew any more. "He'll fill your head with tales of grandeur about how he led an army and raised a dragon, but in the end, a dying old fairy made him run for his life."

The Masked Man scowled at her. "So *you've* heard of me, at least," he said. He looked Hagetta up and down—there was something very familiar about the witch. He was certain their paths had crossed a long time ago, but he didn't want to waste any time recalling it. He had come to the tavern with a purpose, and the witches weren't going to give him much time.

"I haven't come here to impress you; I've come here to establish a *partnership* by offering you a warning," he said.

"We don't need partnerships with the likes of you," Gargoylia said.

The Masked Man continued his pitch despite her unwillingness. "You have the right to be worried," he said. "It's widely believed that a witch is responsible for the missing children, and the villages that lost their young are not taking it lightly. I've lived in hiding for months and even I've heard about their upcoming retaliation. They aren't planning a witch hunt—they're planning an *extermination!*"

The news was heavy for the witches. Was the Masked Man trying to rile them up, or was the situation even worse than what they feared?

"Which is why we need to find the witch responsible while we still can," Hagetta said.

The Masked Man shook his head. "I'm afraid there's nothing you can do to prevent this," he said. "Even if you proved every witch was innocent, this massacre will happen. They don't want justice for the missing children; they want justice for every crime your kind has ever committed against theirs. They're using the missing children as an excuse to seek centuries' worth of revenge!"

The witches went quiet. Relations between witches and mankind had never been easy, and the missing children may have angered the kingdoms of man past the point of no return.

"You try to start wars wherever you go," Hagetta said, desperately trying to belittle the information he was presenting. "We cannot listen to this man! He won't be satisfied until the whole world burns!"

The Masked Man smiled. "There will be battles and fights, but you're giving yourself too much credit if you think there'll be a war," he teased. "Witches won't stand a chance once they're targeted—you're too outnumbered! Soon, your kind will be as extinct as the dragons."

The emotional witch in the back burst into tears again. She hunched over and vomited on the floor. "Sorry," she peeped. "I overwhelm easily."

Colonel Rembert, who stood among the soldiers of the Grand Armée, raised an eyebrow at her. Something about this witch didn't sit well with him.

"I think the Happily Forever After Assembly is behind the kidnappings!" the Masked Man said. "The fairies have always wanted to get rid of the witches, and inspiring a massive witch extermination would do the trick! I wouldn't be surprised if the new Fairy Godmother kidnapped the children herself!"

"The Fairy Godmother would never kidnap two dozen children," said one of the heads of a two-headed witch in the back.

Rat Mary, a mousy witch with thick bushy hair and enormous buckteeth, stood on her seat to get the tavern's attention. "Even if the fairies aren't behind it, I'm sure they'll encourage it!" she said.

"They want to live in a world without witchcraft!" Arboris said.

"They want magic *sssolely* for *themsssselvesss*!" Serpentina hissed.

The witches were easily convinced that the missing children had been a scheme concocted against them, and soon the entire tavern roared with hatred for the fairies. The Masked Man had the witches exactly where he wanted them.

"It's time the witches fought back!" the Masked Man said.

The witches cheered, but Gargoylia shook her head, acting as the voice of reason.

"That would be suicide," she said. "You just said we're outnumbered, especially if the fairies are involved."

The Masked Man rubbed his hands together. "Not if you make the right friends," he said snidely. "With my help, we can raise *another* army!"

The witches cackled at him. The idea seemed ridiculous.

Hagetta quickly reclaimed the floor. "An *army*? An army of *what*?" She laughed. "Besides, you already had an army, and it failed miserably. Who would trust you to handle another?"

The Masked Man jerked his head toward her. Clearly she had touched on a sore subject.

"I'VE NEVER FAILED!" he yelled. "I have spent

my entire life planning a way to abolish the fairies! So far I have succeeded in every step of my plan! The Grande Armée, the dragon, and the attack on the Fairy Palace were never meant to defeat them—just weaken them! Once they thought the fight was over, I snuck into the palace and retrieved a potion I've been after from the very beginning! Now that the potion is in my possession, the real war can begin!"

Beads of sweat soaked through the sack over the Masked Man's head. He took a few deep breaths to calm himself down.

"But before I can begin the next phase of my plan, I need your assistance," he continued. "There was something else in the Fairy Palace I meant to steal along with the potion—a collection of sorts, but the late Fairy Godmother must have gotten rid of it. I need your help finding where she put it. Once we find it and combine it with the potion, I'll be able to recruit the new army."

Gargoylia crossed her arms. "But what *kind* of army?" she asked. "If the Grande Armée and a dragon weren't enough to obliterate the fairies, what is?"

"An army beyond your wildest imaginations!" the Masked Man said with theatrical gestures. "An army that will make the Grande Armée look like a gang of children! I've been dreaming and scheming about it since I was a boy, and with your help we can bring it here. We can lead this army together and this world will be *ours*!"

The witches couldn't tell if the Masked Man was insane or if there was merit to what he was saying.

The emotional witch couldn't contain herself after hearing his speech. "I'm sorry. It's just so nice to see a man so passionate about something," she cried, and tears spilled down her face.

Colonel Rembert eyed the witch suspiciously. As the witch cried, her carrot-like nose was washed away by her tears—*it was a disguise!*

"Sir, I believe we are in the company of more than just witches!" Rembert shouted to the Masked Man. He quickly retrieved his pistol from inside his vest and aimed it at the witch.

Suddenly, the emotional witch leaped into the air and somersaulted toward Rembert, drawing a long sword from inside her cloak. She sliced off the tip of the pistol as she landed at Rembert's feet.

The witch moaned and held her stomach. "Somersaulting is more difficult when you're pregnant," she said.

The Masked Man stared down at the impostor—she wasn't a witch at all.

"GOLDILOCKS!" he screamed.

"Goldilocks, what are you doing in the tavern?" Hagetta said.

"Hello, Hagetta," Goldilocks said. "We followed you here. We knew the Masked Man couldn't resist an audience with the witches."

"*We?*" Hagetta asked.

The Masked Man backhanded Rembert across his face.

"You idiot! You've led us right into a trap!" he shouted. *"Seize her!"*

The soldiers of the Grand Armée rushed toward Goldilocks with their weapons raised.

"NOW!" she yelled.

Four figures in the back threw off their disguises. Jack, Red Riding Hood, Froggy, and the third Little Pig had been among the witches the entire time.

The two-headed witch charged toward the Masked Man, separating into two different people as she closed in—*Alex and Conner Bailey*. The two circled the Masked Man. Alex pointed her crystal wand at him and Conner raised his sword.

"You aren't the only one with masks, dude," Conner said.

Alex didn't say anything. She was clutching her wand so hard, she was afraid it might break in her hand. After months and months of agonized searching, they had finally found him. She would unmask the Masked Man and expose his true identity to the world.

"It's over," Alex told him. "And no one is going anywhere this time!"

Alex flicked her wand at every window and door, and metal bars appeared over them. The twins, their friends, the witches, the soldiers, and the Masked Man were all trapped inside the tavern.

"It's the Fairy Godmother!" Rat Mary screamed, and the tavern erupted in chaos. The witches ran around as if the place were on fire. With no exit, the disorder only grew. It was hard for the twins to keep track of the soldiers and Masked Man with all the panicking women running around them.

It was incredibly overwhelming, and Alex felt her heart beat faster and faster. She couldn't lose the Masked Man again—not after coming so close.

"ENOUGH!" Alex yelled. Her eyes began to glow and her hair floated above her head. Without Alex raising her wand, vines shot out of the ground, wrapped around each witch and Grande Armée soldier, and pulled them to the floor.

Conner looked around nervously. *"Alex, snap out of it!"* he whispered. *"Remember to stay focused so you can control your powers!"*

Alex shook her head and snapped out of the daze her emotions had put her in. Her hair fell and her eyes stopped glowing. She had been having difficulty controlling her powers in recent months, but she didn't care if the vines were summoned consciously or subconsciously—capturing the Masked Man was the only thing that mattered to her.

"You're a powerful girl, but you're going to make the witches angry if you treat them like this," the Masked Man said, looking around the tavern for any possible escape.

"I'll take my chances," Alex said.

"Very well—*so will I!*"

The Masked Man leaped toward the cauldron and pushed it over. The liquid spilled all over the floor and went dim, causing the tavern to go pitch-black. Alex waved her wand and torches appeared on the walls, restoring the light—but the Masked Man was gone.

"Alex! Look!" Conner yelled, and pointed to the fireplace. "He's going up the chimney! He's headed for the roof!"

She looked just in time to see the Masked Man's feet disappear up the fireplace. Alex dashed toward it and climbed up after him.

The witches fought against the vines restraining them. Serpentina, Tarantulene, Rat Mary, and Charcoaline broke free and zeroed in on Conner and the others.

"We will not be disrespected in our own tavern!" Rat Mary yelled. She stretched out her hand and a broomstick flew into it. She hopped aboard and flew in circles around Conner, scratching and smacking him as she went.

"OUCH!" Conner yelled. "Knock it off, rat lady!"

He grabbed her broom handle and the two of them zoomed around the tavern, bouncing off the walls and ceiling like a Ping-Pong ball.

Serpentina crawled across the walls like a lizard and lunged for Goldilocks. The expectant mother swung her sword and sliced off the witch's left arm. Goldilocks looked at the severed arm on the floor and burst into tears.

"I'm so sorry!" she sobbed, but her tears quickly disappeared. "Wait a second, no I'm not! *Damn these hormones!"*

It was a good thing she came to her senses, because

Serpentina's arm grew back almost instantaneously. Her tongue rolled out of her mouth and whirled around Goldilocks like a slimy red whip. It wrapped around Goldilocks's foot and jerked her to the ground.

Jack ran across the tavern to help his wife, but Arboris stood in his way. Hundreds of insects crawled out of the witch's tree-bark skin and attacked him, biting and stinging him all over his body. He dropped to the floor and rolled around, frantically brushing them off.

Tarantulene had her sights set on Froggy. She chased him around the tavern, firing blasts of web at him as they ran.

"I hate spiders! I hate spiders!" Froggy shouted as he leaped away from her. "I can't believe I agreed to do this tonight! I have a kingdom to run!"

Instead of running to her friends' aid, Red had a seat with the third Little Pig and placed a thick binder between them.

"Since everyone is busy, I think we should take this moment to plan the final details of the wedding," she said cheerfully, and flipped through the binder.

"Of course, Your Former and Future Majesty," the third Little Pig said.

"Darling! I don't think this is a good time to plan our wedding!" Froggy said, barely dodging the web being shot at him.

"The wedding is *days* away, Charlie!" Red said. "We've spent so much time helping the twins track down the

Masked Man, I've barely had time to plan anything! Now let's see, oh yes, I have to pick out the right fabric for the tablecloths. . . ."

She pulled out three samples of red fabric that were tucked neatly in the binder.

"What do you think, sweetheart? Should we go with the rubyrock, the blushington, or the blood-blossom?" she asked, and held up the samples to show him.

A rogue string of web shot toward Red, knocking a fabric sample out of her hand and sticking it to the wall.

"Oh, nice suggestion!" she said. "Rubyrock it is!"

"Yes, ma'am," the third Little Pig said, and took note of the decision in a small pad.

Conner couldn't hold on to the broomstick any longer. He let go and he and Rat Mary spun in opposite directions. Rat Mary crashed into Serpentina just as she was about to pounce on Goldilocks, and they both hit the floor.

Conner landed on top of Charcoaline. The witch roared at him and her entire body glowed from the lava building up inside her. She opened her mouth and a fiery jet erupted from it like a dragon. Conner dove behind the sideways cauldron, barely missing the inferno.

"I could use a little help over here! Things are getting heated!" Conner yelled to his friends.

Hagetta kneeled down and placed an open palm on the floor. She closed her eyes and concentrated. A rumbling traveled from directly beneath Hagetta to under Charcoaline. A geyser of water shot out of the ground under her, blasting her to the other side of the tavern. Hagetta redirected the rumbling and another geyser erupted under Arboris, sending her across the tavern, too.

Goldilocks ran to Jack's side and helped him brush the insects off of his body. She suddenly hunched over in pain.

"Goldie, are you all right?" Jack asked.

"The baby is kicking," she said. "I think it wants to join the fight. Boy or girl, it sure has a strong kick."

"Just like its mother," Jack said with a smile.

At the other side of the tavern, Red was losing patience with Froggy.

"What should we use as the centerpiece for the tables?" Red asked. "Candles or flowers?"

There was no response. Froggy was still frantically jumping away from Tarantulene. He was panting and slowing down. Each shot of web the witch aimed at him was a closer call than the one before.

"Charlie, why do I feel like I'm the only one who cares about this wedding?" she asked. "The least you can do is give me an answer."

She looked over her shoulder and saw that Froggy was stuck to a wall, twisted in Tarantulene's sticky web. The spider witch walked toward him with her fangs exposed. Froggy turned a shade of pale green.

"I won't taste good!" Froggy yelled.

"Nice try, but frog is my favorite!" Tarantulene growled.

Just as she was about to sink her fangs into him, Red hit her over the head with a chair. The witch fell to the floor and didn't move.

"Well done, darling!" Froggy cheered.

Red dragged the chair close to him and had a seat. "Charlie, since I finally have you pinned down for a moment, I think now is a good time to talk about the guest list."

Froggy sighed. There was no avoiding the wedding plans now.

Meanwhile, the Masked Man crawled through the opening of the chimney and stepped onto the roof. He ran along the edge, looking for a way down. Alex was right behind him, but as she squeezed through the top of the chimney, her arms became trapped at her sides and she couldn't reach her wand.

The Masked Man got to his hands and knees and carefully started climbing down to the ground.

"YOU'RE NOT ESCAPING THIS TIME!" Alex yelled. Just as they had before, her eyes glowed and her hair floated above her. Suddenly, the entire tavern began to sway. It rocked back and forth, then departed from the creek entirely and rose into the air like a giant balloon.

"Alex! I hope you're doing this on purpose!" Conner said. When there was no response, he crawled up the chimney after her.

The tavern floated higher and higher into the air, flying

above the trees of the Dwarf Forests and into the clouds. The chimney around Alex broke away brick by brick and she was freed. There was no way the Masked Man could escape. This was finally Alex's chance to ask him about what she had been obsessing over for months.

"Just tell me *why*!" she said. "Why did you lie to us? Why did you pretend to be dead?"

"Life would be so dull if we knew all the answers," the Masked Man said, eyeing the ground below as it disappeared from view.

"How could you do this to your own family?" she asked desperately. "We loved you!"

The Masked Man laughed. "You're learning it the hard way, just like I had to," he said. "There is no such thing as *love*. Families are just strangers who share blood. They claim to love you unconditionally, but in the end, they always betray you the most. My mother taught me that lesson, and now you're learning it from me."

Alex shook her head. "You're sick," she said. "I don't know how you ended up like this, but Conner and I can help you!" She extended an open hand, but the Masked Man just glared at it.

Conner crawled through the broken chimney and cautiously joined his sister's side.

"Alex, are you taking us to the moon?" he said.

They were thousands of feet in the air now, well above the clouds. Alex hadn't noticed how high the tavern had floated, and she didn't care.

"Face it, you don't have a choice," Alex told the Masked Man. "There's only one way down and you're coming with us!"

The Masked Man reached into his jacket pocket and pulled out a small book with a gold cover and a blue potion bottle. Alex immediately recognized the small vial as the bottle he stole from the Fairy Palace.

"You're wrong," he said softly. "There's always a choice."

The Masked Man rolled off the roof and plummeted back to the earth. The twins screamed and ran to the edge of the roof to look over it. The Masked Man fell through the clouds below and disappeared from sight.

"I can't believe it!" Conner said. *"He killed himself!"*

Alex shook her head in disbelief. *"No!"* she said. "It wasn't supposed to end this way! We were supposed to help him!"

A thousand feelings spiraled through her like an emotional tornado. She was so overwhelmed that she could barely focus on anything. Her hair fell back into place and her eyes returned to normal.

The tavern suddenly dropped through the sky. The twins and everyone inside the tavern began to scream. Conner held on to the broken chimney with one hand and his sister with the other so they wouldn't fly off it.

Pieces of the tavern broke off as it fell. A large chunk of the roof flew off and the twins could see their friends inside, holding on to anything they could.

"I'd like to get married in one piece, please!" Red screamed.

"Alex! Do something!" Conner yelled at her.

It was hard for Alex to get a grip on her wand as they fell. When she did, she raised it above her head and cracked it like a whip just before they reached the ground. As if the tavern were connected to an invisible bungee cord, it jerked back upward and then crashed on top of Dead Man's Creek—imploding into a large pile of sticks.

"Is everyone alive?" Conner asked as he and Alex brushed the debris off themselves.

Their friends, the soldiers, and all the witches moaned—everyone was covered in bits of the former tavern. Goldilocks sat up and vomited again.

"Is that from the baby or the drop?" Jack asked.

"I'm not sure," Goldilocks said.

Gargoylia roared, still fighting the vines wrapped around her. "You've destroyed our tavern!" she yelled. "You'll pay for this!"

"Bill us," Conner said, and helped his sister and friends to their feet.

"What happened to the Masked Man?" Froggy asked.

Conner looked at Alex, but she couldn't bring herself to say it. Her friends had given up months of their lives to help her search for the Masked Man, only to go home with nothing. The guilt was unbearable, and Alex felt like her life was just as wrecked as the tavern.

"He's gone," Conner told the others. "Like, *really gone*."

Within the hour, Sir Lampton and a small fleet of Charming Kingdom soldiers joined them at the wrecked tavern. They had been stationed in the woods nearby in case the twins needed them. They rounded up the remaining Grande Armée soldiers and the witches and put all of them in restraints.

Alex sat on a boulder by the creek decompressing from the night's events. Conner walked over to her and put a hand on her shoulder.

"If anything good comes from tonight, at least we know none of these witches are behind the missing children," he said.

Although she would never admit it, the missing children couldn't be further from her mind.

"I never expected he would rather take his own life than face us," she said. "I never would have made the tavern float if I thought he'd jump."

"But did *you* actually make the tavern float, or did it just *happen*?" Conner asked. "A lot of things have just been *happening* lately."

Alex rolled her eyes and walked away from him, but he followed her.

"Ever since you saw the Masked Man's face, you've been having a difficult time controlling your powers," he said. "It's just something you should be careful of—"

"Why are you still calling him the Masked Man?" Alex yelled. "He's our *father*, Conner! I know what I saw! Why don't you believe me?"

"I wouldn't have spent the last five months helping you search for him if I didn't believe you saw *something*," he said. "I just can't fully accept that he's our father until I see his face for myself."

Alex sighed. "Well, he's dead, so neither of us has to worry about him ever again," she said. "I just wish I could have gotten to him in time to help him—to change him back to the man we knew."

Conner nodded. "Now you can just focus on fixing yourself."

He wasn't nearly as upset as his sister, because in truth, he had never believed that the Masked Man was their father. No matter how many times she reenacted the story, he knew their dad could never do what the Masked Man had done to the fairy-tale world. Although, Conner could never bring himself to tell his sister how he really felt.

"What should we do about the Grande Armée and the witches?" Sir Lampton called out to the twins.

"Take the Grande Armée soldiers to Pinocchio Prison," Alex instructed. "But let the witches go—I want to set the record straight that I have nothing against them."

"Yes, Fairy Godmother," Sir Lampton said.

A Charming Kingdom soldier emerged from the woods and ran to Sir Lampton's side.

"Sir, we searched the forest, but there is no sign of the Masked Man," he said. "We searched the area we were certain he had fallen to, but we didn't find his body or any trace of him."

Alex and Conner looked at each other in shock.

"What?" Alex said. "Could he be alive?"

"How could he have survived the fall?" Conner asked.

Alex's eyes darted around the creek and landed on Colonel Rembert. She charged toward him. Her eyes began to glow and her hair floated above her head. Once again, her anger had taken control.

"Alex? What are you doing?" Conner asked, and ran after her.

Before he could stop her, the trees around the creek suddenly came to life. They grabbed every person at the creek except for Alex with their branches and held them tightly to their trunks. Conner, his friends, the witches, and the soldiers of the Grande Armée and Charming Kingdom were all prisoners of Alex's subconscious.

The tree holding Colonel Rembert detached itself from the ground and held him in the air in front of Alex.

"How did he survive the fall? You must know!" she yelled.

"I assure you, mademoiselle, I do not," he said.

The tree tightened its grip around his body—but it wasn't the only one. All the trees at the creek squeezed their captives tighter.

"Alex! Calm down! You're hurting us!" Conner pleaded.

His sister was practically in a trance—he had never seen her so angry. Nothing existed around her but Colonel Rembert and the answers she needed from him.

"What does the potion he stole from the Fairy Palace

do?" Alex asked. "And what else does he need to recruit the army he spoke of?"

"He never told us!" Rembert said. "He was very secretive!"

The branches wrapped around Rembert's throat and choked him.

"Then you must know where he's headed!" Alex exclaimed. *"Tell me!"*

Rembert was gagging and could barely speak. "I... don't... know..." He coughed. "I swear!"

"ALEX, KNOCK IT OFF!" Conner screamed.

Alex came to her senses and the trees returned to normal, dropping their captives to the ground. She looked around the creek in bewilderment at what she had just caused—it was like she had become another person entirely.

Her brother and her friends all stared at her in shock. None of them, including Alex, knew she was capable of such a thing.

"I'm so sorry!" Alex said, and tears came to her eyes. "I don't know what came over me!"

She covered her face and ran into the forest. Her brother didn't even try following her; it was obvious she wanted to be alone.

"I'm afraid our search for the Masked Man is far from over," Froggy said, breaking the tension.

Conner nodded, but continuing their search for the Masked Man wasn't what any of them were afraid of—*they were afraid of his sister.*

CHAPTER TWO

"DO YOU ACCEPT
THE CHARGES?"

E mmerich Himmelsbach stood at the kitchen sink
washing stroganoff stains off a stack of plates. It was
the hundred and forty-sixth night in a row he had
washed dishes (not that he was counting), and if his mother
was serious when she punished him, Emmerich had about
two thousand more nights to go.

As far as Frau Himmelsbach knew, five months ago
Emmerich ran off with an American delinquent for a few
days of childish fun. When he returned, he was scolded,

lectured, stripped of all privileges, and given dish duty until he was old enough to leave home. But Emmerich thought it was a small price to pay for embarking on what he considered *the adventure of a lifetime*. And having to keep the truth of his excursion a total secret proved to be the real punishment.

Emmerich spent every moment of every day thinking about the amazing people he met and all the incredible places he saw in the fairy-tale world. He desperately wished he could talk about his adventures with someone, but the only person he could safely reminisce with lived on the other side of the globe.

He was halfway through the dishes when the kitchen phone started ringing. Emmerich didn't answer it at first, expecting his mother to pick up in the next room. After the seventh ring he dried his hands and picked up the receiver.

"Hallo?" he said.

"Emmerich Himmelsbach?" an American woman asked.

"Yah?" the young German boy replied, curious as to how this stranger knew his name.

"You have a collect call from Miss Bree Campbell in the United States," the operator said. "Do you accept the charges?"

Emmerich didn't completely understand what she meant, but if Bree was trying to contact him, he figured it was best to accept. "I guess so," he said.

He heard a click, and then a frenzied, stressed, but familiar voice came on the phone.

"Emmerich? Is that you?" Bree whispered.

"Bree! I...I...I was just thinking about you!" Emmerich said. He was so excited to speak with her that he could barely remember English.

"I've been thinking about you, too," she whispered.

"Why are you whispering? Are you all right?" Emmerich asked.

"I'm fine, but I don't have long to talk," Bree said. "It's still morning over here. I'm hiding in the janitor's closet at school. This was the only place I could find any privacy. Where are you? Are you someplace safe?"

Emmerich looked around the kitchen and shrugged. "Yes, I'm safe."

"Good," Bree said. "I've been dying to talk to you! My parents grounded me until college for sneaking away from the school trip. I just convinced them to give me back my cell phone. By the way, thanks for accepting the charges of this call—my parents would have seen it on our phone bill if you hadn't."

"I've been in trouble since we got back, too," Emmerich said. "My mother's made me do dishes every night since we got back! How bad did you get it?"

Bree sighed. "I got dishes, vacuuming, yard work, and any other agonizing task they can think of," she said. "But listen, I've really got to talk to you about something! I've been thinking a lot about our trip to the fairy-tale world—"

"It's all I ever think about!" Emmerich said. "Not a day goes by that I don't wish we could go back somehow."

"I feel the same way!" Bree said. "I've been missing the fairy-tale world so much, I started plotting a way back to Neuschwanstein to travel through the portal again."

"I wish we could," Emmerich said. "But to activate it we would need someone of magic blood to play the panpipe—and we don't have either of those."

"My thoughts exactly," Bree said. "So I started thinking of other ways the portal might be activated—which made me think about the portal itself, how it worked, and everything we learned about it—and I know I read too many mystery novels, *but I think I've discovered a major plot hole in what we were told!*"

Emmerich was confused. "You found a hole into the fairy-tale world?" he asked.

"Not an actual hole—a hole in the explanation we were given," she said. "I've been thinking a lot about the portal we traveled through to get into the fairy-tale world, and something doesn't add up."

"What is it?" Emmerich asked.

"The Grande Armée was trapped in the same portal for over two hundred years," Bree said. "So here's my question—if the Grande Armée was trapped for so long, how did *we* manage to cross through it so quickly? Shouldn't *we* have been trapped in the portal for just as long as General Marquis and his men?"

Emmerich closed one eye and scrunched his forehead as he thought about it. "But Conner and Mother Goose used the portal, too, and they never got stuck."

"Exactly!" she said, forgetting to whisper. "So what separates Mother Goose and Conner from the Grande Armée?"

Emmerich took a wild guess. "They aren't French?"

"No," Bree said. "They could cross through the portal without problems because they had magic in their blood! *Meaning you and I must have magic in our blood, too!* It's the only explanation!"

His mouth dropped open. He didn't understand how this could possibly be true, but he wanted to believe it with every fiber of his being.

"But how?" Emmerich said. "We aren't related to any-one from the fairy-tale world."

"That's where my theory gets a little tricky," Bree said. "If I'm remembering it correctly, Mother Goose trans-ferred some of her blood into Wilhelm Grimm so he could play the panpipe and trap the Grande Armée into the portal—"

"Should I be writing this down?" Emmerich asked.

Bree continued while he looked for a pen and paper. "You and I are both from German heritages," she explained. "Meaning it's possible we may be *descendants of Wilhelm Grimm!*"

Emmerich gasped. *"Ach mein Gott,"* he said, and his rosy cheeks went pale. "That would mean you and I are distant family!"

Bree was grinning ear to ear—she had waited a long time to share this discovery with someone else. "And we may be capable of opening a portal to the fairy-tale world ourselves!"

Emmerich turned on the garbage disposal so he could squeal without his mother hearing. "But how can we prove it?"

"We'll have to trace our family trees," she said. "It'll be difficult for me, since I've been grounded from pretty much everything under the sun, and I can't exactly tell my parents why I'm suddenly so interested in our ancestry— but we've got to try!"

A bell rang on Bree's side of the phone.

"I have to go," she said. "I'm already late for my next class. I'll call you back after I do a little research on my family. Try to find out what you can about yours, too."

"I will! *Viel Glück!* That means *good luck* in German!"

"I know," she said. "*Viel Glück* to you, too!"

Bree hung up her phone and sighed with relief. It felt like a ton of bricks had been lifted off her shoulders now that she had finally talked to Emmerich, but the weight was replaced with adrenaline. Bree and Emmerich were on the verge of the greatest discovery of their young lives.

She stood up from the bucket she had been sitting on and exited the tiny janitor's closet. When she opened the door, Bree was accosted by four girls she had the misfortune of sharing a grade with.

"The closet is an odd place to make a phone call, don't you think?" Mindy asked with a judgmental eyebrow.

Mindy, Cindy, Lindy, and Wendy—the four members

of the reading club, aka the Book Huggers—were lined up in the hallway waiting for Bree to come out. She tried to push past them, but they blocked her from leaving the closet.

"You guys have been following me around for months," Bree said with an agonized eye-roll. "You've got to stop this—you're starting to creep me out!"

"Who were you talking to, Bree?" Cindy asked. Her voice always had a slight vibration due to a mouthful of metal braces.

"That's none of your business," Bree said, and tried pushing past them again.

"Actually, it is," Lindy said, hovering over her like a streetlamp. "We've been appointed *hall monitors* this semester by Principal Peters—everything that happens outside of class between school hours is our business."

Wendy, who had never been known to make a sound, crossed her arms and nodded along.

Bree closed her eyes tightly, trying not to roll them again. "I don't know how you'll find the time to monitor the hallways in between the reading club and *stalking me*," she said.

"We're not running the reading club anymore," Mindy said. She tossed each of her trademark pigtails as if they had been promoted to something much greater.

"We decided to take a break from books and focus our energy on another passion," Cindy said. "So we started a brand-new club."

"The Conspiracy Club!" Lindy was happy to share. "Now our little hobby of keeping an eye on suspicious events can be an extracurricular activity!"

Bree let out a long, anguished sigh. It didn't matter what they called themselves; they would always be the Book Huggers to her.

"For the thousandth time, Alex and Conner transferred to a school in Vermont," she said. "They weren't abducted by aliens, or kidnapped by Bigfoot, or swallowed by a man-eating plant, or whatever you obsess over."

Mindy glanced at the others. "A man-eating plant? Hmmm . . . we never thought of that. . . ."

"The point I'm trying to make is that they're completely fine! All four of you need to get a life!" Bree said.

"How come everyone we talk to says that?" Cindy asked. "Mrs. Peters, the district supervisor, the police, our parents . . . they all say we need to find something better to do with our time! How come we're the only ones who realize something fishy is going on?"

If they hadn't been driving her nuts for months, Bree would have felt bad for lying to them. They were so fixated on the Bailey twins; keeping information from them was like hiding chew toys from a bunch of teething puppies.

"Well, this has been fun, but I'm late for class," Bree said, and finally squeezed through them.

"You can't go to class without a pass," Lindy said, and all four of them shared a malicious grin.

"So write me a pass, then," Bree said, but she could tell

from their self-righteous faces that it wasn't going to be that easy.

"Bree, Bree, Bree," Mindy said as she shook her head. "We've known you since kindergarten. You're like a sister to us."

"I don't want to be your sister."

"So we'll make you a deal," Mindy continued. "We'll do you a favor and not tell Mrs. Peters that we caught you talking on your phone in the closet if you just tell us where Alex and Conner are. Plain and simple."

"But you can't prove I was on my phone," Bree said. "You have no evidence."

Mindy jerked her head to the other three—none of them had thought of that.

"I've got a counteroffer for you," she said. "Why don't you write me a pass, excusing me for being late to class, and I'll tell you where Alex and Conner really are."

The Book Huggers were shocked by her willingness.

"Really?" Mindy asked.

"Totally!" Cindy said.

"Yeah, coming right up!" Lindy said.

Wendy nodded her head so fast, she almost pulled a muscle.

All four of them whipped out their pads and wrote her a pass. Mindy was the quickest and handed it over. Bree inspected the pass and then shrugged.

"Cool, thanks, guys," she said, and turned to leave.

"Wait! You have to tell us where they are!" Mindy said.

The Book Huggers were bobbing with so much anxiety, they looked like they were about to wet their pants.

"Oh, I'm not telling you *today*," Bree said. "That wasn't part of our agreement—but I will *eventually*. If you're going to be a conspiracy club, you've got to pay better attention to the details."

Bree proceeded down the hall to class. The Book Huggers looked like a pack of wild hogs about to charge at her.

"Don't worry, girls," Mindy said to calm her friends. "This isn't over—even if it's the last thing we do, we *will* find out what really happened to the Bailey twins."

CHAPTER THREE

THE UNGODMOTHERING

I t has been two weeks since I last heard from you!" Charlotte yelled from the magic mirror. "Do you know what it's like to be a parent and not hear from your children? One day I hope you have kids who disappear for weeks and months at a time just so you know what you and your sister constantly put me through!"

Conner sat in his sister's chambers at the Fairy Palace, wishing he were anywhere else in the world. "No, Mom, I don't," he said. "I'm sorry we haven't been good about keeping you informed."

"I WILL NOT tolerate this anymore!" she said. "If I don't hear from you at least twice a week, I am coming into the fairy-tale world and bringing you both home!"

"Mom, you can't come into the fairy-tale world without magic—" Conner said, and quickly realized he shouldn't have.

Charlotte raised both eyebrows and gave her son the dirtiest look he had ever seen her make. "You don't think I can come into the fairy-tale world, Conner?" she asked, and swiveled her head. "I don't care how thick the border is between dimensions; nothing is going to keep me from my children. Magic or no magic, I will crawl right through this mirror and drag you both back home if I have to!"

It was obvious there was nothing he could say to make the situation any better. The twins were guilty of neglecting their mother, and now Conner was getting an earful about it.

"Mom, you have every right to be mad, but please chill out—"

"Conner Jonathan Bailey, don't tell me to chill out!" she said. He knew he was in serious trouble whenever she used his full name. "How am I supposed to chill out when my fourteen-year-old children are fighting armies and dragons in another world?"

"Actually, Grandma is the one who fought off the dragon," he said.

"That dragon is going to look like a bunny compared to me if I have to come over there," Charlotte warned. "And where is your sister? Why isn't she talking to me?"

The twins had agreed it was best to keep the details of their latest escapades as basic as possible when they talked to their mother. If she was this mad at them for not contacting her regularly, Conner couldn't imagine how she might react if she found out the man they were hunting down could potentially be her deceased husband.

"Alex is in a meeting with the Fairy Council," Conner said. "She's not trying to upset you. She's just got a lot on her plate now that Grandma's gone."

It was difficult for Conner to keep the truth from his mother, especially as he watched how it had affected Alex. He half wished his mother *would* find a way into the fairy-tale world and somehow retune his sister.

"I don't care how important or powerful you two become. I am your mother and I deserve some respect!" Charlotte said. *"If presidents and kings manage to call their mothers, my children can, too!"*

There was a knock on the door. Froggy and Jack poked their heads into the chambers. Conner figured they must have been eavesdropping, because they looked much more concerned than usual.

"It's okay, guys, you can come in," Conner said. "My mom is just chewing me out for not calling her more." He tried to laugh it off, but their expressions didn't change.

"You should come to the grand hall," Froggy said.

"Things are pretty heated between your sister and the council," Jack said.

Conner sighed—there never seemed to be a moment's

rest, especially around the palace. "Mom, I'm sorry, but I've got to go put out a fire," he said. "I promise to talk to you at least twice a week. I'll drag Alex in front of the mirror next time if I have to."

Charlotte crossed her arms. "One last thing before you go!" Conner braced himself for her last remark—he was positive this one would really sting.

"I love you both so much. Please be safe," Charlotte said softly.

It broke Conner's heart. He wondered if she had planned to end their conversation like this all along. His mother was a master at making him feel guilty.

"We love you, too, Mom," Conner said. "And don't worry; we've got a lot of people looking after us. Please tell Bob we said hello."

Charlotte's image disappeared from the mirror. Conner followed Froggy and Jack out of the chambers and down the stairs into the grand hall of the Fairy Palace. He thought things between him and his mother had been tense, but tension was so high in the hall, it was difficult to breathe.

The Fairy Council stood behind their respective podiums as Alex paced in front of them. The entire room was uncomfortable, and Conner could tell his sister was furious.

Alex had changed up her look in recent months, dropping everything that reminded her of their late grandmother. She replaced her blue gown that sparkled like a starry sky with a simpler green dress that grew wildflowers out of the seams. Her hair was longer than it had ever been, and a thin headband did a poor job at keeping it out of her face. She barely used her wand anymore—even that was too reminiscent of her grandmother.

Conner, Jack, and Froggy found Red and Goldilocks standing in the back. Both women were very quiet and stared at the floor.

"What's going on?" Conner whispered to them.

"The council is asking Alex to call off her search for the Masked Man," Goldilocks whispered back. "And she isn't taking it well."

That much was obvious. Alex could barely look any of the Fairy Council members in the eye.

"I don't understand why none of you are listening to me," Alex snapped.

"We *are* listening," Emerelda said. "But we don't agree with you."

"What part don't you agree with?" Alex raised her voice. "The Masked Man is still out there! He is dangerous and we need to find him—end of discussion!"

"The Masked Man is a criminal, but we don't see him as a threat now that the rest of the Grande Armée has been captured," Xanthous said. "We've supported your search for five months. It's unfortunate that he hasn't been captured yet, but it's time to move our attention to more pressing matters."

"There are still twelve children from the Charming Kingdom and twelve children from the Corner Kingdom missing," Skylene reminded the room.

"And I bet the Masked Man is behind that," Alex said. "He said himself he's in the middle of a grand scheme that he spent more than a decade plotting. I wouldn't be surprised if he kidnapped the children to get the witches' attention. He needed their help to recruit another army, so he orchestrated the beginnings of a witch hunt to scare them and convince them they needed protection!"

No matter how logical it was to her, the Fairy Council refused to believe the two were connected. Alex did the best she could to keep her frustration in check, but she could feel it bubbling up inside her like a volcano.

"Yes, you told us," Tangerina said. "The Masked Man plans on recruiting an army *beyond our wildest imaginations* using the potion he stole from your grandmother's chambers."

"We understand why this would concern you," Emerelda said. "However, it sounds like a delusional man's fantasy more than a well-thought-out plan."

Alex shook her head. She was more stubborn than all of them put together. "I'm the Fairy Godmother, and I became the Fairy Godmother by following my heart," she said. "And my heart is telling me that the Masked Man is up to something. I'm not going to change my mind until he's caught."

The members of the Fairy Council eyed one another. This was what they were afraid of.

Emerelda closed her eyes and took a deep breath. "This is not a request, Alex," the green fairy said. "Either you call off the search for the Masked Man or we'll be forced to take action against you."

The tension instantly doubled in the hall. Alex looked back at Conner and their friends, but they were just as stunned as she was.

"Excuse me?" Alex asked, and crossed her arms. "What do you mean, *take action against me*?"

"As members of the Happily Forever After Assembly, it is our job to protect it," Xanthous said. "And if our leader is making decisions we all disagree with, that may be harmful to the kingdoms in any way, we can't stand by and let it happen."

Alex threw her arms into the air. "Let me remind you, if it hadn't been for my brother and me, all of you would be dead! I'm not the enemy—the enemy is out there and you're wasting time!"

"You asked Jack and Goldilocks to form a committee to track down the Masked Man and his men," Rosette said. "Detach yourself from the task so this council can focus on something productive."

"That was before I found out who the Masked Man really was!" Alex blurted out. She had hoped their disagreement wouldn't lead to this.

"Alex, listen to yourself," Skylene said. "Your judgment is clouded because you think this man is your father."

"I *know* he's my father! I saw his face with my own eyes!" she said. "After all the times my judgment and intuition has saved this world, why are you fighting me on this?"

"Your father died four years ago in the Otherworld," Xanthous said. "The Masked Man was in Pinocchio Prison for over a decade. This couldn't be the same man—it isn't possible."

"You said you saw your father just two days after your grandmother passed away," Emerelda said. "Sometimes when we're overwhelmed, we see what we *want* to, rather than what's actually there."

Alex was appalled that Emerelda would suggest such a thing. She could feel her blood boiling in her veins—she didn't know how much longer she had until she lost control of her anger.

"You think I *wanted* to see my father under that mask?" she asked. "Do you think I've *wanted* to lie awake every night wondering how my father became a murdering thief? Or why he lied about his death to his children? I know the facts don't add up, I know it doesn't make sense, but four years ago, if you'd told me the fairy-tale world existed, I wouldn't have believed that, either."

The Fairy Council members either rolled their eyes or sighed in exasperation. Alex couldn't believe how difficult they were making this.

"If you all think what I'm saying is impossible, then we

could be dealing with some seriously dark magic—perhaps magic we've never dealt with before. I know with all my heart that if we ignore this, we'll regret it," she said.

Conner closed his eyes and took a deep breath. It was hard watching his sister have to practically beg for respect. However, he wouldn't believe her if he were in their shoes.

Emerelda must have sensed his uneasiness, because she suddenly redirected the room's attention to him. "Conner, what do you think? Do you think your sister saw what she thinks she saw?"

Conner's insides tightened from being put on the spot. His sister looked back at him with big pleading eyes; if anyone could convince the council Alex wasn't being irrational, it was him. He had been at her side since before they were born.

"I...I...I don't know," Conner mumbled. He stepped closer to her, trying to have a private word in a crowded room. "Alex, in just a few days you had your heart broken by that Rook guy, we fought an army, we lost Grandma, and you became the leader of the fairy-tale world. Maybe Emerelda is right? Maybe you didn't actually see what you think you saw?"

Alex felt like she'd had the wind knocked out of her. She didn't have a single ally among them, not even in her own brother. He had proven what the Masked Man said to her on the roof of the Witches' Brew—it was family who betrayed her the most.

A few tears rolled down Alex's face without her realizing. Still, she wasn't ready to give up.

"I don't care how delusional you all think I am," she said. "I'm going to find the Masked Man and prove you wrong, with or without your help."

Each of the council members nodded to Emerelda. The moment they were all dreading had finally come.

"Then I'm afraid we have no choice," Emerelda said. "Alex, the council feels you are blinded by your emotions and not fit to lead the Happily Forever After Assembly. For the first time in history, we hereby *ungodmother* you."

"WHAT?" Conner yelled. He couldn't believe his ears. *"How is that allowed?"*

"As your new superiors, we order you to stop your search for the Masked Man at once," Xanthous said. "We believe continuing your pursuit will do more harm than good, so anything you do from here on out against the council's wishes will be considered a crime."

"You can't do this!" Jack shouted.

"She hasn't done anything wrong!" Goldilocks said.

"We were hoping to avoid this, but you heard her yourselves," Emerelda said.

Everyone turned to Alex. All the blood drained from her face and she was eerily quiet. It was like she was having a bad dream. The people she once considered friends and colleagues were treating her like a criminal.

Alex couldn't suppress her feelings anymore. She felt her frustration, her anger, and her agitation begin to surface from deep within her. As emotion surged through her body, she went numb and completely lost herself to rage.

"Oh, no," Conner whispered to his friends. "This isn't going to be good."

Alex's eyes started to glow and her hair floated above her head. She howled with laughter and levitated in the air. The Fairy Council was terrified—they had never seen her like this before.

"What's happening?" Xanthous asked anxiously.

"She's just a little overwhelmed, that's all!" Conner said. He put himself between Alex and the council, desperately trying to defuse the situation. "Just give her a minute and everything will be fine—"

Alex jerked her head up and reached toward the sky. A series of lightning bolts rained down from the clouds and hit the council's podiums until each of them exploded. The members of the council dived to the floor for safety.

Everyone in the entire hall looked to one another in panic—none of them knew what to do.

"Seize her!" Emerelda shouted.

The Fairy Council flew into the air and surrounded Alex from all different angles. Alex waved her hands around her body and a tall wall of flames circled her, blocking their approach. The flames shot into the air with the power of a large rocket. The blast was so strong that Conner was knocked clear across the room. The flames disappeared and Alex vanished into thin air.

The grand hall became so quiet, you almost could hear

everyone's hearts racing in unison. Emerelda sprinted toward Conner. He struggled to get to his feet, but she didn't offer him a hand.

"How long has this been going on?" she demanded. Her eyes were wide and her nostrils flared.

"On and off for a couple of months," he said. "But she's never done anything like *that* before!"

"Why didn't you bring this to our attention?" Emerelda said. She used the same tone his mother did in Alex's chambers.

"Oh, come on now," Red said, trying to lighten the mood. "She's just a teenage girl! I used to throw little tantrums like that all the time! Granted, I never disappeared into blazing infernos."

"That was not a tantrum!" Emerelda said.

"Then what's going on with her?" Conner asked.

"My guess is your sister is so drained from chasing the Masked Man that she has lost touch with herself," Emerelda said. "She has no control of her powers!"

"Tell me something I don't know!" Conner said. "So how do we help her?"

Emerelda ignored him and turned to the other members of the Fairy Council. "I want all of you to contact the kings and queens of the Happily Forever After Assembly at once," she instructed. "Tell them all to cease contact with Alex immediately. We must put all of our efforts into finding and capturing her, by any means necessary."

Conner felt like he had whiplash. In one meeting his

sister had gone from the Fairy Godmother to the most wanted person in the fairy-tale world.

"Whoa, whoa, whoa," Conner said, putting himself between the council members. "That's *Alex* we're talking about! She had a breakdown—what's the big deal?"

Conner wasn't the only one anxious to know. The Fairy Council, Jack, Froggy, Goldilocks, and Red huddled around Emerelda.

"We all know Alex is a very powerful person, perhaps the most powerful fairy we've ever known," Emerelda said. "Her magic is fueled by heart, and whatever happened in the Fairy Godmother's chambers between her and the Masked Man five months ago has broken her emotionally. If we don't stop her—if she can't get a grip on her emotions—she may lose control of herself forever."

"Okay," Conner said. The grave look in Emerelda's eyes was scaring him. "Then what can I do?"

"Find her before it's too late," she said. "I've seen this happen only once before. All it took was a broken heart to turn one of the most gifted fairies I had ever known into a foul and dangerous creature. The situation was very different, but all the signs are there."

Conner gulped. "Who was it?" he asked.

Emerelda paused, hesitating to tell him. *"The Enchantress,"* she said.

CHAPTER FOUR

GOOSE ON THE LAM

Alex opened her eyes. To her astonishment, she was standing on a cloud in the center of a ferocious storm. Rain blew from every direction and soaked her to the bone. She wrapped her arms around her body and shivered in the freezing wind. Lightning flashed in the clouds below her feet. The thunder was deafening, as if dozens of cannons were being fired all around her.

She had no idea where she was or how she had gotten there. Her memory was spotty at best. The last thing Alex remembered was standing in the grand hall of the Fairy

Palace. She was arguing with the Fairy Council about the Masked Man...the longer their discussion went on, the angrier Alex became...Emerelda questioned Conner about Alex's reliability, and that's when her memory faded completely.... She could recall only quick glimpses of what had happened, but it didn't take long to put the pieces together.

"Oh, no!" Alex gasped. *"What have I done?"*

It was like recalling a nightmare. The Fairy Council had dethroned her as Fairy Godmother. Alex's anger took control of her body and she retaliated *by attacking them!*

The more lucid she became, the more the storm around her began to calm and dissipate. The rain stopped and the cold wind came to a halt. Alex looked around, trying to determine her whereabouts, but all she saw were thick gray clouds for miles and miles.

Alex chose a direction and walked through clouds like fluffy quicksand. In the distance she could barely make out the silhouette of a massive structure with several towers. When she squinted she saw a large wooden door. Alex recognized this place immediately.

"It's the giant's castle!"

Alex's stomach dropped. The castle instantly reminded her of the time she and her friends narrowly escaped being clawed and eaten by the giant cat that lived inside. Despite her initial instinct to run in the opposite direction, Alex figured the castle might be the best place to go, given the circumstances. She doubted the Fairy Council would look for her *there*. Perhaps that's why she had taken herself to the sky all along.

She continued toward the castle, and her feet eventually found a solid path that curved up to the castle's enormous front door. Alex almost crawled under the door, like she and her friends had before, but luckily she had learned a few tricks since then. She waved her hand over the door, and it began to open.

Once the door had opened wide enough, Alex went inside and the door shut behind her. The castle was exactly as Alex remembered. The stone tiles of the floor were the size of swimming pools. Each step of the massive staircase was the height of a building. You could probably fit the entire Fairy Palace into the entrance hall alone.

However, one thing was very different. The last time she was in the castle, the floor had been covered in hundreds of bird carcasses (victims of the giant cat's appetite), but now it was completely clean. In fact, the whole castle had a very "lived-in" feel.

Alex gulped nervously—more than just the giant cat was living in the castle now.

She walked into the room to the right of the entrance hall and found the castle's sitting room. Each piece of furniture was the size of a house. A pile of timbered trees burned in the fireplace like logs. An enormous armchair had been placed close to the fire. Its back was facing Alex, but she could tell someone or something was sitting in it.

"Squaaa?"

66

Alex jumped. Perched at the very top of the armchair was a familiar goose. The bird was enormous, but still dwarfed in comparison to the giant's castle.

"Lester?" Alex said. "What are you doing here?"

The goose ruffled his feathers excitedly. *"Squaaa!"*

"What is it, boy?" a raspy voice said from the chair. Alex sighed with relief; she was among friends.

"Mother Goose? Is that you?" Alex called up.

"Alex?" Mother Goose said. "What are you doing here?"

"I was going to ask you the same thing."

"Lester, be a dear and help our girl up here," Mother Goose instructed.

Lester glided to the ground and Alex climbed on his back. He flew her to the seat of the armchair, which was like a balcony looking over the fireplace. Mother Goose sat in a rocking chair, her large traveling basket at her side, and she sipped from a large thermos that was undoubtedly filled with her favorite bubbly beverage.

"HISSSSSSSSSS!"

Alex shrieked. The giant cat was seated on the armrest of the chair. He glared at her and arched his back as he hissed. Obviously, he remembered Alex from when they first met. He raised a paw and extended his claws, ready to strike.

"Easy, George Clooney," Mother Goose said to the cat. "She's a friend—she's not going to harm you! Don't make me spray you with water again!"

The giant cat retracted his claws and slouched, still

sending Alex a nasty look. She was surprised to see how obedient he was. "Is the cat *yours* now?" she asked.

"I was never planning on it, but someone has to teach this giant sack of gluten some manners," Mother Goose said. "He almost ate Lester the first time we came here. But I put him on a strict fish and grain diet."

The cat glanced at Lester with hunger in his eyes. Clearly he was still tempted.

"And you named him George Clooney?" Alex asked with a laugh.

"Yes, after one of my favorite boyfriends from the Otherworld," Mother Goose said.

"He was your *boyfriend*?" Alex said with a raised eyebrow. Of all the stories Alex had heard over the years, how had Mother Goose managed to keep that to herself?

"Oh, I keep forgetting you're from the Otherworld." Mother Goose chuckled. "An old gal can dream, can't she?" She snapped her fingers and another rocking chair appeared beside hers. "Have a seat, kiddo! It's good to see you."

Alex had a seat, also happy to be reunited. For the last couple of months, Mother Goose sightings had become fewer and fewer. For some reason, she avoided the Fairy Palace as much as possible these days, and the twins were worried the day would come when she disappeared forever.

"We haven't seen you in months," Alex said. "Is this where you've been hiding?"

"It is," Mother Goose said with a heavy sigh. "I'm sorry I've been MIA, Alex—I miss you and your brother like crazy, but it's difficult being around the palace now that your grandmother is gone."

Alex knew exactly how she felt, so she couldn't blame her. "Believe me, I know. Why come here of all places?"

"I love this place," Mother Goose said. "It's got high ceilings for Lester to fly around, it's very quiet, it has great views on a clear day, and the late giant and I have similar tastes in bubbly." She pointed to the giant's teacart in the corner of the room, where a dozen bottles taller than Alex were filled with Mother Goose's favorite drink. "That's a lifetime supply for me!"

"We sure miss seeing you around—will you ever come back?"

Mother Goose hesitated to answer. "I don't know. I haven't decided. Every night I hope I'll wake up the next day with the desire to rejoin humanity, but no luck so far. I just need more time, I guess."

Mother Goose took a long swig of bubbly. Alex noticed a small leather-bound book resting on her lap.

"What are you reading?" Alex asked.

"Oh, this?" she said. "It's just my old diary. Boy, I've had some adventures in my time. I used to write down everything—I always hoped one day when I was old or finally locked up for good, there would be someone there who would appreciate it."

"May I?" Alex asked, reaching for the diary.

Mother Goose smiled and handed it to her. Alex flipped through the old pages. There were hundreds and hundreds of entries dating back hundreds of years into the Otherworld and the fairy-tale world. There were pictures, flowers, leaves, and letters folded in between the pages.

"You've certainly lived," Alex said, impressed by the artifact.

"Certainly did," Mother Goose said. "Certainly did . . ."

Her choice of words concerned Alex. *"Did?"* she said. "Why are you talking like it's over? You're not ready to throw in the towel yet, are you?"

Mother Goose sighed and her gaze drifted to the fireplace. She seemed sad, at least sadder than Alex had ever seen her before.

"Getting old is not for wimps, I'll tell you that much," Mother Goose said. "When I was young, I wanted to live forever. There wasn't a bridge I didn't want to cross, or a stone I wanted to leave unturned. Then I reached a certain age and everything started disappearing. My friends started to die one at a time until none of them were left. The world is always changing, but one day you wake up and realize that it's changed *without* you—and there's no chance of catching up to it. Your adventures are over, and you find yourself all alone with nothing left but the memories. Then you just wait . . . and wait . . . and wait until it's your turn to meet your maker—or 'return to magic,' as your grandmother always put it. And when that day comes, you pray someone you know will be waiting for you when you get there."

It broke Alex's heart to hear her say such a thing. "But, Mother Goose, that can't be true," she said. "You have more life in your pinkie than most people do in their entire body. The adventures aren't over, they'll just be different."

"Thank you, sweetheart," Mother Goose said with a smile. "I certainly hope that's the case. Now it's your turn— what brings you to the Casa de Giant?"

Alex closed her eyes tightly, willing herself not to cry. "I've been *ungodmothered* by the Fairy Council. I've ruined everything."

Mother Goose choked on a swig of bubbly. *"What?"* She coughed. "Can they do that?"

"Apparently so."

"Why in the world would they do that?" Mother Goose said. "You're one of the brightest fairies this world has ever seen!"

"They believe my search for the Masked Man has gone too far and they think I've become destructive," Alex said.

"Oh, I doubt that," Mother Goose said. "They've always thought *doing nothing* is better than doing something that *might* be harmful or make them look bad. But that's politics for you."

"No—it's true," Alex admitted. "Lately, whenever I get overwhelmed, I completely lose control of myself and my powers. I attacked the council with lightning when they made the decision! It was like someone else had taken over my body and I was just watching from inside."

"Wow," Mother Goose said. "I'm sorry I missed it."

"Maybe they were right to demote me," Alex said, suddenly filling with self-doubt. "Maybe it's best if I'm not the Fairy Godmother. Now they can focus on finding the twelve missing children from the Corner Kingdom and the twelve missing children from the Charming Kingdom."

"I remember another time when a bunch of young people went missing—we called it *Woodstock*, but that's a different story," Mother Goose said. "You're not going to quit looking for the Masked Man, though, are you?"

Alex shook her head. "I can't stop," she said. "No one believes me, but I know he's my dad. No matter how many times the Fairy Council tries to convince me I was just hallucinating, I know what I saw. He had my dad's eyes, his nose, his mouth...who else could it have been? I won't be able to function properly until he's found."

Mother Goose looked at Alex with large sympathetic eyes. There was so much she wished she could tell her, but she had made the late Fairy Godmother a promise shortly before she passed away, a promise she intended to keep.

Mother Goose took Alex's hand. "I believe you, honey."

Alex looked up at her with big bright eyes. "You do?"

"I've seen some pretty incredible things in my lifetime," Mother Goose said. "They didn't always make sense and they weren't always what people wanted to hear, but that doesn't mean they didn't happen. If you say you saw your father, *then you saw your father*—end of discussion."

Alex was so thankful someone was on her side that it brought tears to her eyes. "But what do I do now? I'm the most wanted person in the kingdoms. The council's hunting me down as we speak."

Mother Goose rolled her eyes and waved the thought off. "If I had a nickel for every time the council got their panties in a ruffle over me, I could afford to pay back all my gambling debts in both worlds. If I were you I'd consider it a blessing. You're no longer the Fairy Godmother or associated with the Fairy Council—*great!* That means you can start playing by your own rules. Let people be afraid of you for now; that fear will only turn into admiration when you find the Masked Man and prove you've been right all along. And what will the council have to say when that happens? They'll never be able to hold you back again."

Mother Goose took another swig of bubbly and nodded, content with her advice.

"And you know what?" Mother Goose added. "I'm going to help you."

"You will?" Alex asked.

A mischievous smile grew on her face. "I've always wondered what it would be like to see those uppity, colorful know-it-alls get proven wrong. Count me in."

For the first time in a very long while, Alex smiled. "And we'll be playing by our own rules. I like the sound of that."

CHAPTER FIVE

POTIONS AND PREDICTIONS

A small wagon traveled through the woods in the dead of night. It was pulled by a single mule and transported three women: a brunette, a redhead, and a blonde. The women were middle aged, but they were so tired from traveling, they looked much older.

The brunette woman had never steered a wagon before and struggled to keep her grip around the reins. The red-headed woman glanced back and forth from a map to the path ahead, and the blonde woman held a lantern to illuminate the woods. They watched the trees nervously—not afraid of what they might see, but of who might see them.

None of them had ever been so far away from home, and they hoped no one from home would ever know where they were headed.

"Are you sure we're going the right way?" the blonde fussed.

"I'm following the map as best as I can!" the redhead said.

"Quiet, you two!" the brunette whispered. "Look! It's the Dwarf Forests!"

After traveling all night, they had reached the border between the Corner Kingdom and the Dwarf Forests. They were certain because the trees ahead were thicker and eerier than any woods they had ever seen. Just the sight of it sent chills down their spines.

"Are we sure we want to go in *there*?" the blonde said, getting cold feet.

"The witch's house is just a little ways inside," the brunette said. "We'll be there in no time."

The wagon crossed a small bridge and traveled into the unsettling forest. A mile or so in, the women found a house sitting on the edge of a river. It had a tall hay roof and a watermill that turned slowly as the river ran through it. It was exactly as it had been described.

The women helped one another down from the wagon and tied their mule to a tree. They linked arms and cautiously approached the front door of the house. Each woman nudged the other, but they were all afraid to knock on the door.

"May I help you?" said a voice behind them.

The women screamed and turned around. Another woman was standing behind them. She was beautiful, with dark hair and bright red lips. She wore long black robes with golden trim and snakeskin high-heeled boots. She would have looked like any other woman except for the large ram-like horns that grew out of her head and curled along the sides of her face.

The women figured this was the witch they were looking for.

"Are ... are ... are you Morina? The beauty witch?" the blonde asked with a trembling jaw.

"That depends," the witch responded with a fierce scowl. "What are you doing here?"

"We don't mean any harm," the redhead said, using her friends as a shield. "A mutual acquaintance recommended your ... *services*."

Morina's scowl slowly morphed into a smile. "Oh, you're *customers*! Welcome, ladies. Forgive me for being rude; one can never be too careful when a witch hunt is on the horizon. Please, come inside."

Morina pointed to the door and it flew open. She put her arms around the women and escorted them inside her home.

The front room of the house was an elegant shop. It had marble floors, a crystal chandelier, and pillars supporting the high ceiling. Everything was white, including a large desk and chair in the center of the room. Shelves holding small glass bottles filled with colorful liquids lined the walls. The women felt like children in a candy shop.

"Now, ladies, what brings you to my neck of the woods?" Morina asked.

"We heard you've invented a potion that reverses the signs of aging," the brunette said.

"The rumors are true," Morina said. "Only, it's not just *one* potion. My shelves are filled with concoctions guaranteed to rejuvenate, revitalize, or refresh—depending on your specific needs."

The women looked around the room as if they had died and gone to heaven. Could the potions around them really restore their youth? It seemed too good to be true.

"Are these the potions you sold to the Evil Queen?" asked the blonde. "We heard you were one of the beauticians who provided her with beauty regimens."

"Indeed," Morina said. "For years she was my exclusive client and a dear friend. It's a shame what happened to her, but I assure you, her fate should not reflect on the quality of my products."

"How do we know your potions work?" the redhead asked.

Morina's smile grew; this was always her favorite question when making a sale. Morina crossed to the corner of the room and pulled on a tassel. Curtains parted on the wall, revealing a large mirror with a golden frame.

"Do any of you know what this is?" Morina asked.

"A mirror," the blonde said.

"Yes, but it's not an ordinary mirror," Morina said. "When someone steps in front of it, they will see the reflection of who they are *inside*. It was a gift from the Evil Queen herself, who, as you know, had a fascination with magic mirrors. They call it a Mirror of Truth."

Morina stepped in front of the mirror and the women gasped. Her reflection transformed into a hideous young woman with warts, a hunchback, and a clubfoot. The ramlike horns were the only similarity the witch and the reflection shared.

"But that couldn't possibly be you," the brunette said.

"It *was*," Morina said. "My grandfather was a troll, so naturally with witch and troll blood in my veins, I was destined for ugliness. I constantly had my heart broken by men who couldn't love me because of my appearance. But instead of dwelling in self-pity, I decided to do something about it. I spent years of my young life mixing and matching potions, creating concoctions that altered my looks little by little until I was satisfied. And since my own transformation was so successful, I decided to share my creations with others ... *for a price*."

She turned back to them and the ugly reflection faded away. Morina took each woman gently by the hand and placed her in front of the mirror. They covered their eyes, afraid of what the mirror might show.

"Go on," she encouraged. "Take a look. I promise you have nothing to be afraid of."

The women looked up at the Mirror of Truth and their eyes filled with tears. Three young, beautiful, and vibrant women stared back at them—reflections they hadn't seen in decades.

"Why be another victim of nature's cruelties when you can put a stop to it?" Morina said. "Let the women inside you be reborn so the world can see who you truly are. With the help of my potions, you can be reunited with the beauty and self-confidence that time has stolen from you."

The witch didn't have to say any more—the women were sold.

"Now, one at a time, tell me what each of you is specifically looking for," Morina said.

One by one, each woman stepped forward and confessed her deepest and darkest insecurities to the witch. Luckily for them, Morina had a product for everything. After she determined what products they needed, the bottles flew off the shelves and into three white bags that appeared on the desk. By the time Morina was done diagnosing the women's needs, each bag was filled with dozens of potions.

"How much is this going to cost us?" the brunette asked.

"It's a different amount for each customer," Morina said. "I charge half of your individual fortunes to use my potions."

The women eyed one another. They had been told the fee was expensive, but none of them thought it would cost them *this* much. Luckily, they were prepared to pay any price. They looked back into the Mirror of Truth for inspiration and each placed a heavy bag of coins on Morina's desk.

"Excellent! Now, let me warn you," Morina said. "The potions have been bewitched to reverse their intended effects if a customer is lying about her finances."

The women grew paranoid and handed over all the money they had in their possession. A satisfied smirk spread across Morina's face and she slid her proceeds into the large drawer of the desk.

"Thank you, ladies," she said. "It's been a pleasure doing business with you."

Morina escorted the women out of her home and waved them off as they traveled away on the wagon. When she turned back to her home, she noticed something odd. The front door was swinging ever so slightly, as if someone had quickly run inside when she wasn't looking.

Morina charged into her house horns first, slamming the door behind her. There was no visible sign of an intruder, but she knew she wasn't alone.

"Show yourself!" she demanded.

When there was no movement, Morina spun her finger in a quick circle. An aggressive whirlwind appeared and twirled around her shop. It found a man crouching behind her desk and trapped him inside its vortex. The whirlwind spun the man so fast, he couldn't make a sound.

The witch sighed and then snapped her fingers once she realized who it was. The whirlwind disappeared and dropped the Masked Man at her feet.

"Lloyd," Morina said. She may have been the only person in the fairy-tale world who could recognize the late Fairy Godmother's son in his disguise. Over the years she had spent so much time detesting every fiber of his being, she recognized the pale blue eyes under the mask immediately. They had history together, history that didn't end well.

"Hello, Morina," the Masked Man said. He was so dizzy, he almost became sick and had difficulty standing.

"You pathetic excuse of a man," the witch said. "I knew it was only a matter of time before you slithered your way back into my life. What are you doing here?"

The Masked Man hesitated to respond, knowing the answer would infuriate her. "I came to ask for your help," he said.

"MY HELP?" Morina yelled, outraged by his audacity. "You think you can sneak into my home and request a favor from me after what you did?"

"I understand why you'd be angry," the Masked Man said.

"Anger is nothing compared to the feelings I have toward you," she said. "You *lied* to me! You *stole* from me!"

"Please, allow me to explain—"

"There's nothing to explain!" Morina said. "We had an arrangement! I supplied you with hundreds of love potions!

In return, you promised me a king-sized fortune, but you failed to hold your end of the bargain!"

"I know I didn't deliver it as fast as I promised, but that doesn't mean it can't happen," he said. "Please hear me out! If you help me now, I swear I'll be able to give you a *kingdom* in return!"

"You are the scum of the earth and I will not listen to another word you say! Get out of my house before I drop you into the river piece by piece!"

Morina pointed to the door and it flung open. The Masked Man reached into his jacket pocket and pulled out the small blue potion bottle, holding it up like a badge.

"What is *that?*" she asked.

"It's a potion my mother created when I was a child," the Masked Man said. "This small vial is what I've been after my entire life. It could very well be the most powerful potion in the world. Just a few drops turn any book into a portal to the world it possesses."

Morina grunted and rolled her eyes—she couldn't believe the Masked Man was still feeding her more lies.

"I know it seems impossible," the Masked Man said. "Watch this."

He removed a small golden book from his jacket pocket and placed it on her desk. Morina read the title: *A Boy's First Dog.* The Masked Man opened the book to the first page and carefully poured three drops of the potion on it.

As if the book had suddenly transformed into a

spotlight, the pages glowed and a bright beam of light shot directly out of it toward the ceiling.

"Look inside it," the Masked Man said eagerly. *"Please."*

Morina reluctantly leaned into the beam. Her head was no longer in her shop. Everywhere she looked, she saw words spinning around her. She tried to read them, but they moved too fast. The words randomly dispersed and morphed into the objects they described, gaining color and texture. Soon Morina found herself in a pleasant field covered in wildflowers. In the distance, a young farm boy happily played fetch with a puppy.

"My goodness." Morina gasped and leaned out of the beam. He was telling the truth.

"Remarkable, isn't it?" the Masked Man said.

Morina slid into the chair behind her desk—he had her attention. "You have five minutes. Explain yourself. What are you planning to do with this potion? And why do you need my assistance?"

The Masked Man put the potion and the book back into his pocket and had a seat on her desk.

"Long story short, ever since I was a boy it's been my life's mission to overthrow my mother and the fairies," he explained. "And this potion is going to help me achieve it."

"That's a peculiar goal for a child to have," Morina pointed out.

"It was a peculiar situation," he said. "My mother always favored my older brother, John. I knew he was destined to take her place and he was known as her *heir of magic.* So I started fantasizing about a world where I was the leader. They were just childish daydreams, but somehow my mother discovered these dreams. Fearing that one day I might act on them, she committed the cruelest act a mother could commit on her own son."

"Did she send you to bed without dinner?" Morina said with a laugh.

"She drained all the magic from my body, turning me into a human," the Masked Man said, and his voice cracked as he recalled it. "I was punished for crimes I had never committed. It was my birthright to participate in magic, and she stripped it from me. So I vowed one day to destroy her and everything she had created.

"I knew the only way I could defeat her was by regaining power, not in a magical sense, but in a military sense; I needed an army. A typical army of men would never do. I needed one that was more powerful than any force this world had ever seen. By using the potion my mother created, I could recruit an army of *literary villains*. I could control and unleash what the world had only seen in their nightmares. I could be unstoppable."

The more farfetched his plan became, the less it interested Morina. "Then why did you ask me for love potions?" she asked.

"By the time I developed this plan, I had been banished from the Fairy Kingdom," the Masked Man said. "I knew there was no way I could sneak into my mother's chambers without a colossal distraction to occupy the fairies—*I needed a dragon egg.* I searched for one for years, researching everything I could about the beasts. It led me to the Snow Queen, who had preserved one from the Dragon Age. When she turned me down, I knew I would need better resources to obtain one.

"I used the love potions you provided on Little Bo Peep. My plan was to seduce and marry her, and then convince her to challenge the Red Riding Hood throne. Once Little Bo was elected queen, I would have been king. I could give you what I promised and form a crusade to find a dragon egg."

"How did you wind up in Pinocchio Prison instead?" Morina asked.

"Because I got impatient and paranoid," the Masked Man said. "Manipulating Little Bo was much harder than I expected. So, in a moment of weakness, I snuck into the Fairy Palace and tried to steal the potion by myself. I was caught and my mother sentenced me to life in prison. She gave me this sack to wear over my head so no one would know I was her son.

"Ten long years later, an army from the Otherworld led by a man called General Marquis invaded the prison. We shared the same goal—destroy the fairies—so the general was easy to convince that a dragon was what they needed to do so. I knew his army and a dragon would never be enough to destroy the fairies, but I knew it would distract them long enough so I could get my hands on the potion."

"Your objective is as insane as you are," she said. "What makes you think these literary characters will listen to you?"

"I'm rather persuasive," the Masked Man boasted. "The Grande Armée was proof of that."

"You still haven't told me how I fit into all of this," Morina said.

"Oh yes, I'm getting there," he said. "When I retrieved the potion, I discovered all my old books had been relocated. I need your help to find them. Once we locate them I can begin recruiting the army I spoke of!"

"And how am I supposed to find these books?"

"Do you still have that crystal ball?" the Masked Man asked. "If I recall, you used to be very good at giving predictions."

"Fortune-telling is a hobby I gave up a long time ago," Morina said. "I'm a potion mistress now. It's much more lucrative."

"Understood and respected. But, Morina, if you help me locate these books, I promise you I will give you any kingdom you want when I've conquered the world."

His offer lit a spark of excitement inside of her and she was almost embarrassed to acknowledge it. This wasn't the first time she had been offered a kingdom.

"The Evil Queen was going to declare me as her successor once her huntsman killed Snow White," Morina said. "Obviously, it didn't work out in my favor. So I'm not very eager to get my hopes up again."

The Masked Man got to his hands and knees. "Then please look into your crystal ball for validation. Let it convince you that my plan will work if you help me."

As much as she despised him, Morina knew it wouldn't hurt to humor him. Worst-case scenario, the Masked Man would continue being a pebble in her shoe. But the proposition of her own kingdom was something she couldn't let go to waste.

She stood and crossed to a door in the back of her shop. A dozen locks bolted and chained the door shut. She waved her hand over the locks and one by one they unlocked, unbolted, and unchained themselves. The door opened and the Masked Man saw a staircase that led down into a dark basement. He stood to follow her.

Morina held up her hand. "Absolutely no one is allowed in my basement but me, understood?"

The Masked Man knew there was no negotiating this and nodded. Morina climbed down the stairs and the door shut behind her. The Masked Man paced around the shop as he waited, inspecting and pocketing the products Morina had for sale. A few moments later the door opened and Morina appeared with a crystal ball.

She placed the crystal ball on her desk and had a seat. The witch blew off a thick layer of dust covering the ball.

"This may take a moment," Morina said. "It's been a long time."

The witch stared into the crystal ball, deep in

concentration. White clouds appeared inside it and began to spiral. Glimpses of the future began to show themselves to her.

"Interesting," Morina said with large eyes.

"What do you see?" the Masked Man asked, desperate to know.

"I see winged creatures, ruthless men, and soldiers bearing symbols," she said. "It appears your madness will pay off. You *will* recruit a literary army, overthrow the fairies, and take over the world."

The Masked Man jumped into the air and cried with joy. His life's work would not be a waste. Despite his mother's efforts to stop him, he would obtain the power he had desperately desired since childhood.

Morina squinted as the crystal ball began showing her something else, something she had never seen before.

"What do you see now?" the Masked Man asked. Her expression made him nervous.

"I'm not entirely sure," she said. "I see buildings that stretch into the sky . . . machines of extreme capabilities . . . billions of people, all of difference races . . ."

"I know what that is," he said with a frown. "You're looking at the Otherworld."

Morina was so fascinated by what she saw, she barely heard him. Images of the Great Wall of China, the Eiffel Tower, the Nile, and New York City flashed before her eyes. She had heard references and rumors of the Otherworld before, but until now she never could have imagined how grand it was.

"Impressive," Morina said. "This world is operated completely without magic."

"Just man and machines," the Masked Man said. "My mother and brother loved it dearly, but it never interested me."

Clearly, Morina was mesmerized by it. "So someone capable of magic could potentially do very well there...," she said softly. "They could be a *god*."

"Potentially, I suppose," the Masked Man said. "But it's a miserable place—destined to destroy itself, if you ask me."

The images in the crystal ball changed, distracting Morina from her new fixation.

"Are you aware you have *family* in the Otherworld?" she asked.

The Masked Man crossed his arms and let out a long and aggrieved sigh. "Don't remind me. It's where my late brother lived and where his children are from."

"Your *family* could pose a threat to you in the near future," Morina said.

"I can handle my niece and nephew," the Masked Man said. "They're young and naïve—my niece is even convinced I'm her late father. They'll be the first to die once I'm in power."

The witch was being vague on purpose. Alex and Conner weren't the family she was referring to. Apparently, the

Masked Man had family he was unaware of, and knowing this could be very useful to her.

"Now that you've seen I'm destined to form the army, can you locate my books for me?" the Masked Man asked.

Morina looked harder into the crystal ball and the location became clearer and clearer.

"I see a library in a castle," she said. "A few years ago, your mother gave your books away as a gift for helping her grandchildren. This castle is filled with decorations. It looks like the servants are preparing for a celebration as we speak. A *wedding*, it seems."

"It must be Red Riding Hood's wedding to King Charlie," the Masked Man said. *"My books are in their castle!"*

Morina looked up from the crystal ball for the first time. *"King Charlie* you said? As in the *long lost Charming prince?"*

"Yes. He's a king now," the Masked Man said. "He was elected king by the people of the Little Bo Peep Republic after Little Bo died."

Morina's cheeks flushed. "Well, isn't that *something…*," she said with a tight jaw.

The Masked Man couldn't tell if she was angered, saddened, or both by the news. Rather than questioning her reaction, he composed his plan to retrieve the books.

"The books shouldn't be difficult to steal while the wedding is under way," he said. "The entire kingdom will be attending it."

Morina stared off into the distance, making plans of her own.

"The wedding won't be enough," she said. "You'll need another *dragon* of sorts to make sure the kingdom's attention is completely captivated. And I know just the thing...."

Morina smiled at him. If the Masked Man were wiser, he would have questioned her sudden cooperation, but the only thing on his mind was getting to those books and forming his army.

"Thank you, Morina. I swear to you, when I am in power, you can have whatever kingdom you want."

For the first time in her life, Morina was glad the Masked Man had stopped by. While looking into her crystal ball she had seen much more than his future. Morina had discovered a world of opportunities for herself, and if she played her cards right, she could get much more out of this partnership than a *kingdom*.

CHAPTER SIX

THE BAD FAIRIES

Conner and his friends returned to Dead Man's Creek much sooner than any of them would have liked. He and Jack rummaged through piles of the destroyed Witches' Brew while Red and Goldilocks searched the woods nearby. Porridge and her son, Oats (who was nearly the size of his mother now), helped Conner and Jack by kicking over the larger pieces of the wrecked tavern.

"I only see sticks," Jack said. "Are we looking for anything in particular?"

"Anything," Conner said desperately. "Anything that could lead us to the Masked Man. Alex isn't going to stop looking for him because the Fairy Council forbade her to—she'll be even more determined to prove herself now. We've got to get to him before she does. I'm afraid of what she might do when she finds him."

Conner tried to tell himself he had done everything he could to help his sister, but he knew that wasn't true. If he had been honest with her from the beginning about her obsession with the Masked Man, perhaps they wouldn't be in this predicament.

Now, on top of being overwhelmed, Alex was all alone and probably thought the entire world was against her (including her brother). Conner just wanted to find her so he could help her rebuild everything that had been lost, but even if they found her, he wouldn't know where to start.

"It's such a shame," Red said, shaking her head as she searched the ground. "The people you depend on and trust always disappoint you the most."

Goldilocks nodded. "I agree. I can't believe the Fairy Council did that to Alex, especially after all she's done for the kingdoms. Who cares if the Masked Man is her father or not; you'd think they would learn to trust her instincts by now."

Red glanced at her awkwardly. "The Fairy Council? I was talking about the caterers for the wedding. They canceled on us *this* morning. Do you know how difficult it'll be to find someone to cook for five hundred people with two days' notice?"

Goldilocks found Red more annoying than ever when she talked about her wedding. The last thing Red needed was *more* entitlement.

"I'm glad Jack and I had a small wedding," Goldilocks said. "No fight or fuss, just simple and quick."

Red rolled her eyes. "I suppose it was easy sending invitations since your *guest list* and the *most wanted list* were one and the same. Unfortunately, when you're respected as much as Charlie and I are, you have no choice but to throw an extravagant but elegant celebration. Our people are *depending* on a spectacular wedding—it teaches them how to dream."

Goldilocks took a deep breath, fighting the temptation to throw something at her.

"If you still have wedding plans to make, why are you here?" Goldilocks asked.

"I don't like planning anything without Charlie, and he was busy with a bunch of *king nonsense* today. Apparently the citizens are very anxious about what he'll rename the kingdom now that he's on the throne."

"Is he going to name it after himself, like you and Little Bo did?" Goldilocks asked.

"No," Red was disappointed to report. "He's determined to give the kingdom a name it can keep beyond his reign. I believe he's settled on *the Center Kingdom*. It's a bit boring, if you ask me, but I suppose the kingdom will save a fortune not constantly reprinting maps."

Red suddenly stopped in her tracks and pressed her finger to her lips. Goldilocks was very familiar with this pose—Red did it every time she was about to ask a favor.

"I almost forgot," Red said. "I have something I wanted to ask you, Goldie."

"Oh, no," Goldilocks sighed.

"Since Alex will *still* most likely be in hiding at the time of the wedding, will you please be my *matron of honor*?" Red asked excitedly. "*Oh, please say yes!* I can't think of anyone else I've been through more with. We're like *sisters*—the kind of sisters who have almost killed each other at one point in time."

Goldilocks stared at her blankly for a few moments and then burst into tears. Red became teary-eyed at the sight and threw her arms around her.

"I didn't know you would be so touched!" Red said.

"I'm not," Goldilocks said, and wiped her eyes on Red's sleeve. "It sounds awful—but I can't think of a reason to say no. And everything seems so much worse when you're pregnant."

Red quickly dropped the embrace and joined the boys.

"I'm sorry, Red! That was rude of me. Of course I'll be your matron of honor," Goldilocks apologized. "I can't filter a word I say, because of the hormones."

Their search for clues leading to the Masked Man continued for a couple more hours, until Conner's frustration got the best of him. He grunted loudly and began kicking the debris around him.

"This is pointless!" he yelled. "There's nothing here! We've got to look somewhere else."

"This is the only location where we've seen the Masked Man in five months," Jack said. "Where else can we search?"

Conner didn't have an answer. He walked down to the creek and sat on a boulder as he thought it over. He looked into the sky for clarity, but instead he found a distraction. What he saw was very strange, and he rubbed his eyes to make sure it wasn't a hallucination.

"Guys?" Conner said to the others. "What's *that?*"

A *book* was flying through the air—and it appeared to be flying toward *him*. As the book flew closer, Conner saw three tiny objects hovering around it: one purple, one green, and one orange. Each had a pair of colorful wings.

"Are those insects? I didn't bring any repellant," Red said.

"No, they're fairies!" Goldilocks said.

"INCOMING!" one of the fairies yelled. *"We can't hold it any longer!"*

The book slipped from their tiny grip and smacked Conner right in the face. He temporarily lost sight in his left eye, but when his vision returned, he saw three fairies land on a boulder beside him. They were sweating profusely and out of breath.

"So sorry, Conner!" one of the fairies said. "We've carried that all the way from the Fairy Kingdom!"

Conner instantly recognized her—although he hadn't seen her in years.

"Trix? Is that you?" he asked.

The fairy had dark hair and blue wings and wore a dress made of purple leaves. She smiled up at him and batted her big eyes, so pleased that he remembered her name.

"Hello, Conner!" Trix said. "We've been looking everywhere for you! These are my friends Merkle and Noodle."

She gestured to the other fairies and they waved at him. Noodle was plump for her size and her stomach stuck out of her orange dress. Merkle was as thin as a pencil and glanced around nervously as she vigorously rubbed her hands together.

"We shouldn't have done this!" Merkle said. "We're going to get into so much trouble!"

"Merkle, calm down before your hands catch on fire," Noodle said. "No one knows we're here!"

"What *are* you doing here?" Conner asked.

Trix flew up to his face so she could look him in the eye. "We know about your sister!"

"Trix, the entire world knows about her," Conner said. "Overnight she went from the Fairy Godmother to the most wanted person alive. It's pretty newsworthy."

"No, I mean we were *there* last night at the Fairy Council meeting!" Trix said. "We saw the entire thing!"

"We were sitting in the windowsill; no one ever notices

us there," Noodle said with a wink. "We've never missed a Fairy Council meeting—it gives us something to talk to the other fairies about. We know all about the Masked Man and we think Alex is right to be worried about him!"

"We shouldn't have been there!" Merkle said, and covered her face in shame.

"And most of the fairies we've talked to are on her side!" Trix said. "We think it's the council who blew things out of proportion!"

Conner was glad his sister had support from someone.

"I appreciate that, Trix, but it's very complicated—"

"The council will banish us from the Fairy Kingdom if they find out what we've stolen!" Merkle suddenly exclaimed. "We're bad fairies! VERY bad fairies!"

The poor thing looked as if she was about to have a heart attack.

"Okay, *pause!*" Conner said. "What did you guys steal?"

Trix and Noodle eyed each other mischievously.

"Remember the time you and your sister saved me from banishment?" Trix asked. "Well, it's been three years, but I've always planned on returning the favor. So I wanted to help your sister prove herself, and Noodle and Merkle agreed to assist me."

"Biggest regret of my life!" Merkle said.

"At the council meeting, your sister mentioned that the Masked Man stole a potion from the late Fairy Godmother—one he claimed was very powerful," Trix said. "The Fairy

Council isn't worried about it, but if *Alex* is concerned, then *we're* concerned!"

"So, we did a little snooping around the Fairy Palace on her behalf and found out *she was right!*" Noodle said. "The late Fairy Godmother did invent a potion that was *very powerful*! And we think it's the one the Masked Man stole!"

Given the sources, Conner didn't want to get his hopes up, but what they were telling him was very intriguing. "How do you know this?"

"Just show him the book already! I can't stand the anticipation!" Merkle yelled, and her eyes almost bulged out of their sockets.

Trix and Noodle each grabbed a corner of the book they had transported and dropped it into Conner's lap. He opened it and flipped through the pages. It was filled with entries, sketches, and diagrams—it was a log of experiments. At first Conner assumed the neat and feminine handwriting belonged to a scientist, but it looked very familiar. It was the same handwriting Conner had seen in birthday cards and letters.

"This is my grandma's!" Conner said. "I've never seen it before."

"We found it tucked away in her former chambers at the palace," Trix said. "She recorded the ingredients of all the spells and potions she created inside it."

"And we stole it!" Merkle gasped. She had never been so ashamed.

"Yeah, we *stole* it!" Noodle said with a smile. She was tickled by their naughtiness.

"And we think the last entry is the potion the Masked Man stole!" Trix said. "It's *very* powerful—much more powerful than any other potion she created."

Jack, Goldilocks, and Red gathered closer to Conner and the fairies, anxious to hear it themselves. Even Porridge and Oats seemed interested by what the fairies discovered.

"I think that's worth taking a look at," Jack said.

"I agree! Listen to the insects, Conner!" Red said.

The fairies fluttered with so much excitement, they buzzed like bees.

"Just read the last few pages! The part about the Portal Potion," Trix instructed.

Conner turned to the last entry of his grandmother's book and read about the creation.

The Portal Potion

Success! After weeks and weeks of trying, I've finally discovered the correct ingredients for the potion I'd hoped to create for my son! With just a few drops, the potion turns any written work into a portal to the world it describes. Even with my ability to create portals to and from the Otherworld, I never thought it would be possible to create a substance that allowed me passage to any world I wished.

My son will get to see the places and meet the characters he's spent his whole childhood dreaming about! And best of all, I'll get to watch his happiness soar as it happens!

The ingredients are much simpler than I imagined, but difficult to obtain. Their purposes are more metaphysical than practical, so it took some imagination to get the concoction right.

The first requirement is a branch from the oldest tree in the woods. *To bring the pages to life, I figured the potion would need the very thing that brought the paper to life in the first place. And what else has more life than an ancient tree?*

The second ingredient is a feather from the finest pheasant in the sky. *This will guarantee your potion has no limits, like a bird in flight. It will ensure you can travel to lands far and wide, beyond your imagination.*

The third component is a liquefied lock and key that belonged to a true love. *Just as this person unlocked your heart to a life of love, it will open the door of the literary dimensions your heart desires to experience.*

The fourth ingredient is two weeks of moonlight. *Just as the moon causes waves in the ocean, the moonlight will stir your potion to life.*

Last, but most important, give the potion a spark of magic to activate all the ingredients. Send it a beam of joy straight from your heart.

The potion does not work on any biographies or history books, but purely on works that have been imagined. Now, I must warn about the dangers of entering a fictional world:

1. Time only exists as long as the story continues. Be sure to leave the book before the story ends, or you may disappear as the story concludes.

2. Each world is made of only what the author describes. Do not expect the characters to have any knowledge of our world or the Otherworld.

3. Beware of the story's villains. Unlike people in our world or the Otherworld, most literary villains are created to be heartless and stripped of all morals, so do not expect any mercy should you cross paths with one.

4. The book you choose to enter will act as your entrance and exit. Be certain nothing happens to it; it is your only way out.

The Fairy Godmother had drawn an illustration of a small vial at the end of the entry. It looked exactly like the bottle Alex had seen the Masked Man steal, and exactly like the bottle Conner had seen him holding on the roof of the Witches' Brew.

"Holy smokes," Conner said. His head was spinning so fast, he felt like the ground was moving. "That's how he survived the fall when Alex made the tavern float! He activated that small book with the potion and must have gone inside it before he hit the ground!"

The situation was becoming clearer but more confusing at once. Was it possible Alex had been right this entire time?

"Your grandmother said she made the potion for her son—*your* father," Goldilocks said. "When the Masked Man stole it, he told Alex he was taking something that was *owed to him*."

Conner nodded. "I almost hate to say it—but Alex's story is starting to make sense," he said, although he still wasn't ready to believe the impossible.

"The Masked Man told the witches he needed their help finding something, and once he did, he could recruit an *army beyond their wildest imaginations*," Jack recalled. "He said it was a *collection of sorts* and was supposed to be with the potion, but the late Fairy Godmother had gotten rid of it."

"He must have been talking about a collection of books," Conner said. "We've got to find Alex and fill her in on this. She may know which books he's talking about."

They all looked at one another, more determined to

find her than ever. However, Red did not reciprocate their enthusiasm. She had zoned out of their conversation and was staring peculiarly at the creek.

"Red, what's wrong?" Jack asked.

"Nothing, I'm fine," Red said, but she never looked up. "But I swear I just saw the creek's current change direction—"

Red let out a high-pitched squeal. She covered her mouth with one hand and pointed down the creek with the other. Two wooden caskets eerily floated in from another part of the Dwarf Forests. Red and the others stared at them in complete silence until the caskets gradually washed ashore nearby.

"What are those doing in the creek?" Trix asked. She and her fairy friends had never seen such a macabre sight.

"They don't call it Dead Man's Creek for nothing," Jack said.

"You don't think there are *bodies* inside, do you?" Red peeped.

Goldilocks withdrew her sword. "Only one way to find out."

Without any hesitation, Goldilocks approached the caskets and sliced off the latches. She opened them and then had to cover her mouth from the smell.

"Yup, there are bodies inside, all right," she said. "Come take a look! I've never seen corpses like these before."

"No, thank you!" Red was quick to say. "I'll take your word for it!"

Conner and Jack went to have a look for themselves. Each casket contained the body of an elderly person. They were so pale and wrinkled, they looked like white raisins. They were also so shriveled, their gender couldn't be identified. It was as if the bodies had been completely drained of life.

The fairies hovered over Jack's shoulders, too scared to look, but too curious not to.

"Oh, no!" Merkle cried. "This is an omen! It's an omen, I tell you!"

It was so ghoulish, Conner thought the paranoid fairy might be right. "Yeah," he said. "But an omen of what?"

CHAPTER SEVEN

ANSWERS IN THE ATTIC

As soon as Bree finished her Biology homework, Mrs. Campbell sent her up the narrow pull-down stairs to organize the attic. It didn't necessarily need organizing, but there were only so many times Bree could clean the kitchen or mow the lawn. And since Bree was still grounded, her mom was forced to get creative with the tasks she assigned, and the Campbell house had never looked better because of it.

The attic was dark and dusty. Besides a little light

cleaning, there wasn't much Bree could do. So, she figured she would just move boxes from one end of the attic to the other until her mom called her down for dinner.

At first she tried arranging all the storage by season, but that stopped when she couldn't decide which season the box of baby clothes belonged in. She then started organizing items by color until she found the box of Christmas lights and quickly lost interest in the amount of work that would take. The themes to her organization changed repeatedly, until she ended up just stacking boxes in the shapes of famous structures.

Bree had been so taunted by questions and theories lately, she actually enjoyed the mindless activity. She never expected to find something in the attic that would make those questions more daunting.

She stacked a pile of boxes too high and it toppled over, spilling all the contents on the floor. One of the items was a small treasure chest Bree had never seen. She could tell it was old from the faded floral design painted over the wood.

She blew off a layer of dust covering the chest and discovered the name *Anneliese* carved into the lid.

"Anneliese?" Bree said as she inspected it. "Oh, this must have belonged to Grandma!"

She was Bree's German grandmother, and since Bree had been questioning her heritage a lot recently, she wondered if she could find any information among her grandmother's things.

She opened the chest and a strong perfumed scent filled the attic. The chest was full of letters, photos, and newspaper clippings her grandmother had saved over the years. One of the clippings caught Bree's eye. It had yellowed with age and was very stiff to the touch. It announced Anneliese's engagement to Stephen Campbell, Bree's grandfather.

Directly under the clipping was a letter addressed to her grandmother, and Bree's heart stopped when she read the return address.

Cornelia Grimm
1729 Mystic Lane
Willow Grove, CT

"Grimm?" Bree said, and opened the letter as fast as she could. This was *exactly* what she was looking for.

A black-and-white photograph fell out of the envelope. It was of two young women posing on the front steps of a very large house. The one on the right was Bree's grandmother, so she assumed the woman on the left was Cornelia.

Cornelia looked a few years younger than Bree's grandmother. She had long blonde hair all the way down to her waist and the same smile as Anneliese. Bree figured the two must have been related. She carefully unfolded the letter and read it.

Dearest Cousin Anneliese,

I recently found this photo of you and me when I was cleaning out my desk. I want you to have it. It was taken the day you came to live with us at the house. Can you believe that was almost five years ago? Seems like only yesterday we picked you up from the harbor.

We hope married life is treating you well! Tears come to my eyes every time I remember your beautiful wedding. Stephen is a wonderful man. Are there any children for you two on the horizon? We certainly hope so!

The house isn't the same without you, but we're getting by. The Sisters and I continue the family work and have so many amazing things to tell you next time we meet.

We know this isn't what you intended would happen when you moved to the United States, but we are so happy you've found such a wonderful life.

We miss you and think about you often.

Love, Cornelia and the Sisters

Bree put the letter down and stared at the floor, a little bit in shock. Grimm wasn't a common last name, so if

Cornelia was her grandmother's cousin, then it was very possible her theory about being related to Wilhelm Grimm was true! The letter practically proved it!

She searched the chest for more correspondences between her grandmother and Cornelia, but they must have lost touch over the years, because she didn't find anything. But it didn't matter; this small piece of information made Bree feel like a thousand fireworks had been ignited inside of her.

Bree whipped out her cellphone from her pocket, eager to tell Emmerich. She didn't care how late it was in Bavaria; she had to share this information with someone else before she combusted.

"Bree, dinner is almost ready," Mrs. Campbell said as she climbed into the attic. "Well, it certainly looks *different* in here."

"I had some difficulty organizing it," Bree said. "I can finish it after dinner."

"No, honey, you don't have to," Mrs. Campbell said. "Your dad and I were just talking, and we've decided you're off the hook. You're not grounded anymore."

"Really?" Bree asked. She was very surprised at the exciting turn her afternoon had taken. "Why?"

"Because your little sister cut off her classmate's ponytail today at school," Mrs. Campbell said. "You've done such a great job with all the chores, we have no way of punishing *her*. And also, we think you've learned your lesson."

Bree nodded. "Definitely have," she said eagerly.

Mrs. Campbell tried to stop herself from saying what she said next, but it boiled up so much inside of her that she had no choice. "Why did you have to do something so stupid, Bree? I love all you girls equally, but you're my *smart daughter.* What were you thinking running around Europe?"

"I told you, Mom," Bree said. "I just wanted to have a little fun. And if it's any consolation, I just read about this study that says severe jet lag alters a person's judgment. So that might have had something to do with it."

"Well, whatever it was, don't ever do it again," Mrs. Campbell said. She noticed the chest and letter in Bree's hand. "What did you find there?"

"I found some of Grandma Anneliese's old letters," Bree said. "This one is from someone named Cornelia Grimm. Does that name sound familiar?"

Mrs. Campbell thought about it. "Oh, I think that was one of the ladies from your grandma's old *coven.*" She laughed.

Bree was certain she misheard her. *"Coven?"* she said with a gulp. "Did you just say *coven*—as in a house of witches?"

"At least that's how your dad and his brothers joke about it," Mrs. Campbell said.

"Wait—are you telling me Grandma was a *witch*?" Bree asked.

It was starting to concern Mrs. Campbell how seriously her daughter was taking this.

"Sweetheart, witches don't exist," she said. "When your grandmother came to this country she moved into a big house somewhere in Connecticut with a bunch of distant relatives. Apparently they used to do a bunch of kooky things together—probably just European stuff. Your grandma was very secretive about her life before she met your grandfather."

Hearing this made Bree's mouth fall open.

"Well, maybe one of us should go there and figure it out," Bree said. "It doesn't matter how distantly we're related—if we have family up there it would be nice to meet them."

Mrs. Campbell stared at her daughter as if she were coming down with an illness.

"Sweetheart, no one is going to Connecticut. Those women probably aren't even alive anymore. You've been grounded too long. I want you to make as many plans with friends as possible for the next couple weeks, okay? I think it'll be good for you."

Mrs. Campbell returned downstairs, unaware of the state she was leaving her daughter in. Bree had so many thoughts at once, she had forgotten how to move. She sat in silence as her body caught up with her racing mind.

She definitely had plans to make, but none of them had anything to do with friends. Bree had to find a way to *Connecticut*....

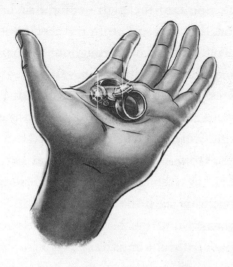

CHAPTER EIGHT

THE ONLY OBJECTION

The day of Red and Froggy's wedding finally arrived and the newly christened Center Kingdom was in a daze of celebration. Despite the constant setbacks, Red managed to finish all the planning her perfect day required. And thanks to a great amount of self-control on Goldilocks's part, Red had lived to see it.

The former Hall of Progress had been transformed into a beautiful altar. Five hundred chairs had been set to face a pulpit on top of a large platform. Risers were built for a two-hundred-piece symphony. A massive organ with pipes stretching into the high ceiling had been carefully constructed. Tall vases of pink, red, and white carnations were arranged and placed throughout the hall. White pillars and rosy silk drapes lined the walls.

Goldilocks had spent the entire morning helping the castle servants put everything together and was very proud of their work. However, when Red arrived to make her final inspections, Goldilocks discovered that her true task as matron of honor wasn't just helping the bride, but protecting everyone *from* the bride.

Red stormed into the Hall of Progress wearing nothing but a pink bathrobe and fuzzy slippers. She had curlers in her hair and no makeup on. Her eyes were much larger than usual and a scowl was frozen on her face—she had never looked so anxious.

"This is WRONG, it's all WRONG!" Red yelled. "The chairs are too close together—the women's dresses will get caught! The pulpit is too far away—I'm getting married, not making a pilgrimage! Tell all the musicians they are not allowed to eat any of the food—the caterers only had time to prepare enough for the guests! The pillars and drapes need to match—this place looks like a giant rib cage!"

Red didn't even look at anything long enough to properly see it. She flung her arms around, yelling and pointing at anything she could.

"Red, this is exactly as you planned it," Goldilocks said. "You need to calm down."

"Please tell me *that's* not what you're wearing to the wedding," Red hollered, targeting Goldilocks next.

"No, I'm wearing something much uglier that you chose for me," Goldilocks said. "Remember? The pink dress with the puffy shoulders?"

Red wasn't listening to a word she said. She began pacing and mumbling to herself.

"Did you sleep last night?" Goldilocks asked.

"*Sleep?* How was I supposed to sleep when there's so much to do?" Red asked. "Wait, are you saying I look puffy? *OH GOD, I LOOK PUFFY! The wedding is canceled! Everyone, go home!*"

Goldilocks removed the flowers from the nearest vase and dumped the water over Red's head to cool her off. The bride-to-be screamed.

"Listen to me very carefully," Goldilocks said, and leaned threateningly close to her. "Everything in this building is *exactly* how you wanted it to be. You're just having *pre-wedding jitters*. There is *nothing* you need to fix or adjust. What you *need* to do is go back to the castle and start getting ready and *enjoy* the day, because if I hear one more complaint from you, this *wedding* will turn into your *funeral*! Is that clear?"

Red frowned, her jaw trembled, and she nodded slowly. "Yes." She turned to face the rest of the room. "My apologies, everyone. Well done! As a reward for your efforts, I'd like to invite you all to the reception at the castle following the ceremony—*just don't eat anything!*"

However, Red wasn't the only one feeling pre-wedding jitters. Froggy, Conner, and Jack were dressed up in nice suits and kept one another company in the library of the castle while they waited for the ceremony to start. Froggy stood motionless at the window. He stared out at the kingdom and watched as the citizens lined the streets. They were bubbling with excitement and anticipation, hopeful for a glimpse of the royal wedding.

"It's funny how times change," Froggy said softly. "Four years ago I was living in a hole, afraid that if I showed my face to the world it would hate and fear me. I never thought love was an option for me. Now here I am, the elected king of a kingdom, about to marry one of the most beautiful women in the world—and she's technically the one who proposed."

"If there's one thing life is good at, it's surprising you," Jack said. "And sometimes it surprises you in the best ways."

Conner was sitting in an armchair, staring at the floor, oblivious to what they were saying. His mind was still fixated on their search for his sister and the Masked Man.

He quickly looked up when the room went quiet. "I'm sorry, what did you say?" Conner asked. He was supposed to be Froggy's best man, and so far, he was failing at it.

"Just an observation, nothing important," Froggy said. He gulped and loosened his collar. "Why does everyone rethink their decision to get married on the day of their wedding? I've been fine with the idea for months, but only now do I feel like I'm getting cold feet."

Conner laughed. "But, Froggy, you're an amphibian. Your feet are always cold!"

Froggy turned to him and smiled. It was a nice way of putting things into perspective.

There was a knock on the door and the third Little Pig poked his head into the library.

"Your Majesty, the former and future queen is almost ready. The ceremony will begin shortly."

Jack patted Froggy on the back. "This is it. Are you ready?"

"Ready as I'll ever be," Froggy said. "Gentlemen, please join me in my last steps as a bachelor."

They followed him out of the library, but Conner lingered in the doorway. A bad feeling grew in the pit of his stomach and he looked back at the empty library. It felt as if he was forgetting something, but he couldn't figure out what it was.

He didn't want to keep the others waiting, so he caught up with them, but the feeling stayed with him. Perhaps he was just having jitters of his own.

Meanwhile, in Red's chambers, the bride-to-be was taking an impossibly long time to put on her wedding dress. Goldilocks tried fussing with the sleeves of her matron of honor dress as she waited, but there was only so much she could do.

"Hurry up, Red," Goldilocks instructed. "You don't want to be late to your own wedding."

"Perfection can't be rushed," Red called out from her changing room.

As if Red were wrestling a giant fabric monster, Goldilocks heard rustling and tussling from the changing room as Red's handmaiden struggled to get the dress on her. When the handmaiden stepped out of the changing room her face was so flushed, she looked like she had run a marathon.

"What a dress," the handmaiden said. She was going to have nightmares about it for the rest of her life.

"Come on, Red," Goldilocks said. "I'm dying to see it."

The wedding dress was so massive, the front of it emerged from the changing room a few moments before Red followed behind. It was a white mountain of ruffles and lace, lined with red trim and covered in ridiculous red bows. The veil was messy and exploded from the top of Red's head like a volcano.

Goldilocks was speechless, and not in a good way. Clawdius leaped from his bed and barked at the dress as if it were a wild beast.

"Well, what do you think?" Red asked with a hopeful smile.

"Well, you said you wanted the wedding to be a spectacle, right?" Goldilocks said.

Red marched across her chambers to the mirror and had a look for herself. Judging from her reaction, the dress wasn't at all what she had expected.

"I look like a blizzard!" Red gasped. *"I don't understand—it looked so pretty in Granny's sketch!"*

"You didn't try it on beforehand?" Goldilocks asked.

"I didn't have time!" Red said. "I was too busy helping the twins find the Masked Man!"

"Maybe there's a way to *simplify* it?" Goldilocks suggested.

The handmaiden hooted. "It's so tightly stitched, it would take hours to alter it. She might be better off walking down the aisle naked."

Red had a massive panic attack. She walked around in circles and fanned her tears with her hands so her makeup wouldn't run. As far as she was concerned, the wedding was ruined.

"Maybe I can help?" said a familiar voice.

They all turned to see Alex standing behind them. None of them noticed when she appeared. Clawdius charged forward to pounce on her, his traditional way of greeting someone he liked, but Alex waved her hand and the wolf froze in midair. Despite being suspended, he still managed to lick the side of her face.

"Alex!" Goldilocks said, and gave her a hug. "You had all of us so worried. Thank God you're all right!"

"Well, I've been better," Alex said.

Red cleared her throat. *"Excuse me!"* she said, redirecting their attention. "Alex, it's nice to see you, but *I'm in the middle of a wedding crisis!* I could use a fairy's touch!"

"I think you need more than that." Goldilocks laughed.

"Can you help me or not?" Red yelled.

Seeing Red in such a frantic state made Alex forget about her own problems, but she was hesitant to help her.

"I don't know if I should," Alex said. "You saw what I did to the Fairy Council. My powers have a mind of their own—there's no telling what I might do to you."

Red had never looked so desperate. "I don't care if you turn me into a big ball of fire and lightning," she said. "Even *that* would look much better than this dress."

"All right." Alex shrugged. "But I'm going to need your help, Red. I can supply the magic, but you'll need to focus. Think of exactly how you want your wedding dress to look—what you want Froggy to see walking down the aisle toward him."

Red nodded and closed her eyes. Alex extended her hands toward her and light began swirling around the hideous dress. Red concentrated as hard as she could, thinking about the dress she had always dreamed of getting married in.

"Oh, my word," Goldilocks gasped, and covered her mouth.

"I've never seen such a gorgeous thing in my life!" the handmaiden said.

Red refaced the mirror to see for herself. She went into shock because of how stunning it was.

The fabric was so soft and fluffy, the dress looked like a cloud. Appropriately, a *hood* had replaced the veil, and it turned into a long train that flowed down Red's back and onto the floor. The whole dress twinkled like a starry sky.

"I think it needs one more thing," Alex said. She

snapped her fingers, and rather than a traditional bouquet, a *basket* of flowers appeared in her hand.

"I look *beautiful*," Red whispered. For the first time that day, her eyes filled with tears of joy. "Thank you so much for coming, Alex! It means the world to me!"

At first, Alex was planning to avoid Red's wedding altogether, not wanting to create a scene or cause any more damage. But seeing how happy Red was on her wedding day made Alex ashamed to have even *thought* about missing it.

"I just wish I could see the ceremony," Alex said. "But I'll probably cause a major fuss if I step onto the altar—"

"Oh, that shouldn't be a problem," Red said. "The organ isn't real—it's a little secret room. I had them build it just in case any of my friends were on the run and didn't want to be seen."

Alex and Goldilocks shared a quick look. Had they heard her correctly?

"You were *planning* on one of us being on the run?" Goldilocks asked.

"Are you *new*?" Red asked. "One of us is always in trouble or running from something or someone. It's just a given in our group. So I planned for it."

Alex and Goldilocks stared at her, amused but bewildered.

"We should get going, Your Former and Future Highness," the handmaiden said.

Clawdius whined—he was still frozen in the air. Alex waved her hand and he landed on the ground.

"Sorry, Clawdius, you're staying in the castle until you learn the difference between children and chew toys," Red said. "It's a long story, but thank goodness we got there in time."

Red had one last look at herself in the mirror and headed for the door. The handmaiden helped Red through the doorway, making sure her dress didn't snag on anything. The dress was hard to walk in, so Goldilocks pulled Alex aside while they let Red get a head start.

"Have you talked to your brother?" Goldilocks asked.

"I don't want to talk to my brother," Alex said. She was still upset he hadn't come to her defense at the Fairy Palace.

"Well, what he has to say might surprise you," Goldilocks said. "We found out some information about the Masked Man."

"What did you find?" Alex asked.

"The potion he stole from the Fairy Palace is something your grandmother invented when your father was a boy," she said. "It turns any written work into a portal to whatever world it describes. Knowing what he told the witches, we think he's going to use the potion to recruit an army from a collection of books your grandmother used to own."

"What?" Alex asked. She knew the potion must have been powerful, but she had no idea such a thing was even possible. "What kind of books is he after, then?"

"We were hoping you would know," she said. "Can you think of anything off the top of your head?"

Alex thought about it as hard as she could, but the only books she remembered her grandmother having were spell books.

"I can't think of anything," Alex said. "But regardless of what books he's after, we won't be able to stop him unless we know where he is."

Goldilocks nodded. "We'll find him much faster if we work together again."

"I know," Alex said. "But after what I did to the Fairy Council, I'm afraid to be around you guys. I couldn't live with myself if I ever lost control and hurt one of you."

Goldilocks put her hands on Alex's shoulders and looked directly into her eyes.

"Alex, for the last six months I have been at the mercy of *raging* hormones," she said. "One minute I'm devastated, then the next I'm obnoxiously happy. I'm either overly sympathetic or vengefully spiteful, but never anywhere between. Yesterday, Jack told me I looked beautiful and I *punched* him."

"Why are you telling me this?" Alex asked.

"Because I know what it's like not being in control of your emotions," Goldilocks clarified. "And if I can get through today without killing Red, I have no doubt that *you* can learn to control yourself, too."

Alex appreciated Goldilocks's faith. "I'll work on it."

"Yoo-hoo!" Red sang from the hall. *"Come on! It's showtime!"*

Alex and Goldilocks headed out of Red's chambers and followed the happy bride down the hallway.

"Are you excited, Red?" Alex asked.

"Honestly," Red said, "I never thought I could be this happy. Who would have thought marrying a frog would bring me so much joy?"

The wedding guests had all arrived and taken their seats. The musicians played a pleasant song as they waited (except for the organist, who couldn't figure out why the organ wasn't working). All they needed was the bride, and the wedding could begin.

Froggy stood on the platform and looked quite anxious. Every second he waited made him more paranoid that Red might have had second thoughts. He was afraid that at any moment Red's handmaiden would run inside and tell the room the bride had called it off.

All the royal families had come to support Froggy and Red. Froggy's brothers, King Chance, King Chase, and King Chandler, gave him thumbs-ups to calm his nerves. His sisters-in-law, Cinderella, Snow White, and Sleeping Beauty, blew him kisses.

Queen Rapunzel sat with her long braid piled in her lap, as it had tripped all the guests seated near her. The people sitting behind Empress Elvina were upset because her giant crown made of tree branches blocked their view, but they were too afraid to ask her to remove it.

Red's granny and the Little Old Woman who managed the Shoe Inn sat on either side of the empress, chatting her ears off.

"I've heard that elves aren't the best tailors," Granny said. "You should let me come to the Elf Empire and give sewing lessons. I've made all of Red's clothes ever since she was a little girl. Her wedding dress is the best one I've ever made! At least I hope it is. I lost my glasses a few weeks ago."

The Fairy Council was also in attendance, and Conner avoided making eye contact with them as much as possible. Unfortunately, he couldn't avoid *everyone* he wanted to.

"Weddings are so romantic. Don't you think, Butterboy?"

Conner's whole body went tense at the sound of the voice. He looked up and saw Trollbella had chosen the closest possible seat to him.

"It reminds me of the time we almost got married," Trollbella said. "Remember that, Butterboy? It was the best ten minutes of my life!"

It was a memory Conner had tried repeatedly to forget. "It rings a bell."

"Of course, we were so young and foolish then. We weren't mature enough for marriage," Trollbella said.

"That was only two years ago," Conner reminded her.

"Feels like yesterday, right?" she said. "I'm so glad we didn't go through with it. We needed time apart before we made that leap. We needed to live a little and have more experiences in love. Thankfully, I got all of that out of the way with Gator—*may he rest in Troblin heaven*. I'm sure you feel the same way about that *blonde girl*."

"You mean Bree?" Conner said. "We weren't *dating*. I haven't even talked to her in a couple months."

Even though they hadn't spoken in a while, Conner would be lying if he said he didn't think about Bree often. In fact, Bree was the only thing he actually *liked* thinking about these days.

"Funny how the *flames* of love diminish so quickly," Trollbella said with a deep sigh. "Luckily, I've learned the difference between a *flame* and a *fire*. I didn't know it at the time, but Gator was just a flame. I'm done with *flames*, what I need now is a *fire*."

She looked up at Conner and batted her big eyes. Conner's stomach started to turn—he thought they were past all of this.

"Well, I hope you find one," Conner said, and patted her on the shoulder. "Excuse me."

Conner walked away from her as quickly as possible and joined Froggy on the platform.

He wished Trollbella had never brought up Bree. If he were honest with himself, he might admit how much he missed her, but he ignored the feeling whenever it arose, afraid it would grow if he gave it any attention.

Conner was glad she wasn't around—or so he told himself. He had already exposed her to a dangerous expedition around Europe and a two-hundred-year-old army. Wherever she was, she was much better off without him. Danger seemed to follow Conner and affect anyone associated with him.

Knowing that, Conner wondered if he could ever get married himself. Would it be selfish to expose someone he loved to a life as crazy as his? Would someone willingly exchange rings with *him* knowing it was a risk?

Conner abruptly slapped his forehead. *"The rings!"* he whispered to himself. *"That's what I forgot!"*

"What's wrong?" Jack asked.

"I left the rings in the library."

"Do you want me to retrieve them?"

"No, I know right where I left them," Conner said. "I'll be right back. I'm the worst best man ever."

Conner rushed out of the House of Progress and made a mad dash for the castle. It was hard to run through the village with all the people lining the streets. The crowds began to cheer as Red rode by in a golden carriage.

"Crap!" Conner said. "It's gonna start!" He ran as fast as he possibly could, determined to get the rings back in time.

The golden carriage arrived at the House of Progress and all the villagers gathered at the front steps. Red and Goldilocks were escorted out of the carriage and the people cheered at their first glimpse of her wedding dress.

Hearing the crowd outside as Red arrived was the cue for the wedding to begin. The third Little Pig was to officiate at the ceremony, so he took his place behind the pulpit. Jack stood on the steps of the platform just below Froggy, a promoted groomsman until Conner came back.

"Where did Conner go?" Froggy asked.

"Bathroom," Jack said. "He'll be right back."

Alex magically appeared in the small room inside the organ and no one was the wiser. She was so grateful that Red had gone to such lengths. As she looked around the room she saw the wedding was filled with people she didn't want to see—although she didn't see her brother anywhere.

Goldilocks walked down the aisle and took her place across from Jack. Red appeared in the doorway in all her glory and the room got to their feet. She moved toward the pulpit and the doors were shut behind her. She walked so delicately, it seemed like she was floating down the aisle.

Froggy felt like time stopped once he saw Red. He forgot where he was and how he had gotten there. As far as he was concerned, she was the only thing in existence. He had never seen such a beautiful sight in his life, and his big glossy eyes became even glossier.

Red had to remind herself to breathe as she walked. She couldn't believe this moment had finally come. The wedding felt absolutely perfect and everything seemed right in the world.

"You may be seated," the third Little Pig announced when Red reached the pulpit. He gave a little opening speech, making the guests laugh a couple of times. Red and Froggy were lost in each other's eyes and didn't hear a word of it.

Jack worried more as the ceremony went on. Conner was still nowhere to be found.

"What's wrong?" Goldilocks mouthed to him.

"I don't have the rings," Jack mouthed back.

"And now it's time for the rings," the third Little Pig announced to the crowd.

Goldilocks turned to the organ and pointed to her finger. *"Rings,"* she whispered, hoping Alex would hear her.

To Jack's relief, two sparkling rings magically appeared in his hand. He gave one to Froggy and the other to Red. They were oblivious to everything but each other and had no clue anything was wrong.

The quick save wasn't entirely unnoticed. Emerelda eyed the rings suspiciously—she knew Alex must have been close by. She looked around the room, searching for where she might be hiding.

"Get out of here," Goldilocks whispered at the organ.

Alex wanted to stay for the entire ceremony, but she knew it was best to make a peaceful exit while she still could. She gazed at her friends one final time, and quietly disappeared into thin air.

"With this ring, I thee wed," Froggy said as he slipped the ring onto Red's finger.

"With this ring, I thee wed," Red said, doing the same.

"King Charlie Charming, do you take Red Riding

Hood to be your wife and queen for as long as you both shall live?" the third Little Pig asked.

"I do," Froggy said. He was so emotional, he let a *ribbit* slip.

"Do you, Red Riding Hood, take Charlie Charming as your husband and king for as long as you both shall live?"

"I do," Red said. "And even beyond that."

Their hearts were overflowing with so much joy, they could have flooded the House of Progress. There wasn't a dry eye in the room. All the observing couples held each other a little tighter.

"Then unless there are any objections, I hereby pronounce you—"

BAAM! The doors burst open with a blinding flash of light. A gust of wind blew through the hall, knocking over all the vases and pillars. The guests screamed and covered their heads. A horned creature entered the hall and leisurely strolled down the aisle. As it moved closer to the platform, Froggy and Red realized it wasn't an animal, but *a woman*.

"Forgive the intrusion, but *I object*," Morina said with a menacing smile.

The room erupted into a wave of murmuring. No one knew who or what the woman was.

"How dare you!" Froggy said. *"Who are you?"*

"You don't recognize me, Charlie?" Morina said with a playful frown. "After all we've been through together?"

Even though she didn't have horns herself, Red was about to charge the intruder. "Charlie, do you know this woman?" she asked.

Froggy tried to remember who she might be but couldn't recall a time their paths had crossed. "I've never seen her before in my life. *Identify yourself, woman!*"

Morina cackled so loudly, the hall vibrated from the echo. "Why, I'm your *fiancée*," she said. "Your *other* fiancée."

The entire room erupted in booing and hissing. They couldn't believe this woman had the nerve to barge into a wedding and proclaim such a distasteful lie.

Everyone was outraged, except for Froggy. He became stiff as a board and turned pale green. He knew who she was after all, but he never thought he would ever lay eyes on her again.

"*Morina...*," he said. "*You've changed....*"

The witch was delighted to see how affected he was by her transformation. "It's been a very long time. Yet you're exactly how I left you."

Red grabbed Froggy's hand, fearing the worst. "Charlie, what is she talking about?"

Froggy was trembling, as if he were seeing a ghost. "It's been years since I saw her," he said. "She was my first love, but I was afraid of what my family would think if they found out I was courting a witch, so I ended it. She was convinced I ended it because of how she looked at the time, even though I swore it had nothing to do with her appearance.

She cursed me to look like a frog so it was my *own* face I would be ashamed to show them."

Red felt as if she was going to be sick. The Charming Kings all stood at once.

"Guards!" King Chance yelled. *"Seize this woman! She is a criminal!"*

"Oh, sit down!" Morina said, and with a flick of her finger each of the Charmings were compelled to sit against their will. "You don't have proof I was the witch who did this to him. Although it does *sound* like me."

"Why are you here, Morina?" Froggy asked. "What do you want?"

"Isn't it obvious?" she said. "I've decided I want you back. I've missed you so much over these years. Why else would I so rudely interrupt your wedding?"

"Over my dead body!" Red screamed, putting herself between Morina and Froggy.

The witch rolled her eyes at the affectionate gesture. "That can easily be arranged," she said. "You have two options, Charlie. Come with me now, and return to the life we started so long ago. *Or* choose to stay and watch me curse your bride with a fate far worse than yours. The choice is yours."

The Fairy Council leaped to their feet at the threat.

"If you even *attempt* to curse anyone, we will personally escort you to Pinocchio Prison," Emerelda said.

"Relax, I haven't done anything illegal yet," Morina said. "It's entirely up to Charlie. So what will it be?"

The hall waited with bated breath, but Froggy didn't know what to do or say. The witch had a paralyzing effect on him.

"Fine," he said with a quivering jaw. "I'll go."

The room gasped. Morina laughed and clapped her hands.

"What?" Red yelled. "Charlie, you can't be serious! I'm not letting you go!"

"I have to go, darling," he said. "I won't let her harm you."

Red put her hands on his face and tears spilled down her own. "Let her curse me, I don't care," she said. "There's isn't a curse in the world that would be worse than living without you!"

"Red, she's much more powerful than she seems," he said. "This is the only way I can protect you."

"She's livestock with lipstick! I can handle it!" Red cried. *"I won't let her take you from me!"*

"I'm so sorry, my love," he said with tears of his own. "I have to go. . . . I have to. . . ."

Red grabbed hold of him with all her might. Froggy kissed her forehead and forced her off of him and joined Morina in the aisle. The witch linked arms with him and they headed to the door together.

Tears were flowing out of Red's eyes like a fountain. "Emerelda, do something!" Red said. "You can't let her do this!"

"She hasn't done anything," Emerelda said. "He's leaving of his own free will."

"THEN, SOMEONE DO SOMETHING!" Red hysterically cried. "PLEASE, I'M BEGGING! SOMEONE STOP HIM!"

Everyone in the hall looked at one another desperately, but there was nothing to be done. When no one came to her rescue, Red ran after Froggy, but she tripped on her dress and fell to the floor.

"CHARLIE, WAIT! COME BACK!" she pleaded. "PLEASE COME BACK!"

Red crawled down the aisle as she cried for him, but Froggy never looked back. He and Morina reached the door and disappeared into a puff of dark smoke.

Red lay on the floor and sobbed hysterically. Goldilocks ran to her and kneeled beside her. Cinderella, Snow White, Sleeping Beauty, and Granny joined Goldilocks on the floor, but Red was beyond comforting.

The Charming Brothers stood over her by their wives.

"We'll find him, Red," Chase said.

"We won't let this witch take our brother from us again," Chandler said.

"But she didn't take him this time...," Red cried. *"He left me.... He left me at our wedding...."*

Red was so devastated, she became delirious.

"Is this a dream, Goldie?" Red asked. *"Please tell me this is a dream...."*

Goldilocks had no words to comfort her. Red rested her head on Goldilocks's lap and sobbed herself to sleep. With nothing left to see and no way to help, the Fairy Council disappeared one at a time. The other guests took their lead and filed out of the Hall of Progress.

"What ever happened to Butterboy?" Trollbella said as she walked out with the others.

Jack looked around the hall, but there was still no sign of him. "I'm going to find Conner," he said to Goldilocks. "Something must have happened to him."

He left the Hall of Progress as fast as he could. The eager crowds outside weren't aware of what had occurred and they cheered every time someone walked out, expecting their newly married king and queen to emerge at any moment.

Jack squeezed through the villagers and retraced what he assumed would have been Conner's path to retrieve the rings. He made it all the way back to the castle with no sign of him. However, as soon as Jack stepped into the library, he discovered his instincts were right.

All the furniture had been knocked over and the paintings were crooked. The windows were shattered and most of the shelves were broken. The floor was covered in books and glass.

"Conner!" Jack yelled.

He heard grunting and found Conner curled up in the corner. He had a black eye and a busted lip, and he was clutching his stomach. Jack gently lifted him up to a seated position.

"Conner, what the hell happened?" Jack asked. "Who did this to you?"

He was still shaken up and had a hard time speaking. "He was here...," he said.

"Who was?" Jack asked.

"The Masked Man," Conner said. "When I came back for the rings...he was in the library...he was stealing books...I tried to hold him down...but he fought me off...."

Conner raised his arm and showed Jack a sack he was clutching tightly in his fist. He had managed to grab hold of the Masked Man's mask.

"I saw his face...," Conner said. "Alex was right all along....*He's our dad!*"

CHAPTER NINE

———◆✦◆———

A MOTH OF MEMORIES

Alex stood in a window that was so large, a ship could sail through it. She had chosen to occupy this bedroom at the giant's castle because of this very window and the beautiful view of the stars it had at night. Also, it was the farthest bedroom from Mother Goose's room and the only place you couldn't hear her snoring.

Every night she would stare up at the stars and pretend she was talking to her grandmother. The castle was above the clouds, so Alex had an unobstructed view of the moon and constellations. Wherever her grandmother was, Alex felt much closer to her here.

"You said that fairies don't die and that you'd always be with us," Alex said. "So if that's the case, please send me a sign to show you're there. Please send me something that lets me know I'm not really as alone as I feel."

It was a request Alex asked of her grandmother every night, and every night she waited for a response. Eventually she became too tired to stand and would crawl into the giants' football field–sized bed and try to sleep. However, tonight Alex never became tired, and the longer she waited for a response, the angrier she became.

"The whole world thinks I've lost my mind, Grandma," she told the sky. "And I can't blame them—I've lost control of my powers and I'm obsessed with finding a man I think is my dad. It would be much easier if I believed I was crazy, too, so why can't I? Why am I so certain of what I saw? I'm begging you, please send me something to give me some clarity—I hate feeling this way."

Luckily for Alex, someone *was* listening tonight. Just when she was about to give up and go to bed, something among the stars caught her attention. It was bright and grew bigger and bigger the longer she watched it.

Alex would have assumed it was a plane if she were in the Otherworld, but she had no clue what was headed her way. Soon, Alex saw the object had wings, not like a bird or a fairy but like an insect. It was a giant moth, proportionately sized in scale of the giants' castle, and it was made entirely of white light.

The moth landed on the windowsill beside Alex. She had no reason to trust the moth, but for whatever reason, she knew it wasn't going to harm her.

"Where are you from?" Alex asked.

The moth looked up to the stars.

"Did my grandmother send you?" she asked.

The moth wiggled its feathered antennae, and Alex took that as a yes.

"Why did she send you?"

The moth lowered its wings and made them flat against the windowsill. Even though it never said a word, Alex knew exactly what it meant.

"You want me to climb on your back?" Alex said.

The moth stayed put—so she took it as a yes. Alex wasn't sure if it was even possible, but when she stroked the moth's wing, she found it was as solid as a real moth despite being made of light. Alex climbed onto its back and the moth fluttered into the night sky, leaving the giant's castle behind.

The moth glided through the cool night air and down into the clouds. Alex could see the entire fairy-tale world once they flew beneath them.

"Where are we going?" Alex asked, but the moth never gave any indication.

Everything was dark, but judging from the terrain she could see, Alex figured the moth was descending somewhere between the Fairy Kingdom and the Charming

Kingdom. They landed in the middle of a forest. There was a dry riverbed and a few tree stumps but nothing very special about this part of the woods.

"Why did you bring me here?" Alex asked as she climbed down from the moth's back.

The moth suddenly separated into a dozen orbs that then dispersed throughout the woods. A few of the orbs flew to the tree stumps and morphed into the rest of the missing trees. Some of the orbs turned into water and flowed down the empty riverbed. It was like they had turned into holograms to show what the forest had once looked like.

The remaining two orbs flew farthest into the forest and became the silhouettes of a woman and a young boy. They walked hand in hand to where Alex was standing. The boy reminded her so much of Conner when he was younger, and the woman looked like a younger version of her grandmother.

"Oh my gosh," Alex said as she glanced around the forest. "This is a *memory*. That's Grandma and Dad!"

Her dad and grandmother were in the middle of a conversation as they walked. Their voices sounded overexposed, like an old recording was playing.

"Why are you taking me into the woods, Mother?" the boy asked. "You know I hate the outdoors."

"Because fresh air is good for you," the Fairy Godmother said.

"I don't see how that's possible with all the bugs," the boy said. "I wish you let me stay in my room."

He was a very spiteful and unhappy child—nothing like Alex had imagined. The twins were told their entire lives how energetic and adventurous their dad was as a boy. But the child Alex was watching now couldn't be more different than that. Was the memory she was witnessing of a rough time?

"I wanted to show you something I found the other day when I took a walk," the Fairy Godmother said. She put her hands on his shoulders and moved him in front of a tree. "Do you see that big hole in the tree? There's a squirrel's nest inside there."

"Fascinating," the boy said, and rolled his eyes. "Can we go home now?"

"Not yet—I want you to see it," his mother insisted. "The last time I was here a mother squirrel had just given birth to babies. One of the babies had very sharp claws and was scratching itself and all its siblings, so the mother chewed its claws off."

"Why would she do something so barbaric?" he asked.

"Because she was trying to protect it and the other babies from getting hurt," she said. "It may make it more difficult for the squirrel to climb trees and defend itself later in life, but the mother did what she knew she had to. All mothers have to make tough decisions regarding their children; it's just part of nature. Why don't you peek in and see how much they've grown?"

The Fairy Godmother gave him a little push toward the tree. The boy reluctantly looked inside.

"It's empty, Mother, I don't see anything," he said.

"Perhaps an owl attacked the nest and ate all the babies during the night. Now *that* is something I wish I could have seen."

The boy turned back around and saw his mother pointing her wand at him. *POW!* Ropes blasted out of the tip of her wand and wrapped her son around the tree. He screamed and struggled against them, but he was confined.

"Mother, what's the meaning of this?" the boy yelled. *"Let me go!"*

"I'm so sorry, my darling," the Fairy Godmother said tearfully. "This is the hardest thing I will ever do, but I have no choice."

"What are you talking about?" the boy said. *"What are you doing to me?"*

"I know what you dream of when you're asleep," the Fairy Godmother said. "I know your heart's greatest desire is to grow up and take over the world, but I can't let you use your magic to hurt or kill anyone. So, I have to *chew your claws off.* I have to kill your magic."

"No, Mother!" the boy screamed. *"Don't do this! Please!"*

The Fairy Godmother pointed her wand at him again and hit her son with a bright blast of light. A few moments later, a sparkling silhouette his exact shape and size fell out of him. The Fairy Godmother waved her wand and chains wrapped around the silhouette. She dragged it into the river and held it under the water.

The silhouette squirmed and convulsed as the Fairy Godmother drowned it, splashing water everywhere. The task was more difficult to perform than the Fairy God-mother had expected, and she closed her eyes. Little by little, the silhouette faded in the water until it washed away completely.

Both the Fairy Godmother and her son were crying, but for very different reasons. Alex was choked up, too—it was one of the saddest things she'd ever witnessed. This couldn't be a real memory—this must have been someone's nightmare. But why was her grandmother showing it to her?

"One day you'll forgive me," the Fairy Godmother said, and climbed out of the river.

"I will never forgive you!" her son cried. *"I will hate you until you die!"*

He stared up at her with so much hatred, he was obviously telling her the truth. He would never love her again.

"That's your decision," she said. "But even if you do, I will never stop loving you, Lloyd."

Alex felt like she had been punched in the stomach. *"Lloyd?"* she said.

"You never would have done this to John...," Lloyd cried. "You'll always love him more... always..."

The trees, the river, the Fairy Godmother, her son, and everything the orbs projected vanished, leaving Alex alone in the forest. It was so still and quiet, Alex could hear her heart beating. Her grandmother's spirit supplied her with more clarity than she could have asked for.

"So that *was* a memory," she said. "Dad had a *brother!*"

CHAPTER TEN

MAKING AMENDS

The following morning, Alex was still in the forest the moth had taken her to. She sat on a tree stump and stared at the dry riverbed across from her. The events that had taken place here a few decades before constantly replayed in her mind. She was so fixated on them, she hadn't even noticed the sun had risen.

For months she had tortured herself with theories to validate what she saw in the Fairy Palace. She spent hours of each day trying to understand how her wonderful father had become such a monster and been in two places at once.

And although it didn't bring her any joy to learn the truth, it was the best answer she could have hoped for: It wasn't her father, but she hadn't hallucinated, either.

Alex and Conner had an uncle—an *uncle Lloyd*, to be exact. And based on the little she knew about him, Alex couldn't blame her dad and grandma for keeping him a secret.

She was very eager to tell her brother what she had discovered. Now that she had confirmed her sanity was intact, it was much easier to forgive her brother for not believing her. Perhaps she had expected too much of him. Had the roles been reversed and Conner claimed *he* saw their deceased father come back from the dead, she probably would have treated him exactly as he had treated her.

Alex was looking forward to regrouping with her friends. Goldilocks was right; they worked much better together. And now that she had the answers she had been looking for, she wasn't nearly as worried about her emotions getting the best of her.

A stomping sound came from somewhere behind her in the woods. She turned and saw a chubby unicorn with a broken horn in the distance.

"Cornelius?" Alex said. "Is that you?"

She was certain it was her old steed—how many misfit unicorns could there be in the world? Cornelius bucked excitedly when he saw her, but then ran in the opposite direction.

"Well, that was strange," Alex said.

A few minutes later, Cornelius came racing back, galloping faster than any horse. The unicorn wasn't alone. A very handsome young man with wispy hair was riding on Cornelius's back.

"Rook?" Alex said. "What are you doing with Cornelius?"

He was the last person she expected to bump into in the woods, but Rook was overjoyed to find her.

"Alex!" he said. "Cornelius and I have been looking *everywhere* for you!"

She knew why the rest of the world was searching for her, but Rook's motives were a mystery. "What for?"

"It's a long story—but we've been following the Masked Man!" he told her. "We know where he's been hiding!"

Alex's heart began to race— she prayed he wasn't mistaken. "But we've been looking for months! How did you find him?"

"Cornelius and I have been trailing him," Rook explained. "We figured it wouldn't hurt to have two more men on the job. We weren't going to bother you unless we found something worth bringing up—but a few days ago we saw him running through the Dwarf Forests! We followed him and found a *cave* he's been living in!"

"Rook, that's amazing!" Alex said. "Where is the cave?"

"Northwest, between the Elf Empire and the Northern Kingdom," he said. He retrieved a folded paper stuck in his boot and handed it to her. "Here, this map has his exact whereabouts."

Alex looked it over—Rook had circled the exact spot in the Northern Mountains where the cave was located.

"There's something else you should know," Rook said, and his tone became much more serious. "We checked on the cave yesterday to make sure he hadn't moved. His mask was gone, but he had a large bag of books with him. One by one he took a book out, laid it open on the ground, and poured this strange liquid on it from a blue bottle. It made the books glow *and then he disappeared inside them.*"

"What kind of books did he do this to?" Alex asked anxiously. He must have found the collection he was after.

Rook closed one eye as he remembered. "They were really specific titles—I had never heard of them before," he said. "The first one was called *20,000 Leagues Under the Sea*. He spent a couple hours inside that one, then returned from it soaking wet. A giant tentacle came out after him and tried to pull him back inside, but he managed to shut the cover and it went away. The second book was called *The Jungle Book*, and he was inside that one for only a few minutes before he crawled out of it with scratches all over his body."

Alex covered her mouth. She never expected the Masked Man was after literature from the *Otherworld*. No wonder he had such a hard time locating the collection.

"The third book was about a wonderful warlock of some

kind," Rook said. "He was from a place with two letters—I think it started with an *O*."

"You mean Oz?" Alex asked. "He went inside *The Wonderful Wizard of Oz*?!"

"Yes! That's the one!"

"And how long did he stay inside?"

"He's still in there as far as I know," Rook said. "He traveled into it a few hours before sunrise. He took the whole bag of books with him. Cornelius and I have been searching for you all morning—we didn't want to do anything until we found you. It's a miracle we did!"

Alex was so enthralled that she was shaking. "I've got to find my brother. Thank you so much, Rook!"

She gave Rook a huge hug and kissed him on his cheek—but as soon as she did, she regretted it. She pulled away from him and he blushed. It was an insensitive thing to do, given their history.

"You could have been killed," she said. "Why would you risk going after him?"

Rook was shy about telling her, but he forced himself to. "I'm just trying to make amends for hurting you. I'll never stop caring about you, Alex."

Alex appreciated it, but it didn't change how she felt about him. During the war with the Grande Armée, Rook knowingly put the world at risk to save his loved ones. She understood that he had been thrown into a terrible situation and just did what he thought was right, but it was still difficult to forgive him.

Unfortunately, Alex's world was filled with terrible situations and difficult decisions, and she had to trust anyone who came close to her unconditionally. And just like her brother had feared, she didn't think she would ever find someone she was comfortable enough to share that burden with.

"Well, don't waste any more time on my account," Rook said. "Go find your brother."

Alex gave Cornelius a hug and left the forest. She headed for the Center Kingdom, hoping her brother and their friends were still there.

Conner was lying in bed in a guestroom of the Center Kingdom castle. Hagetta sat by his side, setting his injuries ablaze with the flames of her magical healing fire. Goldilocks and Jack stood over the bed, very intrigued by the process.

"Thanks for coming, Hagetta," Conner said. "This sure beats waiting for everything to heal naturally."

"If only it healed wounds of the heart, too," Hagetta said. "How is Red holding up?"

Goldilocks sighed. "She won't eat or come out of her room."

"In good news, the kingdom felt so sorry for Red, she's been reelected queen in Froggy's absence," Jack said.

"I can't believe he left her at the altar," Conner said. "That doesn't sound like the Froggy we know."

"He's overcome the curse but not the spell she cast over him," Hagetta said. "I hate to say it, but he did the right thing. Morina is a very powerful witch and she's infamous for the grudges she keeps. He probably saved Red's life by leaving with her."

She raised a burning stick toward Conner's black eye, but he held up his hand to stop her.

"I kind of want to keep that one," he said. "It makes me look tough."

Hagetta applied the flames anyway and the bruising disappeared within a few seconds. She looked over his injuries one last time and shook her head. "I don't understand what kind of father could do this to his own son."

"You're positive the Masked Man is your father?" Jack asked.

Conner nodded. "I feel so ashamed of myself. I know Alex better than anyone—of course she was telling the truth! She wouldn't have believed it herself unless she was absolutely sure of what she saw. I should have supported her more. What kind of brother am I?"

There was a bright flash and Alex appeared in the middle of the room. It gave everyone a fright and Conner almost fell out of bed.

"I don't know when you learned to do that, but I wish you wouldn't!" he yelled. "Wait—*Alex!* You're *here!* Thank God, we have so much to tell you!"

Alex was so glad she had caught Conner and their

friends together. "And I have so much to tell you! Where are Froggy and Red? Did they go on their honeymoon?"

They exchanged depressed looks and Alex knew something was horribly wrong.

"Conner, you're *hurt*," Alex said, noticing the patches of flames covering his body. "What happened?"

Goldilocks broke the bad news to her. "Shortly after you left, a witch named Morina stormed into the wedding and threatened to curse Red unless Froggy left with her."

"What?" Alex said. "But *why*? Who is this witch?"

"She's the witch who cursed Froggy to look like a frog all those years ago," Hagetta said. "It must have infuriated her that he found happiness despite his appearance, something she could never achieve."

"But the Fairy Council was there. Why didn't any of them stop her?" Alex asked.

"The Charming Kings tried, but he wasn't being *kidnapped*," Jack said. "There wasn't anything anyone could do. He left of his own free will to protect Red."

Alex couldn't believe she had missed all of this, but she was glad she'd left the wedding when she did. Had she stayed, she definitely would have lost control of herself and done something she regretted.

"Conner, please tell me you injured yourself trying to fight her off," she said.

"Oh, just wait, the story gets better," Conner said sarcastically. "While all this was happening, I came back to the castle because I had forgotten the rings. I caught the Masked Man—*oh yeah, remember him?*—stealing books from the library! I tried to hold him down, but he attacked me. I yanked his mask off just before he left and I saw his face! You were right, Alex—*it's Dad!* I'm so sorry I never believed you!"

Alex looked from side to side uneasily. "Err...no, I wasn't."

"No, Alex, it's okay!" Conner said. "We all know you're not crazy or confused! We believe you now—I saw him with my own eyes! Dad is alive and he's been wreaking havoc on the fairy-tale world! It's my fault for not trusting you from the beginning—*why are you looking at me like that?*"

She didn't seem nearly as relieved to hear this as he had expected. Instead, Alex just nodded along and impatiently waited for him to stop apologizing.

"First off, thank you for your trust. I appreciate it," she said. "But I was wrong. The Masked Man is not Dad—*it's Dad's brother!* I just found out!"

Conner raised an eyebrow. "Who told you that?"

"Well," she said, not knowing how to describe what she experienced. "Um...a *moth* did."

Conner squinted at her and his mouth fell open. He was expecting a much better answer than that. "A *moth* told you?"

"Yes—but it wasn't a regular moth, it was more like an angel."

"An angel moth?"

"Well, it came from somewhere in the stars. I think Grandma sent it."

"Grandma sent you an angel moth from outer space?"

"Kind of! Anyway, the moth took me to a forest and then turned into a bunch of orbs that re-created a memory—stop looking at me like that, Conner! The point I'm trying to make is that the Masked Man is not our dad!"

The others looked back and forth at the twins like they were watching a tennis match. It was the most absurd conversation they had ever heard.

"Guys," Conner said to them, "I take back everything I said before. I think Alex has lost her mind and I might be next."

"Hold on a second," Alex said, and crossed her arms. "You just said you should have believed me from the beginning! Why don't you believe me now?"

"Because you sound ridiculous," he said.

Alex closed her eyes and made a fist with both hands. "Conner, who cares how I found out! The Masked Man is actually our uncle Lloyd! Grandma had two sons!"

"IT'S ABOUT TIME YOU FIGURED IT OUT!" shouted a voice that didn't belong to anyone in the room.

Mother Goose suddenly appeared outside the window, flying on Lester's back. The gander knocked the window open with his beak and they flew into the room and landed with a loud *thump*.

"Alex is right, Conner," Mother Goose said as she

climbed off Lester's back. "You have no idea how long I've been waiting for you to put the pieces together!"

"You've known this entire time?" Alex asked.

"It was your grandmother's dying wish that I not tell you," she said. "I swore to her that I would keep it from you. That's one of the reasons I've been keeping such a low profile! I knew if I hung around you kids while you looked for him, what I knew would slip out eventually. Thankfully, the rooster is out of the henhouse now!"

The twins wanted to choke her for keeping information from them *yet again*, but they knew Mother Goose cherished her friendship with their grandmother too much to break her promise to her.

"Does anyone else know about our uncle?" Alex asked. "I mean, the Fairy Council must have known Grandma had two sons."

"Well, it's complicated," Mother Goose said. "When Lloyd was a teenager he ran away from the Fairy Palace and your grandmother told the council he was dead— she even staged a funeral that the council attended. She didn't see him until years later on the *first* night he broke into the palace to steal the potion. The Fairy Godmother received an anonymous letter that warned her he was coming for it, so she was expecting him. Thanks to the Hall of Dreams, she already knew what he was planning to do with the potion, so she sentenced him to life in Pinocchio Prison. *She* gave him the mask he wears so no one would ever know he was her son."

The story of the Masked Man was getting more complex as time went on, and there still were so many things they didn't know.

"Mother Goose, do you know where he's been hiding?" Jack said.

"I don't, but Alex does," Mother Goose said. "Alex's old *squeeze* found her in the woods and told her he had found the cave Lloyd has been hiding in."

Everyone jerked their heads toward Alex. They couldn't believe it had taken this long for one of them to bring it up.

"Wait, how do you know that?" Alex said.

"I've been following you since the moth showed up," Mother Goose said. "Yes, Conner, there really was a moth—and yes, your grandmother most likely sent it from wherever she is. I wish she had sent a letter instead. Giant insects give me the creeps no matter how angelic they are."

"Will one of you just tell us where he is already?" Conner yelled.

Alex filled the others in about her encounter with Rook and Cornelius in the woods. She told them everything Rook told her, and what he had witnessed.

"Those are the books I caught him stealing!" Conner said.

"Grandma gave Froggy the books as a thank-you for helping us survive our first trip into this world," Alex said. "They must have been the collection our uncle was asking the witches to help him find. He must have found them on his own and stole them when everyone in the castle was at the wedding."

"So the army he's planning to recruit isn't from one story," Conner said.

He gasped as he remembered something he and his sister had seen several months earlier. At the time it seemed meaningless, but now that he knew his uncle's plans, it was spookily significant.

"Alex, do you remember his cell in Pinocchio Prison?" Conner asked. "He had all those strange carvings on the wall, of monsters, and pirates, and soldiers! Now think about the books he has in his possession. He's planning to recruit an army of *literary villains!*"

It was an unsettling thought for everyone. The damage the Masked Man could cause if he unleashed an army like that onto the world would be catastrophic. There wouldn't be a force powerful enough to stop it. All the armies in the fairy-tale world were still recovering from the war with the Grande Armée.

"So what's the plan?" Jack asked. "How do we stop him?"

"We need to go to the cave," Alex said. "We'll wait for him to go into a book, if he's not inside one already, and destroy it. That should trap him inside it forever, right?"

"According to the rules of your grandmother's potion journal, it should," Goldilocks said. "She made it very clear to be protective of the book, as it's the only way in and out of a story."

"Great," Alex said with a sigh of relief. Getting rid of her uncle might be easier than she expected. "Then we should hurry."

Everyone seemed convinced except for Conner, who shook his head. "Alex, you're forgetting one thing," he said.

"What's that?" she asked.

"We need the Masked Man to clear your name," he said. "The only way we'll be able to prove to the Fairy Council that you've been right all along is if they see him with their own eyes. They need to admit they were wrong for doubting you and reinstate you as the Fairy Godmother."

"Conner, I don't care about being the Fairy Godmother anymore—"

"But I do!" he said. "You were born to lead, protect, and help the people of this world, and you can't do that if you spend the rest of your life hiding. You and I both know that if this world gets left to the council alone, it's going to fall apart."

Alex was very touched by her brother's words, but she couldn't ask them all to put themselves in danger for the sake of her reputation. However, as Alex looked around the room, she saw it wasn't up to her. Everyone was nodding in agreement with Conner.

"He's right," Goldilocks said. "We have to capture your uncle and bring him back—even if it means going into the books ourselves."

"*We're going to go inside the books ourselves?*" Mother Goose said, and everyone turned to her at once. "Sorry—that wasn't an objection. It would be very *adventurous*, even for this group."

Their support almost moved Alex to tears. In less than a day she had gone from feeling like the loneliest person in the world to the luckiest.

"I'm assuming everyone is in?" Conner asked. He put his hand in the middle of the group and one by one the rest of them joined in. Even Lester joined and stuck the tip of his wing in.

"To the cave!" Jack said.

"And beyond the kingdoms!" Goldilocks added.

There was a soft knock on the bedroom door. It opened and everyone was happy to see Red standing in the doorway. Her eyes were swollen from crying and she held a handkerchief tightly in her hand.

"I couldn't help overhearing." Red sniffled. "I'm not positive where you're planning to go, but I hope you'll let me come along. I could really use an *adventure*."

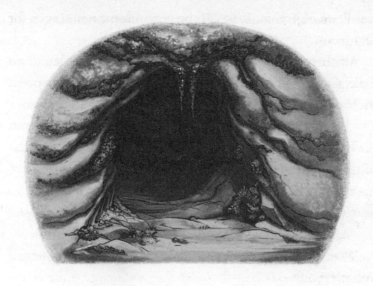

CHAPTER ELEVEN

THE CAVE

The twins and their friends left for the cave minutes after forming their plan. Alex didn't trust her powers enough to teleport everyone by magic, so they traveled by horse instead. They galloped northwest at full speed, knowing time was of the essence.

Jack and Goldilocks rode Porridge while the twins steered Oats, who was more than excited for his debut journey. Oats's father, a large stallion named Buckle, had been brought out of the Center Kingdom stables for Hagetta to ride. One minute aboard the infamously rambunctious horse was all it took for Hagetta to cast a calming spell on him.

Mother Goose and Red traveled aboard Lester and flew in circles above the others so they kept the same pace. Mother Goose was self-appointed to navigate and occasionally shouted directions down at the others. She also used the trip as an opportunity to play therapist and tried making Red feel "better" with stories of her own heartbreak.

"I've been left and left others at the altar many times myself," Mother Goose told her. "The day I was supposed to wed King Henry VIII was the day he met Anne Boleyn. Needless to say, I went home alone—but boy did I dodge a bullet!"

"Was this recent?" Red asked her.

The mountains in the northwest weren't very far away from the Center Kingdom and they were expected to reach the cave by midnight. Traveling at a horse's pace really made Alex miss her days with Cornelius, but she was happy he had found a companion in Rook.

To pass the time, Conner told Alex everything he had learned about the Portal Potion from their grandmother's book.

"The potion's ingredients were pretty simple," Conner said. "You just need a branch from the oldest tree in the woods, a feather from the finest pheasant, and a liquefied lock and key from someone you love. Then you let it simmer under two weeks of moonlight, add a splash of magic to mix it up, *and presto—potion galore!*"

"That's all it takes?" Alex asked. "You'd think the ingredients would be more complex for such a powerful substance. This is kindergarten stuff compared to the Wishing Spell."

"The ingredients are more symbolic than specific," Conner said. "Grandma had to be really imaginative when she was creating it."

"That's the beauty of magic—there's really no science to it," Alex said.

After the sun set, Mother Goose enchanted a swarm of fireflies to illuminate the land as they traveled across it. As predicted, they arrived at the cave just before midnight. Alex was grateful Rook's map had been so detailed; the cave blended into the mountainside so well, they would have never found it on their own.

Lester landed as the others dismounted their horses.

"Porridge," Goldilocks said, "if anyone or anything but us comes out of that cave, I want you, Oats, and Buckle to run into the nearest woods and hide there, understood?"

The cream-colored horse gave her a strong nod. Everyone lingered near the cave's entrance for a moment before stepping inside.

Mother Goose rubbed her hands together. "Well, just like I said to Lewis and Clark, North America ain't gonna explore itself," she said. "Let's get a move on."

She led the others into the cave, pulling a timid Lester along with her. The cave was pitch-black.

"It's so dark and creepy in here," Red said.

"What were you expecting? A chandelier?" Conner said.

"That's actually not a bad idea," Mother Goose said. She whistled and the fireflies flew inside and piled over one another at the top of the cave, forming a large chandelier. "Good thinking, C-Dog."

Now that they had a little light, they could see the cave was very tall but not very wide. A handful of the books stolen from the castle were littered across the ground. They walked around the cave and inspected them, reading the titles they found.

"*Tom Sawyer,*" Jack said.

"*Great Expectations,*" Goldilocks said.

"*Hamlet!*" Red said excitedly. "Oooo! Can we visit *Hamlet*? It's my favorite Shakyfruit play!"

"I think your week has been tragic enough," Mother Goose reminded her.

Conner picked up an older book with a yellow cover. As soon as he opened it, a bright beam with the power of a searchlight shot out of it. It scared him and he dropped the book, causing a couple of loose pages to slip out.

Conner gulped. "I found *The Wonderful Wizard of Oz*," he said.

"Be careful," Alex said. "Every page might count!"

The twins collected the loose pages and carefully stuck them into their pockets. Alex cautiously opened the book with the toe of her shoe and turned to the very first page. Just as before, the bright beam of light shot directly out of the book toward the top of the cave. It was a hundred times brighter than the fireflies.

"I bet our uncle is still in there," Alex said.

"Only one way to find out," Goldilocks said. "Let's take a peek and see."

"One of us should stay behind and keep an eye on the book," Jack said. "If anything happens to it while we're inside, we'll be stuck."

"I'll stay," Hagetta volunteered. "I'll guard it with my life. The rest of you go, and please be careful."

They gathered around the book and stared down at it like parachutists waiting to jump from a plane.

"Here goes nothing," Conner said. He stepped into the beam and vanished from the cave.

Conner found himself in a bright and endless space. There was absolutely nothing to see except for words floating, spinning, and jumping all around him.

"Wow," he said. "I've never seen *this* before."

Alex appeared beside Conner. She was followed by Goldilocks, Red, Jack, and finally Mother Goose, who yanked Lester inside the book behind her. None of them could believe the world of words they had entered.

As if their presence had activated something, the words suddenly vibrated to life and shot in all directions. They dispersed randomly and began forming shapes—stretching and multiplying to perfectly outline whatever they described.

The twins and their friends watched in amazement as

a world was crafted around them. A bleak little house with only four walls and a tiny barn appeared in the distance. Grassy fields stretched into the horizon everywhere they looked. Everything from the land to the sky was dreary and gray.

"Alex, I don't think we're in Kansas anymore," Conner whispered to his sister. "And by that, I mean we're actually *in Kansas*."

CHAPTER TWELVE

THE CYCLONE

Despite their prior experiences of traveling between dimensions, Alex and Conner were absolutely astonished. In a matter of seconds the vast prairies of Kansas had been created around them, and their mouths were as wide-open as their awestruck friends'. Even Lester's jaw dropped at the sight of it all.

"It worked!" Alex said. "Not that I wasn't expecting it to—but I still can't believe it actually worked!"

"It's *remarkable*," Goldilocks agreed.

The only thing that traveled with them from the

cave was the *Wonderful Wizard of Oz* book itself. It was lying open on the ground and emitting a bright beam of light, exactly as it had done in the cave. Conner stuck his head through the beam and saw Hagetta standing in the cave.

"Well?" Hagetta said.

"It worked!" he said, and gave her a thumbs-up. "Wish us luck."

Conner leaned back into the story and shut the book. The beam disappeared, but reappeared as soon as he opened it. He closed it again and tucked it safely into the back of his belt.

Red looked around the fields as if she had never seen anything so bleak. "So this is the Otherworld?" she asked.

"It's L. Frank Baum's interpretation of it," Alex said. "But technically, yes."

"Well, it's just *lovely*," Red said, but her face told differently. "It reminds me of my kingdom—if all the happiness and color had been drained from it."

The lack of color was quite depressing and it immediately put the group in a somber mood. In fact, *they* were the only colorful things in this world.

They heard barking and a child's laughter coming from inside the farmhouse. It was nice to know *some* cheerfulness existed in this place. The door of the house opened and an old man with a white beard stepped out onto the front lawn. He stared up at the sky uneasily.

"The sky is awfully gray today, Em," the man called back to the house. "Grayer than it usually is."

A frail farmer's wife walked out of the house and began sweeping the porch.

"Oh, Henry, stop it," Em said. "The sky looks no different than it did yesterday or the day before that."

A little girl appeared behind the screen door. She was adorable and wore pigtails and a dainty dress. She held her scruffy little dog in her arms and lovingly stroked his fur.

"No, I've got a bad feeling about this," Henry said. "We may have a cyclone on our hands."

"You'll worry Dorothy if you keep talking like that. Now, go inside," Em ordered.

The little girl held her dog a bit tighter and stared up at the sky with the same concern as her uncle—it was too late.

"Who are those sad people?" Red asked the twins. "And what's a cyclone? Is he talking about a one-eyed man?"

Alex and Conner didn't respond. This wasn't the first time they had seen their favorite childhood storybook characters come to life, but it was an enthralling sight nonetheless.

Dorothy spotted them and shrieked with joy.

"Auntie Em! Uncle Henry!" she said. "Look over there! *It's other people!*"

It must have been a long time since the girl had seen another soul besides her aunt and uncle. She was more excited to see the twins and their friends than they were to see her. Dorothy ran across the field to greet them. Henry and Em were so surprised by the visitors, they didn't move.

"Hello there!" Dorothy said. "What brings you to our farm?"

"Hi there, Dorothy," Conner said.

Dorothy gasped. *"How did you know my name?"* she asked with large eyes.

Alex shot Conner a dirty look and he panicked. "Because . . . because . . ." He struggled.

A huge smile grew on Dorothy's face. "I know," she said. "You're a *fortune-teller*, aren't you? I knew it from the moment I saw you—*you're a traveling circus!*"

With nothing better to say, everyone just nodded.

"Indeed," Conner said, and instantly broke into an outrageous character. "I am *Master Connermoondo*—psychic extraordinaire. The men, women, and bird behind me are part of the world-renowned Bailey Traveling Circus."

Dorothy excitedly jumped up and down. Toto barked at them; even he seemed overdue for some entertainment. This was the most exciting thing that had ever happened to them.

"Allow me to introduce my friends," Conner said with overdramatic gestures. "Meet *Jack*, the circus strong man; *Goldie*, the sword juggler; *Red*, the uptight mistress of the tight rope. Straight from the wild Madagascar jungles, meet the *Lestersaurus*—and his tamer, *Madam Goose*. And last but not least, my sister, *Alexandra the bearded lady*."

"What?" Alex said.

"But she doesn't have a beard," Dorothy pointed out.

"She shaved this morning," Conner said.

Alex rolled her eyes—nothing was ever easy when she traveled with her brother.

"We were on our way to Kansas City and stumbled upon your humble abode," Conner said.

"That's putting it nicely," Red said.

"I'm so glad you did!" Dorothy said. "Nothing exciting ever happens around here."

It tickled the twins and they exchanged a smile. They knew more about her than she knew about herself.

"Won't you please stay for supper?" Dorothy asked, then turned to her aunt and uncle. "Can they join us, Auntie Em? Oh please say yes!"

Auntie Em and Uncle Henry looked at each other and shrugged.

"I suppose," Uncle Henry said.

"Hope you like corn," Auntie Em said.

Conner quickly looked back at the others, but none of them objected.

"Supper sounds like a good idea," Mother Goose said. "I'm a little hungry, and if Lester doesn't eat every four hours he gets really crabby. *Don't look at me like that, Lester; I wouldn't say it if it weren't true.*"

Dorothy escorted her visitors into the farmhouse. The house was so small; it was only one room. It had a stove, a cupboard, two beds, a table, and four chairs, forcing everyone but Conner to eat on the beds and on the floor. True to her word, Auntie Em served corn—*and that was all.*

"Please tell me about all the places you've been to!" Dorothy requested at dinner.

"Well, I have good memories of Baton Rouge and Jefferson City," Mother Goose said. "But if you want to make a few bucks, Texas is where the money is."

The others gave her a strange look. How did she know that?

"What?" Mother Goose said. "You think *this* is the first circus I've been in?"

Uncle Henry and Auntie Em never looked up from their corn, but Dorothy was all eyes and ears. Living on the Kansas farm must have been such a dull life, but the adventures that awaited her would definitely make up for a lifetime of boredom.

"You folks certainly get around," Uncle Henry said.

"Speaking of *getting around*," Jack said, "have any of you noticed an awkward man around these parts?"

"He might go by *Lloyd* or *the Masked Man*," Goldilocks said. "He's a friend of ours from the circus. We're looking for him."

"Can't say we have," Auntie Em said. "Y'all are the only visitors we've had since, well, since as far back as I can remember."

This was disappointing and also confusing to the

twins. If there was no sign of their uncle in this story, had he already traveled into another book?

"He must be *somewhere else*," Conner said. It was a loaded statement, but luckily only his sister and friends caught on.

"I wish I was somewhere else," Dorothy said with a sigh. "Sometimes I dream about joining the circus just so I can see the world, but I don't think Toto and I will ever get out of Kansas."

A strong wail of wind came from outside, followed shortly by a high-pitched whistling. The sounds were alarming and Dorothy, Henry, and Em froze solid. The tiny house began to rock as the wind grew stronger and stronger outside.

"It's a cyclone!" Henry yelled, and stood up from the table. "I'll free the animals!"

He jumped from the table and ran out of the house in a panic. Not knowing any better, Mother Goose, Lester, Red, Goldilocks, and Jack quickly followed him.

"What are you guys doing?" Conner yelled.

"We need to stay inside the house!" Alex called after them. "They have a storm cellar!"

It was too late—their friends were already outside, and they didn't hear a word Conner and Alex said over the strong winds. Em dove to the center of the room and rolled up the rug, revealing a square door built into the floor.

"Quick, Dorothy! Follow me into the cellar!" Em ordered.

She pulled the door open and climbed into the storm cellar under the house. Toto was frightened and jumped off of Dorothy's lap and hid under her bed.

"Toto!" she said. "Come here, boy!"

While Dorothy tried to retrieve her dog, Alex and Conner ran outside to retrieve their friends. The sky was so gray, it was almost black. The wind blew from every direction and was so strong, it was almost impossible to stay standing.

The twins found their friends in the barn helping Henry set the farm animals free. The cows and horses ran out of the barn and into the fields, away from the approaching storm.

"You guys! We've got to get back into the house!" Conner yelled. "Trust us! This is going to get nasty!"

"The storm cellar is the only guaranteed chance we have to survive this!" Alex said.

They figured the twins knew what they were doing since they knew the story, and so they followed the twins out of the barn and back toward the house but came to a quick halt. They screamed and pointed to the sky. Spiraling down from the black clouds was an enormous tornado.

The tornado touched the ground and headed directly for the small farmhouse. The twins and their friends had to grab one another's hands to stay on their feet.

"We don't have time to get to the cellar!" Conner yelled.

Alex screamed. "CONNER! LOOK OVER THERE!" she shouted, and pointed to a nearby field.

Running as fast as humanly possible against the wind was Alex and Conner's uncle. His stolen bag of books was slung over his shoulder and he was bolting for the farmhouse. Even more shocking was that he hadn't replaced the mask Conner had ripped off in the library, so for a split second the twins thought they were seeing their father.

Lloyd leaped onto the porch and saluted the twins. He had been in Kansas the entire time, just waiting for the storm to break.

The tornado was only a few yards away from the house and Lloyd ran inside. The farmhouse was ripped off its foundation and flew into the air. Like a gigantic cloudy monster, the cyclone swallowed the house and it disappeared into the vortex.

"Dorothy!" Henry shouted, and ran toward the twister.

"Henry! Wait! Stay with us!" Jack yelled after the farmer.

"No, Jack!" Alex said. "Leave him! He'll be okay!"

"How do you know?" Jack said.

"Because I've read the book!" Alex said.

The wind was deafening and only grew louder as the tornado drew closer. At first Conner thought they should all travel back through the *Wonderful Wizard of Oz* book and into the cave, but he would have lost it in the powerful winds if they tried.

"Everyone, back into the barn!" Conner yelled. It was their only option of survival now.

The terrified group pulled and pushed one another

until they all made it back into the barn. Once they were inside, they slammed the doors shut and grabbed hold of anything they could wrap their arms around. Conner clutched a post with one arm and the book with the other.

The tornado smashed into the barn and tore the roof off. The barn began to sway and creak. It tilted back and forth, leaning farther each time.

"Houston, we have liftoff!" Mother Goose shouted.

The barn spun into the air, flying higher by the second. Their feet dangled in the air. There was no way of telling which way was up or down. The tornado was so powerful, gravity didn't apply.

The barn doors were sucked off their hinges. Red lost her grip and was pulled out of the barn.

"RED!" the twins screamed in unison.

"Lester! Go get her!" Mother Goose ordered.

The goose let go of a stable door he had been clutching with his beak and flew into the storm. The wind blew him in circles around the tornado. Every so often he would see a big ball of red fabric pass him—*it was Red*. Lester spread his wings so the wind blew him faster and he managed to catch a piece of Red's dress in his mouth.

"LESTER, HELP ME!" Red screamed. "DON'T LET ME DIE IN SUCH AN UGLY PLACE!"

The barn was flying directly at them. Lester pulled Red close to his body and wrapped his wings around her, turning himself into a big feathery ball. He smashed straight through the barn wall, returning to the others.

"Great work, Lester!" Mother Goose shouted.

"I thought being left at the altar would be the worst part of my week!" Red yelled.

The barn flew uncontrollably around in the air as the storm continued. Occasionally the twins could spot the farmhouse bobbing up and down in the center of the tornado, but there was no way they could reach it.

The cyclone sped even faster, flinging the barn in one direction and the farmhouse into another. The world spun so fast outside the barn, no one could make out where they were headed. For the first time bright colors could be seen somewhere in the distance, but they couldn't tell if it was the ground or the sky.

The barn kept spinning and spinning... falling faster and faster... but they had no idea *what* they were falling into....

CHAPTER THIRTEEN

THE TIN WOODMAN

Is everybody alive?" Conner asked. A series of grunts, moans, and squawks answered his question. It was a miracle they had all survived.

After what seemed like an eternity of falling, the barn had come to a sudden and harsh stop when it hit the ground. What was left of it imploded on impact, and the twins and their friends struggled to push away the wreckage piled on top of them.

"That was much rougher than I was expecting," Alex said.

"Hold on a second—you were *expecting* that?" Goldilocks said.

They all shot her dirty looks and she smiled guiltily. Alex had completely forgotten her friends weren't as familiar with *The Wonderful Wizard of Oz* as she and her brother were. They had no idea a *cyclone* was on the menu.

"Yeah, sorry about that," Alex said. "In the story a big tornado picks up Dorothy's house and sends it to the Land of Oz. I probably should have filled you all in on that."

"But if the tornado sent them to Oz, where did it send *us*?" Conner asked.

They helped one another get to their feet and emerged from the collapsed barn. At first they had to shield their eyes—everything was so much brighter than it had been in Kansas. The sky was a vivid blue and they were surrounded by a forest of green trees. Even the dirt was more radiant than before.

"Whoa," Conner said. "Did someone adjust the contrast settings?"

"Where are we?" Jack said.

Alex didn't have to think twice. "You guys, we're in OZ!" she excitedly declared. "We didn't end up in Munchkinland like Dorothy, but the cyclone definitely sent us here, too."

A soft moaning sound suddenly filled the forest.

"Does anyone else hear that?" Red asked.

They looked around the trees, but they didn't find the source.

"Where is that coming from?" Mother Goose said. "Lester, is that your stomach?"

The goose shook his head. He was just as curious as everyone. The sound continued and appeared to grow more agitated as time went on. Conner gasped and his eyes grew very wide—he knew where it was coming from.

"Oh, no!" he said. "The sound is coming from under the barn! We landed on someone—just like Dorothy does! Quick, we've got to help them!"

Conner and the others quickly dug through the pieces of barn. They figured they were getting closer to whoever it was, because the moaning became louder and louder.

"Please don't die—help is on the way!" Conner shouted into the wreckage. "Glinda, is that you? Oh God, if we killed Glinda I will never forgive myself!"

To Conner's relief, they didn't find the beloved Good Witch of the South but uncovered a man instead. He was unusually tall, and very thin. He had a long, pointed noise and wore a pointed cap. As they brushed the debris off of him, they discovered that everything from his clothes to his skin was made of metal.

"Oh my gosh! It's the Tin Woodman!" Alex said.

"Is he a friend of yours?" Red asked.

"No, he's one of the main characters in the story," Conner whispered. "This is a big deal!"

The Tin Woodman was so heavy, it took all of them to

pull him up onto his feet. He was as stiff as a statue and frozen in a position with his axe raised. His eyes were very large and darted around at the strange people helping him. He continued to moan, but his mouth was shut tightly.

"What's wrong with him?" Goldilocks asked. "Is he petrified?"

"No, he's rusted!" Alex said. "He needs oil."

"Do think there's a body shop nearby?" Mother Goose said.

"No, he should have an oilcan around here somewhere," Alex said.

She looked around the trees and saw a tiny cottage a little ways into the forest. She ran to it and went inside, returning to her friends a few moments later with an oilcan. She immediately oiled the joints around his prominent jaw and it fell open.

"AAAAAAHHHHH!" The Tin Woodman's moans turned into screams now that his mouth was open, and they didn't stop.

Everyone covered their ears and looked to the twins to do something about it.

"Is there a way to turn him off?" Red asked.

"Dude, chill out!" Conner said. "Why are you screaming?!"

"BECAUSE A BARN JUST FELL OUT OF THE SKY AND LANDED ON TOP OF ME!" the Tin Woodman yelled. "I DOUBT YOU'D BE TAKING IT ANY BETTER IF IT HAPPENED TO YOU!"

Goldilocks slammed the Tin Woodman's mouth shut until he calmed down.

"Are you going to stop screaming now?" she asked, but he didn't move. "Well? Give us a nod."

"He can't nod unless he has oil," Alex said. She oiled the joints around his neck and the Tin Woodman nodded. Goldilocks pulled his mouth open again.

"That feels so much better," the Tin Woodman said. He was so relieved, he forgot what he had been screaming at. "Would you be so kind as to oil the rest of me? Please?"

Alex oiled his joints from the neck down. Slowly the Tin Woodman's body began to relax. His shoulders fell and he dropped his axe to his side.

"Thank you," he said with a long sigh. "I've been holding that thing up for a year!"

"You've been stuck like this for a year?" Jack asked.

"Most uncomfortably," the Tin Woodman said. "I always keep an oilcan close by me in case I start to rust. The one time I left it in my cottage, a huge rainstorm caught me by surprise. I've been here ever since."

"That sounds terrible," Mother Goose sympathized. "I know the feeling. I was buried alive for *two weeks* once— boy, was I glad to get out of that mess! That's when I learned to ask questions *before* participating in a religious ritual, no matter how cute the islanders are."

The Tin Woodman glanced at them all nervously. "Who are you people? Where did you come from?"

Conner pushed his sister forward. "Alex, I'm going to

let you take this one since I always seem to say the wrong thing."

Alex looked into the Tin Woodman's curious eyes. If the barn was any indication, the truth would be way too shocking for him to comprehend. She needed to come up with a story he could believe but wouldn't frighten him away if they needed his help.

"We aren't supposed to tell anyone," Alex said. "But we're on a secret mission for *the Wizard*. We were traveling through the air when our barn lost its balloon—something the Wizard put together for us—and we fell into this forest. Luckily we had you to break our fall."

The Tin Woodman was instantly captivated. His jaw dropped open and he put both hands on top of his head. "You know the Wizard of Oz?" he asked in bewilderment.

"We work for him!" Alex said. "There's a ruthless criminal on the loose and the Wizard asked us personally to track him down. He's come to Oz in hopes of recruiting an army! The Wizard wants us to stop him before any innocent people are hurt."

"Why, that's terrible!" the Tin Woodman said. "But what kind of army would he be looking to recruit?"

"I was hoping you could tell us," she said. "We aren't from around here. Would you happen to know of anyone or anything that might help this criminal overthrow the Wizard?"

The Tin Woodman scratched his head as he thought it over. "There are the guards of the Emerald City, but they would *never* betray the Wizard," he said. "Wait! I know! He'll probably team up with the Wicked Witch of the West! Everyone knows she's wanted to get rid of the Wizard since he came to Oz!"

The twins and their friends gulped in unison. They didn't have to be familiar with the story to know that the Wicked Witch of the West was one of the most terrifying villains in the history of literature. Naturally, the twins' uncle had come to Oz to partner with her.

"Well, that's not *that* bad, right?" Conner said, desperately trying to make light of the situation. "She's just one witch and a couple of flying monkeys."

"The flying monkeys aren't all she has in her control," the Tin Woodman said. "She has forty great ferocious wolves, a flock of forty frightening crows, swarms of killer bees, and an army of Winkies."

"Yep, that sounds like something Lloyd would be into," Mother Goose said.

"Wait, what's a Winkie?" Red asked.

"A Winkie is how my parents told Alex and me apart when we were infants," Conner said, and laughed hysterically at his own joke—although no one joined him. "Sorry, not the time."

"The Winkies are the people who live in the western half of Oz," the Tin Woodman explained. "The Wicked Witch of the West enslaved them when she took over the Winkie Country, and now she rules the land mercilessly from her castle."

The news bothered everyone except Alex—she was delighted to hear it.

"Alex, why are you smiling?" Conner asked. "This is *terrible* news for us. We can't compete against that."

"No, this is *great* news for us!" she said. "It doesn't matter *who* or *what* our uncle is after as long as we know where he's headed. We can stop him before he reaches the witch. And if he landed in Munchkinland with Dorothy, and we're in the forest with the Tin Woodman, that means we've got at least a day or two of a head start."

"You're right!" Conner said joyfully. "We'll just hide out close to the witch's castle, then tackle him before he gets inside!"

"But who's going to take us there?" Goldilocks said. "None of us know this land well enough to navigate through it alone."

They all turned to the Tin Woodman at once, thinking the same exact thing. As soon as he caught on, the Tin Woodman put his arms up defensively.

"Don't look at me!" he said. "I'm not going anywhere near that place!"

"Oh, come on!" Red said. "If this man gets to the Wicked Witch before we get to him, thousands of innocent people might die! Have a heart!"

Alex leaned in to whisper in Red's ear. "That's not going to work, Red. Part of the story is that the Tin Woodman doesn't have a heart—"

"What do you mean he doesn't have a heart?" Red said

loudly. "That's absolutely ridiculous! Everything has a heart!"

The Tin Woodman quickly grew paranoid. "How did you know I don't have a heart?"

"Because the Wizard told us!" Conner said, thinking fast. "The great and powerful Wizard knows everything! He told us if we crossed paths with a man made of tin to offer him a heart in exchange for helping us."

"So if I escort you to Winkie Country, the Wizard will give me a heart?" he asked.

"He sure will—"

"Excuse us for one moment," Alex interrupted. Before he could say any more, Alex quickly pulled her brother aside. "Conner, what are you doing? We don't have a heart to give this man!"

"We'll papier-mâché one if we have to!" Conner said. "Even the Wizard gives him a fake one at the end of the story, and he's perfectly happy with it!"

"Good point," she whispered. "As you were."

Conner walked back to the Tin Woodman and offered him a handshake. "One heart in exchange for guidance to the Wicked Witch's castle. Do we have a deal, Mr. Woodman?"

The Tin Woodman was very conflicted. Could he face his biggest fear in return for his greatest wish? He certainly wouldn't get a heart waiting around in the forest.

"Deal," he said, and shook Conner's hand.

"Fantastic," Mother Goose said. "How are we getting there?"

"We'll take the *yellow brick road*, of course," he said matter-of-factly.

A quiet little gasp slipped out of Alex and she grabbed her brother's hand.

"Is it far?" Jack asked.

"It's just beyond the forest," the Tin Woodman said. "We'll take it all the way to the Emerald City and then travel through the Winkie Country to the witch's castle. Everyone, follow me—and someone bring my oilcan."

He led the way, and Mother Goose, Red, Jack, Goldilocks, and Lester followed closely behind him. Alex pulled Conner a few steps back and let the others get a head start.

"Did you hear that, Conner?" Alex said. She had bright eyes and a huge smile. "He's taking us to the yellow brick road! *The yellow brick road!* My inner six-year-old self is flipping out!"

Conner smiled, too. "*There* she is," he said with a happy sigh.

"Where is it? Do you see it already?"

"I'm not talking about the yellow brick road, I'm talking about *you*." Conner laughed. "It's nice to see you *excited* about something again. I've missed it."

CHAPTER FOURTEEN

TROUBLE ON THE YELLOW BRICK ROAD

T he Tin Woodman guided his new acquaintances through the Ozian forest and they found the magnificent yellow brick road winding through the heart of the woods. Even against all the effervescent colors in the Land of Oz, the bright and majestic road stood out.

Alex began skipping as soon as her feet touched it—she couldn't help herself. "When in Rome," she told her brother before he could tease her.

As they traveled down the most famous path in literature, the land changed drastically around them. The landscape of Oz was even more diverse than the fairy-tale world. With every turn, the yellow brick road curved into a different terrain. One minute they were in a thick forest, the next a wide-open field. They crossed over streams and rivers, ponds and lakes, farmland and little villages, only to end up in another forest.

Mother Goose found the continuously changing land very entertaining. Even *she* had never been someplace so unpredictable.

"This place is a hoot!" she said. "It's more random than your mood swings, Lester!"

"Squaaa," the large bird replied, as if to say, *"How dare you."*

Jack and Goldilocks kept a watchful eye on everything they passed. They had never been someplace they had such little knowledge about. They wanted to be prepared at all times, but didn't have the slightest clue of what to be prepared for.

Red was more interested in the Tin Woodman than the scenery. No matter how long she studied him, she couldn't figure out how he *worked*. She was half expecting to find an on switch sticking out of his back.

"Have you always been a Woodman?" she asked.

"Oh yes," he answered. "My father was a Woodman before me, and his father before him."

"Were you all made of tin, or is your family a variety of metals?" Red asked, but then quickly apologized. "Forgive me, I hope that wasn't insensitive. I've never met someone of your . . . um . . . *element*."

"No, I'm the only one made of tin," the Tin Woodman said. "But I was a real man once."

"Oh, so it's a curse!" Red said. "I'm very familiar with curses. My fiancé was cursed to look like a frog—or at least he *was* my fiancé once upon a time. I'm not sure what to consider him now."

"It wasn't a curse but the result of a spell," the Tin Woodman said. "I fell in love with a beautiful Munchkin girl who agreed to marry me. But she lived with a mean old woman who didn't want to live alone, so she bribed the Wicked Witch of the East to hurt me. She cast a spell on my axe, causing it to slip out of my hand and cut off my limbs one at a time, eventually severing my head and splitting open my body. A local tinsmith rebuilt me one appendage at a time until I was made entirely of tin."

Red was very disturbed by his ghastly story. "Why on earth didn't you just get a new axe?"

The Tin Woodman went quiet for a moment. "I never thought about it," he said.

"Then whatever happened to the Munchkin girl you were going to marry?" Red asked.

"I don't know," he said. "The body the tinsmith built me was hollow. I never had a heart to miss her with, so I forgot all about her. I suppose she still lives with the mean old woman."

"Trust me, you're better off without a heart," Red said.

"I speak from experience. Not having a heart means you'll never have to worry about heartbreak. And believe me, *it's awful*."

"But living without a heart means you cannot *feel* at all," the Tin Woodman said. "It may spare you from grief, or loneliness, or misery, or longing, or fear—but you do not enjoy, or laugh, or excite, or love. And one who cannot love is just an object."

Red scrunched her forehead. "But if you can't *long* for anything, how do you know you want a heart?" she asked. "And if you don't *fear*, then why were you so scared when the barn landed on you?"

The Tin Woodman went quiet again. He didn't have an answer, but Red was making him think.

Conner cleared his throat. "Excuse us, Mr. Woodman," he said, and pulled Red aside to where the Tin Woodman couldn't hear them. "Red! What are you doing? You need to shut up!"

"Why? This man clearly has a heart, he just doesn't realize it," she said.

"Obviously!" Conner said. "But he's not supposed to learn that lesson until the end of the story! If he learns that now, we're going to lose our guide!"

Red crossed her arms and tried to be silent.

The yellow brick road took the traveling party through a few obstacles, but nothing they couldn't handle. At one point the road disappeared into a deep ditch, but the Tin Woodman chopped down a tree and they used it as a bridge.

They also came to a stop when there was no bridge to connect them to the yellow brick road on the other side of a wild river. Lester acted as a boat and transported each of them across the water one at a time. He squawked loudly when it was the Tin Woodman's turn, as it was difficult to stay afloat with the heavy man on his back.

Alex and Mother Goose weren't using magic on purpose. To the twins' knowledge, the only people in Oz capable of *real* magic were the witches, and they didn't want the Tin Woodman thinking they had anything to do with the Wicked Witches of the East or West.

All in all, their journey was rather easy compared to how they'd arrived in Oz. Jack and Goldilocks started to relax little by little, but the effortlessness only worried the twins—it was *too easy*.

"I remember Oz being a lot more dangerous in the book," Conner told his sister.

"Me too," Alex said. "I remember there were all kinds of scary plants and animals. Maybe we're missing them all."

The twins nodded, but they knew they were never that lucky, and the next few miles of the yellow brick road would prove that.

"What was that?" Goldilocks said, and stopped in her tracks.

"What did you see?" Jack asked.

"It was a big shadow," she said. "It ran through the trees just to my right—"

Red screamed. "I just saw something, too. There, in the trees to my left!"

The Tin Woodman gripped his axe with both hands, inspiring Jack and Goldilocks to retrieve their own weapons. Alex and Mother Goose shared a look—they would use magic if they had to.

The shadows moved quickly from tree to tree in the forest around them, but never in the same place twice. Something—or several somethings from the looks of it— was *hunting* them.

"What are they?" Conner asked.

"Kalidahs," the Tin Woodman said, and anxiously eyed the woods.

"Come again?" Red peeped. "What are Kalidahs?"

Unfortunately her question was answered when a pack of eight monstrous beasts emerged from the trees and surrounded them. They had bodies like bears and heads like tigers. Each was nine feet tall and exposed their ferocious fangs and claws.

"Holy hybrid!" Mother Goose yelled.

The Kalidahs growled at the trembling travelers.

"These guys don't happen to be herbivores, do they?" Conner asked.

"They are, actually!" the Tin Woodman said.

Conner was shocked. "Well, that's a relief!"

"Wait—herbivores eat meat, right?" the Tin Woodman asked.

"No, those are *carnivores*!"

"Oh," the Tin Woodman said. "My mistake. These are *definitely* carnivores."

The Kalidahs lunged toward them. Jack and the Tin Woodman struck two with their axes. Goldilocks gashed one with her sword and kicked another in the stomach. Mother Goose flicked one on the nose.

"Bad hybrid!" she chastised. "Very bad!"

Their defenses only angered the Kalidahs and they salivated at the mouth. Alex hit the yellow brick road with her fist and tree roots shot out of the ground and wrapped around the monsters' feet.

"Run!" she yelled.

The twins and their friends ran down the yellow brick road as fast as they could. The roots slowed the Kalidahs down for only a couple seconds and they raced after the travelers on all fours. Alex and Mother Goose stayed in the back of the fleeing group, enchanting the forest as they ran to protect their friends.

Alex waved her hands and the trees bent down, trapping the Kalidahs in their branches. They were too strong to be contained for long, and the savage beasts tore through the branches like they were very tiny sticks.

Mother Goose raised her hands into the air as if she were lifting something heavy and dropped them with gusto, sending a strong wave through the yellow brick road like a rug, knocking the Kalidahs off their feet.

"Yahtzee!" Mother Goose said with a fist pump.

Still, it wasn't enough to scare the beasts away. They avoided the road and ran through the trees on either side of the yellow brick road and were gaining ground. The Tin Woodman, Jack, and Goldilocks slashed their paws as they clawed after the group.

The forest was starting to thin out and the yellow brick road curved into a flowery meadow ahead. The meadow was wide-open—they would have no trees to shield them from the Kalidahs. Alex started to panic; they were too powerful and there were too many of them to fight off.

"Conner, when we get to the meadow, make sure the others keep running," she said. "Get them as far away from me as possible! I'm going to stay behind!"

"But the Kalidahs will kill you!" he said.

"No they won't," Alex said. "I'm getting *overwhelmed*."

Conner was frightened to hear this, but he knew it might be their only chance to make it out of Oz alive. He and the others ran into the meadow, and Alex stayed at the edge of the forest. She turned to face the Kalidahs—they were so close to her, she could see the whites of their eyes and the tips of their fangs.

Alex closed her eyes and tried to think of the most over-whelming thoughts possible. If she could reach the point of losing herself the way she did in the Witches' Brew and the Fairy Palace, she knew she could scare the Kalidahs away.

Fortunately, she didn't have to. All eight of the beasts came to an abrupt stop at the edge of the forest, inches away from her. They whimpered and ran off in the opposite direction. Alex couldn't believe it—she hadn't even done anything yet—*or had she?*

The others saw it, too, and came to a halt in the middle of the meadow.

"What happened?" Conner yelled.

"I have no idea," Alex said with a laugh. "They just stopped and ran the other way!"

She joined her friends in the meadow, and together they watched in utter confusion as the cowardly creatures retreated into the woods.

"That must have been one dirty look you gave them," Mother Goose said. "Atta girl!"

They all congratulated Alex with hugs and pats on the back, but she wasn't sure she deserved it. She was certain it must have been something else.

The Tin Woodman was astonished. "So you and the old woman are capable of *magic*?"

"Who are you calling old, *rusty*?" Mother Goose snapped at him.

"Only a few tricks the Wizard taught us," Alex said with a guilty laugh.

Thankfully, the Tin Woodman found it highly intriguing, not frightening.

Their escape from the Kalidahs must have taken a toll on them, because everyone looked exhausted. They panted and panted, but none of them could catch their breath. Lester lay on the ground and went right to sleep.

"Look at all these beautiful flowers!" Red said, admiring the scarlet flowers covering the meadow. "They match my dress perfectly."

Red picked one and placed it in her hair. She gathered more for a small bouquet and suddenly screamed.

"What is it, Red?" Jack asked.

"It's a skeleton!" she screamed. "Right there, lying under the flowers!"

They all went to inspect it but paused when they felt crunches under their feet. The meadow wasn't just covered with flowers; it was also littered with skeletons. It was horrifying, but none of them had caught their breath enough to scream—in fact, the longer they stood in the meadow, the more exhausted they became.

"What is this place?" Goldilocks asked breathlessly.

The Tin Woodman didn't seem nearly as tired as the rest. "Oh, no," he said with alarmed eyes. "It wasn't *us* that the Kalidahs were running from; it was the flowers! We've entered the field of deadly poppies!"

The twins heard a *thump* behind them, quickly followed by another. One by one their friends dropped to the ground, fainting from the poppies' poisonous fumes.

"Conner," Alex panted. "What are we going to—"

She fell into the flowers before she could finish her sentence.

Conner was the last one of his friends standing. He fought the anesthesia for as long as he could, but the poppies were too strong. The scent made him dizzier and more fatigued than he had ever been in his life. He was almost too tired to breathe.

With no lungs in his chest, the Tin Woodman was the only one not affected, and he watched in horror as Conner slowly lost consciousness.

"Get . . . *help* . . . ," Conner whispered to him.

Conner collapsed on the ground. His eyes fluttered shut and he fell into a deep, possibly eternal sleep. . . .

CHAPTER FIFTEEN

THE WITCH'S CASTLE

Alex and Conner awoke to the sound of sniffling. They were so groggy, they couldn't tell if they were awake or still dreaming.

"They're dead.... They're dead and it's all my fault," someone cried. "I should have known better than to take them into that poppy field. Now they'll never make it to the witch's castle and I shall never get a heart."

The twins sat up and looked around. They were in a grassy field beside a stream. All their friends were sound asleep on the ground near them. Mother Goose was snoring so loudly, it was a wonder the others could sleep through it.

The Tin Woodman was sitting on a boulder by the stream, crying buckets and buckets of tears into his hands. The twins helped each other to their feet and walked over to him.

"Mr. Woodman, are you all right?" Alex asked.

"No, I'm not all right," the Tin Woodman cried, but never looked up. "I just led the Wizard's associates straight to their doom! They breathed too much of the deadly poppy poison and now they'll never wake up! I'll never get a heart and I will never love, or fear, or laugh, or be sad again!"

Alex and Conner shared a smile.

"Mr. Woodman, you can dry your tears!" Alex said happily. "We're awake!"

"Is that you, Alex?" the Tin Woodman asked, but still didn't look up.

"Yes, it's me," Alex said. "My brother and I are up and I'm sure the others aren't far behind."

"Oh, that's wonderful!" he said. "I thought I had lost you all forever!"

Despite the good news, the Tin Woodman stayed in the same sorrowful position with his hands covering his eyes.

"Dude, are you okay?" Conner asked.

"I'm afraid I've cried myself into a rust," the Tin Woodman said. "Be a friend and fetch my oilcan, will you?"

Conner retrieved the oilcan tied to Lester's reins and oiled the Tin Woodman's joints. He was so happy to see the twins were awake, he gave them each a tight squeeze. The others started waking up, too. They yawned and stretched and grew curious once they realized their surroundings had changed.

"What happened to us?" Jack asked.

"The deadly poppies put you to sleep," the Tin Woodman said. "I carried all of you as far away from the meadow as I could—I was afraid it was too late! But you're all alive and all is well!"

The Tin Woodman jumped happily, causing a loud *clank* when his metal body hit the ground.

"You carried all of us here by yourself?" Goldilocks asked.

"Oh, certainly not," the Tin Woodman said. "The field mice helped me."

Everyone suddenly froze. They hadn't realized at first, but the ground was covered in thousands of tiny mice that blended into the dirt. Red let out a piercing scream and all the mice scattered into the nearby trees.

"How did you convince a bunch of field mice to help you?" Jack asked.

"As I was dragging the twins out of the meadow first, I came upon the Field Mice Queen," the Tin Woodman explained. "She was being chased by a wildcat and it almost caught her, but luckily I intervened and sliced off the wildcat's head before it ate her. As a thank-you, she ordered all her subjects to help me bring you all to safety."

"Oh," the twins said in unison. They had forgotten the field mice helped Dorothy and her friends escape the poppies in the original story. Still, it was an odd thing to comprehend.

"You let MICE touch me while I was sleeping?" Red yelled. "Who do I look like? CINDERELLA? That is absolutely disgusting! You should have just left me in the meadow!"

Mother Goose got to her feet and did a couple wind-mill stretches. Her joints popped like firecrackers. "What a snooze! How long were we out for?"

"Two days," the Tin Woodman said.

"Oh, no!" Conner shouted.

"That's terrible!" Alex said, and she started to panic. "That means we've lost our head start on Lloyd! He could already be there by now recruiting the Wicked Witch and her army!"

"Then let's get to the Winkie Country right away!" Goldilocks said.

Without wasting another minute, the Tin Woodman raced to the yellow brick road and the others hurried after him. They sprinted as fast as their bodies would carry them and ran off the remaining drowsiness from their poppy-induced sleep.

"Look! The Emerald City!" The Tin Woodman pointed out. "Winkie Country is just on the other side of it! We're nearly there!"

A bright greenish glow filled the sky above the city in

the horizon. A massive gate had been built around the city and was covered in emeralds and jewels that twinkled so brightly in the sun, it was almost blinding. Alex wished with all her heart that she could travel beyond the gates and see the spectacular city for herself, but they didn't have a moment to spare.

Perhaps in the future, she and her brother could return to Oz under more enjoyable circumstances and see the Emerald City. But the longer it took them to get to Winkie Country, the less likely it became.

They traveled past the Ozian capital and journeyed a few miles west. The grassy fields around them became less and less lush until the grass died out completely. All they could see in the distance were rough, rocky hills. They knew immediately when they had entered Winkie Country because the yellow brick road came to a dead end.

"Why is there no road through the Winkie Country?" Goldilocks asked.

"Because no one wishes to go there," the Tin Woodman said matter-of-factly.

"Then how will we find the Wicked Witch if there is no path?" Jack asked.

"Usually the Wicked Witch knows you've entered her country from the moment you step foot on Winkie ground," the Tin Woodman said. "She has one eye, but it is as powerful as a telescope, and she can see many miles away from her castle. We won't have to find her—she'll find us."

They all paused before going any farther, and fearfully

looked out at the unfriendly land ahead. No one wanted to take the first step.

"Don't everyone go at once now," Mother Goose said.

"I nominate the Tin Woodman to go first," Red said. "It's his world, after all."

"We can't lose our guide," Jack said.

"Then I'll go first," Alex said. "But no one is going into the Winkie Country unarmed."

She snapped her fingers and buckets of water appeared in all their hands and Lester's beak. Her friends looked down at them curiously.

"What are these for?" Goldilocks asked.

"Spoiler alert," Conner said. "Water melts the witch."

Alex tiptoed to the very edge of the yellow brick road. She took a deep breath and stepped onto the dirt of Winkie Country. The entire group suddenly gasped and shielded themselves—but nothing happened. A few moments passed and there still was no sign of the Wicked Witch.

"Perhaps the border receded," Red said. "Take another step."

Alex took a second step. Once again, everyone covered themselves, but it was unnecessary. She walked several feet into Winkie Country, but there was no retaliation.

"The witch is a no-show. What's plan B?" Mother Goose asked.

"I've heard you can find the witch's castle if you just follow the sun as it sets in the west," the Tin Woodman said.

"Okay, then," Mother Goose said. "You all heard the man—*onward ho!*"

The twins and their friends traveled straight into Winkie territory together. It was some of the most stressful steps any of them had ever taken. They expected to be attacked at any minute by one of the Wicked Witch's wolves, or crows, or bees, or flying monkeys, but an assault never came.

They traveled for miles and miles into the west with no sign of *anything*. The dry and uneven land was completely deserted—they didn't even see a single Winkie. As the sun started to descend, it was easy to predict where it would set and they headed in that direction. Just as the sun disappeared into the horizon, the witch's castle came into view.

"There it is!" the Tin Woodman called to the others.

The castle was not the dark and intimidating fortress they had expected, but was rather pleasant and traditional. It had towers and flags and sat on top of a cliff overlooking the West Country. Even more surprising, there was nothing to stop them from nearing it.

The twins and their friends inched up a steep path to the castle's entrance. The drawbridge had already been lowered and they cautiously crossed it and entered the castle without any trouble. The entire country was *empty*.

"I don't like this one bit!" Conner said. "This is definitely a trap! Any minute now we'll be attacked by the witch's horrible creatures!"

Even as his anxious voice echoed through the halls of the castle, not a single soul revealed itself. They traveled through the vacant castle and found a long throne room. It had high windows that offered impressive views of the dreary land surrounding it.

"I don't get it," Conner said as he looked around the throne room. "Where is everyone?"

"Isn't it obvious?" Alex said with a sigh. "Our uncle got here before us. He recruited the witch and her army. We're too late!"

Defeated, Alex had a seat on the Wicked Witch's throne. Suddenly, a winged creature flew out from under the seat in a panic. It was frightened and moved so fast, none of them could tell what it was. It flew toward a window but didn't realize the window was closed, and it smashed into the glass.

The creature fluttered to the floor and started whimpering. They gathered around it and stared in awe. It was a small monkey, no larger than a cat. He had plump rosy cheeks, brown fur, and wore a tiny vest. A pair of bat-like wings grew out of his back.

"It's a baby flying monkey," Red said with delight. "Hello there, little fella! You are the cutest thing I've seen since we got here."

The baby screeched and lunged at them, trying to defend himself from the newcomers. However, the monkey was more frightened than anyone, and his efforts only made him seem more adorable.

"That's all right, little guy, we aren't going to hurt you," Conner said.

A banana magically appeared in Alex's hand, and she handed it to him. The monkey was very grateful for the food and ate the whole thing in just a few bites. Alex got to her knees and smiled at him.

"Can you talk?" she asked.

"Yes," the monkey said with a high voice like a toddler's.

"What's your name?"

"Blubo," the monkey said.

"What happened, Blubo?" Alex asked. "Why are you here all by yourself?"

She was calm and friendly. He knew there was no reason to fear her.

"A man came to see the witch in the castle," Blubo said. "He had a bag of books with him and a pair of sparkly silver shoes. He told the witch he had killed the Wicked Witch of the East and taken them from her, and if the witch wanted them, she would have to help him."

"You're doing a great job, Blubo," Alex said. "Can you remember what the man asked the witch for?"

The monkey batted his eyes at her. "Can I have another banana first?" he asked.

"Certainly," Alex said.

She snapped her fingers and a bowl of bananas appeared. Blubo went to town as he finished the story. He was much more animated now that he had something in his stomach.

"The man told the witch he knew she wanted the silver

shoes," the monkey said. "He said if she let him use her army of Winkies, and wolves, and crows, bees, and flying monkeys, he would give her the shoes. The wicked witch agreed and they all left—*these are great bananas, by the way!*"

"Do you know where they went?" Alex asked.

"The man took a book out of his bag and poured this funny blue water on it," he said. "The book magically lit up! Then all the Winkies, and wolves, and crows, and bees, and flying monkeys, and the Wicked Witch followed the man inside!"

The twins looked at their friends with worried eyes. This was what they'd feared.

"Why did you stay behind?" Conner asked.

"The Wicked Witch wears a golden cap that controls the flying monkeys," Blubo said. "But I am young and the cap has no control over me. I stayed behind, but my family was forced to go against their will. I hope they'll be all right."

"Did they leave the book behind?" Alex asked.

"The man had the Wicked Witch order me to throw it off the castle's balcony when they were gone," he said. "The man said he had to get rid of it because others would be looking for it."

"Why is Lloyd discarding the books he's traveling into?" Jack asked. "Your grandmother said the books are the only way in and out of each story."

"He saw us in Kansas during the cyclone," Conner said.

"He knows we're following him into the stories. He must have another way home if he's getting rid of the books."

"But how is that possible?" Goldilocks asked.

They all fell silent for a moment as they each thought about it. What else could the twins' uncle have that would give him access to the fairy-tale world?

"I know," Red said. "Charlie had a book called *A Treasury of Fairy Tales* in his library. It had all of our stories inside of it—although, I didn't care for the illustrations of me. I bet he's going to use the Portal Potion on it to get back to our world."

This gave their uncle an even greater advantage. He could move freely between worlds, rather than following the rules of the potion like the twins and their friends were forced to.

Conner went to the nearest window and searched for the balcony. "We have to find the book," he said. "That might take us forever!"

"No, it won't," Blubo said. "Like I said, the golden cap doesn't work on me, so I didn't have to follow the witch's orders. I hid the book instead."

"Where?" Alex asked. "May we see it?"

The monkey thought it over. "If I give it to you, will you defeat the Wicked Witch and free my family from her?"

He looked up at them with large, desperate eyes. The twins couldn't promise him anything, but they needed the book desperately.

"We can promise to *try*," Alex said. "There are a lot of

people we're hoping to save by going after this man—a lot of families just like yours we'll be helping."

Blubo looked back and forth at them. He reached into his vest and pulled out a small book with a green cover. He handed it to Alex and she read the title. Her eyes grew wide.

"Peter Pan," she told the others. "He's going to Neverland next."

"What's in Neverland?" Goldilocks asked.

"Captain Hook and the pirates are," Conner said with a heavy heart.

The others didn't have to ask the twins any questions to know this made their situation go from bad to worse.

"Then let's go after them," Jack said. "We won't solve anything by sitting around the castle."

They huddled together and formed the next phase of their plan.

"Since we don't have an alternative way home like our uncle, someone needs to stay in Oz and keep an eye on the *Wonderful Wizard of Oz* book and the *Peter Pan* book we travel into," Conner said.

"I'll stay," Goldilocks said.

"Then I'm staying, too," Jack said.

"Jack, I'll be perfectly fine in the castle," she argued. "They'll need *one of us* with them."

"I'm not leaving the mother of my unborn child," Jack said. "If they should need us, we'll only be a book away."

It was settled. Conner pulled out the yellow book

tucked in the back of his belt and gave it to Jack and Goldilocks to look after. Alex placed the green book on the floor in the center of the room and flipped it open. As expected, a bright beam of light shot directly out of it and up to the high ceiling of the castle.

"I have a feeling there's a lot more to you people than what I've been told," the Tin Woodman said. He had been quiet up to this point, but seeing the book magically light up forced him to break his silence.

"We *may* have skipped a few of the details," Conner said sheepishly.

"Can you still give me a heart as promised?" he asked hopefully.

"*Sure,*" Conner said. "But it may take us a little longer than we realized."

"If I assist you further in your quest, could it get me a heart faster?" the Tin Woodman said.

Alex and Conner looked at each other and shrugged. "It couldn't hurt," Alex said.

"Then I am at your service," the Tin Woodman said.

The twins, Red, Mother Goose, Lester, and the Tin Woodman stood in a circle around the beam of light.

"Is everyone ready?" Alex said. The others each gave her a confident nod.

"Here we go again," Conner said. "Next stop, *Neverland!*"

CHAPTER SIXTEEN

DITCHING THE DARLINGS

Alex and Conner stepped through the beam of light and left the witch's castle and the Land of Oz behind. They waited as the words from the new story built an entirely new world around them. The Tin Woodman, Red, Mother Goose, and Lester arrived a moment later and observed their newest location in wonder.

"*Extraordinary,*" the Tin Woodman said. "I've never seen a place like this."

"It's spectacular!" Red said, and placed a hand over

her heart. "Look at all the elegant buildings! The lamps! The paved streets! I wasn't expecting Neverland to be so *sophisticated*!"

"Guys, this isn't Neverland," Conner said. "We're in *London*."

They were standing in a small square park bordered by streets and rows of tasteful town houses. It was very late and all the streetlamps were lit. The twins were very amused by how much the classic English neighborhood enchanted their friends. The Tin Woodman and Red didn't care what this place was called; it was still just as marvelous and foreign as anything else they might have seen.

"Hello, London!" Mother Goose said. "Boy, we've had some good times here, haven't we, Lester?"

Lester nodded with large eyes. He remembered things very differently. Conner picked up the copy of *Peter Pan* and tucked it safely into Lester's saddle.

A horse and buggy passed them on the street. The driver wore a tall top hat and had a thick mustache. Red and the Tin Woodman gave the driver a friendly curtsy and bow. He stared at them very strangely, as if his mind was playing tricks on him, and continued down the street without acknowledging them.

"What year does this story take place?" Mother Goose asked. "Is it before or after the Great Fire of London— *purely curious, not that I had anything to do with it*."

"The early nineteen hundreds," Alex said.

"Mother Goose, have you been in this story before?" Red asked.

"London is a city in the Otherworld, and it's where this story begins, just like Kansas," Alex explained.

"Then I'm afraid to ask how we get to Neverland," Red said, already dreading it. "Hurricane? Earthquake? Sinkhole?"

"Of course not," Conner said. "That would be ridiculous. We *fly* to Neverland."

"Fly what?" Mother Goose asked.

"Mother Goose, I can't believe how unfamiliar you are with these stories," Conner said. "After all the time you've spent in the Otherworld, how do you not know about Peter Pan?"

"I was too busy spreading stories with your grandmother and the other fairies to read any of them," she said. "So who is this Pan fellow? Is he a pilot?"

"Right now, he's our only hope of finding and stopping Uncle Lloyd," Alex said. "Come with me, we've got to look for him."

Alex hurried down the street and the others followed behind her. She carefully looked over every town house they passed. Occasionally she would climb over a gate and peer through a window to see the inside of a house.

"What are we looking for?" the Tin Woodman asked.

"The Darlings' house," Alex said. "Peter visits the Darlings' nursery in the beginning of the book. I should know it when I see it—*everybody, quiet!*"

Without warning, Alex pushed her brother and Red into the flowerbed and dragged the Tin Woodman, Mother Goose, and Lester behind the pillars of the porch they were inspecting.

A man and a woman emerged from the town house across the street. The man promptly locked the door of their home and escorted the woman down the street. They were dressed up in a suit and gown and were in mid-conversation.

"I'm telling you, George, I know what I saw," the woman said.

"Mary, your imagination has run off with your mind." George laughed.

"I was not imagining it," Mary insisted. "Last night, after I read the children a bedtime story, as I sat sewing while the children fell asleep, I saw him—a boy outside the window of the nursery!"

"My dear, there is nothing outside the window of the nursery but air," George said.

"Then he was *floating*," Mary said. "Nana saw him, too! She snapped the window shut and he disappeared."

"Imagine that," George said.

"Don't mock me, George, I wouldn't say such things if they weren't true. Anyway, he left his shadow behind. I put it in a drawer for safekeeping. I do suppose he'll be coming back for it."

"His *shadow?*" George couldn't believe the words coming out of his wife's mouth. "Mary, I've heard enough. You've been cooped up with the children for far too long and you need a break. Now, let's enjoy the rest of our night without any more talk of such nonsense, I beg you."

George and Mary turned the corner and disappeared down another street.

"The wife sounds like a loon," Mother Goose whispered.

"No, she's telling the truth," Alex said. "Any minute now Peter Pan and a pixie named Tinker Bell will appear at the windows of the nursery. I have to admit, I'm excited to see them!"

Everyone stared at the tall windows at the very top of the town house and waited for the boy and the pixie to appear. They waited and waited, but nothing was happening. They watched the windows until their necks started to ache. The others had seats on the steps of the town house, but Alex stayed put—she wasn't going to miss anything.

"Any minute now!" Alex said cheerfully. "We'll grab him, ditch the Darlings, and head to Neverland!"

A couple of long hours later, there was still no sign of Peter Pan or Tinker Bell. Then they heard a couple of voices and everyone's heart jumped—*this was it*. They quickly resumed their positions behind the pillars and in the flowerbed. However, it was only George and Mary returning to the street on their way home.

"This isn't right," Alex said. "They're not supposed to be back yet! Peter Pan should have taken Wendy, Michael, and John to Neverland by now."

As Mr. and Mrs. Darling walked up the front steps of their town house, Conner felt a soft breeze. He looked down the street and saw a young boy peeking out from behind a neighboring town house's chimney. He flew from one chimney to the next, creeping closer to the Darlings' home.

"Guys!" Conner whispered. *"Look! It's Peter!"*

They all turned in the direction Conner was pointing and saw "the boy who wouldn't grow up" himself. He had messy auburn hair, rosy cheeks, and clothes made of green and brown leaves.

Peter hovered behind the chimney of the Darlings' neighbors' house until George and Mary went inside their home. As soon as they shut the door, he dashed to the windows of the nursery, all the while never casting a shadow on anything below him.

Alex pointed at the window and it locked before Peter got there. He pulled on the window, but it wouldn't budge. He grew very worried and looked inside. When he didn't see anything moving, he lightly knocked on the glass.

"Tink?" Peter whispered. *"Tink, are you in there? Did the woman trap you with my shadow?"*

When there was no response, Peter's posture sank and he dropped a few feet in altitude. He quickly flew off into the night, searching the sky and streets around him.

"After him!" Alex told the others. "We can't lose him!"

They followed Peter on the streets below, chasing after him as if he were a loose balloon. It became increasingly difficult to keep up with him; the longer he searched, the less inclined he was to stay in line with the streets. He flew over several streets at once, jumping from neighborhood to neighborhood.

"We're not going to find him at this rate!" Red said.

"I agree, we're rats in a pigeon chase," Mother Goose said. "Lester, fly after him!"

"Wait!" Conner said when something caught his eye. "Look over *there*."

He pointed to a small park in the center of the neighborhood. Peter Pan was sitting on the very top of a statue. His face was buried in his crossed arms and he appeared to be crying. The twins and their friends snuck into the park as quickly and quietly as they could, which was especially difficult with the Tin Woodman's heavy metal boots.

"Should I say something to him?" Conner asked.

"No, let me," Alex said. "I know exactly what to say."

She tiptoed right up to the statue where he was seated. Peter was so upset, he didn't hear her coming.

"Boy, why are you crying?" Alex asked, quoting the story she knew by heart.

She startled him and Peter abruptly shot into the air. When he saw she was just a girl, he posed in midair with his hands on his hips and slowly descended to the ground.

"Who are you?" Peter asked.

"My name is Alex," she said. "And these are my friends."

She gestured to her brother and the others and they walked farther into the park.

"Pirates!" Peter screamed when he saw them. He

shielded Alex and pulled out a small dagger. "Don't worry, Alex! I shall protect you!"

"These aren't pirates, these are my friends," Alex said. "They aren't going to hurt anyone."

"*All* adults are pirates," Peter said, and waved his dagger at Conner and the others.

"But I'm only like a year or two older than you," Conner said.

"*I'm only like a year or two older than you,*" Peter repeated with a funny voice and ugly face.

"Are you mocking me?" Conner asked.

"*Are you mocking me?*" Peter said.

"Dude, stop it."

"*Dude, stop it.*"

"Gosh, you're immature!"

"*Gosh, you're immature!*"

Conner was beyond annoyed and grunted heavily. "I know staying young is your thing, but you *really* need to grow up!" he said.

"*I know staying young is your thing—*" Peter stopped mimicking him and looked at him curiously. "Wait, how did you know that?"

Alex took this as an opportunity to reposition herself between Peter and the others. "We know all about you and Neverland," she said. "We were waiting for you at the Darlings' house, but you were super-late—well, later than you were supposed to be. What took you so long?"

Peter put his dagger away but continued to eye them

curiously. "I was looking for Tinker Bell. She's a friend and a pixie. Last night, Tink and I were listening to Mrs. Darling read a fairy tale to the children. Mrs. Darling saw me outside the window, so I left in a hurry—I left so fast, my shadow stayed behind. Usually Tink is right beside me, but I couldn't find her anywhere! I've searched the entire city, but she's *gone!*"

"Do you have any idea where Tinker Bell might have gone?" Alex asked.

"Would she have gone back to Neverland?" Conner asked.

"No, Tink doesn't like to fly alone," Peter said sadly. "Now I'm all alone without a pixie or a shadow."

"Why is the shadow such a big deal?" Conner asked.

Peter looked at him as if he had insulted a family member. "A shadow is a friend that never leaves you!" he said.

"But *yours* did," Conner pointed out.

"It wasn't his fault," Peter said. "He was hoping the Darling children would wake up and their mother would read them another bedtime story. Shadow loves fairy tales."

A perky smile came to Red's face. "Which fairy tale was it?" she asked, and ran her fingers through her hair.

" 'Cinderella,' " Peter said.

Red slumped. "Oh...," she said with a disappointed sigh. "You didn't miss much—she dies in the end."

Peter's mouth was agape and his eyes became watery. Alex grabbed Conner's arm and pulled him aside.

"Are you thinking what I'm thinking?" she asked.

"This kid is psychotic?" he asked.

"No, about *Tinker Bell*," she said. "It's not a coincidence she came up missing the same time our uncle entered the story."

"Oh, right," Conner said. "Obviously Lloyd kidnapped her. He probably used her pixie dust to travel to Neverland and recruit Captain Hook."

"That's not all he's using Tink for," she said. "Just like he used the silver shoes on the wicked witch, he's got to have leverage to bargain with Hook, and what does the captain want more than anything?"

"He wants to kill *Peter*," Conner said, trying his best to remember the story. "Uncle Lloyd's going to give Tinker Bell to Captain Hook so he can use her as bait for *Peter*."

"Precisely," Alex said.

The twins quickly rejoined their friends and the age-defying boy.

"Peter, we know where Tinker Bell is!" Conner said.

"Where?" Peter asked. He was so excited, he flew a few feet into the air and hovered right in front of the twins.

"A very bad man has kidnapped her," Alex said. "He's using her to recruit Captain Hook and the pirates into a special army he's forming. Will you take us to Neverland? With your help, we might be able to stop him and save Tinker Bell, but we won't know until we get there."

"Of course!" Peter said. "Follow me!"

Peter shot into the sky like a rocket and disappeared

from sight. He had completely forgotten to take the others along.

"This kid has some serious ADHD," Conner said.

They waited for a few moments and were relieved when Peter finally returned.

"Sorry, I forgot to give you the magic *pixie dust!*" he exclaimed. He reached into a small pouch on his belt and threw a handful of shimmering dust on each of them. *"Pow! Bam! Kaboom! Shazam!"* he said playfully, and pelted them with dust until he had none left.

"None for me, thank you," Mother Goose said when it was her turn. "The last time I had pixie dust was 1964, and the next day I woke up on top of the Brooklyn Bridge with a tattoo of John Lennon on my ankle. If we're going to fly to Neverland, I'll just ride Lester."

"Suit yourself," Peter said. "The rest of you, think lovely, wonderful thoughts!"

This was easier said than done. The group had had an exhausting and stressful couple of days, and thinking of something cheerful enough to fill their bodies with joy was rather difficult.

"Oh, come on," Peter said. "None of you can think of a single happy thought? You must be the saddest bunch I've ever met!"

"But I *can't* think of happy thoughts," the Tin Woodman said. "I would need a *heart* to do that—*WOOOO!*"

Just by mentioning a heart, the Tin Woodman rose a few feet off the ground. He hovered with his limbs spread out like an astronaut and spun like a wheel. It was a very odd feeling and he wasn't sure if he liked it.

The twins and Red were very impressed by their levitating friend. Still, manifesting a thought of pure happiness was like finding water in the desert. Peter became antsy—he had never had such trouble teaching someone to fly before.

"If you can't think of happy thoughts, try thinking of a happy memory," he advised. "I hope you at least have *one* happy memory."

They closed their eyes and searched their memories, looking for that one special moment in their past when they had been the happiest.

"I'm thinking of the time Mrs. Peters told me I was a good writer," Conner said.

"I'm remembering the time when Grandma told us we had magic in our blood," Alex said.

Alex and Conner slowly rose into the air and grabbed each other's hands to steady themselves. The weightless sensation made the twins laugh. They felt like they were swimming in a pool and on a roller coaster at the same time.

"Nice work!" Peter said. "Now it's your turn, Princess."

"It's *Queen*, thank you very much," Red replied.

Red was having the most trouble of anyone, which wasn't surprising after the devastating week she had endured. She was afraid if she became too in touch with her emotions, she might sink into the ground instead.

"Come on, Red," Conner encouraged. "You can do it!"

"Forget about the wedding," Alex said. "Remember the time you were the most happy!"

Red closed her eyes tightly. "I'm thinking about the day I became queen of my own kingdom," she said. She opened one eye to see if it had worked, but sadly, she was still on the ground.

A memory wasn't going to work for her. Everything she thought of only reminded her of Froggy and how much she missed him. So instead of looking into the past for happiness, Red looked into the future.

"I'm thinking about the day I get Charlie back, and get to slaughter Morina like the cow she is!" Red declared.

The young queen propelled into the sky like a firework, screaming as she went, and rose higher than anyone. Her friends cheered and clapped for her. Red twirled through the air, fighting to keep the layers of her dress down. Eventually she managed to straighten herself out and looked down at the others in fright—she couldn't believe how high she was.

"And away we go!" Peter said, and flew off into the night sky. Mother Goose hopped onto Lester's back and they followed the boy.

Alex, Conner, Red, and the Tin Woodman just bobbed up and down in the air like parade balloons. Floating was the easy part, but learning to *fly* took some work.

At first they tried *swimming* through the air, but they only tired themselves out. Eventually, they discovered that by putting pressure on their feet, as if they were pushing against an invisible kickboard, they could maneuver through the air. A few moments into it, they got the hang of it, and soared after Peter and Mother Goose.

Peter definitely took the scenic route on the way to Neverland. They circled above the Tower of London and looped through the Tower Bridge, narrowly avoiding a steamboat passing under it. They flew above the Thames River as it snaked through the heart of the city. Peter got so close to the water, he splashed the twins behind him.

They zigzagged through the steeples of Parliament and spiraled up to Big Ben. Peter playfully kicked the small hand of the giant clock, setting London back an hour and causing it to send a powerful chime through the city.

Because of his size and stiffness, the Tin Woodman wasn't flying as agilely as the others and kept bumping into things. He ricocheted off the roof of Parliament like a pinball.

"Sorry! Pardon me! Excuse me! My fault!" he apologized to the steeples, and chimneys, and flagpoles he slammed into.

They flew down Whitehall and over St. James Park and toward Buckingham Palace.

"Oooo, what is that?" Red yelled when she saw the palace.

"That's Buckingham Palace," Alex said. "It's where the monarchy resides."

Red was mesmerized. "What a stylish and tasteful place! Look at that beautiful statue out front of it in the middle of the street! That looks exactly like the statue I wanted to build in celebration of Charlie's and my wedding!"

Red left the others and flew down to the gate. She peered through the bars at the palace in delight. She had to hang on to the bars tightly because the fairy dust was making her drift back to the sky.

One of the palace guards on duty saw Red and stared at her in disbelief. It wasn't every day he saw a floating woman at the gate.

"Yoo-hoo!" Red called to him. "I just love your hat! Please tell the current monarch that Queen Red of the Center Kingdom says hello—"

Conner flew to the gate and pulled Red's hands off the bars. "Red, come on. You're gonna get left behind!"

The palace guard fainted and Red and Conner rejoined the others. Peter led them higher and higher into the sky. They left London behind and headed for the stars.

For a few minutes, the twins forgot all of their worries. They didn't feel the angst of tracking down their uncle, or the burden of stopping him, or the fear of what would happen if they failed. All the twins felt was *freedom* and the cool night air against their faces. Their spirits soared as high as their bodies. They shared a smile, knowing this was an experience they would remember for the rest of their lives.

They looked back and saw not just London but the whole world beneath them. They had left the earth's atmosphere, but the air traveled with them.

"Say, where is this Neverland, anyway?" Mother Goose asked.

"It's the second star to the right, and straight on until morning!" Peter called out.

Just as he said it, an unusually bright star appeared in the night sky ahead. The closer they flew to the star, the more they could make out a small island floating in space.

"We've made it!" Peter said. "Welcome to Neverland!"

CHAPTER SEVENTEEN

ADVENTURES WITH
THE LOST BOYS

Peter Pan and his fellow fliers hovered above a large
fluffy cloud as they viewed the breathtaking sights of
the mystical island below them.

There was a prominent mountain range in the center of
Neverland, and the rest of the island was made up of hills
and beaches. It was covered in forests and jungles, and
there were waterfalls, rivers, streams, and bays. The water
flowed through the island and spilled into an ocean that

surrounded Neverland and then faded into the starry sky beyond it.

Neverland was a child's paradise, with adventure and discovery around every corner. It was everything the twins had imagined and much more.

"Do you see that smoke trail in the hills?" Peter asked, and pointed to it. "That's the Indian Camp! And over there is Mermaid Lagoon! And right there in the middle, that's where the Lost Boys and I live!"

"What about Captain Hook and the pirates? Where are they?" Alex asked.

"They're aboard the *Jolly Roger* in Pirates Bay on the other side of Neverland," he said. "Come with me, I'll show it to you!"

"No, wait!" Conner said. "We can't risk the pirates seeing us! They can't know we're here until we've formed a plan to keep them from leaving the island."

"Then we'll have to spy on them by *land*," Peter said, and seemed very excited by the challenge. "We must team up with the Lost Boys and travel to the pirate ship straightaway! If we go anywhere near the pirates, it's better to have safety in numbers!"

He dived through the cloud and flew to the island. The others followed him, except for the Tin Woodman, who went around the cloud, fearing it might cause him to rust. They carefully surveyed the land as they descended, hoping their presence went undetected.

Peter guided them to a tropical area in the heart of Neverland. The region was covered in sand and large plants with enormous leaves. Peter crowed like a bird, letting the Lost Boys know he had returned home.

Just as they were about to land, Conner heard a soft *whooshing* go past his face. He didn't think much of it at first, but then the sound continued and increased—it was happening all around them now. He turned to his sister to ask if she was hearing it, too, when he saw something very small and thin fly between them.

"What on earth—EVERYONE, LOOK OUT!" Conner yelled.

It was the sound of *arrows* being shot at them from the trees below. The twins and their friends dodged them the best they could, but the arrows were so thin, they barely saw them coming. They hit the Tin Woodman and bounced in all directions.

"OUCH!" Red screamed. The twins looked back and saw an arrow sticking out of her behind. "I'VE BEEN SHOT!"

Red went pale and her eyes fluttered shut. She fell the rest of the way to the island and crashed on the sandy ground. Peter, the twins, the Tin Woodman, and Mother Goose and Lester landed and rushed to her side.

"Red, are you all right?" Alex asked.

Mother Goose had a good look at the arrow sticking into Red and yanked it out. Red instantly came back to life and sat up.

"EASY! That hurts!" she said.

"Relax—your dress is so thick, it was barely touching your skin," Mother Goose said.

"Peter, what's happening? Are the Indians attacking us?" Conner asked frantically.

Peter had a look at the flimsy arrow. "Nope," he said. "Indian arrows would have killed you."

A group of six young boys charged out from the trees. They were howling animal noises and chanting war calls as they ran. They raised handmade bows and arrows, swords, hammers, and clubs into the air. All of them were filthy and wore clothes made of leaves, bark, animal skin, and whatever else they could find on the island.

The boys came to a stop when they saw Peter standing with the newcomers.

"Peter!" they all said in unison.

"Hello, boys!" he said. "I've returned to Neverland!"

They cheered and jumped for joy—they seemed fairly easy to please.

"Lost Boys, let me introduce you to my new friends," Peter said, but he wasn't good with names. "New friends, these are the Lost Boys: Tootles, Nibs, Slightly, Curly, and the twins."

Each of the Lost Boys gave the newcomers a ferocious look and growl as Peter called their name. They each tried *out-growling* the previous one, but it wasn't intimidating in the slightest. No matter how loud they growled, they were still just little boys.

Tootles was the oldest of the boys and wore a pair of thick glasses. Nibs was very scrappy and was missing the most baby teeth of all of them. Slightly was the most sophisticated of the bunch and wore a tie made of vines.

Curly was the chubbiest of the boys and his clothes were very tight. The Lost Boy twins were identical and the youngest. They moved in such perfect synchronization, it was like they shared the same brain.

"Look, it's the giant bird we tried to shoot down!" Tootles said, and pointed to Lester.

"Let's get him before he flies away!" Nibs shouted.

"We'll cook him and eat for days!" Curly said.

"It's been ages since we had a proper meal," Slightly said.

"Attack!" the Lost twins said.

The Lost Boys licked their lips and ran after Lester like savages. Lester hid behind Mother Goose and Peter blocked the boys from attacking him.

"Boys, leave the bird alone!" Peter commanded. "He's a friend of Alex, and any friend of Alex is a friend of mine!"

The Lost Boys slumped and kicked the sand. "Yes, Peter," they said together. Their excitement quickly returned as soon as they saw the Tin Woodman.

"Look at that man!" Tootles said.

"He's made of metal!" Slightly said.

"We could turn him into an oven!" Curly said.

"And weapons!" Nibs said.

"Attack!" the Lost twins said.

The Lost Boys chased the Tin Woodman and tackled him to the ground. They chanted war calls and beat him with their weapons.

"Hey! Stop that! Knock it off!" the Tin Woodman said.

The others couldn't believe what they were seeing. The Lost Boys were the worst-behaved children in the universe. It was as if they were playing characters in a wild game of pretend, but the game never ended.

"And *that's* why I never reproduced," Mother Goose said.

"I don't think these children are qualified to help us," Red whispered to the twins.

The twins were getting frustrated—they couldn't afford to lose any more time. Alex waved her hand and a strong wind blew the Lost Boys off the Tin Woodman. They got to their feet and huddled in fear.

"She's a witch!" the Lost Boys yelled, and pointed at her.

"I'm much scarier than a witch," Alex said. "And if any of you brats try to hunt, shoot, or attack one of my friends again, I'll turn you all into birds and hunt you myself!"

"Peter, why would you bring a witch back to Neverland?" Tootles asked.

"I can't believe Tink let you do this," Nibs said.

"She's going to give me nightmares!" Curly confessed.

"Wait a second, where *is* Tink?" Slightly asked.

"Tinker Bell?" the Lost twins asked.

The Lost Boys looked all around the island for their pixie friend, but she was nowhere to be found.

Peter broke the news. "Tinker Bell has been kidnapped. I brought Alex and her friends back to Neverland to help us rescue Tink from the man who stole her!"

"Kidnapped?" Curley said in shock.

"Not Tinker Bell!" Tootles said, and burst into tears.

"He'll pay for this!" Nibs said with a vengeful scream.

"But *who* kidnapped her?" Slightly asked.

"Yeah, who?" the Lost twins asked.

Peter looked at Alex and Conner—perhaps it was best if one of them explained.

"He's a terrible man who wants to recruit Captain Hook and the other pirates for a special army," Alex said. "We've got to find and stop him before he leaves Neverland with the pirates and Tinker Bell!"

The Lost Boys shook with rage—they were furious someone would do this to their friend.

"We'll leave for the *Jolly Roger* at once!" Nibs said.

"We'll stop them from leaving with Tinker Bell!" Tootles said.

"We'll show those pirates no mercy!" Slightly said.

"We'll take no prisoners!" Curly said.

"Attack!" the Lost twins said.

Each Lost Boy was more passionate than the next. They didn't need much explanation to get excited about something.

"Guys, calm down, it's not that simple," Conner said. "This man we're talking about isn't alone. He has wolves, and crows, and bees, and flying monkeys, and an army of

Winkies with him. We won't stand a chance if we just barge onto the ship and start a fight. We need to see the ship and come up with a plan to stop them."

Once again, the Lost Boys slumped and they kicked the sand. All they wanted to do was attack *something* today—was that too much to ask?

"You heard him, boys!" Peter said, and flew into the air. "Let's lead our new friends to the pirates and see what we're up against!"

He flew into the trees and the Lost Boys ran after him. The twins looked at the others and shrugged.

"I guess we should follow them," Alex said.

"This is going to go horribly wrong," Red said.

"There's not much else we can do," Mother Goose said. "Let's just follow the Boy Scouts from Hades and hope for the best."

They exchanged looks, each more apprehensive than the last, but Mother Goose was right. Peter quickly returned with some information he had forgotten to share.

"A friendly warning to watch your step," he said. "The Lost Boys like setting traps."

They carefully followed Peter and the Lost Boys to the other side of the island. The Neverland jungles were filled with grotesque reptiles and repulsive insects—a little boy's dream. Red almost had a panic attack at the sight of them. She closed her eyes and let the twins guide her so she could pretend she was somewhere else.

They arrived at Pirates Bay and hid behind a row of

boulders on the beach. The *Jolly Roger* was an enormous ship made of red and black wood and took up the majority of the bay. Alex and Conner never had too much experience with pirate ships, but Captain Hook's was by far the most impressive one they had ever seen.

They heard lots of voices and activity coming from the ship, but the *Jolly Roger* was so tall, they couldn't see anything happening on deck.

"Can we get any closer?" Conner asked.

"Not without the pirates seeing us," Peter said.

A small rowboat was lowered off the ship. It only had one passenger and the twins didn't need to be any closer to recognize him.

"Conner, look!" Alex said. "It's Uncle Lloyd!"

"What's he doing?" Conner asked.

He didn't appear frustrated or defeated, as if the pirates were kicking him off their ship. On the contrary, he looked rather excited.

Lloyd rowed the boat to the center of the bay and stopped. He waved a white handkerchief at the ship. A pirate watching from the crow's nest waved a handkerchief back and then whistled to the pirates on deck.

The sails were raised and they filled the sky, soaking up the ocean breeze. The *Jolly Roger* crept into the bay, heading directly for Lloyd and the rowboat. Lloyd pulled out the blue potion bottle from his lapel pocket and poured a few drops of it onto a red book. A bright beam shined directly out of it and toward the sky.

"He and the book are going to get crushed if he doesn't get out of the way!" Mother Goose said. "Granted, my knowledge about ships isn't that great; I was only on the *Mayflower* for a weekend."

The twins watched in anticipation—what could their uncle possibly have up his sleeve now? To their astonishment, the *Jolly Roger* rose out of the water and flew into the air!

"How is that possible?" Red gasped.

"They must have used Tink's pixie dust on the entire ship!" Peter said.

It flew over the rowboat and into the beam of light. The entire ship, the pirates, and everyone else on board disappeared from Neverland and entered the red book's story. Lloyd cheered from the rowboat as he watched the ship vanish: Another phase of his plan was complete.

The twins' uncle wrapped a heavy chain around the book's back cover. In one swift move, he jumped into the beam himself and dropped the book into the ocean. Lloyd disappeared and the red book sank to the bottom of the bay.

The twins and the other onlookers ran out from behind the boulders and stared at the bay in disbelief.

"I can't believe he did it," Alex said. "He left with not only Captain Hook and the pirates, but with their whole ship, too!"

"Did they just travel inside a magic book?" Peter asked the twins.

"Don't start asking questions now, kid," Mother Goose said. "Your head will explode."

"We've got to get that book," Conner said, eyeing the water. "All right, raise your hand if you're a good swimmer! Nibs, I'm assuming it's you."

"The bay is too deep for any human to reach the bottom," Peter said. "But I know something that can. Boys, let's take our friends to the *lagoon!*"

CHAPTER EIGHTEEN

MERMAID LAGOON

Peter and the Lost Boys led the others to another part of Neverland where Mermaid Lagoon was located. The lagoon was the most serene place they had been to on the island by far.

The shallow water was separated from the ocean by a reef wall. It was shaded entirely by tall willow trees that grew around the edge of the water. Boulders were sprinkled throughout the water, allowing Peter, the twins, and the Lost Boys to hop from rock to rock until they reached the center of the lagoon.

Mother Goose, Lester, and Red waited on land, where they knew it was safe. Conner leaned over his rock and looked into the water, but all he saw were small fish swimming between the boulders.

"Do you think they'll be willing to help us?" Alex asked.

"I'm not sure; we've never asked them for help before," Peter said. "They like me, but usually they try drowning the Lost Boys whenever they get too close."

"Can you repeat that?" Conner asked with a gulp.

Suddenly, a webbed hand with long nails shot out of the water and grabbed Conner's foot. More hands appeared throughout the lagoon and tried pulling the twins and the Lost Boys into the water, but they helped one another kick the hands away. Dozens of mermaids had arrived, and they were nothing like the twins had expected.

Unlike the colorful and angelic mermaids in the fairytale world, the mermaids of Neverland were nasty and sinister-looking creatures. Their skin was slimy and so pale, it practically glowed. They had red, slanted eyes and thin, flat nostrils. Instead of hair, they had long fins that stuck straight up like Mohawks. They had several piercings and wore small fish bones as jewelry.

"I thought the Neverland mermaids were supposed to be beautiful!" Conner whispered to his sister.

"Beauty is in the eye of the beholder," Alex whispered.

"What are you doing in our part of the island?" the

mermaid closest to Conner hissed. She wore a necklace of shells that the others did not, so he figured she must have held some authority among the other mermaids.

"We don't mean any harm," Conner said. "We've come to your lagoon to ask you a favor!"

The mermaid blinked a couple times and flared her nostrils. She exchanged a confused look with the other mermaids, but none of them understood what he was talking about.

"What's a *favor*?" the mermaid asked.

"It's something you do for someone else when they need help," Alex said.

The mermaids took a moment to process this and howled with laughter, exposing their jagged little shark-like teeth.

"We don't do favors," the mermaid said. "Especially with the *Lost Boys*!"

The lagoon erupted in chaos as the Lost Boys and the mermaids insulted one another. The twins couldn't let this continue any longer—it was wasting time, and the mermaids were their only hope.

"SILENCE!" Alex yelled. "I want all the Lost Boys to go back to land, and my brother and I will talk to the mermaids *alone*!"

The boys separated from the creatures, exchanging a couple more insults and splashes as they went.

"We aren't going to get anywhere with favors," Alex said to the mermaids. "So why don't we negotiate a *trade*?"

"That depends," the mermaid said. "What is a *trade*?"

"It's when you give something and get something in return," Alex explained.

"We can't blame you for not liking the Lost Boys," Conner said. "We just got here and *we* can't stand them, either. But if you could pick one thing that the Lost Boys did that annoys you the most, what would you choose?"

The mermaids looked at one another and thought it over. They spoke to one another in high-pitched growls and clicks—apparently they had their own language.

"They take all of our fish!" the mermaid hissed. "They have plenty of food to hunt on land and in the sky, but we're limited to the fish in the waters."

"Wonderful," Alex said, and clapped her hands. "So if we convince the Lost Boys to stop fishing in your waters, will you do something in return for us?"

"What do you want in return?"

"There's a book wrapped in a chain at the bottom of Pirates Bay," Conner said. "We need you to retrieve it for us."

Once again the mermaids exchanged growls and clicks. Their language sounded like a mix of dolphin and bat sounds.

"Yes," the mermaid said. "That is a trade we are willing to make."

"Great!" Alex said. "Hold that thought."

The twins hopped across the boulders back to land and filled the Lost Boys in on the trade they had negotiated with the mermaids.

"What? We'll never stop fishing!" Peter said. "Fishing is one of the Lost Boys' favorite things to do!"

"Do you want to see Tinker Bell again or not?" Conner yelled.

Peter and the Lost Boys all sighed and nodded their heads. The twins returned to the mermaids with the good news.

"It's settled!" Alex said. "Enjoy your fish!"

The mermaids looked back and forth between the twins and the Lost Boys—they weren't sure if they liked this whole *trading* thing, but they weren't going to be the first ones to break their end of the bargain.

"We'll meet you at Pirates Bay," the mermaid told the twins. She clicked at the other mermaids and they dived below the waters.

The twins and their friends returned to Pirates Bay as quickly as they could. The mermaids were waiting for them in the water when they arrived. Alex and Conner told them exactly where they had seen the book sink and the mermaids went to retrieve it. They resurfaced a few moments later and handed the twins the book.

"Thank you so much!" Alex said. "We promise the Lost Boys will keep their end of the trade—*right?*"

"Right," the Lost Boys repeated unenthusiastically.

The mermaids splashed them one more time and swam away. Alex unraveled the damp book from the chain and read the title to the others.

"*Alice's Adventures in Wonderland*," she said. "Lloyd

must be going after the Queen of Hearts and her card soldiers next!"

The Tin Woodman mistook this as good news. "The Queen of *Hearts*?" he said with a smile.

"Don't get excited—she's loud and awful," Conner said, and then let out a long sigh. "This trip just keeps getting better and better, doesn't it?"

"Are you going to travel inside the magic book like the *Jolly Roger* did?" Peter asked.

Alex and Conner nodded. "We don't have a choice," Alex said. "It's the only way we're going to stop them—if we even can at this rate."

"Then I'm coming with you!" Peter declared. "I will not rest until Tinker Bell is back in Neverland with me and the Lost Boys!"

"That's awfully brave, Peter, but it's going to be very dangerous," Conner said. "You could get seriously hurt or even get killed!"

Peter retrieved his dagger and raised it to the sky. "To die will be an awfully big adventure!" he proclaimed.

Alex and Conner looked at each other, thinking the same thing—they weren't going to get rid of him. Rather than spending time arguing, the twins went right into forming the next phase of their own plan.

"One of us needs to stay in Neverland and look after the books," Alex said. "Who's it going to be this time?"

The twins, the Tin Woodman, Mother Goose, and Lester all turned to Red. Her eyes grew large and her whole body tightened—every part of her rejected the idea.

"Don't even think about it," Red said. "I'm not staying on this island."

"Red, I don't mean to sound rude, but you're the least *useful* in the group," Conner said. "We need you to stay here and make sure nothing happens to the books."

"These *savages* have already shot me," Red said, and pointed at the Lost Boys. "What do you think they'll do to me when I'm alone?"

"Red, I promise you'll be safer here than in Wonderland," Alex said.

Red couldn't believe her ears. She might as well have been persuaded to walk off a cliff. The twins didn't give her any more chance to argue. Before she knew it, Conner was handing her their copy of *Peter Pan* as if the decision was final.

"Boys, I order you to listen to Miss Red," Peter instructed. "I want you to protect her and make her very comfortable while we're away. Treat her like you would your own mother."

The Lost Boys were very excited by this idea. Red looked like she was going to be sick.

"Yes, sir!" Tootles said, and saluted Peter.

"Now just wait one minute! Am I supposed to sleep in the jungle?" Red asked, but none of her friends were listening anymore.

"Of course not; we'll build you a home!" Nibs said.

"I don't like the sound of that!"

"I've always wanted a mother," Slightly said.

"Well, keep dreaming!"

"Can we call you Mother, Miss Red?" Curly asked.

"Certainly not!"

"Mother!" the Lost twins shouted.

"We have a mother! We have a mother! We have a mother!" the Lost Boys chanted.

Red felt like her friends had just fed her to a pack of hungry wolves. She tried to fight the decision, but it was too late. The twins, the Tin Woodman, Mother Goose, Lester, and Peter were already gathered around the next book.

Alex opened *Alice's Adventures in Wonderland* and a beam of light shot into the sky. "We'll have to get to the queen's palace as quickly as possible," she said. "If we don't catch up with Lloyd in this story, we may *never* stop him."

They entered the beam and departed Neverland, hoping with all their hearts that Wonderland would be their final stop.

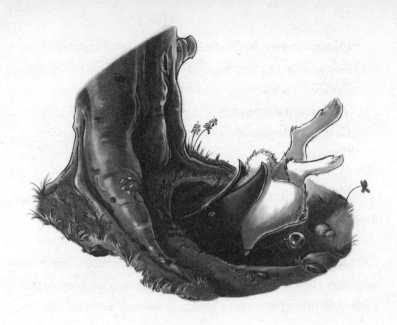

CHAPTER NINETEEN

DOWN THE RABBIT HOLE

The twins and their friends traveled into *Alice's Adventures in Wonderland* safely and took in the newly formed environment. Once again, Conner picked up the book and tucked it safely away, this time into Lester's saddle.

"To quote my friend Amelia Earhart, *boy am I glad to get off that island!*" Mother Goose said. "I wouldn't be surprised if Tinker Bell got herself kidnapped on purpose just to get away from those awful children."

"Is this Wonderland?" the Tin Woodman asked.

"Doesn't look very *wondrous* to me," Peter said, and crossed his arms. "In fact, it looks just like the English countryside."

"That's because it *is* the English countryside," Alex said. "Trust me, once we get to Wonderland, you'll know it."

The countryside was very picturesque. Rolling green hills and trees of all kinds surrounded them and a quiet river ran beside them. It was very comfortable outside, and judging from the different shades of golden leaves, the twins figured it was the beginning of autumn.

They heard noises coming from down the river and realized they weren't alone. A young woman escorted a little girl out of the trees and across a stone bridge. They appeared to be in the middle of an argument. The twins and their friends hid behind trees and eavesdropped.

"We mustn't leave the bank at a time like this," the little girl fussed. She was a very pretty child and held a small cat in her arms. She wore a bow in her hair and a lacy apron over her dress.

"Alice, I'm taking you home to Mother so she can put you down for a nice nap," the young woman said. She was pretty, too—an older version of her sister.

"You're the worst sister in the world!" Alice said. "If you had seen the flying pirate ship, I would have believed you! Dinah saw it, too, and it gave her quite the shock, the poor dear!"

She kissed the cat's forehead and cradled her tightly. In Alice's defense, the cat looked utterly freaked out.

"Then I'm afraid you've both gone mad," the sister said. "Now come along. If you mention the pirate ship one more time, I'm going to have a word with Father. "

The sister took Alice by the hand and they crossed the bridge and headed home.

"We're definitely in the right place," Conner said.

"Certainly are," Alex said. "All we need now is the—"

Something white and fluffy suddenly dashed across the countryside in the distance and caught their attention.

"What is that?" the Tin Woodman asked.

"That's our ticket to Wonderland," Alex said. "Quick, everyone follow that rabbit!"

The twins, the Tin Woodman, Peter, Mother Goose, and Lester sprinted into the countryside after the furry animal. He hopped along a dirt path and then dashed into the trees. It was hard to follow him with all the leaves and tall grass obstructing their view, but luckily the White Rabbit paused every few hundred yards or so. He would remove a golden watch from the pocket of his waistcoat and check the time.

"Oh, dear! I'm terribly late!" the White Rabbit said, and raced deeper into the countryside.

They chased the White Rabbit over a tall hill and into a small valley. They all gasped and came to a halt. The enormous *Jolly Roger* was lying on its side in the valley. Thankfully, the ship appeared to be vacant, as if the pirates had parked it there.

The White Rabbit hopped to a hedge and climbed into a wide hole under the hedge's roots. The twins and the others caught up to the hedge just a moment before the rabbit disappeared. They stared into the rabbit hole while they caught their breath.

"Before we go down there, it's important for everyone to know a few facts about Wonderland," Alex said.

"Oh, *now* she decides to give us a heads-up," Mother Goose said.

"Wonderland is a place of trickery and confusion," Alex said. "Nothing makes sense and nothing is as it seems. We have to stay together at all times, so never travel too far away from the group. Don't trust a word anyone says, no matter how friendly they seem. Wonderland will drive you mad if you aren't careful."

They all took a deep breath and rallied up some courage.

"On the count of three we'll jump inside," Alex said. "One ... two ... *three!*"

They jumped into the rabbit hole and fell down a long dirt tunnel. They fell and they fell, faster and faster, but there was no end in sight. They started seeing cupboards and bookshelves peculiarly placed along the walls of the tunnel as they went. They assumed this meant they were getting close, but they were sadly mistaken.

"Are you sure this is the right rabbit hole?" the Tin Woodman asked. "This one appears to be endless!"

"I'm positive," Alex said.

"Then let's speed things up," Mother Goose said.

She shaped her hand to look like a gun and fired an invisible bullet into the space above them. *BAAM!* A huge explosion went off, pushing them down the tunnel at rocket speed. The blast rattled the tunnel, and all the cupboards and bookshelves fell off the dirt walls and down the tunnel after them.

The twins and their friends finally reached the end of the tunnel and landed on a soft pile of leaves and twigs. They looked up and saw an avalanche of carpentry headed straight for them.

"LOOK OUT!" Conner yelled.

They jumped to their feet and dived away from the pile of leaves. The cupboards and bookshelves from the tunnel crashed to the ground and created a mountain of broken wood, glass, and teacups. It piled so high, it blocked the rabbit hole.

"I hope we weren't planning to go back that way," Mother Goose said.

They found themselves in a long and low hall. The walls were lined with doors of all shapes, sizes, and colors—there wasn't a single doorknob that was alike. Mother Goose, the Tin Woodman, and Peter tried opening the doors, but they were all locked.

"None of these doors will open," Peter said.

"It's all right," Alex said. "We're not using any of them."

Alex went to the back of the hall where a curtain was hung. She moved the curtain aside and revealed a tiny door that was about a foot tall. She looked through the tiny keyhole and saw a beautiful garden on the other side—*Wonderland*.

"This is the door we need!" Alex said. She got to her

feet and looked around the hall. "Now, there should be a golden key somewhere."

Alex found a glass table pushed to the side, but there was no key on top of it like she was expecting.

"Oh, no," she said. "Uncle Lloyd must have taken the key with him when he passed through. We'll have to find another way in. Everyone, stand back, I'm going to enchant it—"

CRASH! Without instruction, the Tin Woodman kicked the small door open.

"Apologies," he said. "I figured this would be faster."

Alex looked like she was about to kiss him. "Good thinking."

"How are we going to fit through the door?" Mother Goose said. "Lester will never squeeze through something that small."

Lester gave her a dirty look as if to say, *"But YOU will?"*

"There should be a bottle somewhere that makes us shrink—oh, here it is!" Conner said. He found the bottle, with a ribbon tied around it, on top of the glass table. The ribbon read:

DRINK ME

Conner uncorked the bottle. "Bottoms up!" he said.

Just as he was about to take a sip, Peter knocked the bottle out of his hands. It hit the floor and shattered, the liquid spilling everywhere.

"What did you do that for?" Conner yelled. "We needed that!"

"Conner, look at the floor!" Alex said.

The others backed away from the spill. The liquid rotted the floor, turning the checkered tile into a nasty brown.

"I knew that bottle wasn't from this place!" Peter said. "It's from Hook's ship! It was poison! They must have switched the bottles knowing we would be following them."

The twins sighed with relief—they were so glad Peter insisted on coming along.

"How are we going to fit through the door?" the Tin Woodman asked.

"I'll shrink us," Alex said.

It had been a while since her powers backfired on her, and she hoped this wasn't the moment that would break that streak. She closed her eyes and focused as hard as she could. Alex pointed to each of them and light swirled around their bodies, shrinking them all to under a foot tall. Once she changed them without trouble, she shrunk herself.

"Nice job!" Conner said, and gave his sister a hug.

The freshly shrunk group hurried through the smashed doorway and entered the gardens of Wonderland. Just as Alex had said, the others knew where they were the very second they laid eyes on it.

They felt like they had entered a painting. It was bright and colorful, but everything was oddly proportioned, as if the world were filled with abstract pieces of art. Everything moved slightly, too, as if it were swaying in a breeze, but there was no wind.

"Look at those flowers!" Peter said, and pointed into the garden ahead.

The flowers were as extraordinary as they were disturbing. Each flower grew as tall as they were. They were gorgeous colors and had beautiful plump petals. However, each flower also had a *face*. They turned to the newcomers and watched them as they walked by.

"Remember, they love tricking people in Wonderland," Alex whispered. "Don't talk to any of them."

"Hello there," a rose said.

"Welcome to the garden," said a tulip.

"Wouldn't you like to stay and hear us sing a song?" an orchid asked.

The group took Alex's advice to heart and walked past the flowers without making eye contact. They kept their eyes on the ground until they were out of the garden.

"If I haven't seen that in a nightmare before, I definitely will now," Conner said.

They looked up and their hearts beat with excitement. In the distance, on the edge of a wood of very tall trees, they saw the White Rabbit. He had paused to look at his watch.

"Oh, dear, I am so late!" the rabbit said frantically. "I must hurry to the castle before the queen leaves!"

He dashed into the woods and they chased after him. The rabbit hopped down a paved path, but it was very difficult to follow him because the path had a mind of its own.

It went sideways, it curled upside down, it coiled up trees, and sometimes it ended for no reason and they had to turn around.

Unfortunately, they lost track of the White Rabbit and he vanished from sight. They took the path in the direction they last saw him and came to a fork. The path split in two different directions, and there was a large silver fork stuck in the ground.

"Which way do we go?" Conner asked.

"I don't know," Alex said. "We might have to ask for directions."

"But you said not to trust anyone here," Peter said.

"I know, but we don't have much choice now," Alex said. "We'll take the path to the right and ask the first person, plant, or animal we see."

They followed the path to the right and traveled out of the woods, and they found themselves entering a forest of another kind.

There were mushrooms everywhere they looked. They varied from the size of normal mushrooms to the size of houses. There were polka-dot mushrooms, plaid mushrooms, rainbow mushrooms, and mushrooms of every pattern and color imaginable.

"This place is nuts!" Conner said.

An odor filled the air as they continued into the mushroom forest.

"I recognize that smell," Mother Goose said. "It reminds me of *Morocco!*"

They figured *someone* must have been causing it, so they followed the scent off the path. Eventually they found the source of the smell and they couldn't believe what they were seeing.

In the middle of the fungal forest, they found an enormous caterpillar lounging on top of a mushroom and smoking from a hookah. He was blue with dark spots and was very obese, even for caterpillar standards. His antennae were wrapped around his head like a turban. The caterpillar's eyes were glazed over as if he was half-asleep, and he blew smoke rings into the air.

"Excuse me, Mr. Caterpillar?" Alex said, approaching his mushroom. "I hope we're not bothering you, but would you kindly point us in the direction of the Castle of Hearts?"

"*Who* are you?" he asked the group in a drowsy voice.

"My name is Alex, this is my brother, Conner, and our friends Mother Goose, Lester, Mr. Woodman, and Peter."

"*What* are you?" the caterpillar asked.

"Well, we're all different," she said. "I'm a girl, those two are boys, she's an old woman, that's a goose, and he's a man of metal."

The caterpillar giggled. "Different, but the same."

"Huh?"

"Different, but the same," he repeated, but found it just as funny the second time. "Or so it appears."

Alex turned back to the others, but none of them had any clue what he was talking about.

"I'm afraid I don't understand," she said.

"Lost," he stated.

"Was that a question?" Alex asked.

"A question to you, 'tis fact to me," the caterpillar said.

Alex was so confused, she shook her head. The others felt their sanity slipping from their brains just by being in proximity to the caterpillar.

"This is going *great*," Conner said with a massive eye roll. "This worm is clearly insane; let's find someone who can actually help us."

"Let me handle this one, kids," Mother Goose said. "He's not crazy, the hookah is just making his brain sleepy. I might understand him if I get on his level."

Mother Goose walked up to the caterpillar and had a bouncy seat on the mushroom beside him.

"May I?" she asked, and gestured to the hookah.

The caterpillar passed it to her and Mother Goose smoked it. After a few moments, her eyes became as glossy as his and she also spoke in complete nonsense.

"Who are you?" Mother Goose asked the caterpillar.

"What I am," he said.

"Where are you?" she said.

"Here with you," the caterpillar said.

"And if this were the Castle of Hearts?" Mother Goose asked.

"We'd be there," he said.

"But where?" she asked.

"In the castle," he said.

"Ah, so there would be here," she said, and they nodded together.

"Here would be what's left." The caterpillar nodded.

"Am I what's left?" she asked.

"You're what's right, of course."

"But what's right is wrong."

"And what's left is right."

"I understand completely," Mother Goose said. "Thank you so much, Mr. Caterpillar."

The others stared at them absolutely dumbfounded. Mother Goose hopped down from the mushroom and moseyed back to them.

"The caterpillar said to go back to the fork and take a left," she said.

"He did?" Alex asked.

"It's all about the keywords," Mother Goose said. "I used to be friends with a sultan who enjoyed the hookah, too. Lester, I'm going to need you to carry me the rest of the way—I'm awfully tired."

They left the mushroom forest and returned to the fork in the path, and traveled left instead of right. They followed the path through Wonderland until they came to a sign that read CASTLE OF HEARTS and pointed to a road that went up a very steep hill. An enormous structure was perched at the top of the hill. The windows were shaped like hearts, and the flags flying from the towers bore hearts, too.

"That's it!" Alex said. "It's the Queen of Hearts's castle!"

They ran up the hill to the castle and found themselves in the queen's gardens.

There were rosebushes throughout the garden. Most of the roses were red, others were white, and there were some that looked like a mix of the two. After further inspection the twins realized that all of the red flowers had been *painted*. It was only then they noticed that the garden was littered in brushes and paint cans. It was as if the project had come to an abrupt stop—and the twins were pretty sure they knew why.

"Let's go inside the castle," Alex said. "Maybe the Queen of Hearts and her card soldiers will still be there."

They walked across the drawbridge and entered the Castle of Hearts. Much to the Tin Woodman's delight, there were hearts everywhere. The rugs were covered in hearts, the wallpaper was hearts, and all the art was of hearts. Even the doors and arches throughout the castle were shaped like hearts.

"Gosh, it's like Valentine's Day threw up in here," Conner said.

Despite the decor, they found the castle very *disheartening*. Just like in the Wicked Witch's castle, they didn't find a single soul.

"No one's here!" Alex said, and tears came to her eyes. "We're too late again! Uncle Lloyd has already taken everyone! We'll never catch up to him!"

"Yes, we will," Conner said. "Even if we have to travel into every book that's ever been written, we'll find him and

stop his army. Everyone, keep your eyes open for a book—
he could have stashed it anywhere."

They searched every corner of the castle but came up
empty-handed. They walked down a long corridor and
through a pair of enormous heart-shaped double doors.

The room behind the doors was massive and square.
There was a giant throne at the other end of the room and
a large platform in the center with a heart-shaped axe resting on top of it. Above them, the room was lined with rows
and rows of benches. It was big enough to seat thousands of
people.

"What is this place? A stadium?" Conner said.

"It's a courtroom," Alex said. "This must be where the
queen has people beheaded."

Alex walked closer to the throne and she accidentally
kicked something. A flat object slid across the floor. She
looked down and saw it was a *book*. It was covered in a blue
jacket with the title *A Treasury of Fairy Tales*.

"I found it!" Alex called to the others. "It's the treasury
Red was talking about! Conner, they've returned to the
fairy-tale world already!"

The twins felt sick to their stomachs. Their uncle had
succeeded. He had formed the army of literary villains he
had been dreaming about since he was a child, and now he
was leading it into the fairy-tale world to destroy it.

"Okay, we've got to get back as soon as possible,"
Conner said. "They must have *just* entered the fairy-tale
world—they couldn't have gotten very far. We'll regroup

with Jack, Goldilocks, and Red and go straight to the Fairy Council. We'll show them Peter and the Tin Woodman—they'll have to believe us! We'll round up the armies of the kingdoms together and we'll take our uncle down."

Alex opened the *Treasury of Fairy Tales* and a bright beam of light shined up from its pages.

"We'll save time if we split up," Alex said. "Mother Goose and I will go to the Fairy Council and show them the Tin Woodman and Peter. Conner, you travel back into Neverland and Oz and gather up the others. Travel back to the cave and start warning the kingdoms of what's coming."

Everyone nodded. It was the best plan they could make, given the time and the circumstances. Conner retrieved their copy of *Alice's Adventures in Wonderland* from Lester's saddle.

"Alex, be careful," Conner said, and gave her a hug.

"You too," she said.

Alex, Mother Goose, and Lester quickly traveled into the beam of light and disappeared from the Castle of Hearts.

Conner opened *Alice's Adventures in Wonderland*. However, just as he was about to step back into Neverland, a winged creature swooped through the courtroom and stole the book.

"What the heck?" Conner said.

The creature vanished as quickly as it had appeared. Conner looked around the courtroom but didn't see anything. The creature reappeared a moment later and stole the treasury just as the Tin Woodman and Peter were about to follow Alex and Mother Goose inside.

A sinister laugh echoed through the courtroom, but it didn't come from any of them.

"What's happening?" Peter asked.

Conner felt like his heart was beating out of his chest. "We're not alone." He was just as terrified to say it as they were to hear it.

A *thump* echoed in the courtroom. Like condensation evaporating from a window, a shield of invisibility disappeared from thousands and thousands of figures that had been inside the courtroom the entire time. Lloyd and his villain army hadn't traveled into the fairy-tale world after all—they were *here*.

"Well, well, well," Lloyd said. "It looks like my brave little niece and nephew have come all this way for nothing."

Conner's uncle appeared by the throne. He was standing with Captain Hook, the Queen of Hearts, and the Wicked Witch of the West.

Captain Hook was a tall man with long, dark, curly hair. He wore a large black hat and a heavy coat with massive shoulders. Notoriously, his right hand was missing and had been replaced by a sharp metal hook.

The Queen of Hearts was a hideous woman. She had an abnormally large head and wide mouth and her face was unpleasantly flushed at all times. She wore a golden crown and a large unflattering gown with mismatched patterns of hearts. Her scepter and all her jewelry were hearts as well.

The Wicked Witch of the West was short and feisty. She had one large visible eye and another that was covered with an eye patch. She had three braids of thin hair and wore a pointed golden hat that allowed her to control the flying monkeys. She held a magical umbrella and used it as a cane when she walked.

The seats above them were filled with their infamous subordinates, who cheered for their respective commanders.

There were thousands of men and women in yellow armor that made up the Winkie army. They stared off into space, as if the Wicked Witch had brainwashed them. The witch's wolves, crows, bees, and flying monkeys stood and flew among them.

There were hundreds of pirates. They were all monstrous and ragged-looking men. Hook's infamous sidekick, Mr. Smee, was among them. He was an awkward, fat, and balding man with a gray beard and striped blue pants.

The Queen of Hearts's playing-card soldiers were stationed through the courtroom as well. They were each eight feet tall and four feet wide. They bore numbers and symbols of hearts, clubs, spades, and diamonds. The White Rabbit was among them and was so terrified by the creatures around him, he covered his eyes with his ears.

If all the children in the Otherworld combined their nightmares, they would be where Conner was standing right now. The Wicked Witch tapped her umbrella on the floor, creating the *thump* they had heard earlier, and a flying monkey landed at Lloyd's side. The monkey handed him the copies of *Alice's Adventures in Wonderland* and *A Treasury of Fairy Tales.*

"You've made a big mistake," Conner said to his uncle. "As soon as Alex realizes you haven't entered the fairy-tale world yet, she'll know something is wrong. She'll come back with the fairies."

Lloyd laughed. "Sadly, Alex will never return from the place I sent her." He peeled the treasury jacket off the book and Conner saw the two didn't belong together. *Alex had been tricked into another story!*

"Where did you send her?" he yelled.

"That doesn't matter anymore," Lloyd said. "What matters *now* is where I'm sending the rest of you."

"I say OFF WITH THEIR HEADS!" the Queen of Hearts shouted.

"I told you, Your Majesty, you can chop as many heads off as you like once we conquer the fairy-tale world," Lloyd said. "I have something even better planned for these three."

Lloyd nodded to the Wicked Witch and she tapped her umbrella again. Six flying monkeys swooped down and grabbed Conner, the Tin Woodman, and Peter by the arms. They flew them high into air and the entire villain army roared with delight.

Conner's uncle removed another book and the blue potion bottle from his lapel pocket. He placed the book on the platform in the center of the courtroom and poured the potion onto it. A beam of light shined straight out of the book and toward the ceiling.

"You'll never get away with this!" Conner said.

"But I already have," Lloyd said with a menacing smile. "Throw them in!"

"NOOOOO!" Conner yelled.

The flying monkeys threw Conner, the Tin Woodman, and Peter into the beam and they vanished from the Castle of Hearts. The villain army erupted in applause.

Lloyd stacked the book he had tricked Alex into and the book he threw Conner into on top of their copy of *Alice's Adventures in Wonderland*. He gave the Wicked Witch another nod. A fiery geyser blasted from the tip of her umbrella and she burned the books until they were nothing but a pile of ashes.

This outraged Captain Hook, and he hooked Lloyd by his collar. "You said *I* would be the one to kill Peter Pan!" he yelled in his face. "*That* was our agreement!"

"James, relax," Lloyd said. "I've simply put him in a place he can't escape from for the time being. Once you and your men have successfully aided me in conquering my home, I will retrieve the boy for you."

Captain Hook released him from his hook and Lloyd patted him on the shoulder. Hook wasn't convinced Lloyd would keep his word, but only time would tell.

Lloyd stood on top of the platform to address the entire army.

"The time has come!" he shouted. "Now that the children are gone, there will be nothing to protect the kingdoms of my home world! We will return to the ship and set sail at once! Together, we will conquer the fairy-tale world and destroy anything that stands in our way!"

The villains roared in favor. Lloyd looked proudly over the army he had formed. His whole life had led up to this very moment. The boy whose powers had been stripped from him was now standing as the most powerful man in the universe. He had accomplished the impossible, and nothing was going to stop him now.

"But first," Lloyd said, "to ensure victory, there is another story I'm interested in recruiting from.... We have one more stop to make."

CHAPTER TWENTY

THE STORYBOOK GRILL

It was after school and instead of spending time with friends like her mother had insisted, Bree was sitting alone in a booth at a diner. She sipped a vanilla milk shake and stared down at the letter written by Cornelia Grimm that she had found in the attic. She hoped by reading it over and over again, she might discover something new that could answer one of the many questions percolating in her mind. Unfortunately, there were no clues or subliminal messages to find.

Bree took a break from overanalyzing the letter and

watched the diner's staff around her. There were two waitresses in the diner that afternoon, but only one seemed to be working. She actively waited on the patrons while the other sat at the counter and took notes from a thick textbook.

"Petunia, order's up for table number four," the working one said to the other.

"Rosemary, for the *twentieth time*, I told you I'm studying for my Zoology exam," Petunia said.

"I've got my hands full with tables two and seven," Rosemary said. "Your homework can wait *one* minute!"

Bree knew the waitresses had to be sisters. They spoke to each other exactly like Bree and her sisters did. She looked at the menu and her suspicion was confirmed. In bold letters, the menu clearly said:

STORYBOOK GRILL
A FAMILY ESTABLISHMENT

Naturally, when Bree decided to go for a walk after school and came across the diner, she had to check it out. The diner was filled with cartoonish fairy-tale art and knickknacks but still had a classic 1950s vibe, complete with a jukebox.

"That's one Ogre Burger cooked medium rare, one Beanstalk Salad with ranch, a Cinderella Club Sandwich on Snow White Bread, three orders of Charming Curly Fries served Goblin Style, the Spinning Wheel Sliders to start, and the Gingerbread House Pie for dessert," Rosemary said, repeating the order for the family at table seven. "Will that be all?"

Bree had never heard of this place before, and to no surprise, she found it very comfortable. She wished she were still in contact with Alex and Conner so she could tell them about it.

"Petunia, seriously?" Rosemary said when she discovered her sister hadn't moved from the counter. "Table four's food is getting cold! No wonder you got fired from the animal hospital!"

"How dare you!" Petunia fired back. "You know perfectly well I left to go back to school!"

An older woman stepped out from the back of the diner. "Girls, stop fighting!" she said. "*I'll* take table four their food." The woman was authoritative but easily annoyed, so Bree assumed she must have been the waitresses' mother.

The mother delivered the food to the table. On her way back, Bree caught her eye. The woman and Bree were instantly drawn to each other, as if they had known each other in a previous lifetime.

"Are you enjoying your Midnight Milk Shake?" the woman asked.

"It's delicious, thank you," Bree said.

"Could I interest you in some Charming Curly Fries or Three Little Pigs in Blankets? On the house," she said.

"No, thank you," Bree said. "I've never seen this place before—is it new?"

"Next month the girls and I will be celebrating our second year of business," the woman said. "I never thought I'd own a restaurant so late in life, but it's kept us busy."

The woman was very easy to talk to. It had been a while since Bree was *engaged* in a conversation.

"Why did you choose a fairy-tale theme?" Bree asked.

"We wanted something that reminded us of home. Fairy tales have a special place in our hearts."

Bree definitely could relate. "I know the feeling."

The woman took the empty seat across from her. "My name is Iris, what's yours?"

"Bree Campbell." She shook Iris's hand. "It's nice to meet you."

"Forgive me for being nosy, but what's that you're reading?" Iris asked, and pointed to the letter.

"It's a letter I found that was written to my grandmother a long time ago," Bree said.

"Oh," Iris said. "And it's significant to you?"

"Sort of," Bree said. "I've been thinking a lot about family lately, and it answers some questions that have been on my mind."

"Every family should have a few good mysteries," Iris said. "May I take a look?"

Bree slid the letter across the table. Iris put her reading glasses on and read it.

"Beautiful penmanship," she said. "They certainly don't teach people to write like *this* anymore." The sender's name seemed to intrigue Iris as much as it had Bree. "Cornelia Grimm is a cousin of your grandmother's?"

"I think so," Bree said. "My grandma isn't alive to confirm it, unfortunately."

"Grimm is an unusual name, isn't it?" Iris said. "Any relation to the Brothers Grimm, by chance?"

"That's actually exactly what I'm trying to figure out," Bree said. "If she's still alive, I want to find this Cornelia woman and ask her, but my parents would never go for it. Things got a little crazy the last time I went on a trip."

Iris found this quite curious. "You seem very interested in the possibility. Would a relationship with the Brothers Grimm mean more to you than just a bragging right?" she asked.

Bree didn't know how to explain it without sounding like a total lunatic.

"It would mean... It would mean...," she said, struggling to find the right words. "I suppose it would feel like I had a little piece of magic somewhere inside me. It would make me feel like I was part of something bigger than myself—like I was meant for greater things than I realize."

"I hope you would feel that way regardless of any association," Iris said.

"It's more than an association," Bree said. "It would clarify things, help me understand where I belong, and give me a purpose. I know it sounds crazy, but I'm constantly worried that if I don't find out, I'll be tortured by it forever. And living with that fear has started to change me. I've become less interested in school, I ignore my friends, and I'm meaner to my little sisters that I've ever been before. It's like I can't enjoy anything until I figure it out."

She couldn't believe she had just spewed so much information to a stranger. It had been so compressed inside her, it all spilled out the moment she started talking about it.

"I'm sorry." Bree laughed. "I sound like such a teenager—so many emotions, such little time."

Iris understood more than Bree realized. This was about much more than just DNA; Bree was on a delicate road to self-discovery.

"You don't want to spend your life searching for relevance," Iris said. "It will only lead to mistakes. Those mistakes will harden you and make you bitter. You'll start resenting people who have found happiness. You'll spread misery, hoping it will destroy your own, but it won't. If you have a chance to validate something within yourself, then do yourself a favor and take that chance. You don't want to live with a piece of your heart missing—it'll turn you into a monster. It's better to be the hero of your own story than to become the villain of someone else's."

"So you're saying I should find this Cornelia woman?" Bree asked.

"If it'll bring you peace, I recommend you do," Iris said. "Even if you don't get the answers you're looking for, you'll never be poisoned with regret."

Bree understood and agreed with her completely, but being a teenager, there was only so much she could do.

"But she lives all the way in Connecticut," Bree said. "There's no way I could make it there on my own."

Iris raised a mischievous eyebrow. "Where in Connecticut?"

"Willow Grove," Bree said. "Have you heard of it?"

Iris checked the postmark on the envelope. "What a coincidence," she said. "The powdered buns we call Snow White Bread come from a factory in Connecticut. It's not in Willow Grove, but the zip code looks very familiar."

Iris winked at Bree, but she didn't understand what she was getting at.

"The delivery truck will be here next Friday," Iris said. "We're always their last stop of the week before it turns around. The deliveryman is sweet but gets distracted *very* easily. He has a crush on my daughter Petunia."

Bree couldn't believe it. Was Iris implying what she thought?

"Iris, are you trying to get me to sneak to Connecticut on a delivery truck?" Bree asked, and couldn't help but smile at the thought.

"I have absolutely no idea what you're talking about, Ms. Campbell," Iris said, and stood from the booth. "But I'm going to get you another Midnight Milk Shake while you think about it."

CHAPTER TWENTY-ONE

THE WIZARD AND HIS APPRENTICE

Alex braced herself as the words from *A Treasury of Fairy Tales* formed the fairy-tale world around her. She had no idea what part of the fairy-tale world the book would place her in or what kind of mess she might be stepping into, so she was prepared for the worst. She just hoped she could get Peter and the Tin Woodman to the Fairy Council before the villain army did any damage.

An overcast sky appeared above her. Green hills

stretched into the horizon and were covered in boulders and stones. There was a forest of thick mossy trees in the distance. The air was salty and Alex could see the ocean nearby beyond a great cliff.

Alex was alone in the area, so she felt safe for the time being, but she had no idea where she was. She knew the landscape of each kingdom by heart, so she was certain she would know exactly where she was the moment she arrived. However, there was nothing about the land she recognized, and the area was an absolute mystery to her.

Mother Goose and Lester also came out of Wonderland fearing the worst. They charged into the scene with their fists and wings raised but quickly relaxed when they saw there was no one to fight. The new environment puzzled them, too, and they looked around the land curiously.

"Where are we?" Mother Goose said.

"I have no idea," Alex said. "I thought I had been to every part of the fairy-tale world, but I've never been to this place before."

They scanned the area and looked for a clue as they waited for the Tin Woodman and Peter to step out of the beam of light, but neither a clue nor their friends presented themselves.

"That's strange," Alex said. "I wonder what's keeping them."

She went to the treasury and right as she was about to poke her head inside the beam of light, it vanished. A moment later the book burst into flames and Alex jumped back from it. In just a few seconds it burned into nothing but a small clump of ash.

"What in the world just happened?" Mother Goose asked.

"They must have destroyed the treasury in Wonderland," Alex said. "But why would they burn it? The Tin Woodman and Peter were supposed to follow us."

The twins made their plan so fast, Alex was worried she or her brother may have misheard each other. But there was nothing that could have misled them to destroy the book. They both knew it was the Tin Woodman and Peter's way into the fairy-tale world, and that the two book characters needed to convince the Fairy Council of their uncle's approaching army.

Alex gazed at the unfamiliar land surrounding them and a very troubling thought entered her mind. The color drained away from her face. Her knees went weak and she fell to the ground. She was trembling and she felt her heart beat in the pit of her stomach.

"Oh, no," she gasped.

"Alex, what's wrong?" Mother Goose asked. "You look like you left a small child at the grocery store."

"Peter and the Tin Woodman won't be joining us in the fairy-tale world because *we're not in the fairy-tale world!*" Alex said. "Mother Goose, we've been tricked! Our uncle knew we were following him and conned us into the wrong story!"

Mother Goose turned white and Lester's head hung

so low, it almost touched the ground. They didn't want to believe it, but it did explain why neither of them recognized where they were.

"How do we get back?" Mother Goose asked.

"We can't," Alex said. "The book acts as the entrance and the exit to each story! We're trapped without it!"

"But Conner and the others must have seen the book get destroyed," Mother Goose said. "They'll know we've been marooned!"

"Maybe," Alex said. "Unless something happened to them, too! They could be trapped in another story for all we know!"

Alex broke into tears. She couldn't believe their journey had taken such a miserable turn. They had been so careful up to this point, and now they were trapped, *possibly forever.*

Mother Goose decided Alex was panicking enough for the both of them. She took a deep breath and tried being positive by playing devil's advocate.

"There's no way of telling what happened to your brother," she said. "But it's very possible he crossed into Neverland safely and we're worrying for nothing. And if he did, once he arrives in the fairy-tale world with the others, it won't take them long to realize something happened to us. Even if he doesn't, I have no doubt someone *will find us.* It may take time, and it may throw off our plan, but I promise you we won't be trapped here forever."

Mother Goose pulled a handkerchief from her pocket

and dried Alex's tears. Alex gave her a small smile and nodded. "You're right." She sniffled. "This isn't indefinite, it's just a delay."

"Atta girl," Mother Goose said. "Since we're here, why don't we find out what *here* is? I certainly hope there's a tavern somewhere in this story—I'm going to need a drink."

Mother Goose helped Alex to her feet and they journeyed into the land, looking for evidence of what story they were deserted in.

They walked through the forest, but it went on for miles. The trees were ancient and grew into the sky. Their roots were enormous and had completely unleveled the ground, making it difficult to walk over. Unfortunately, the woods were empty and offered nothing to put them at ease.

"Walking isn't doing us any good," Mother Goose said. "Lester, let's see if we can find anything from the sky. Alex, you keep searching the forest. We'll be right back."

She hopped on Lester's back and they flew above the trees and disappeared into the overcast sky.

Alex had a seat on a tree root while she waited. She felt herself slipping into another spiral of despair and tried to fight it off. Being upset about the situation wouldn't solve anything, but staying positive was a real challenge. Thankfully, her doubting was interrupted by a sound coming from the forest—it was footsteps, and they were headed straight toward her.

"Mother Goose?" Alex said. "Is that you?"

The footsteps continued, but there was no sign of Mother Goose or Lester. The steps echoed through the trees, so Alex couldn't tell where they were coming from, but they were definitely getting closer. She got to her feet and looked around, hoping who or whatever the steps belonged to could help her determine their location.

Alex climbed a steep mound and crashed into a man running the opposite way. They tumbled down the mound and landed on top of each other in a shallow ditch. Alex screamed and they both quickly got to their feet.

The man was tall and muscular. He wore a red shirt, a brown leather vest, and a knight's helmet. He carried a shield and a wooden sword.

"Forgive me, miss," he apologized, and removed his helmet to look her in the eye. "Are you hurt?"

Alex wasn't sure—the man was so attractive, she went completely numb. The man was only a year or two older than she was. He had short sandy blonde hair and blue eyes that Alex immediately became lost in.

"Miss, are you hurt?" he asked again.

"Nahimmaokay," Alex mumbled—it was all she could manage.

"Oh, you don't speak English—DO NOT FEAR, I COME IN PEACE!" he shouted with large gestures.

"Not speaking English doesn't make me hard of hearing," Alex said playfully. Her remark was surprising to herself—she had just met the man and she was already *flirting with him!*

The man smiled at her. "Pretty *and* witty, I see," he said.

Alex started to blush just as a thunderous roar came from the forest. Apparently the man had been running from a creature, and it just caught up with him. Alex was relieved; hopefully the man would just think she was blushing because she was scared.

"Excuse me one moment," the man said, and put his helmet back on.

He climbed out of the ditch and Alex followed him. A massive black bear was standing just a few feet away from them. It raised its claws and bared its teeth. The bear roared again and it was so loud, Alex and the man almost fell back into the ditch.

"I'll handle this, don't worry," the man said.

Alex wasn't worried at all. With just a snap of her fingers she could turn the bear into a harmless poodle if she needed to. The bear charged toward them and the man blocked its paws with his shield. Alex sat by a tree and watched the battle—it was much more amusing than using magic.

"Remember, you must always be one step ahead of your enemy!" said an airy voice that resonated through the trees. Alex looked around the forest but didn't see who or where it was coming from. Perhaps it was a spirit?

The man seemed to be taking the voice's advice. He used the bear's head as a springboard and jumped into the air. He grabbed hold of a tree branch and pulled himself into the tree.

"A step AHEAD, not step ON their head!" the mysterious voice clarified.

The bear climbed the tree after him. It tore the branches off as it went, making it impossible for the man to climb down.

"When in trouble, use your surroundings as a tool!"

The man climbed to the very top of the tree and the bear followed. The tree bent from their weight. The man waited until the bear was right behind him and then leaped off. The tree flung the bear into the woods like a catapult, and it crashed to the ground a few yards away.

Alex clapped for the man and he gave her a quick bow. The bear was furious and breathed heavily from its flared nostrils. It got to its feet and charged after him.

"Use your opponent's anger against them! Taunt them until they are blind with rage!"

The man zigzagged between the trees and kicked dirt into the bear's eyes as it chased him. The bear was blinded and pawed its eyes to get the dirt out. The man ran toward it, about to strike it with his wooden sword.

"Never be fooled by false injuries!"

The bear suddenly opened its eyes and knocked the man across the woods. He landed by the tree Alex was seated on.

"Are you a knight or something?" Alex asked.

The man pulled himself up to a seated position beside her. "Or something," he said.

"I don't think you're going to win this fight with a

wooden sword," Alex said with a cheeky grin. "Do you need a hand?"

"Of course not," the man said, insulted she would even ask. "That bear is exactly where I want him. This isn't the first beast I've slaughtered."

The bear was running straight for them—coming in for the kill.

"But it might be your last," Alex said.

The man pointed his wooden sword at the bear, but it might as well have been a toothpick—the bear ran so fast, nothing was going to stop it.

"Most importantly, never involve innocent people in your dueling—"

The mysterious voice was mysteriously interrupted. Just as the bear was about to pounce on the man and Alex, metal chains wrapped around the bear's body and pulled it inside a large cage that magically appeared behind it.

The man took off his helmet and stared in amazement. "Are you seeing this, too, or did I hit my head?"

Alex was just as surprised as he was—*her* magic wasn't trapping the bear. This enchantment was coming from someone *else*. A gust of wind came from above them and they looked up to the sky. Mother Goose and Lester descended into the forest and landed beside the caged bear.

"I leave you alone for five minutes and you almost get clawed to death by a bear?" Mother Goose said.

"I could have handled it if I was worried," Alex said.

Mother Goose hopped down from Lester's back. The

man quickly got to his feet and looked back and forth between the old woman and the large bird. It wasn't every day he saw a person flying on the back of a giant goose.

"Lester and I didn't see anything but more trees from the sky—Hey, who's the heartthrob?" Mother Goose asked when she noticed the man.

"We haven't been formally introduced," Alex said, and turned to him. "I'm Alex. These are my friends Mother Goose and Lester."

"Pleased to meet you, cutie," Mother Goose said, and winked at him.

"Pleasure," the man said with a polite smile. "My name is Arthur, and the bear you just chained up is actually my friend Merlin."

Alex and Mother Goose weren't sure they heard him correctly and looked to the other to confirm it. "Did he say *Merlin?*" they asked together.

WHOOSH! A whirlwind of dirt and leaves surrounded the caged bear, and the beast disappeared. An old man with a long silver beard and thick silver eyebrows appeared in its place. He wore glasses, a blue robe, and a matching pointed hat. He stared down at his arms and legs in bewilderment.

"Madam, that was one *brilliant* enchantment!" Merlin said, and applauded Mother Goose. "I've never seen someone enchant something so effortlessly!"

Mother Goose batted her eyes. "Well, when you've been *enchanting* for as long as I have, you get lots of practice," she snickered.

Merlin took off his hat, exposing his bald head, and bowed to her. "It is a great pleasure to make your acquaintance," he said, and kissed her hand. "You are a goddess of sorcery!"

Mother Goose blushed at the compliment, even more than Alex had earlier. Lester rolled his eyes and looked away.

Alex couldn't believe what she was seeing and hearing. Were these really the legendary characters of *King Arthur* standing before her? She had to clarify it before they went any further.

"Hold on a second," Alex said. "Are you *the* Arthur and Merlin—as in *Camelot?*"

"Shhhh!" Merlin shushed her and quickly covered Arthur's ears. "The boy doesn't know about that yet! You're going to give it away! I'm having a hard enough time keeping him focused on combat lessons—Wait a moment, how do you know about Camelot?"

Alex and Mother Goose went quiet—they didn't know what to tell him. Merlin was a wizard, after all; he might understand the truth if they gave it to him. Arthur looked at Alex and Mother Goose with a curious smile.

"Can you predict the future like Merlin?" he asked.

"Come again?" Mother Goose asked.

"Merlin is training me to be the next King of England," Arthur explained. "He says he's certain I'll be the king in the future because he's prophesized it. Although, I've never met anyone *else* who believes it."

"Well, he's right," Alex said, and received a dirty look

from the wizard. "Sorry, Merlin! I didn't mean to give anything away."

Arthur's eyes lit up. "So it's true," he said. "I really am going to be king! You must be wizards, too!"

"Technically, I'm a fairy," Alex said. "And Mother Goose is—well—I'm not sure what to call her."

"Experienced," Mother Goose said. "I've never been into labels—and I don't want to burst your bubble, Artie, but we can't predict the future. People are just very *knowledgeable* where we come from."

"We're practically from a different world," Alex said with nervous laughter.

"Avalon?" Merlin asked.

"No, we're *literally* from a different world," Mother Goose said.

"Oh, *France!*" Merlin said, and nodded confidently.

Alex and Mother Goose sighed—perhaps Merlin wouldn't understand after all.

"We're from a different *dimension*," Alex said, giving it one last try. "I know it's hard to believe, but we're trapped in this world until someone figures out where we are and rescues us."

Merlin and Arthur shared the same fascinated look—the kind of expression Alex was used to people making once they understood.

"And what dimension might that be?" Merlin asked.

"Wait—you believe me? You don't think I sound totally insane?" she asked.

"You don't sound mad at all," Arthur said. "Merlin has always said the universe is far more complex than we realize, and you're proving it. What do you call your dimension?"

"Well, there are two, actually," Alex explained. "There's the Otherworld, and there's the fairy-tale world. I suppose we're from both—but I should probably stop while I'm ahead. It's a long and complicated story."

Alex was worried for nothing; the wizard and his apprentice seemed very excited by what she was telling them. Meeting Alex and Mother Goose was the most thrilling thing that had happened to them in a while.

"You both must join us for tea, and I won't take no for an answer," Merlin said. "We want to hear everything about your world, or *worlds*, and how you found your way into ours."

Alex and Mother Goose didn't have a reason to object. Being stranded meant their schedule was clear, and they had never had tea with a wizard before. Merlin offered Mother Goose his arm and she linked it with her own. Arthur offered Alex his arm, too, and the men escorted the women (and Lester) through the woods to Merlin's home.

Merlin lived in a modest cottage a few miles farther into the forest. When Alex and Mother Goose walked through the front door, they couldn't tell which part of the house they were entering; every surface and piece of furniture was covered. There were potions, plants, cauldrons, candles, and thousands of books stacked to the ceiling.

There was everything you'd expect to find in a wizard's home, but there were also stacks of sketches of very familiar machines and contraptions. Alex recognized a spinning jenny, a sewing machine, a typewriter, and a record player. She could have sworn she even saw a drawing that looked like a cell phone in his collection, but didn't want to seem nosy. Clearly, they were objects Merlin had seen in his visions of the future.

"Merlin, you're a hoarder," Mother Goose said.

"Forgive the mess," he said. "It's been a couple centuries since I had guests."

Merlin snapped his fingers. A broom, a mop, and a bucket leaning in the corner came to life and began cleaning the cottage around them. He cleared a space engulfed in books and revealed a table buried beneath. They had a seat and Arthur poured them each a cup of tea. He made a bucket of vegetables for Lester, who waited outside—the giant gander was too big to fit inside the cottage.

"Now, tell us about the Otherworld and the fairy-tale world, and don't be shy about the details," Merlin said.

At first, Alex and Mother Goose were very vague in their explanations. They told them all about the fairy-tale world and how the late Fairy Godmother had discovered the Otherworld. Mother Goose told them how she and the other fairies spread the stories of their world around the Otherworld to give the children something to believe in. Alex explained how she and her brother discovered the fairy-tale world by accidentally traveling through their grandmother's storybook.

However, explaining how they entered the world of *King Arthur* was difficult without details, and the specifics started to spill out. Alex told them how she and her brother defeated the Enchantress and the Grande Armée the following year, and how they formed the Happily Forever After Assembly. She told them they recently discovered that a criminal called the Masked Man was actually their secret uncle and how he stole the Portal Potion from the Fairy Palace.

Alex told them that she had been the Fairy Godmother until she was *ungodmothered* by the Fairy Council, when they refused to believe that her uncle was a threat to the kingdoms. Mother Goose filled them in on their travels as they followed Lloyd from story to story and tried stopping him from recruiting an army of literary villains, only to end up stranded.

Merlin and Arthur were a great audience. Alex and Mother Goose talked for hours and hours without any interruption. Arthur's eyes were glued on Alex as if she had cast a spell on him. He was fascinated by every word she said.

"It's astonishing, absolutely astonishing," Merlin said, and stroked his silver beard. "To think, this world exists in others as *a fable*. It endorses my theory that *we are all but*

characters in the books of God's library. Or perhaps someone else said that and I'm forgetting who. The best part
about predicting the future: I'll always say it first."

Mother Goose looked around at all the things Merlin
had collected throughout the centuries. A framed sketch on
the wall caught her attention.

"Merlin, is that a sketch of *a flying machine*?" she asked.

Merlin had forgotten the sketch was there and left the
table to get a better look. "It appears so," he said. "Is it
familiar to you?"

"A friend of mine designed one just like that in the fifteenth century," Mother Goose said. "He lived in Italy
and was named Leonardo da Vinci. Did you see him in a
vision?"

"Madam, I can barely keep the names straight of people living in *this century*," Merlin said. "You can't expect
me to remember the names of people from the *fifteenth
century*."

Mother Goose giggled like a schoolgirl. Alex had never
seen someone amuse her so much. Merlin sat back down
but scooted his chair much closer to Mother Goose than it
was before.

"Perhaps this world is just the past of your world," he
said. "Let's take it century by century. Give me the names
of your friends and I'll give you the names of people I've
predicted. It'll be good fun!"

"Oh, Merlin, I knew so many people, we could be playing this game for days!" Mother Goose laughed.

"Terrific! It'll entertain us while we wait for someone to rescue you," he said.

Watching Mother Goose and Merlin journey down memory lane made Arthur and Alex feel like two third wheels.

"Can I interest you in a walk?" Arthur whispered to her.

"Sure," Alex said with a smile.

Arthur and Alex left Merlin's cottage and took a stroll through a part of the woods she hadn't seen. It was a more pleasant area, with younger trees and a much smoother ground. The sun had set while they were in the cottage and the moon was their only source of light. Alex might have found it romantic if she hadn't been thinking about so many other things.

"I'm glad to know a little more about you know, seeing as how you already know everything about me." Arthur laughed. "Your worlds sound incredible. I can't believe how much you've accomplished at such a young age. It's very inspiring."

"I have wonderful friends who've helped me," Alex said. "You're very inspiring yourself, and a bit of a legend."

Arthur chuckled. "Am I? Do tell."

"Oh no, I did it again!" she said. "You'd better be cautious around me—I'll spoil your destiny if you're not careful."

"Oh, I will," Arthur said, and shrugged like he didn't care, but he wasn't convincing. "If there's one thing I absolutely *don't* want to hear about, it's my future. I want to be totally surprised. Knowing I'll be the King of England is enough—but you're positive that happens?"

"Yes, you become king," she said. "But that's all I'm going to tell you, so don't ask me any more! Besides, you already knew that."

"Indeed," Arthur said. "*But*...no one has said I'll be a *good* king. It would be a relief to know I don't go mad or bad before the end."

Alex sighed, but with a smile. She knew Arthur was prying information out of her just to tease her, but two could play *this* game.

"You're a *good* king, don't worry," she said, and then looked sadly to the ground. "At least you are once you heal from...*the incident*."

"What *incident*?" Arthur asked.

Alex shook her head somberly. "Well, if Merlin hasn't told you, then I probably shouldn't."

"Oh, right—*the incident*," he said, pretending to know. "Old Merlin's told me about that plenty of times."

"Good," Alex said. "So you know all about *the leeches*."

Arthur gulped. "Yes...I do," he said nervously.

"Luckily by then you've already been captured by the Saxons and your legs have been ripped off," Alex said. "So there aren't *too* many leech wounds."

Arthur gulped. "It's the definition of *luck*," he said.

"It's a shame you lose both your arms in the battle before you get captured," Alex said. "But you aren't known as *Arthur the Limbless* for nothing."

"*Arthur the Limbless?*"

"Oh, yes," Alex said. "A lesser king would have let the

title belittle him, but you still manage to instill fear in all your enemies. Then again, that could be because of your future wife, Queen Girtha. Of course, Merlin has told you about her...."

"Naturally," Arthur said. "She's that nasty woman, right? So hideous, people are afraid to look at her. Now remind me, how many terrible children do we have?"

"Just the one," Alex said. "And who would have expected *you* to die during childbirth?"

"*I* die in childbirth?" Arthur asked with a quiver in his voice. "How is that possible?"

"Isn't that obvious?" Alex asked. "That's why they call your wife *Girtha the Strong Handed*. Did you never make that connection?"

"Oh, that's right," Arthur said. "I made that connection once before, but I forgot about it."

"I don't blame you," Alex said. "I would have blocked it out of my mind, too."

Arthur stopped walking for a moment while he thought it all over.

"Wait a second, if I'm *limbless* when I become king, how do I manage to pull *that* out?" he asked, and pointed into the trees ahead.

Alex turned to see what he was talking about and saw a grassy clearing in the forest ahead. In the middle of the clearing was a stack of rocks covered in ivy, and a large boulder in the center had been stabbed with a bright sword.

Alex covered her mouth. "It's *the sword in the stone*!" she gasped.

Arthur was very amused by her excitement. "I thought you'd like to see it."

"You knew I was fibbing this whole time, didn't you?" Alex asked.

"Since the leeches," Arthur said with a guilty smile. "But you were very convincing, don't get me wrong."

Alex playfully punched his shoulder and went into the clearing. She walked around the sword in the stone and admired its magnificence. She could practically feel the splendor radiating from it. It had a blue handle and a bright silver blade. There was a square plaque on the rock that read:

HE WHO REMOVETH THIS SWORD FROM THIS STONE

SHALL REVEALETH HIMSELF THE TRUE KING OF ENGLAND.

"Do you want to give it a try?" Arthur asked.

"What? You want *me* to try pulling the sword out of the stone?" she asked, pointing to herself.

"Why not? People travel from all over the world to give it a try," Arthur said. "Who knows, maybe it's *your* true fate to be the next King of England."

"I doubt that, but if it pleases you, I'll give it a go," she said.

Alex stood on the rocks behind the sword and wrapped her hands around the handle. As she connected with one of the most important objects in mythical history, she felt a spur of energy move through her body. She bent her elbows and tightened her grip, preparing to give the sword a strong tug.

"BOO!" Arthur yelled inches away from her ear.

"AHHHHH!" Alex screamed. *"What's wrong with you? I could have had a heart attack!"*

Arthur laughed so hard, he fell to the ground. He looked up at her fuming face and only laughed harder.

"I'm sorry, I couldn't help it!" He laughed. "You should have seen the look on your face!"

Alex was furious. She wanted to take the sword out of the stone and make *Arthur the Limbless* become a reality. However, with every passing second the scare faded away and the humor set in. Alex fought the giggles growing inside, but once they surfaced, there was no turning back. She held her stomach and laughed until tears filled her eyes. It felt so good—she couldn't remember the last time she laughed so hard or cried from joy.

"Do you forgive me?" Arthur said.

"I suppose I had it coming," she said. "You should give it a try next. Maybe tonight's the night you're supposed to become king."

Arthur's smile faded and he shook his head. "I know it

won't budge. It'll happen when I'm ready to be king, but I'm not ready yet. I'll feel it inside before I even touch the sword."

For the first time since Alex arrived, the *once and future king* seemed a little sad.

"Arthur, what's wrong?" she asked. "Are you afraid you'll never be ready?"

At first Arthur shrugged it off, but Alex looked at him with so much compassion, he felt like she might understand. She was the first person he had ever known who made him want to confess his feelings rather than suppress them.

"I suppose I'm just worried I'll disappoint people," Arthur admitted. "Merlin says I'm going to be a legendary king—I just wish I was confident enough to agree. And now that I know the legend of my reign stretches into other dimensions, it seems impossible that I'll ever live up to those expectations, or worse—"

"The expectations you put on yourself?" Alex said, finishing his sentence.

Arthur went quiet and nodded. "You too?"

"My legacy isn't written in the stars like yours, but when I first became the Fairy Godmother I almost drowned in the expectations other people put on me," Alex said. "I wanted to believe in myself as much as the rest of the world did, so I put so much pressure on myself; I became harshly disappointed every time I made a simple mistake. I felt like I would disappoint the world if I was ever exposed as—"

"Human," Arthur said, finishing her sentence this time.

"Yes," Alex said. "My biggest fear was disappointing someone, and then after one moment of weakness I ended up disappointing the entire fairy-tale world. I went from being the most beloved person in the Happily Forever After Assembly, to the most feared and hated. But rather than fighting the world that discarded me, I chose to continue saving it. So maybe greatness isn't about being immortal, or glorious, or popular—it's about choosing to fight for the greater good of the world, even when the world's turned its back on you."

Arthur looked into her eyes like no one had before. They shared a special kinship, an understanding, and an outlook on life unlike anyone else they had connected with, and possibly ever would.

"I don't know what forces brought you into this world, but I am so grateful they did," Arthur said.

"Me too," Alex said. "It's nice to know I'm not as alone as I thought."

"Let's make a pact," Arthur said. "We'll both continue living lives of *true greatness*, despite how we're remembered in the end."

"Deal," Alex said.

They shook hands and exchanged warm smiles. The energy Alex felt from the sword in the stone was nothing compared to the touch of Arthur's hand. They remained hand in hand for a few moments, and separated just before the handshake could turn into anything else.

"We should head back to Merlin's cottage before it gets too late," Arthur said.

They broke eye contact and both put their hands in their pockets. Alex felt something strange in her pocket—a paper she had completely forgotten about. She pulled it out of her dress and unfolded it. Her entire face lit up with excitement.

"Oh my gosh," Alex said. "This is a page from *The Wonderful Wizard of Oz!*"

"Isn't that one of the stories you traveled into?" Arthur asked.

"Yes—my brother and I collected the loose pages that fell out before we went inside," she said. "I think I can use this page to get back to Oz and then travel back home!"

"Don't you need the Portal Potion to do that?"

"I know the recipe—I can make the potion," Alex said. "And if my brother has the other pages, that means he can travel back into Oz, too! I've got to tell Mother Goose!"

Arthur and Alex excitedly ran back through the woods to Merlin's cottage to tell him and Mother Goose the good news. By the time they arrived, Merlin and Mother Goose were three-quarters deep into a large bottle of ale and she was still reminiscing through the centuries.

"I had a fling, with Emperor Constantine—but only one date, with Alexander the Great," Mother Goose said with a hiccup. *"The world gets it wrong, about Genghis Khan—the world's biggest pain, is that jerk Charlemagne."*

"I don't know why you're rhyming, but it sure is fun," Merlin said and hiccupped himself.

They jumped when Alex and Arthur rushed through the door.

"Mother Goose, I have wonderful news!" Alex said, and showed her the paper she'd found in her pocket. "It's a page from *The Wonderful Wizard of Oz*! We can use it to go into Oz and then back to the fairy-tale world!"

Mother Goose was so excited, she went into a fit of hysterical hiccups and couldn't speak.

"Wouldn't you need the Portal Potion to do it?" Merlin asked.

"Yes, but we can make it here," Alex said. "The ingredients are very simple. We need a branch from the oldest tree in the woods, a feather from the finest pheasant in the sky, a liquefied lock and key from a loved one, two weeks of moonlight, and a zap of magic."

Mother Goose had an idea. She pointed her finger and opened her mouth to share it with them, but only a hiccup came out. Instead of explaining, she decided to just do it herself. She stood from the table and went outside. They heard Lester squawk loudly outside and Mother Goose returned with a handful of his white feathers.

"Have your pick of a feather; there's no finer pheasant than Lester—HIC!" Mother Goose said.

Alex chose a particularly long feather. "Great! One down, four to go!"

"That certainly seems doable!" Merlin said. "Arthur,

as part of your training, I insist you help the lovely young lady collect the ingredients she needs for the potion. In the meantime, I will entertain Mother Goose."

"It'll be my honor," Arthur said. "I'd like to spend as much time with you as possible before you leave."

He winked at her and she smiled from ear to ear.

"Likewise," Alex said.

She was so thrilled by the discovery of the page, she hadn't realized until now that their time together was limited—and she was very surprised how sad it made her. Alex spent the entire day worrying how she would escape the world of *King Arthur*. She never imagined she would end the day with the future king himself, or that he might be someone worth staying for.

CHAPTER TWENTY-TWO

THE MERRY MEN OF SHERWOOD FOREST

Once Conner, the Tin Woodman, and Peter were thrown into the book, it didn't take long for the words of the story to form a world around them. A word stretched beneath Conner's feet. Before he had time to read it, the word turned into liquid and Conner sank into a large body of water.

A strong force pushed him deeper and deeper into the water. He was so discombobulated, he didn't know which way the surface was, or if there was even a surface to be found. He stretched his arms and legs out as far as he could to find something to grab—but he was alone in this world of water. Conner was drowning in the ocean of a literary world.

Just as Conner was fearing the end was near, he felt a hard hand grab the back of his shirt and lift him upward. The next thing he knew, he was lying on a wooden floor. He rolled to his back and saw the Tin Woodman and Peter looking down at him.

"Conner, are you all right?" the Tin Woodman asked. "You landed in the stream and had quite a fit."

"I was afraid I landed in the ocean of *Moby-Dick* or *The Swiss Family Robinson*," he said.

"It's not even that deep," Peter said. "You must be a terrible swimmer."

Conner sat up and looked around. He and his friends were on a narrow bridge over a shallow stream. They were in the middle of a forest with tall and thin trees, but there was nothing unique enough to help him recognize which forest it was.

"Does this place look familiar?" the Tin Woodman asked.

"No," Conner said. "Quick, we need to find the book! It's got to be here somewhere!"

They spread out and searched the woods.

"Conner! I found it!" Peter said. He pointed to a green book floating down the stream.

"After that book!" Conner shouted.

He dove into the stream and swam after it. Peter flew

above the water and tried to grab it, but the stream's current picked up and sloshed it around. Just as they both narrowed in on it, the book burst into flames, even though it was soaked and surrounded by water. It burned into ashes and the stream washed them away.

Conner felt like the wind had been knocked out of him. His uncle must have destroyed it in Wonderland. They were trapped!

"What happened?" the Tin Woodman asked. He watched them from the bank, where it was dry.

"The book's gone," Conner said, and shook his head. "We're stuck here. And that means my sister and Mother Goose are probably stuck wherever they are, too. We'll never get to the kingdoms in time to warn them—they'll never have time to prepare for the army coming!"

Conner crawled out of the stream, sat on the ground, and covered his face with his hands. The Tin Woodman lowered his head and placed a hand over where his heart should be.

"Don't worry, lads!" Peter said. "The Lost Boys will come for us!"

"They're in a different dimension, Peter!" Conner snapped. "How do you expect them to rescue us?"

"How do you expect them to rescue us?" Peter mocked him.

"This is serious, Peter!" Conner yelled. "We might be trapped here forever!"

"We might be trapped here . . . wait, *forever?"* Peter said. The reality of the situation hit him and he descended to the

ground. "So I may never see Neverland or the Lost Boys again?"

Conner sighed. "I'm afraid so."

Peter sat on the ground with his legs spread out in front of him. His mouth fell open and his eyes filled with tears.

"There must be *something* we can do," the Tin Woodman said.

"I suppose the best thing to do is figure out where we are," Conner said. "Hopefully we'll find someone who can help us."

They journeyed deeper into the forest but found nothing for miles. Peter flew into the sky for a better view and saw a large stone structure in the distance. They figured it was their best option for the time being and headed toward it. Along the way they spotted a long piece of parchment pinned to a tree. It read:

WANTED DEAD OR ALIVE

THE THIEF, VANDAL, AND OUTLAW

ROBIN OF LOXLEY

BY ORDER OF THE SHERIFF OF NOTTINGHAM

REWARD IF CAUGHT

Conner read the poster a few times just to make sure he wasn't imagining it. Of all the places to be stranded, he figured it could have been much worse.

"Guys, we're in *Robin Hood*," Conner said.

The Tin Woodman and Peter were excited to hear it, but their smiles quickly faded.

"Who?" the Tin Woodman asked.

"Is that Red Riding Hood's brother?" Peter asked.

"No, but this is good news!" Conner said. "Robin Hood is a hero—if anyone can help us in this world, it'll be him! We've got to find him!"

The Tin Woodman and Peter eyed the poster suspiciously.

"If he's a hero, why is he wanted by the Sheriff of such and such?" the Tin Woodman asked.

"The Sheriff of Nottingham is the bad guy in this story," Conner explained. "Robin Hood steals from the rich and gives to the poor—he's the guy we want to find."

"I say we capture Robin Hood and turn him in for the reward," Peter said. "Surely being rich would help us more than a criminal can."

"I think the boy has a point," the Tin Woodman said.

On the spot, the Tin Woodman and Peter began making plans to capture the outlaw. They ignored Conner, who frantically shook his head at the idea.

"Guys!" Conner said. "We are not going to kidnap or kill Robin Hood!"

FEEESHT! An arrow came out of nowhere and pinned

Conner to the tree. He screamed in agony but stopped once he realized the arrow was stabbing through his sleeve and not his arm. *FEEESHT!* Two arrows pinned both sides of Peter's pants to the tree beside Conner. *FEEESHT!*

"INDIANS!" Peter screamed.

"There are no Indians in Sherwood Forest!" Conner said. "Besides, the correct term is *Native Americans!*"

FEEESHT! An arrow hit the Tin Woodman's back, but it broke on impact. *FEESHT!* A bundle of arrows pelted the Tin Woodman. *FEEESHT!* The arrows only bounced off his metal body. *FEEESHT!* The Tin Woodman retrieved his axe and sliced the oncoming arrows in midair.

"THE KNIGHT IS IMPENETRABLE!" a voice called from somewhere in the treetops. "MERRY MEN, ATTACK!"

Before they knew it, four men and five horses charged through the forest. The men jumped off their horses and circled Conner, Peter, and the Tin Woodman with their weapons raised.

One of the men was enormous, standing seven feet tall at least, and he held a long staff. A rather flamboyant man, who wore clothes made of red silk and a large feathered hat, held a sword in each hand. A short and plump padre was among the men and held a crucifix and a Bible like a sword and shield. There was also a thin musician, who didn't have a weapon, either, but he strummed chords on a mandolin threateningly while giving the boys a nasty look.

"Well, look what we have here," the large man said in his gruff voice.

"The sheriff must be getting desperate if he's only sent one knight and two children into the woods," the man in silk said, and then tossed his hair.

"Oh, heavenly Father, what kind of coward sends children to do his sinful work?" the padre said, and shook his head.

Conner almost didn't recognize the men circling them. They were much more weathered and aggressive than he was expecting.

"PIRATES!" Peter yelled.

"There are no pirates in Sherwood Forest, either!" Conner said. "These are the Merry Men of Sherwood Forest—they work with Robin Hood!"

"Looks like they found us before we could find them," the Tin Woodman said, completely distrustful of the men around him. "Which one is Robin Hood?"

"DID YOU HEAR THAT, MEN? THE KNIGHT HAS REQUESTED AN AUDIENCE WITH ME!" shouted the voice from above.

A man suddenly dropped down from the treetops and landed on his feet. He was tall and handsome with a red beard and a bright smile. He wore dark green clothing, a feathered cap, and tall boots. He held a bow in one hand, and a quiver of arrows was strapped to his back.

"Robin Hood!" Conner said excitedly. "We were just talking about you—"

"AND PLOTTING MY ARREST, OR SO I OVER-HEARD," Robin Hood said. "BUT THERE SHALL BE NO VICTORY FOR YOU TODAY, KNIGHT. YOU ARE NO MATCH FOR THE GREAT ROBIN HOOD AND HIS MERRY MEN!"

Robin Hood rarely made eye contact as he talked, and he spoke as if there were a large audience around him at all times. Conner was very disappointed; the legendary prince of thieves was not the compassionate hero he grew up believing in, but rather a boisterous narcissist who praised himself in the third person.

"Time-out!" Conner said. "First off, you don't have to shout—we're *right here*. Second, this is all a big misunderstanding—"

"DO NOT SPEAK, CHILD ACCOMPLICE!" Robin Hood commanded. "SHAME ON YOU FOR ALLOWING THE SHERIFF OF NOTTINGHAM TO USE YOUR INNOCENCE AS A PLOY FOR HIS WRONGDOING. MY QUARREL IS WITH THE KNIGHT STANDING BEFORE ME, WHOM THE SHERIFF SENT TO CAPTURE AND POTENTIALLY KILL ME."

Robin Hood glared at the Tin Woodman. The Tin Woodman glanced behind himself to make sure he wasn't referring to someone else.

"Me?" he asked softly. "But I'm not a knight."

"DO NOT LIE TO ME, KNIGHT!" Robin Hood warned. "ONLY A MAN WORKING FOR THE SHERIFF WEARS ARMOR SUCH AS YOURS! YOU CANNOT

FOOL ME! DO NOT INSULT YOUR INTELLIGENCE BY TESTING MINE!"

"Oh, I'm not wearing armor," the Tin Woodman said. "You see, where I come from, there was a witch who cast a spell on my axe—"

"DO NOT FILL MY HEAD WITH TALES OF WITCHCRAFT," Robin Hood ordered. "YOU MUST RETURN TO THE SHERIFF AND TELL HIM ROBIN HOOD IS INSULTED BY THIS ATTEMPT TO SEIZE ME! GO NOW, AND I SHALL SPARE YOUR LIFE!"

The Merry Men cheered and the musician played a chord on his mandolin. The Tin Woodman stayed put and eyed the men confoundedly.

"THE KNIGHT LINGERS!" Robin Hood said.

"Sorry, but where am I supposed to go?" the Tin Woodman said. "I told you I'm not a knight—I have no idea where to find the sheriff."

Robin Hood stared at him and stroked his beard. Clearly he was not a knight, but Robin Hood was too cocky to believe he was mistaken, so he had to think of another reason why the Tin Woodman was showing resistance.

"THE KNIGHT IS SO OVERWHELMED BY MY PRESENCE, HE IS *CONFUSED*," Robin Hood told his Merry Men. "LITTLE JOHN, WILL SCARLET— ROUND THEM UP! WE'LL TAKE THE KNIGHT

AND CHILDREN BACK TO OUR CAMP UNTIL THEY REGAIN CONTROL OF THEIR SENSES!"

The Merry Men removed Conner and Peter from the tree and tied their hands and the Tin Woodman's hands together. Robin Hood and the Merry Men climbed on their horses and set off deeper into the woods, pulling their captives behind them.

"Some hero," Peter said under his breath.

"This man is a lunatic," the Tin Woodman said.

"You guys were right," Conner said. "We definitely should have captured him and turned him in for money."

"ALAN-A-DALE, MY FAITHFUL MINSTREL," Robin Hood called to the musician. "PLAY US A CHEERFUL TUNE OF MY COURAGE AND GLORY, TO PASS THE TIME AS WE VENTURE HOME."

The musician played a song on his mandolin and sang along.

"Robin of Loxley, Robin of Loxley,
England's most treasured man.
He takes delight, in leading the fight,
To save good Nottingham.

"Unlike the sheriff, Robin is cherished,
His heart is pure and true.
Loved by the ladies, they want his babies,
And love his merry crew.

"The sheriff grows scared as Robin prepares,
To end Prince John's regime.
If you want freedom, a better kingdom,
Then sing this merry theme!

"Robin of Loxley, Robin of Loxley,
'Tis no one greater than,
Robin of Loxley, Robin of Loxley,
England's most treasured man!"

The Merry Men sang the song over and over again as Robin Hood played conductor, irritating Conner, Peter, and the Tin Woodman to no end. By nightfall they had arrived at the camp, which consisted of half a dozen tents around a small campfire. The Merry Men pulled their captives into a tent and tied them to a pole inside.

The singing continued outside once the Merry Men gathered around the campfire, forcing Conner, Peter, and the Tin Woodman to endure several more hours of terrible lyrics praising a terrible man.

"This is going to drive me insane—and I live on a desert island in outer space with little boys! I've got patience by the ton!" Peter said, and shoved Conner, as if he could do something to solve the matter.

"I don't know why you're shoving me, leaf boy!" Conner said, and pushed him back.

"Because we wouldn't be here if you and your sister hadn't lost control of your uncle!" Peter said.

"Maybe if your friend didn't have a pixie-sized brain, she wouldn't have gotten kidnapped!" Conner said.

With every remark, they shoved each other a little harder.

"Gentlemen, keep fighting!" the Tin Woodman said.

"Why?" Conner asked.

"Because the harder you shove each other, the looser the ropes around my hands become," he said.

Conner and Peter shared an excited look and took turns knocking into each other as hard as they could. They were so desperate to get away from the Merry Men, they didn't notice how much it hurt their shoulders. After a few moments the Tin Woodman was able to pull his hands free from the rope and he untied the boys.

"Conner, there's something sticking out of your pocket," Peter said.

Conner patted his pants and felt a piece of paper coming out of his back pocket. Knocking back and forth into Peter must have pushed it up. He unfolded it and his eyes grew twice their size when he discovered what it was.

"Guys, it's a page from *The Wonderful Wizard of Oz*!" he exclaimed. "We can use it to get back to Oz, and then get back to the fairy-tale world!"

"Don't we need a potion to do that?" the Tin Woodman asked.

"We'll make the potion! I have the recipe memorized!" he said.

Conner was beaming with joy. When he had stuffed the page into his pocket back in the cave, he never imagined it would later act as a lifeboat. And even better, Conner remembered his sister had one, too—he knew it was only a matter of time before Alex found it and used it to escape wherever she was, if she hadn't already.

His celebration was cut short when they heard a fearful sound coming from outside. It wasn't another song, but horses—*hundreds of them!*

Conner, Peter, and the Tin Woodman peeked out of the tent and saw a fleet of soldiers emerge from Sherwood Forest and surround the Merry Men's camp. They arrived so suddenly, Robin Hood and his men didn't have time to retrieve their weapons. A middle-aged man with a dark beard led the soldiers and he wore a bright star over his armor.

"Uh-oh," Conner said.

"Who is that?" Peter asked.

"LOOK, MEN, THE SHERIFF OF NOTTING-HAM HAS COME TO PAY US A VISIT," Robin Hood said, answering the question. "TO WHAT DO WE OWE THIS *DISHONOR*?"

"Robin of Loxley," the sheriff addressed, "you and your men are under arrest for thievery, vandalism, and running from the law. You will come with us to Nottingham, where you will await trail. Any attempt of escape will result in death."

The sheriff nodded to his soldiers. The archers stepped forward and aimed their bows at Robin Hood and the Merry Men. There didn't appear to be any possible escape.

"This is terrible," Conner whispered.

"Why? The man's a nightmare," Peter said.

"No, it's terrible for us!" Conner said. "The sheriff is going to find us and take us back to Nottingham with them."

"But we were captured, we're not associated with them," the Tin Woodman said.

"It doesn't matter," Conner said. "I know the sheriff seems more tolerable than Robin Hood, but he's a seriously bad dude. He'll take us back to the castle and torture us for sport!"

Peter and the Tin Woodman eyed each other nervously. Conner paced around the tent, thinking of some way they could escape. All they had in the tent was a raggedy blanket and a white sheet bundled up on the ground.

"So, what do we do?" Peter asked.

"I've got an idea," Conner said. "It's crazy, but it just might work. Just go along with whatever I say."

Outside, things were becoming increasingly tense. Robin Hood left the campfire and approached the Sheriff of Nottingham.

"YOU ARE VERY CLEVER, SHERIFF," Robin

Hood said. "YOU PLANNED FOR ME TO CAP-
TURE ONE OF YOUR KNIGHTS EARLIER SO YOU
COULD FOLLOW HIM BACK TO OUR CAMP. WELL
PLAYED!"

"You imbecile," the sheriff said. "We found you because
your voice carries for miles."

All the Merry Men slumped—they knew their leader's
volume would get them into trouble eventually.

"DO YOU KNOW WHAT ELSE CARRIES
THROUGH THE FOREST, SHERIFF?" Robin Hood
asked. "*MY LOVE OF NOTTINGHAM!* SO TAKE ME
AWAY, BEAT ME, TORTURE ME, AND KILL ME
IN THE END. YOU MAY RENDER MY BODY LIFE-
LESS, BUT YOU WILL NEVER DESTROY MY—"

"*Spirit!*" Little John screamed.

"YES, THAT'S WHAT I WAS ABOUT TO SAY!"

"No, sir! Look, there's something ghostly coming this
way!" Will Scarlet said.

The Merry Men and the Nottingham soldiers all turned
to the center of camp. Conner had covered himself in the
raggedy blanket. He was hunched over and he limped
toward them with his arms extended like a zombie.

"Who is this?" the sheriff asked. "Declare yourself at
once or I will have an arrow shot through your heart."

Conner gulped—he hoped this would work.

"I do not fear your arrows, for I cannot be killed!" he
said in a ghoulish voice. "I am Connermoondo, the feared
sorcerer of Sherwood!"

"SORCERER?" Robin Hood laughed. "THIS BOY IS A MERE CHILD WE FOUND IN THE FOREST."

"SILENCE!" Conner yelled at Robin Hood. *"You are blinded by arrogance and were easily fooled by my mortal disguise! I come before you now to offer the sheriff and his men a warning! Leave my forest at once, or I shall sic my army of the dead upon you!"*

The sheriff and his soldiers laughed uproariously. Conner wasn't fooling anyone.

"This boy must learn what happens to people who threaten us," the sheriff said. *"Shoot him!"*

"Now!" Conner whispered.

As the archers aimed their arrows at him, the Tin Woodman ran out from the tent—*but without his head!* The Merry Men and the soldiers screamed at the terrifying sight—for all they knew, he was a headless man back from the dead. The Tin Woodman ran toward the soldiers, and many of them retreated into the woods.

"Peter, you're next!" Conner whispered.

Peter shot out of the tent wrapped in the white sheet. He flew above the camp and moaned in agony like a tortured spirit. The Merry Men held one another and screamed— the padre said a prayer and held his crucifix up to the hovering spirit.

"These forests have been conquered by black magic!" the sheriff shouted. *"Forget about Robin of Loxley and his Merry Men—we must return to Nottingham at once!"*

The sheriff whipped the reins of his horse and retreated

into the woods. The few remaining soldiers followed him—many of them ripping off their armor as they hurried away, to run faster.

When the coast was clear of soldiers, Conner took off the raggedy blanket, Peter threw off the sheet, and the Tin Woodman retrieved his head from the tent and screwed it back on like a bottle cap. They burst into hysterical laughter and gave one another high fives.

"Did you see the look on their faces!" Conner asked.

"We petrified them!" Peter said.

"I would have never thought to take off my head," the Tin Woodman said. "Good idea, Conner!"

The Merry Men were trembling and still clutched one another. Robin Hood approached Conner and his friends, despite his men's pleas to stay away. He looked them in the eyes and bowed.

"OH, GREAT SORCERER OF SHERWOOD FOREST," Robin Hood said, "YOU HAVE SAVED MY MERRY MEN AND ME FROM THE GALLOWS! WE ARE ETERNALLY GRATEFUL AND SHALL SPEND THE REST OF OUR DAYS AS YOUR HUMBLE SERVANTS!"

The Merry Men followed his example and bowed, too. The Tin Woodman and Peter grinned and nudged Conner forward. At first he thought about telling Robin Hood and his men the truth about who he was and how he and his friends had come to Sherwood Forest. On second thought, he was afraid the truth would cause their heads to implode; their current situation seemed much more beneficial.

"You're welcome, Robin of Loxley," Conner said. "And I'll take you up on that."

"WE WILL DO ANYTHING FOR YOU, SORCERER, ANYTHING AT ALL!" Robin Hood said.

"Well, in *that* case...," Conner said, "absolutely no more singing about yourself! And you don't have to call me *sorcerer*—it's already getting old. I'm Conner Bailey, this is the Tin Woodman, and that's Peter Pan."

Robin Hood kissed their feet. Had he not been such a pretentious jerk, it might have been a bit uncomfortable, but they enjoyed seeing him so humbled.

"CONNER OF BAILEY, TIN OF WOODMAN, AND PETER OF PAN," Robin Hood said, "ALLOW ME TO FORMALLY INTRODUCE THE MERRY BAND OF MEN BEHIND ME: LITTLE JOHN, WILL SCARLET, FRIAR TUCK, AND MY MINSTREL, ALAN-A-DALE."

Each of the Merry Men stood upright as his name was called and then fell back into a bow.

"YOUR REQUEST IS OUR COMMAND!" Robin Hood declared.

"Fantastic," Conner said, and rubbed his hands together. "First thing tomorrow, I'm going to give you a list of items I'll need help collecting."

"CONSIDER IT DONE!" he said.

Conner had been right all along—Robin Hood would prove to be *very* helpful.

CHAPTER TWENTY-THREE

LOST ADVICE

R ed had only been with the Lost Boys for a couple of days, but she had come around to the idea of being a mother. As soon as the others left her in Neverland, the Lost Boys built her a spacious underground home. As Peter instructed, they followed every order she gave and waited on her hand and foot. She spent the days stretched out on a lounge chair they crafted from palm trees and she sipped coconut drinks they served her around the clock.

All the Lost Boys hoped for in return was a good

bedtime story every night, which Red happily delivered. It was mindboggling to her why so many mothers complained; she found motherhood highly enjoyable.

"Can I get you another coconut drink, Mother?" Tootles asked.

"No thank you, Tobias," Red said. "I'm quite hydrated."

"Would you like me to fan you, Mum?" Slightly asked.

"Sweet Salvador, thank you, but I'm perfectly cool."

"Mommy, can I make you any snacks?" Curly asked.

"I'm not hungry, but thank you, Caesar."

"Is your chair comfortable enough, Mumzie?" Nibs asked.

"Most pleasantly, Nathaniel."

"Would you like us to rub your feet again, Mama?" the Lost twins asked.

"Thank you, my dear Jeffreys, but they're fine for now."

Red took a moment to watch proudly over her temporary sons. She had never expected the savage children she met on her first day in Neverland would turn out to be perfect gentlemen. All they'd needed were new names and someone to serve.

"Boys, you've been wonderful to Mother today," Red said. "So before we go to bed, I would like to treat you to another *bedtime story*!"

The Lost Boys cheered and eagerly sat on the floor around her. Each of them looked up at her with huge smiles, most of which were missing baby teeth. Red had their undivided attention deficit disorders.

"Which story are you going to tell us tonight, Mother?" Tootles asked.

"One that is very close to my heart," Red said. "It's called 'Beautiful and Brilliant Little Blue Riding Hood.'"

Just hearing the title made the Lost Boys excitedly clap.

"Is it a good story, Mum?" Slightly asked.

"It's the best story you'll ever hear," Red said.

"Does Little Blue die in the end like Cinderella, Snow White, Sleeping Beauty, and Rapunzel?" Curly asked. "I just want to know before I get attached."

"Those were such sad stories," Nibs said, and shook his head. "I can't believe poor Cinderella slipped while running down the stairs at midnight, or that Snow White choked on the poisoned apple, or when Sleeping Beauty awoke, she discovered the spindle had given her a staph infection."

"Poor, poor princesses," the Lost twins sniffled.

"Well, these stories are supposed to teach us valuable lessons," Red said. "Never run down stairs, always chew your food, and see a doctor if your skin is punctured by rusty metal."

"Is there a lesson in the story of 'Beautiful and Brilliant Little Blue Riding Hood'?" Slightly asked.

"You'll have to wait and find out," she teased.

The Lost Boys were on pins and needles. Red cleared her throat and began the story.

"Once upon a time, there was a beautiful and brilliant little girl named Red—excuse me—*Blue Riding Hood*,"

Red said. "One day she was traveling through the woods to bring her granny a basket of goodies. The poor woman had a terrible cold, so the compassionate Little Blue wanted to pay her a visit and lift her spirits. But along the way, she was stopped by a humongous and ferocious wolf!"

The Lost Boys gasped and held one another tightly. The Lost twins even covered their eyes.

"Luckily, Little Blue was so beautiful, the wolf couldn't find it in his heart to eat her," Red said. "But the wolf tried tricking Little Blue into telling him where her grandmother lived so he could find the old woman and gobble her up! Thankfully, Little Red—excuse me—*Little Blue* was as brilliant as she was beautiful, and she gave the wolf directions to another cottage in the woods. The wolf left Little Blue and headed to this cottage, only to find out she had misled him to the home of hunters!"

The Lost Boys howled with laughter at the wolf's misfortune.

"The wolf was killed by the hunters, and Little Blue enjoyed an afternoon with her grandmother," Red concluded. "The other villagers were so impressed with Little Blue's intelligence and bravery, they elected her queen of her very own kingdom! And they all lived happily ever after."

The end of the story was met with a warm round of applause.

"Did they really elect Little Blue *queen*?" Curly asked. "Just for tricking a wolf?"

"I may be paraphrasing, but pretty much," Red said.

"What happened to her after she became queen?" Slightly asked. "Did she get married or have children?"

"Funny you should ask," Red said. "Little Blue met a very special prince whom she loved very much, and they were *supposed* to get married. Unfortunately, the wedding didn't go as planned."

"What happened?" Tootles asked. "Did the wolf come back from the dead?"

"Worse," Red said. "A horrible and hideous goat stole the prince away from Little Blue."

"Oh, no!" Nibs exclaimed. "Why didn't Little Blue stop the goat?"

"There wasn't anything I—excuse me—*she* could do," Red said. "The prince was afraid that if he didn't leave with the goat, the creature would just hurt Little Blue. He sacrificed himself for her."

Slightly sighed and batted his eyes. "How romantic."

"I suppose he wasn't her true love, then," Tootles said. "Better to find out it's not meant to be before the wedding, rather than later after years of marriage."

"Quite right," Nibs said.

"The goat did Little Blue a favor," Curly said.

"Very true," the Lost twins said.

All the Lost Boys nodded their heads in agreement. Red was very confused because she couldn't disagree more— perhaps she had forgotten to tell something.

"Of course the prince was Little Blue's true love," Red said. "After years of searching for love in the wrong places, she felt like she had finally found her missing piece. She was looking forward to spending the rest of her life with him. Not a day goes by that she doesn't spend hours thinking about how much she misses him and wishes something could have been done to stop the goat. *Little Blue cries whenever she thinks about the prince!*"

Red burst into tears and blew her nose into Tootles's sleeve. The Lost Boys eyed her suspiciously and then shared a smile. It was pretty obvious why the story meant so much to her.

"Let me ask you this," Tootles said. "If Little Blue had been kidnapped instead of the prince, what would he have done? Would he have sat around crying while he told her story?"

Red never thought about it. "I don't know," she said. "The prince probably would have fought the goat to the death. He would have rather died fighting for her than live another day without her."

"So why didn't Little Blue fight the goat?" Slightly asked. "Did the prince love her more than she loved him?"

Red shook her head. "No, they loved each other the same," she said. "If you had been at the wedding, you would understand. Little Blue begged the guests to help her, but no one would."

"That's a very interesting thing you just said," Curly

said. "No one would *help* her. Do you understand the significance of this?"

"Curly's right," Nibs said. "Seems to me Little Blue is just so used to people doing things *for* her, she expects other people to solve all her problems. Like you said, a kingdom was just handed to her! She didn't even have to campaign or anything."

"If Little Blue truly loves the prince, she would go after the goat herself," Tootles said. "She wouldn't wait for anyone's help, or permission, or approval! She would fight the goat to the death, too, because she would rather die than live without him."

Red wanted to tell the Lost Boys they were wrong, but she couldn't think of a single reason why. *The Lost Boys were absolutely right!* Only Red knew what it was like to live with Red's heartbreak; she couldn't expect others to help her. Red was the only one who could relieve her pain—and she wasn't going to live with it anymore!

The young queen got to her feet and looked over her temporary sons with very determined eyes.

"Boys, get your things," Red ordered. "We're going *goat hunting!*"

The Lost Boys quickly gathered their various homemade weapons. Red retrieved the *Peter Pan* book she was supposed to be watching and opened it. A bright beam of light emitted from it, illuminating the entire underground home.

Red peeked her head through the beam and looked into

Oz. She saw Jack and Goldilocks asleep on the floor of the Wicked Witch of the West's castle. Blubo was curled up beside them and the copy of *The Wonderful Wizard of Oz* was lying next to him.

"Quickly and quietly, boys," Red instructed the Lost Boys. "We're going to go into Oz, then into the fairy-tale world, and then we're going to rescue your temporary father!"

One by one, they carefully went into the beam of light and entered the witch's castle. Red quietly took the *Wonderful Wizard of Oz* book to the other side of the witch's throne room and opened it. Red and the Lost Boys traveled through the next beam and arrived in the cave of the fairy-tale world.

They found Hagetta sitting just outside the cave's entrance by a fire she had built.

"Red, what are you doing back?" Hagetta asked her. "Who are these children?"

"Hagetta, these are my temporary sons," Red said. "Do you happen to know where the witch Morina lives?"

"I believe she has a home in the Dwarf Forests close to the Corner Kingdom border, although I've never been there myself," Hagetta said. "Why do you ask?"

"Because the boys and I are going to get Charlie back!" Red said.

Before Hagetta could interject, Red led the Lost Boys to a grassy patch where Porridge, Oats, and Buckle were grazing. She helped the Lost twins onto Oats, and then climbed aboard Porridge with Tootles. Nibs, Curly, and Slightly mounted Buckle.

"Red, you can't go after Morina," Hagetta said as she ran after them. "She's one of the most powerful witches in the world! You won't stand a chance!"

"She can't be any worse than a pirate!" Tootles said.

"Yeah, we can handle her!" Slightly said.

"We've got to rescue our mother's true love!" Curly said.

"To the witch's house!" Nibs yelled.

"Attack!" the Lost twins said.

"Hagetta, I have to do this," Red said. "I can't sit around and do nothing while some horned lunatic with a cauldron is holding the love of my life captive! Besides, if the roles were reversed, Charlie would do the same thing for me."

Red took Porridge's reins and led the way.

"Oh, and one more thing," Red called back to Hagetta. "If you see Goldie before I get back, tell her we've borrowed her horses."

There was nothing Hagetta could do to stop them—she had to stay at the cave and watch the book. Red and the Lost Boys traveled into the woods ahead and disappeared into the night.

"Oh, dear," Hagetta said. "This isn't going to end well."

CHAPTER TWENTY-FOUR

THE LADY OF THE LAKE

Arthur and Alex awoke the next morning before sunrise. Finding a branch from the oldest tree in the woods would be challenging, and they didn't want to waste a moment of daylight. They headed straight for the woods and searched for hours, traveling well beyond the parts of the forest Arthur was familiar with.

"We should mark the candidates as we find them," Alex said.

She pointed to a particularly old tree they came across and magically marked it with thousands of twinkling lights.

"But how will we know which one is the oldest?" Arthur asked. "Is there some sort of spell you can use to determine each tree's age?"

"Not that I know of," Alex said. "I was just planning to chop them in half and count the rings."

They searched the forest and marked the oldest trees well into the hours of the afternoon. At one point they entered a beautiful meadow and found Merlin and Mother Goose having a picnic. They were looking at the sky and taking turns magically shaping the clouds into objects and animals for the other to guess—a sorcerer's game of Pictionary.

"It's a rabbit—or a squirrel!" Mother Goose guessed. "No, it looks like a duck! Wait, I know what that is, it's Lester!"

"Correct! You're a natural at this, my dear!" Merlin said.

Lester was sitting beside them and was rather offended that the large fluffy cloud was supposed to resemble him. Alex could tell he had had his fill with Merlin and Mother Goose's shenanigans.

"Lester, would you like to help Arthur and me find the oldest tree in the woods?" Alex asked.

"*Squaaa!*" the gander said, and nodded gratefully.

Merlin and Mother Goose sat up once they saw Alex and Arthur had joined them in the meadow.

"Don't look at us," Merlin said. "We may be the most ancient beings in the woods, but you can't have any of our branches!"

"Good one, Merl!" Mother Goose laughed and clinked his cup with hers.

Alex couldn't help but laugh, too—not at Merlin, but at Mother Goose. She had never seen Mother Goose enjoy herself as much as she did when she was with Merlin. She knew it was going to be difficult for her to part from Merlin when it was time to go back home, but Mother Goose wasn't the only one who would be leaving someone special behind.

Alex and Arthur continued their quest with Lester waddling behind them.

"Merlin is going to miss Mother Goose," Arthur said. "I don't think I've ever seen him so happy before."

"Same for Mother Goose," Alex said. "She's been quite sad lately; it's nice to hear her laugh for a change."

"It's probably for the best you two will be leaving shortly," Arthur said. "Can you imagine the mischief they might get into if you stayed?"

"I'm afraid to think about it," Alex said.

"I bet Merlin hopes Mother Goose still keeps in touch, though," Arthur said, and stuck out his bottom lip. "Merlin would be so sad if he never heard from her again."

Alex side-eyed him—obviously they weren't talking about their elders anymore.

"I'm sure *Mother Goose* would love to keep in contact with *Merlin*," Alex said. "But *Mother Goose* also knows that *Merlin* has a destiny to live, and she wouldn't want to distract him from that."

"Ah, yes," Arthur said. "That whole *destiny* thing tends to get in the way of everything. That's very kind of *Mother Goose*, then."

Alex went quiet. She had known Arthur for a day and it was already hard to think about what life would be like without him. She tried to blame the sudden dependency on her age—what soon-to-be fifteen-year-old girl wouldn't be smitten with such a handsome and smart young man like Arthur?

Although Alex had been smitten before, there was something special about Arthur. Perhaps in another lifetime, if they were beings of the same world, there could be more than friendship to explore. But she was very aware of her situation and the situation waiting at home, so Alex didn't let the idea tease her.

Arthur had become very quiet, too. She wondered if he was thinking the same thing. Arthur broke the silence to play another round of his favorite new game—*pestering Alex*.

"Roughly how old am I when I'm crowned king?" he asked.

"Arthur, I told you I'm not telling you anything else," Alex said. "Some things are meant to be discovered in time."

"How about I say an age and you tell me if I'm close?" he suggested. "Twenty?"

"You're relentless," she said, and glared at him.

"Twenty-five?" Arthur asked.

Alex laughed at his persistence, but it only encouraged him.

"Thirty?" he asked. "Oh, come on, please don't tell me it's after forty!"

"To be honest, Arthur, I don't know," Alex said. "There are several versions of your story, and I'm not entirely sure which one I'm in."

Arthur found this prospect very intriguing. "*Versions*, you say?" he said. "So there's more than one of me? Right now there could be other Arthurs walking around other forests? Arthurs who are braver, stronger, and more *dashing* than I?"

"Impossible," Alex said with a smile. "There might be other versions of your story, but there's only one *Arthur* like you."

Arthur was very touched by this. "Do you think there are other versions of you as well?" he asked.

"Oh yes, but they aren't walking around other stories," she said. "There are plenty of versions other than the Alex you see beside you."

"Interesting," he said. "Care to share?"

"I don't want you to think less of me," Alex said.

"Come on, you know so much about me. Tell me the *worst* thing you've ever done. I promise I won't judge you."

Alex was reluctant to tell him anything, but if he was going to be insistent about something, it was better to tell him stories about her life than give anything else away about his.

"There was a period whenever I got overwhelmed or upset, I would unintentionally cause things to happen," Alex confessed.

"Now we're getting somewhere," Arthur said. "Please, continue."

"The first time I saw the Masked Man's face I was convinced he was my father," Alex explained. "No one believed me, but I knew what I saw. I spent months agonizing over how it was possible—how did my dad come back from the dead and become such a monster? The questions were torture and my tolerance was obliterated. Since my powers are fueled by my heart, my emotions would take over my body every time I became angry or sad—I had no control over what I said or did."

"So what happened?" Arthur asked.

"One time my brother and I were chasing soldiers of the Grande Armée," Alex said. "Just as they were getting away, I caused a brick wall to appear in front of them. They slammed into it and broke their noses."

"So it works out in your favor sometimes," Arthur said.

"Rarely," Alex said. "I used to ride a unicorn named Cornelius. He'd take me all over the kingdoms to the people who needed a fairy. When we were looking for the Masked Man I was so desperate, I tried to use Cornelius to track him down. However, unicorns are magical creatures and they can't be used selfishly. So when it didn't work I became really frustrated and vines shot out of the ground and wrapped around him. He was scared of me for weeks but eventually came around, but I've tried to keep my distance ever since."

Despite her obvious guilt, Arthur made light of it. "That's kid's stuff," he said. "I know you've got a better story in you."

"One time I raised a tavern above the clouds and dropped it," she said.

"You're joking! Was anyone inside of it?"

"Yes, *me!*" Alex said. "Not to mention my brother, all our close friends, and about a hundred witches. Luckily I came to my senses in time to save us before we crashed on the ground."

"Anything else?" Arthur said.

Alex was afraid she might scare Arthur away with her stories, but he stayed right at her side, captivated by every word.

"Actually, yes. I may have skipped a few details about the time the Fairy Council ungodmothered me. I might have *accidentally* attacked them with lightning and then disappeared into a wall of flames."

Arthur let out a sound that was half a laugh and half a gasp.

"Alex Bailey!" he condemned, but with a smirk. "Note to self: Never make you mad. I'm sure the council deserved it, though. Have you had any other *episodes* since then?"

Alex thought about it and was very happy to realize she hadn't.

"Not since I found out the Masked Man was my uncle," Alex said. "He looks just like my dad—anyone else would have come to the same conclusion. I suppose knowing I wasn't crazy like the rest of the world did put me in touch with my emotions."

"But you said you *were certain* of what you saw," Arthur said.

"And I was! Believe me."

"So why did you let what others thought affect you so much?" he asked.

Alex had never put the whole experience into perspective. She and her brother had been through countless stressful situations where people often didn't believe them. Why did this one bother her so much?

"I guess that's a question as old as time, isn't it?" Alex said. "Why do any of us let the world dictate our personal truths?"

"Squaaa...," Lester squawked, as if to say, *"Tell me about it!"*

"Well, I only get two weeks with you after we collect the ingredients for the potion," Arthur said. "But I hope to see as many versions of Alex as I can."

Alex scrunched her lips so they wouldn't stretch into another smile, but Arthur saw right through the effort. He was charming even when he didn't mean to be.

"Fighting it only tempts me to make you smile more," he warned.

They eventually discovered a large lake hidden deep in the woods. The water was cleaner and clearer than any other lake Alex had ever seen. There was a small island in the middle of the lake with nothing on it but a decrepit tree, by far the oldest tree they had encountered all day.

"That's it!" Alex said. "That's got to be the oldest tree in the woods!"

"How are we going to get to it?" Arthur asked.

Alex looked back at Lester and a needy smile came to her face. "Lester, would you mind transporting us to the island?"

Lester looked out at the island and sighed. He didn't want to get his feathers wet, but since Alex rescued him from an afternoon of hearing the same stories told over and over again, he owed her one. He waddled down to the water and tested it with his webbed feet, sending a strong ripple through the still water.

The gander had a seat on the water but saw something that made him leap back to the land.

"SQUAAA!" he squawked with fright. *"SQUAAA!"*

Lester was trembling and gestured to the water with his beak. A geyser of water rose out of the lake like a fountain in slow motion, twisting and looping through the air until it formed the shape of a woman. Like a heartbeat, every few seconds a ripple started at her chest and traveled through her whole body.

"No birds are allowed on my waters!" the water woman said. "Shoo! Go defecate someplace else!"

Lester hid behind Alex and Arthur, who stared up at the woman in awe. The woman was surprised to see them, but seemed delighted by the company.

"Oh, hello there," she said. "I hope I didn't frighten you. I work very hard to keep my lake pristine and must scare away the birds before they spoil my water. I didn't realize he was a pet."

Lester gave the woman a dirty look—who was she calling a pet?

"What—sorry—*who* are you?" Arthur asked.

"I know who she is," Alex said. "Arthur, this is the Lady of the Lake!"

The Lady of the Lake was very pleased to be recognized. "*'Tis I!*" she announced happily. "It's been ages since I had human visitors. My lake is so remote, very few people know it exists. What brings you here today?"

The Lady of the Lake seemed nice enough. Neither Alex nor Arthur felt the need to hide their intentions.

"We're searching the forest for an ingredient needed for a potion," Arthur said.

"Do you by chance know how old the tree on your island is?" Alex asked.

"It's been there for centuries," the Lady of the Lake said. "It may very well be the oldest tree in the forest."

Alex and Arthur shared a smile and their spirits soared.

"Beautiful lady, would you kindly allow us to take a piece of it?" Arthur asked.

"Oh, certainly," the Lady of the Lake said. "To be honest with you, it's a bit of an eyesore. Feel free to take as much of it as you want."

"Thank you so much!" Alex said. "It's greatly appreciated."

Alex, Arthur, and Lester approached the water. The Lady of the Lake put her hand out to stop them.

"You two may cross my waters, but the bird may not," she said. She waved a hand and a line of boulders rose out of the water, creating a bridge to the island.

"No problem," Alex said. "Lester, stay here."

The goose watched as Alex and Arthur hopped across the rocks to the island. Arthur retrieved a dagger from his boot and cut off a small branch.

"Let's get back to Merlin's now and start the potion," he said.

"Excuse me? Did you just say *Merlin*?" the Lady of the Lake asked.

"Yes, he's a wizard," Arthur said. "Do you know of him?"

"Of course I do," she said. "But how do *you* know him?"

"He's a friend and mentor," Arthur said.

It was like he'd said something that offended her. Suddenly, their bridge of boulders sank back into the lake. A wall of water shot into the air around the island, trapping Alex and Arthur.

"What are you doing?" Alex asked.

"Friends of Merlin are not friends of mine!" the Lady of the Lake yelled. Her voice no longer had such a cheery disposition, but a scornful tone.

The wall of water around the island began closing in on Alex and Arthur. Alex tried using magic to hold it back, but every time she raised a hand, a jet of water knocked it down.

"*Oy, bird!* Go find Merlin! Tell him the Lady of the Lake requests his presence, and if he ignores my request this time, his friends will drown," the Lady of the Lake ordered.

Lester didn't waste a minute. He flew into the sky and headed for help, squawking as he went.

"Dear lady, I don't know what your quarrel is with Merlin, but it has nothing to do with us," Arthur said. "Please let us go!"

The Lady of the Lake ignored him. Her attention was fixed on her own reflection in the water. She conducted the water, forming her body to decrease and increase in places, giving herself a more attractive shape. Her hair grew longer, her waist smaller, and her hips curvier. She hummed to herself as she made the adjustments, like she was preparing for a *date*.

A few minutes later, Lester returned with Merlin and Mother Goose on his back. They hopped off the bird and charged down to the edge of the lake.

"Merlin, help us!" Arthur pleaded.

"Nimue, what is the meaning of this?" Merlin said to the Lady of the Lake.

"Hello, Merlin," she said. "It's been a long time!"

"Release our apprentices at once!" Merlin demanded.

"Is *that* how you treat all the lovers you haven't seen in two hundred years?" the Lady of the Lake asked.

"Lovers?" Mother Goose said. "What could you possibly bring to a relationship? Hydration?"

"We've been through this a thousand times, Nimue," Merlin said. "We were never together and we never will be!"

"How can you say that after the romantic month we spent in the cave off the shore together?" the Lady of the Lake asked. "Or have you forgotten about that?!"

"I have not forgotten," Merlin said. "You've flooded your brain and washed away all the sense, Nimue! You *imprisoned* me in that cave!"

"But when I released you, you promised to meet me at this lake!" she said. "I've waited here for you for hundreds of years!"

"I *lied* to get out of the cave!" Merlin said. "You forced yourself upon me so much, it's a wonder I didn't *prune* to death!"

The Lady of the Lake's heartbeat raced so fast, her body was rippling out of control.

"Time to let it go, H20!" Mother Goose said. "Let those children go or we'll—"

The Lady of the Lake suddenly grew four times in size, draining half the lake in the process. "OR WHAT?" she asked.

The water crept closer and closer to Alex and Arthur on the island—they were running out of land. They were moments away from being completely submerged. Clearly,

Merlin and Mother Goose's demands weren't getting them anywhere.

"Let's calm down and make an agreement, then," Merlin said. "Take me instead of the children."

"Oh, Merl, you can't let this oversized puddle take you!" Mother Goose said.

"It's all right, I've dealt with damper characters before," he said. "So how 'bout it, Nimue? Will you hand over our apprentices in exchange for me?"

The Lady of the Lake considered it. Her rapidly rippling body calmed down and she reduced in size.

"I can live with that," she said.

The wall of water around the island dissolved and the boulders resurfaced. Merlin hopped across to the island, but before Alex and Arthur had time to cross to the land, the wall of water returned, trapping all three of them on the island.

"Nimue! We had an agreement!" Merlin yelled.

"I know, but I *lied*!" The Lady of the Lake laughed. "Isn't it wonderfully ironic?"

Merlin, Arthur, and Alex all exchanged horrified looks. They didn't know how they were going to get out of this one.

"Hey! *Lunatic of the Lake!* I'm giving you one last warning: Free my friends, or I'm coming in there!" Mother Goose warned.

The Lady of the Lake laughed at her pityingly. "And what are you going to do, Granny?" she asked. "Geriatric aerobics?"

Mother Goose squinted, her jaw fell open, and her cheeks turned red. Lester covered his eyes with his wings—he knew this wasn't going to be pretty.

"Call me *Granny* one more time! I dare you!" she said.

"GRANNY! GRANNY! GRANNY!" the Lady of the Lake sang.

Mother Goose had had enough. She cracked her neck and rolled up her sleeves. It was time to take matters into her own hands.

"That's it, sister!" she said. "You've pushed me to the edge and let me dangle!"

Mother Goose ran into the lake and started punching and kicking the water. The Lady of the Lake just laughed at her attempts to cause harm. She sent several tall waves toward her, each one stronger than the next, knocking Mother Goose under, deep below the surface.

"Mother Goose!" Alex yelled.

"Let her go, you miserable pond!" Merlin ordered.

"Sorry, Merlin, but your friend is all *washed up*!" the Lady of the Lake said.

Just when they feared Mother Goose would never resurface, all the water in the lake gradually began to whirl in a clockwise direction. The flow increased, catching the Lady of the Lake's attention, but she couldn't regain control of it. The water spun around the island faster and faster. Soon it was moving so fast, the Lady of the Lake couldn't keep her human form and dissipated into the rest of the water.

The spinning lake rose into the air, forming a small hurricane. It was a powerful storm, and Merlin, Arthur, and Alex held on to the island tree with all their might so they wouldn't be blown away. They saw Mother Goose standing at the bottom of the lake, twirling the storm into the air like a giant liquid lasso.

"TIME TO EVAPORATE, YOU WET WENCH!" Mother Goose yelled.

She released her grip of the water, and every drop of the lake flew into the sky and turned into rain, misting the forest around them for miles. The lake was nothing but a wide empty hole in the woods now.

Merlin, Arthur, and Alex were in shock—they still grasped the island tree even though the storm was gone. Mother Goose brushed off her hands and placed them on her hips. She found their dumbfounded faces very amusing.

"I don't know about you, but I've worked up quite an appetite," she said. "Let's get some dinner."

Once they had eaten, Merlin let Alex borrow a small cauldron so she could begin making the Portal Potion. She filled it with water and placed it over the fireplace to let it boil. She cut the tree branch into tiny pieces and added it and Lester's feather to the cauldron.

"All we need is a liquefied lock and key from a loved one," Alex said.

Arthur went down the hall of Merlin's cottage. Alex heard two loud *clunk*s and Arthur returned with a lock and key.

"Where did you get those?" Alex asked.

"I just chipped them off of Merlin's bedroom door," he said. "He's like a father to me, so it should work."

Alex put the objects in a separate cauldron and then placed it into the fireplace with the other. Once the lock and key melted, she quickly poured the mixture in with the other ingredients before it became solid again.

"Now all we need is two weeks of moonlight," Alex said.

"I know the perfect place," Arthur said.

After the sun set, Arthur escorted Alex to a very tall and grassy hill a little ways into the woods. They could see the entire forest from the hill and it also gave them the perfect view of the moon and stars. They placed the cauldron on the ground and lay on either side of it while the potion soaked up the moonlight.

"It's so interesting," Alex said. "The moon and the stars look exactly the same here as they do in the fairy-tale world and the Otherworld."

"Perhaps you can take me to your world someday?" Arthur said. "I would love to see the Otherworld and the fairy-tale world."

"I'm not sure that's a good idea," Alex said playfully. "You're very popular there. It would be very easy to snoop around and find out about your destiny."

Arthur went silent and looked a little sad. There was something troubling him.

"What's wrong?" Alex asked. "Did I say something to upset you?"

"Of course not, I just haven't been very honest with you," he said. "I *know* all the answers to the questions I tease you with. Merlin thinks he keeps a tight lip, but all he needs is a little ale in his system and I can get any answer out of him that I want. I know how old I am when I'm crowned and I know I'll be a great king. I also know about Camelot, the Round Table, and Guinevere."

"Then why have you been pestering me so much?" Alex asked.

"Because you're awfully cute when you try concealing information," Arthur said. "Has anyone ever told you that?"

"Can't say they have," Alex said. "Thank you—I'm glad I amuse you so much."

"You amuse me and *amaze* me," he said. "There are a lot of things you make me feel...."

Arthur became quiet. Alex knew they had to change the subject. If they were any more honest with each other, it would only make their eventual farewell that much more painful.

"Can I ask you a question, from someone whose destiny isn't written yet?" Alex asked.

"Of course," Arthur said.

"If you know of all the challenges, all the pain, and all

the heartbreak you'll endure, why stay on the path destiny has paved for you? Why not venture off and try creating a life for yourself that will be more enjoyable?"

Arthur didn't have to think long. The answer was engrained in his heart.

"I'd like to think the choice falls under our pact of *true greatness*," he said. "I believe the people of England deserve a great king. And if I'm meant to be that man—a man whose legacy will inspire the present and the future of the kingdoms here and even beyond the kingdoms of this world, then it's worth every sacrifice."

Alex was so moved and impressed by his answer, it sent chills through her whole body.

"I thought I knew everything about you, Arthur, but you keep surprising me," she said.

He turned his head to her and they stared into each other's eyes.

"Besides, who really knows what the future holds?" Arthur said. "As I learned yesterday, you never know when someone might drop in and change your world forever."

As she looked into Arthur's blue eyes, Alex felt her mind slowly lose control of her body—but this time it was taken over by her heart. She leaned over and kissed Arthur more passionately than she had ever kissed anyone. It surprised her as much as it surprised him.

"I like this version of you," Arthur said.

"Me too," Alex said. "It's new."

There were a thousand reasons why she shouldn't have done it, but nothing seemed worse than not doing it again. But Arthur kissed Alex back before she had the chance. They lay under the stars and kissed each other until there was no moonlight left for the potion to absorb.

CHAPTER TWENTY-FIVE

THE WITCH OF PAPPLENICK

Conner should have known better than to trust the Merry Men. The morning after the Sheriff of Nottingham was scared off, he assigned Little John and Will Scarlet to find two of the ingredients he needed for the Portal Potion. A few hours later, they returned with the exact opposites of what Conner requested.

Little John dragged a freshly chopped tree into camp and proudly presented it to Conner. It was lively and covered in bright green leaves.

"I thought you'd want to choose the branch, so I brought the whole tree," Little John said.

Will Scarlet followed shortly after with a caged pheasant. The bird was so old, all its remaining feathers were gray. It wheezed so heavily, each breath had the potential to be its last.

"I found him just sitting in the woods," Will Scarlet said. "He didn't even put up a fight when I caged him."

Conner sighed and rubbed his eyes.

"Guys, *thank you*," he said. "But you mixed up my instructions. I said I needed a branch from the *oldest tree* in the woods and a feather from the *finest pheasant*."

Little John and Will Scarlet pointed to each other, as if the other was to blame.

"That's what *I* thought you said, but *he* told me you needed the *oldest pheasant*!" Will Scarlet said.

"No, *you* told *me* he needed the *finest tree* in the woods!" Little John said.

"I did not!"

"You did too!"

Conner stepped between them just as they were reaching for their weapons. "Stop fighting!" he said. "You both need to try again. I'll send the Tin Woodman and Peter with you this time so you don't get confused."

The Tin Woodman and Peter followed Little John and Will Scarlet back into the forest. They passed Robin Hood, who was finally returning from an errand Conner sent him on the night before.

"I HAVE RETURNED!" he announced.

"Did you get the lock and key from Maid Marian?" Conner said.

Robin Hood leaped off his horse with a triumphant smile—but his face quickly fell flat.

"NO," he said. "I HAVE FAILED YOU, SORCERER. I SPENT ALL NIGHT OUTSIDE MAID MARIAN'S CASTLE WINDOW. I ANNOUNCED MY PRESENCE AND I CALLED HER NAME, BUT SHE NEVER OPENED HER WINDOW."

"Dang it," Conner said. "Does anyone else in this camp have a girlfriend?"

Alan-a-Dale and Friar Tuck were the only Merry Men left at the camp. The candidates weren't promising.

"Never mind," Conner said. "Robin, can you go back to the castle tonight and try wooing her?"

"ANYTHING FOR YOU, SORCERER," Robin Hood said. "BUT I FEAR THAT MAY NOT WORK. I FEEL AS IF MAID MARIAN AND I ARE DRIFTING APART. THEREFORE, EVEN IF I COLLECTED A LOCK AND KEY FROM HER, THEY MAY NOT BE WORTHY OF YOUR POTION."

Conner slapped his hand on his forehead—he couldn't believe his luck. If he wanted to go home, he would have to solve Robin Hood's relationship problems on top of everything else.

"Robin, let's have a chat," he said.

"WHAT IS A *CHAT*, GREAT SORCERER?" Robin Hood asked.

"It's a *talk*—let's sit down and talk."

Conner had a seat by the campfire and Robin Hood sat across from him.

"Let me ask you a question," Conner said. "When you talk to Maid Marian, *DO YOU ALWAYS TALK LIKE THIS?*"

Robin Hood gave him a funny look.

"THERE IS NO NEED TO SHOUT, SORCERER," Robin Hood said. "MY HEARING IS IMPECCABLE! I HAVE THE EARS OF A FOX."

Conner rolled his eyes. He had never met anyone so clueless in his entire life—Robin Hood made Red look like a Rhodes scholar.

"Robin, I don't know another way to put this, but you're *volume challenged*," he said. "Maid Marian probably needs a break from you so her eardrums can heal. Tonight when you call for her, I want you to speak to her like you would talk to a baby."

"A BABY, YOU SAY?" Robin Hood asked. Conner covered his mouth with his finger.

"Much quieter than that," Conner whispered. *"Pretend Marian is a small, delicate infant with sensitive ears."*

Robin Hood didn't understand the point of this, but he would oblige any request from his sorcerer.

"Next question," Conner said. "What do you and Marian talk about when you're together?"

"THE DOWNFALL OF PRINCE JOHN AND THE RESTORATION OF NOTTINGHAM!" he said.

"Tonight, I want you to start with a simple *how are*

you?" Conner instructed. "Ask her how her day was. Compliment what she's wearing. Ask her if she got her hair cut."

"BUT MARIAN'S HAIR IS ALWAYS COVERED BY A VEIL," Robin Hood said.

"It doesn't matter," Conner said. "Girls like to feel special. They don't always want to hear about your battles or pillages or whatever else you Merry Men do. They want to know about your *feelings*, especially how *they* make you feel."

"MARIAN MAKES ME FEEL LIKE THE LUCKIEST MAN IN NOTTINGHAM," Robin Hood said.

"Bingo!" Conner said. "Make sure to tell her that."

It was obvious by the face Robin was making that being considerate was something he had never considered.

"THANK YOU, O SORCERER," he said, and gave Conner a strong pat on the back. "YOU ARE WISE IN THE WAYS OF WOMEN. IS THERE A *SORCERESS* IN YOUR LIFE?"

Conner smiled. "There might be an iron in my fire."

"SORCERER, YOU MUSTN'T LEAVE AN IRON IN THE FIRE TOO LONG, IT MIGHT BURN YOU WHEN YOU COME BACK FOR IT," Robin Hood said.

Conner couldn't tell if this was another clueless remark or a deep metaphor. Either way, Robin Hood was right.

Friar Tuck tapped Conner on the shoulder. "Sorcerer, forgive my interruption, but may I ask you something?"

"Yes, Padre Tuck?" Conner asked.

"*Friar,*" Tuck corrected. "I made a list of the items

you need for your potion. Should the others return with the correct items, all you would need is moonlight and a *splash of magic*, as you described. Is that something you will need collected, or were you planning to supply it yourself?"

"Oh yeah, I forgot about that part," Conner said. He forgot his sister wasn't there to finalize the potion with magic. "Friar, if the sorcerer was tired, is there anyone else in Nottingham who could supply some magic?"

"Normally, Sorcerer, it isn't my nature to dwell on witch-craft," Tuck said. He looked around the woods to make sure other friars weren't listening. "However, there is a horrid woman living in the castle who I believe has *danced with the devil*, if you will. Her name is Maudlin, known throughout Nottingham as *the Witch of Papplenick*, and she works for the sheriff."

Alan-a-Dale strummed a dramatic tune on his mandolin that made Conner jump.

"She predicts his future,
And curses his enemies,
With devilish concoctions,
She heals his injuries."

"Great," Conner said sarcastically. "And someone would have to sneak into the castle to get to her?"

"I would assume so," Tuck said.

Conner didn't know why he was surprised. It wasn't a real Bailey scavenger hunt unless the fear of capture, tor-ture, and death was a possibility. Conner knew he would have to find her by himself—he couldn't risk one of the Merry Men screwing it up.

"Robin, you're in luck," Conner said. "You'll have a travel buddy tonight. I'm going to the castle with you."

Later that evening, as the sun began its descent, Conner and Robin Hood traveled to Nottingham Castle. They wore dark cloaks to camouflage themselves in the night and traveled from tree to tree in case any of the sheriff's soldiers were wandering the forest. Nottingham Castle was an enormous medieval fortress constructed from large stones.

Most of the windows were very narrow—barely enough room for an arm to squeeze through. Robin Hood led Conner to a larger glass window and stood below it.

"LOVE OF MY LIFE, 'TIS I, ROBIN HOOD!" he called up to it.

Maid Marian appeared in the window. She was pretty and wore a purple veil over her head. She looked down at the ground and when she saw Robin Hood she quickly ducked behind the window, obviously trying to avoid him. Unfortunately, he saw her, and Robin Hood was heartbroken.

"YOU SEE, SORCERER, IT IS JUST AS I TOLD YOU," Robin Hood said. "HER AFFECTION FOR ME HAS DRAINED FROM HER HEART."

"That's because you said hello like there was a stampede running behind her," Conner said. "Try what we talked about—pretend she's a baby!"

Robin Hood looked back to the window and tried again.

"Lovely lady, please open the window so I may see your beautiful eyes," Robin Hood said.

He sounded like a totally different person with a quieter tone. Maid Marian peeked over the windowsill with very large eyes—*was that Robin Hood?* She opened the window and looked down to make sure.

"Robin of Loxley?" she asked.

"My dear Marian, you look so beautiful tonight!" Robin Hood said. "Is that a new veil?"

"Yes, it *is*!" Marian said. She was shocked he had noticed.

"I must say, there isn't another maiden in all the land who looks diviner than thee tonight," Robin Hood said.

He took off his hat and gave her a small bow. Maid Marian blushed and covered her mouth to hide her grin.

"Oh, Robin." She giggled. "Can you even see my veil from all the way down there?"

"Will you let me into your room so I may see it closer?" Robin Hood asked.

"Smooth!" Conner whispered, and gave him a thumbs-up.

Marian lowered a rope of sheets tied together. Robin Hood used it to climb up the side of the castle and sat on the windowsill. They shared a kiss and Robin crawled into Marian's room.

"Nice work!" Conner called to the window. "Don't forget the lock and key!"

He was so relieved—he wondered if he could have a future in couple's counseling. His relief quickly wore off once he realized he still had to find his own way inside the castle to find the Witch of Papplenick.

Conner ran around the castle but couldn't find a door or a window big enough to crawl through. He eventually found the castle's gate and shook it to see if he could pry it open, but it was solid as a rock. Just as he stepped away from it, the gate started rising. Four soldiers appeared behind it, exiting the castle.

With no time to hide and very few places to go, Conner pressed his body as flat as he could to the side of the castle and closed his eyes. He prayed he would magically blend into the wall like a chameleon. Luckily, the soldiers' helmets were so large, their view was obstructed. All four of them walked right past him. Once they were out of sight, Conner dived under the gate and entered the castle.

The castle was fairly empty, and the footsteps of any approaching soldier clanked so loudly, Conner heard them coming long before he saw them. The inside of the castle looked exactly like the outside. It was nothing but long halls of stone walls and small windows.

"Let's see, if I were a resident witch, where would I be?" Conner whispered to himself. "Either the attic or the basement—that's where witches are always hiding out in these stories."

He found a staircase and hurried down it. It led him to a large steel door with spikes on it. He heard a whip crack and then a man scream.

"Nope, that's definitely *the dungeon*," he said, and quickly turned around.

He searched the castle for a way into the towers, assuming the witch had to live inside one of them. He found a spiral staircase and climbed it higher and higher, growing dizzy as it curled upward. At the top of the stairs he found another door—but this one was ajar.

Conner peeked inside a small circular room; without a doubt he had reached the top of a tower. The room was filled with shelves and tables covered by strange things. There were jars of plants, liquids, and small animals. There were cages of larger animals and potion bottles and cauldrons. It was definitely the room of a witch.

Conner crept inside. "Excuse me, Miss Papplenick? Maudlin?"

He found the witch sitting in a chair in the middle of the room. She had thin gray hair, very wrinkled pale skin, and wore black tattered robes. Her eyes were closed and she was as still as a stone. In fact, she didn't even appear to be breathing.

"*Please* be alive," Conner said.

Just as he stepped closer to check her pulse, someone else ran up the stairs behind him and knocked loudly on the door. Conner quickly hid behind a table of potions.

"Maudlin? Are you decent?" a man said at the door.

The witch snorted and stirred to life. "Yes, Sheriff." She coughed. "You may enter."

The Sheriff of Nottingham stepped inside the tower

and slammed the door behind him. He was a tall and regal man, but once he was alone with the witch, he hunched over and burst into hysterical tears like a small child.

"I'm not having a good night, Maudlin," the sheriff wailed.

"There, there, Sheriff," Maudlin said, and stood to give him a hug. "Come sit down and tell Aunt Maud what happened."

She sat the sheriff in her seat and stroked his hair like she would a doll's. Conner couldn't believe his eyes—he was so embarrassed just by *watching* the sheriff that he looked around the tower for a way out.

"I just want M-M-Maid M-M-Marian to love me!" the sheriff cried. "No matter what I do she'll always h-h-hate me! I've given her a nice home, I buy her nice dresses and veils, and she still treats me like I'm her captor."

"Now, now, Sheriff," Maudlin said. "Marian just needs time to come around, that's all. I told you, women love playing hard to get."

"I don't think she's interested in me," the sheriff sobbed. "I just knocked on her door to say good night, and she wouldn't even open it to look at me! I'm afraid Marian might be in love with someone else!"

"Then she's daft, if you ask me," Maudlin said. "Who could possibly be more handsome, or braver, or more powerful than our Sheriff of Nottingham? There isn't a more suitable bachelor around for miles, and if she can't see that, then she doesn't deserve you. Who else could protect

Nottingham better than our sheriff? *No one.* Who else could achieve Prince John's vision of our kingdom? *No one.* Who else could keep that nasty thief Robin Hood at bay but our sheriff? *No one!* Any girl would be lucky to get a look from you."

Her compliments must have done the trick, because the sheriff's tears dried up and his frown turned into a bashful smile.

"I suppose you're right," he said. "Thank you, Aunt Maud."

"You're very welcome, dearie," the witch said.

"I just wish I didn't have to try so hard," the sheriff said. "It makes my stomach turn and gives me a throbbing headache just thinking about it! I haven't been able to sleep for days!"

"Let Aunt Maud take care of that for you," Maudlin said.

The witch searched through her things and placed a glass of water on the table beside the sheriff. She retrieved a root from one jar, a piece of bark from another, and an herb from the next. She crushed each item up and mixed it into the water.

"Alka root to calm your stomach, bark of an aspirin tree to sooth your head, and the wort of St. John to help you sleep," Maudlin said.

She handed the sheriff the glass and he drank the concoction in one gulp.

Conner thought it was a pretty harmless mixture for

such a renowned witch. He took a closer look around the tower and realized the items weren't dangerous at all. There was nothing he saw that he couldn't get in a grocery store in the Otherworld. The small animals weren't sacrifices for future potions—they were pets.

"There's nothing magical about the Witch of Papplenick," he whispered to himself. "She's not even a witch— *she's a pharmacist!*"

"I feel much better already, " the sheriff said.

"Now, let's go to your chambers and I'll tuck you in," Maudlin said. "You'll get a good night's rest and come back to me tomorrow if you need anything else."

"I will," the sheriff said. "Thank you, Aunt Maud."

Maudlin escorted the sheriff out of the tower and down the stairs to his chambers.

Conner was extremely disheartened. Thankfully, magic was the last ingredient the Portal Potion required. He would have two weeks to find someone else who could provide it while the other ingredients brewed in the potion. However, if Maudlin was any indication, someone with magical capability may be hard to find in the world of *Robin Hood*. Conner's stomach turned at the thought of it and he helped himself to some alka root on his way out of the tower.

He quickly and quietly climbed down the stairs and found the castle's gate. He waited until the soldiers returned from their patrol shifts, pressing against the wall as he did before, and snuck outside.

He found Maid Marian's window and threw a rock at it. Robin Hood peered outside.

"Wrap it up!" Conner called out. "We've got to get back to the camp."

"Farewell, my love," Robin Hood said quietly—at least for him. He kissed Maid Marian and then climbed the rope of sheets to the ground. Maid Marian waved him off as he and Conner ran into the forest.

"How did it go?" Conner asked.

"IT WAS A GREAT SUCCESS, SORCERER," Robin Hood said, back to his normal tone. He opened his hand and showed Conner a small lock and key he had acquired from Maid Marian. "THIS SHOULD WORK NOW THAT OUR AFFECTION HAS BEEN RESTORED."

"That's great!" Conner said.

"DID YOU RETRIEVE THE MAGIC FROM THE EVIL WITCH OF PAPPLENICK?" he asked.

Conner sighed and shook his head. "Maudlin isn't going to work out for us," Conner said. "I'll have to figure something else out."

Robin Hood and Conner journeyed through the woods until they arrived back at the camp. They found the Tin Woodman, Peter, and the Merry Men waiting by the campfire.

"Conner, Little John and I brought back a branch from the oldest tree in the woods," the Tin Woodman was happy to share.

"And I flew into the sky and plucked a feather from the finest pheasant I could find," Peter said.

"That's terrific!" Conner said. "And Robin just got his hands on a lock and key from Maid Marian. We have enough ingredients to start the potion."

He borrowed a pot and pan from the Merry Men and went to work. He boiled water in the pot and added the tree branch and the feather. Once the lock and key had been melted in the pan, he poured it into the pot with the rest of the potion.

Little John climbed to the top of a nearby tree and Peter flew the potion to him. Together they rigged the pot to the tree so it would have a better view of the moon and soak up its light.

"We'll bring it down in two weeks," Peter said.

"Did you get the magic you needed?" the Tin Woodman asked.

"No," Conner said sadly. "Modern medicine was considered *magic* in the early centuries, but it's no good to us. Our new task is finding someone of *real* magic capabilities, like my sister."

"It's too bad I'm out of pixie dust." Peter sighed.

"Hold on a moment," the Tin Woodman said. "Why can't you do it, Conner?"

Peter shrugged—it seemed logical to him, too. Conner was already shaking his head before he thought it through, like they had asked him to juggle knives.

"I don't do magic," Conner said.

"But your sister can," Peter said. "So why can't you?"

"I suppose I *could*, I just don't," he said. "Magic is very tricky. There are a lot of layers to it and I've never done it before—at least, not without my sister."

The Tin Woodman and Peter were very confused. Of all things, why was Conner self-conscious about *this?*

"But *could* you if you *wanted* to?" the Tin Woodman asked.

"Yes—I mean, no—I don't know," Conner said.

Conner supposed it was a possibility, given his DNA, but he couldn't make any promises. He had always considered magic to be like math; it was a skill Alex and only Alex had inherited.

"We've only got two weeks before that potion is ready, mate," Peter said.

"You should think it over in case we can't find anyone else," the Tin Woodman said. "If we don't find someone, we'll be stuck with the Merry Men forever."

The more Conner thought about it, the more the pressure increased. It wasn't necessarily *magic* he was afraid of; he was never good in *any* situation when something depended solely on him.

CHAPTER TWENTY-SIX

THE BASEMENT

R ed and the Lost Boys followed Hagetta's directions
and traveled through the Dwarf Forests toward the
Corner Kingdom. The Lost Boys had never been
in such an unnerving place. They were constantly on the
lookout as they journeyed deeper into the mysterious and
thick woods. Red, on the other hand, never gave their eerie
surroundings a second thought. Her mind was fixated on
one thing and one thing only: saving Froggy.

It grew late, and the night was always darker in the
Dwarf Forests. They followed a river as it traveled south.

They discovered a house on the other side with a tall hay roof and a watermill that turned as the river ran through it. The sight of it sent chills down Red's spine and she knew they had arrived.

"We're here, boys," Red said. "That's the goat's house. Porridge, I want you to take Oats and Buckle somewhere safe. I'll whistle for you when I need you—and if you hear one of us scream, go get help."

Red helped the Lost Boys down from the horses and Porridge led her family out of sight into the trees. Red and the Lost Boys crouched behind the bushes and watched the house.

"Is our temporary dad in there?" Tootles asked.

"I certainly hope so," Red said.

"What are we going to do, Mum?" Slightly asked.

"Should we just barge in and take him?" Nibs asked.

"Attack?" the Lost twins asked.

Before she could answer, cellar doors on the side of the house opened. Morina peeked her head up from below the house and looked around the forest. Red and the Lost Boys hit the ground and watched her through the bushes. They were afraid she might have heard them, but the witch wasn't looking for something in particular; she scanned the forest in *all* directions. Once Morina determined the forest was empty, she went back underground.

"That's the goat, all right!" Red whispered.

"Do you think she saw us?" Tootles asked.

Suddenly, a loud sound came from below the house as

something heavy was dragged up the steps. Morina reappeared, pulling a wooden coffin out from under her house. She dragged it to the riverbank and then returned to the cellar. A few moments later, she dragged another coffin out and set it beside the other one.

Morina pushed the coffins into the river and they floated downstream. She went to the watermill and gave it a strong tug, pushing it against the river's current. Slowly but surely, the river magically began flowing in *the opposite direction,* sending the coffins *upstream* into the Dwarf Forests.

The witch waited for the caskets to drift out of sight, then she turned the windmill in the opposite direction. A few moments later, the river began flowing south again. Morina descended back underground and they heard her lock the cellar doors with bolts and chains.

"So *she's* the one behind the bodies of Dead Man's Creek!" Red whispered.

"Dead Man's Creek?" Curly asked, and gulped fearfully.

"I'll tell you about it once you outgrow your night terrors, Caesar," Red said.

Morina exited the house again, this time using the front door. She was wearing a long black-feathered coat and she carried a small bag. She walked down to the river where a small boat was docked and sat inside it. The witch released the boat from the land and it magically cruised down the river toward the Corner Kingdom.

Red waited until Morina was long gone before getting to her feet.

"We're in luck, boys," Red said. "It looks like the goat has left the stable. Let's sneak inside the house and find your temporary father."

The river wasn't very deep, so Red made the Lost Boys get in and carry her across the water so her dress wouldn't get wet. Once they made it to the other side, they tried entering the house through the cellar doors, but they wouldn't budge. They walked around the house to the front door, but it was locked, too.

"Oh dear," Red said. *"Charlie, are you in there?"*

She knocked on the door but there was no response. The Lost Boys exchanged a smile.

"Time for a Curly toss!" Tootles said.

"What's a curly toss?" Red asked.

"We'll show you!" Nibs said.

The Lost Boys each grabbed one of Curly's limbs and raised him off the ground. They swung him in the air and slammed his chubby body against the door, breaking it down.

"Ouch," Curly said from the floor of the house.

"Good boy, Caesar," Red said. "Mama is so proud!"

Red led the way inside, stepping over Curly as she went. They eyed the front room of Morina's house and ogled all the shelves of colorful liquids. It was unlike any place they had ever been. Unfortunately, there was no sign of Froggy anywhere.

"What kind of place is *this*?" Tootles asked.

"It reminds me of a hospital," Nibs said.

"For such a sophisticated place, the juice tastes terrible," Slightly said.

Red and the other boys quickly turned to Slightly and saw him chug down a bottle of pink potion.

"Salvador, don't drink that!" Red warned, but it was too late. Slightly transformed into a toddler before their eyes. He looked up at the others in shock and started crying.

"Amazing!" the Lost Boys said in unison.

"No one touch anything else," Red ordered. "Tobias, look after your new baby brother—hopefully Alex can change him back when she and Conner return."

Tootles picked Slightly up and cradled him until his tears stopped.

The Lost Boys found a tassel on the wall and pulled on it. Curtains on the wall separated and the Mirror of Truth was revealed. Red and the boys looked in at their reflections, but nothing changed. Their outer truth was as real as their inner truth.

Red searched the room, but there was no sign of Froggy anywhere.

"Mother, over here!" Nibs said. "It's a door!"

He directed Red to the door on the back wall covered in a dozen locks. She figured Froggy was probably on the other side of it.

"Oh, Caeeesar?" Red sang.

Before he knew it, Curly was lifted into the air again by the other Lost Boys and his temporary mother.

"Let's give him a really powerful swing this time," Red

instructed. "There are a lot of locks to break. On three... *one... two... three!*"

After a few aggressive swings to gain momentum, they let him go and he slammed through the door. There was a staircase behind it and Curly rolled down into a basement.

"Ouch," Curly said.

"Is there anyone down there, Caesar?" Red asked.

He never responded. Red and the Lost Boys climbed down the steps after him. What they saw in the basement would haunt their nightmares for years to come.

Curly was on his feet, staring into the room in shock. There were twenty-four beds in the basement—twelve lined against one side, and twelve on the other. The last four beds were empty, but twenty of the beds were filled *with sleeping children*. Each child was *glowing*, but as the light emitted from their bodies it slowly drained into potion bottles at the foot of their beds.

The farther back the bed, the older the child looked. The last few didn't even look like children anymore, but petite senior citizens. Their faces were wrinkled and their hair was gray.

"These must be *the missing children!*" Red gasped.

"What's happening to them?" Tootles asked.

Red noticed that the walls were lined with empty coffins. She covered her mouth, and her eyes filled with tears.

"Morina is draining their youth and beauty to make potions!" Red said. "She's a monster!"

Red and the Lost Boys stared around at the cursed

children in disbelief. They wanted to free them from whatever enchantment was draining their life force, but they didn't know how. They were too afraid to touch any of them.

"Why are there empty beds?" Nibs asked.

"Because they died," said a voice that didn't belong to Red or the Lost Boys.

They looked around the basement to see where it was coming from. Propped up in the corner of the basement was a tall mirror with a silver frame, and to Red's horror, Froggy was standing *inside of it.*

"*Charlie!*" Red yelled, and ran to it. She placed both of her hands on the glass and Froggy put his webbed hands against hers.

"Our dad's a giant frog?" Nibs asked. "*Hooray, our dad's a frog!*"

"Red, who are these children?" Froggy asked. "And why are they calling me *Dad*?"

"These are the Lost Boys of Neverland. I've adopted them for the time being—it's a long story," Red said. "Charlie, what are you doing inside a mirror?"

"Morina put me in here so I would have to watch the children," Froggy said sadly.

"So how do we get you out?" Red asked.

Froggy shook his head. "Magic mirrors are irreversible, my darling" he said. "I'm trapped just like the Evil Queen's lover, but since *the wishing spell* doesn't exist anymore, I'll most likely be in here . . . *forever.*"

Red fell to her knees and shook her head. She thought her heart was broken before, but it had shattered into so many pieces now, it might never heal again.

"No...," she whispered. *"No, no, no..."*

Froggy became emotional at the sight of her. "I am so sorry, my love," he cried. "You must take these children and leave before Morina gets back."

"I can't leave you...," Red cried.

"There's nothing we can do." Froggy wept. "Morina wanted to separate us, and I'm afraid she has for good. *The witch has won.*"

CHAPTER TWENTY-SEVEN

THE SISTERS GRIMM

As far as Mrs. Campbell knew, Bree was spending the weekend at her friend Stacey's house. Even though Bree and Stacey hadn't been friends since the sixth grade, Mrs. Campbell was so excited her daughter was socializing again, she didn't ask many questions. Little did Mrs. Campbell know, after only a week free from being grounded, Bree was already planning another great excursion.

Naturally, she thought of calling Cornelia Grimm first, but her phone number wasn't listed in any directory Bree found. She had no choice but to go to 1729 Mystic Lane, Willow Grove, Connecticut, and pray Cornelia was still living there.

Bree planned the whole trip on her computer Thursday after school. She was so thankful for technology—she didn't know how kids managed to run away before the Internet. She found the address of the sourdough factory the Storybook Grill bought from. Willow Grove was only a bus ride away, and Cornelia's house was roughly an hour's walk from the center of town.

Friday morning, Bree packed her bag with snacks and an extra change of clothes. As soon as the school bell rang, she sprinted to the Storybook Grill and waited behind the Dumpster in the back. Just like Iris had said, the delivery truck for Sam's New England Sourdough arrived that afternoon.

The deliveryman was young and round and wore a white uniform with a red bow tie. He raised the back door of his truck and loaded a cart with boxes of bread. He rolled the cart down a ramp off the truck and into the diner.

He took his time once he was inside. Bree peeked in the window and saw him flirting with Petunia. Bree figured this was her chance to sneak aboard the delivery truck. She found a small space behind a stack of damaged boxes and hid there.

The deliveryman returned twenty minutes later and locked the truck up, clueless of the additional passenger. He started the engine, pulled away from the Storybook

Grill, and headed back to the factory. Bree was on her way to Connecticut with no plan of how she would return.

It took two days for the truck to reach the northeastern state. The deliveryman stopped occasionally to eat and rest, but he was very determined to make it back in good time. Bree even heard him lying to a dispatcher about his estimated time of arrival.

The worst part about Bree's journey was sneaking on and off the truck to find a restroom. She waited until the deliveryman was either asleep in the backseat or eating in a restaurant. Every time she left the truck she was terrified it would be gone when she returned.

Despite it being a stressful and cramped way to travel, it still gave Bree quite a thrill. She hadn't had such an adrenaline rush since she traveled around Europe with Conner. She just wished he were with her to keep her company.

Finally, on Sunday morning the truck pulled into the Sam's New England Sourdough factory. As soon as the truck was parked Bree raised the backdoor from the inside and darted out.

"Thanks for the ride!" she said as she passed the deliveryman.

"Hey! How long have you been in there?" he yelled after her. "Come back here!"

He was too slow to chase after her, and Bree ran to the nearest bus stop. She waited only a few minutes for the next bus to arrive. The bus drove into the small and quiet city of Willow Grove and dropped her off in the center of town.

She pulled a map she had printed out of her bag and followed it a little ways out of town, heading for Cornelia's house. The Connecticut countryside was a beautiful place for a walk. There were rolling hills of green trees all around her as far as she could see.

Bree eventually found Mystic Lane. It was a wide residential street with large homes on spacious lots. All the houses were elegant but old. Some looked like they had been there since before the United States was formed.

"1723 ... 1725 ... 1727 ..." Bree read the addresses as she passed them. "Which brings us to *1729!*"

The house had a tall hedge around its yard, making it much more private than all the other homes on the street. Bree went through a small gate and stepped onto the front lawn. It was a large two-story house with big windows and a wide front porch. The house was painted yellow and the front yard was covered in ornaments. There were colorful wind chimes, garden gnomes, birdbaths, and statues of fairies spread throughout the flowerbeds.

It was very homey and Bree felt very comfortable here— strangely comfortable.

"This must be it," she said to herself.

Bree pulled out the old photograph of her grandmother and Cornelia. She held it up to the house and sighed with relief—it matched perfectly, like an old piece in a new puzzle. The house had been fixed up over the years, but Bree was definitely in the right place.

She walked up the porch steps and knocked on the

door. Bree's heart was racing. She prayed she hadn't traveled so far for nothing.

A middle-aged woman with spiky red hair answered the door. She wore a maroon sweater and dangling ruby teardrop earrings.

"May I help you?" she asked.

"Hello, my name is Bree Campbell. I was wondering if a woman named Cornelia Grimm still lived at this address."

"Why do you ask?"

"I think we're cousins," Bree said. "I was hoping she could answer a few questions for me about our family. I'm sorry to barge in like this, but I didn't know how else to track her down. I've traveled a really long way to get here."

"Yes, Cornelia's here," she said. "Come in, I'll get her for you. My name is Wanda."

They shook hands and Wanda escorted Bree inside. Her spirits soared knowing Cornelia was still alive—her journey hadn't been a waste.

The house had floral wallpaper and white trim. There were large vases of flowers placed on every surface. The walls were covered in framed photos, and not a single frame was alike. Each picture was of a different woman or groups of women who had lived at the house over the decades. Bree recognized one of the women immediately.

"That's my grandmother," Bree said. She showed Wanda the picture of Cornelia and her grandmother.

Wanda smiled at her. "Oh, you're Anneliese's grand-daughter," she said. "Cornelia will be thrilled you've come to visit. Follow me, she's in the sitting room."

They entered a room filled with large comfy furni-ture. There were at least six cats that Bree counted, but she assumed there were probably more in other parts of the house. Another middle-aged woman was sitting on a couch reading a book. She was plump and had dark hair that was graying at the temples.

"Frenda, this is Bree Campbell," Wanda introduced. "Bree, this is my cousin Frenda—Cornelia's daughter."

"Hello there," Frenda said, surprised by the company.

"Hi," Bree said, and shook her hand.

"Aunt Cornelia, you have a visitor," Wanda said. "This is Bree Campbell—she's Anneliese's granddaughter."

Cornelia Grimm was seated in the back of the room. She faced an easel and was in the middle of painting a landscape of some kind. She turned to face the girls and Bree instantly recognized her; she was very old now but still looked simi-lar to her grandma's picture. She had long white hair down to her waist. She wore red-framed glasses, and a stylish silk scarf was wrapped around her neck.

Cornelia was delighted to meet Bree. She retrieved her cane and stood to greet her.

"Hello, child," Cornelia said with a sweet smile. "What a lovely surprise. I was just thinking about your grand-mother this morning."

"I'm so happy to finally meet you," Bree said. "You're my grandmother's cousin, is that right?"

"Yes," Cornelia said. "We were very close when we were young, but unfortunately lost touch over the years. Is she well?"

"Actually, she passed away a few years ago," Bree was sad to share.

"Oh, I'm sorry to hear that," Cornelia said with a sigh. "Well, she's in a better place now. What brings you to the house?"

Bree hesitated, not sure how to put it. "I found a letter you wrote to my grandmother with this address," she said. "I have a lot of questions about our family, and since she's not around anymore, I was hoping you could answer them for me. I would have just called, but you aren't listed anywhere."

"I hate solicitors," Cornelia said. "We would be happy to answer any questions you have. Let's have a seat."

Cornelia sat beside Frenda on the couch. Bree and Wanda took the chairs across from them. The women were all ears and Bree could tell they were eager to hear what questions she had. It wasn't every day that a young woman appeared on their doorstep seeking their help.

"I suppose I should just start with the biggest question on my mind," Bree said. "Grimm isn't a common name, so I was wondering if our family was related to the Brothers Grimm."

"As a matter of fact, yes," Cornelia said. "Wilhelm Grimm was Anneliese and my fourth-great-grandfather."

Once again, Bree's spirits soared so high, she could have levitated into the air. This was the answer she was hoping to get—everything made sense now.

"That's incredible," Bree said with relief. "Are you from Germany as well?"

"My grandparents moved to the United States when they were young, but your grandmother was the first in her family," Cornelia explained. "Before she met your grandfather she came to live with us in this house."

"I figured as much from the letters," Bree said. "I noticed all the photos of women in the hall. Was this house some kind of sorority?"

"Sort of," Cornelia said. "The house first belonged to my mother and her sisters. Many of our relatives have lived here over the years and a strong majority of them were women. I'm sure our neighbors have thought we were a *coven* from time to time."

Cornelia, Frenda, and Wanda all shared a laugh, but Bree didn't join them. Instead, she eyed the women nervously.

"*Are* you witches?" Bree asked in all seriousness.

The room went very quiet. The women shared a look that gave Bree an unsettling feeling. There was definitely a secret among them.

"Sorry, I hope that wasn't rude," Bree said. "Whatever you are, it's none of my business. Recently, I learned a lot about the Brothers Grimm—more than most people would believe. I know the Grimm family has *capabilities* that other families don't."

"Are you talking about the magic in our family's blood?" Cornelia asked.

The hairs on Bree's arms suddenly stood up.

"Yes," she said. "You know about that?"

All three women nodded.

"It's a story that's been passed down in our family from generation to generation," Frenda said. "The Brothers Grimm didn't write the stories they published, but were given to them by fairies from another world. In the early nineteenth century, the Grande Armée caught wind of this world and tried to conquer it. So a fairy transferred magic from her blood into Wilhelm Grimm's so that he could help the fairies trap the approaching army. That magic still runs through our family's veins to this day."

"It's not enough magic to cast a spell or an enchantment," Wanda said. "But we know it's inside of us somewhere, and it separates us from everyone else in the world."

Bree stared at them in shock. She thought she was the only person in the Otherworld who knew the story.

"I'm curious how you knew the family secret before you knew you were in the family," Cornelia said with a laugh. "After your grandmother left this house, she was very adamant that she wouldn't tell her future children—magic always frightened her. I'm assuming she changed her mind but left out some of the details in her explanation."

"No," Bree said. "She never said a word about it; I found

out completely on my own. It's a long story, but last year I went into the fairy-tale world."

The women gasped and sat on the edge of their seats. This was a game changer, even for them. Bree was the first person they had ever known who traveled into the fairy-tale world.

"You crossed over?" Wanda asked.

"But how?" Frenda asked.

Bree told her relatives all about her trip to Germany with her school, and her adventures with Conner and Emmerich. She told them how they traveled into the fairy-tale world through a portal inside Neuschwanstein Castle. She explained that once she returned to the Otherworld, she remembered hearing that Mother Goose had rigged the portal to trap any person of non-magic blood inside it for two hundred years. Having magic in their blood was the only explanation of how Emmerich and Bree traveled through the portal so effortlessly—which led Bree to believe she and Emmerich were descendants of Wilhelm Grimm.

It was a long-winded answer, but the women were completely captivated.

"How is your friend Conner related to magic?" Cornelia asked.

"He and his twin sister are the Fairy Godmother's grandchildren," Bree said.

"Fascinating," Frenda said.

"Tell me about it!" Bree said. "They were the first

children born of both worlds, and their birth somehow connected the two. Apparently, time in the fairy-tale world used to run a lot slower, but now the worlds are in sync."

"How old are they?" Cornelia asked.

"Almost fifteen, I think," Bree said. "What does that have to do with anything?"

None of them answered her. Knowing the twins' ages sent Cornelia, Frenda, and Wanda deep into thought.

"I feel like there's something you're not telling me," Bree said.

All three women suddenly stood.

"I think we should show Bree the guesthouse," Cornelia said. "It'll be easier to explain *the sisterhood* there."

"The *sisterhood*?" Bree asked.

"Follow us, sweetheart," Wanda said.

The women escorted Bree through the house and into the backyard. The lawn behind the house was just as decorated as the front lawn. There was a large guesthouse in the very back of their property. It looked like it may have been a barn before it was renovated.

They went through the door and Cornelia flicked on the lights. The guesthouse was one enormous room with a high ceiling. There was a large steel table in the very center and a row of desks in the back equipped with computers, printers, and radio scanners. There was a wall lined with file cabinets and several built-in drawers and cupboards. A giant map of the world took up another wall, and hundreds of locations were pinned with colorful tacks.

Bree looked around the room with large curious eyes. "What is this place, your secret laboratory?" she asked. "Are you secret agents or something?"

"We call ourselves *the Sisters Grimm*," Cornelia said. "Our sisterhood was founded in 1852 by my third-great-grandmother, Maria Grimm. For almost two centuries, the women in our family have monitored magical phenomena that occur in this world."

"What *magical phenomena*?" she asked. "Are you talking about the fairies that spread stories?"

"That and much more," Frenda said.

"For a long time, our family believed we were the only people on earth who had been exposed to magic and knew of the fairy-tale world," Cornelia explained. "However, we were wrong. When Maria Grimm took a closer look at history, she found our world's past is littered with instances where the two worlds have intersected. The fairies who spread stories were just *one* of those instances."

"But Conner's grandmother was the first and only person capable of creating portals between worlds," Bree said.

"According to our records and research, that isn't true," Cornelia said.

Wanda pulled down a large scrim. It was a time line stretching back thousands and thousands of years, covering every era of known history.

"We know the Fairy Godmother first showed up in this world somewhere in the early Dark Ages," Wanda explained, and pointed to the middle of the time line. "However, there is evidence of crossover between worlds long before she showed up."

"Most ancient civilizations were influenced by creatures that are considered *mythical* today," Frenda said. "The ancient people paid tribute to these beings in their art, stories, and sometimes even worshipped them. Despite the obvious presence of these creatures, historians have labeled their existence as *mythology*—simply because they don't meet the biological standards of animals today."

"Ancient Asia was majorly influenced by *dragons*, Europe is crawling with legends of *fairies* and *trolls* living in its forests, the Vikings claimed to witness *merpeople* as they sailed across the oceans, and that's only naming a few," Wanda said. "Ironically, all these creatures existed in the fairy-tale world at one point in time."

"It's more than just a coincidence, don't you think?" Cornelia said.

"So you're saying thousands of years ago these creatures slipped through the cracks of the fairy-tale world and wound up in our world?" Bree asked.

"Precisely," Cornelia said. "But it didn't end there. Let's show Bree the carcasses."

They walked Bree to the built-in drawers and cupboards. Wanda pulled open the biggest drawer at the bottom and Bree screamed. Inside was the skeleton of a mermaid.

"This was found on a Mexican beach in 1938," Wanda said. "And *these* were found in Ireland in 1899."

She opened the drawer above it and showed Bree four metal trays with small fairy skeletons taped to them.

"Luckily, whenever remains are found, most people think they're fake," Wanda said.

"So how are these things getting into our world?" Bree asked.

"During Maria Grimm's research, she determined that, roughly once a month, somewhere in the world a *doorway* opens to the fairy-tale world," Cornelia said. "It lasts only a few seconds. Sometimes people and creatures slip through, sometimes not."

"Since Maria learned this, every time a doorway opens, the Sisters Grimm have been present to make sure no harm comes to anyone," Frenda said. "If someone or something enters our world, we keep it until the next doorway appears, and do our best to release it back into the fairy-tale world."

"Occasionally a creature gets loose from us," Wanda said. "Perhaps you've heard of a few? There's a harmless water dragon living in Scotland that people call the Loch Ness Monster. A family of hairy ogres has made a happy home in the mountains of North America and Nepal—but you might know them better as Sasquatches or yetis."

"How do you know *where* the doorways will appear?" Bree asked.

"We've used the most powerful force of our world to predict the locations of the magical occurrence," Cornelia said. "Science!"

Frenda picked up a yardstick and pointed to the tacks pinned to the large map of the world.

"We've marked the locations of every recorded sighting of a doorway or a magical being that's entered from one," Frenda said. "Notice the pattern?"

Bree studied the map, titling her head to view it differently. "If you connect the dots, it looks like the locations make a perfect spiral around the world," she said.

"Exactly!" Wanda said. "That's how we know where the next doorway will open."

"And a new doorway appears every month?" Bree asked.

"Like clockwork," Cornelia said. "Until fifteen years ago, that is. We were waiting at the location of the next doorway, but it never appeared."

"Why?" Bree asked.

"Because something happened fifteen years ago. Perhaps it was because your friends Alex and Conner were born," Cornelia said. "Let's show her the diagram."

Wanda turned off the lights and Frenda pointed a remote at the ceiling. Bree looked up and saw a large diagram she hadn't noticed before. It lit up and came to life. There were two small orbs, one blue and one green, circling around a large yellow orb. It looked like two earths orbiting the sun. However, the blue orb was circling the sun much faster than the green one.

"Pretend the two dimensions are planets circling the sun," Cornelia said. "The green one is the fairy-tale world and the blue one is our world. Even though they move at different speeds somewhere in the cosmos, every so often their orbit crosses and they collide."

The blue orb suddenly smashed into the green one. A few moments later it happened again. It repeated until Frenda paused the diagram with the remote.

"We believe the Fairy Godmother was born during the exact moment of a past collision, giving her the ability to move between worlds at will," Wanda said.

"The Fairy Godmother told the Brothers Grimm that the fairy-tale world moved much slower than ours, and that information has been passed through our family since," Cornelia said. "That's why the doorways last only a second to us, but they may last hours or days in the fairy-tale world."

Cornelia nodded to Frenda and she hit another button on the remote. The orbs started moving around the sun at the same speeds.

"We figured something had caused the worlds to move at similar speeds when the doorway never showed up fifteen years ago," Frenda said. "But just because the worlds are moving at similar speeds doesn't mean they won't collide again and form another doorway."

The green and blue orbs bumped into each other, and the moment of impact lasted much longer now that they circled at the same speed.

"On the contrary, we're certain another doorway will form," Cornelia said. "But this time it'll stay open much longer, giving the people and creatures of both worlds plenty of time to travel between them."

"When do you think it'll happen?" Bree asked.

"Because the time difference between the worlds was never fully understood, we can't make an accurate estimate," Wanda said. "But based on the information we do know, we've created a chart that predicts it'll happen within the next six months."

"And where will the doorway appear?" Bree asked.

The women shared a distressed look.

"In the middle of New York City," Cornelia said.

They had definitely done the research to support their theory, but Bree had a hard time embracing it. An open doorway to the fairy-tale world in the middle of one of the biggest cities on the planet would cause pandemonium!

Connecticut offered Bree more information than she ever dreamed.

"This is a lot to digest," she said. "Excuse me for a moment. I need to call my friend Emmerich and fill him in."

She took her phone out of her pocket. She had a dozen missed calls from her mother—Mrs. Campbell must have figured out Bree wasn't at Stacey's house. Bree ignored the calls and dialed Emmerich's number.

"Hello?" Bree said into the phone. "Frau Himmelsbach? This is Bree Campbell, Emmerich's friend.... Yes, the American one.... Yes, *that* American.... I am so sorry for calling so late, but...Frau Himmelsbach, I think we have a bad connection, because you sound like you're crying.... What happened? ... Where's Emmerich? ... *Can you repeat that?*"

Bree turned white as a ghost and sat on the floor. Her hands began trembling so much, she could barely hold the phone to her ear.

"Bree, what's wrong?" Cornelia asked.

"It's my friend Emmerich...," she said with wide, frightful eyes. "He's been kidnapped!"

CHAPTER TWENTY-EIGHT

THE UNEXPECTED GOOD-BYE

Alex barely slept for the two weeks she was trapped in the world of *King Arthur*. Each day she was separated from her brother, her friends, and the fairy-tale world, the more she worried about them. The few hours she managed to doze off were only filled with nightmares of the same worries. She couldn't get the image of innocent people screaming and running for their lives as a flying *Jolly Roger* destroyed their homes out of her mind.

It was a complete blessing she had Arthur to distract her, otherwise her helplessness may have driven Alex insane. In fact, the time she spent with him felt like a two-week-long dream—and like all good dreams, Alex didn't want to wake from it.

The more time they spent together, the more they enjoyed each other's company. Alex felt closer to Arthur after just two weeks than to anyone else she had ever known. After every kiss, affectionate glance, and loaded smile, Alex felt the need to remind Arthur she would be leaving soon—but nothing could stop their growing attachment.

There were times when Alex daydreamed about staying in Arthur's world. What if she pretended the fairy-tale world and the Otherworld didn't exist? Could the fairy-tale world defeat her uncle's army without her? Could she live with the guilt of abandoning her friends and family? Alex was ashamed to even think about it; she knew it wasn't a possibility.

They spent every night together on the hill as the potion soaked in the moonlight. Usually, they fell asleep apart but by morning awoke in each other's arms. However, on the night before her departure, Arthur wasn't shy about cozying up next to her.

"You know, I'm leaving tomorrow," Alex said.

"I know," Arthur said. "But I'm going to pretend tonight lasts forever."

"Forever sounds nice," she said.

It was the first night she didn't have nightmares. Instead,

the dream she lived during the day continued through the night as she slept.

The morning arrived much sooner than she was expecting. Alex awoke and realized Arthur wasn't lying beside her. She sat up and looked around the hill, but there was no sign of him.

"Arthur?" Alex called, but there was no answer.

She gathered the potion and searched the woods nearby, but couldn't find him anywhere. Alex found it very odd that Arthur would leave her on the hill alone. She headed back to Merlin's cottage with hopes of finding him there. Mother Goose and Lester were the only ones at the cottage when she arrived.

"Morning," Mother Goose said. "Is the potion ready?"

"It should be after a zap of magic," Alex said. "Have you seen Arthur? I can't find him."

"Merlin took him into the woods earlier for another lesson," she said. "But I'm glad I caught you alone. I have something to tell you."

Mother Goose had a seat at the table and gestured for Alex to sit with her. Whatever it was, it must have been serious.

"What's wrong?" Alex asked.

Mother Goose took a deep breath and then let it out. "I'm not going back to the fairy-tale world with you," she said. "I'm staying in this world with Merlin."

This was the last thing Alex expected to hear. She was practically whiplashed by the news.

"What?" Alex said. "Mother Goose, you can't stay here!"

"I've got to follow my heart on this one, kiddo," Mother Goose said. "It's taken me centuries to find the place I belong. It's not the Otherworld, it's not the Fairy Palace, it's not the giant's castle—it's right *here* with Merlin."

"I think this is very impulsive," Alex said. "I know you've been lonely since my grandmother died, but you shouldn't uproot to another dimension to be with someone you just met two weeks ago."

Mother Goose chuckled.

"You know what's funny? That's the exact answer I was expecting to give you if you wanted to stay here with Arthur. I prepared a long list of reasons why it would be a bad idea. *You can't stay! People are depending on you at home! You have your whole life ahead of you!* Then I realized none of those things applied to me—so why wasn't I staying?"

"That isn't true," Alex said. "My brother and I both need you—we need your help stopping our uncle's army!"

"Having an old lady tagging along isn't going to help," Mother Goose said. "I'm good for a wisecrack now and then, but I can't defeat your uncle or his army—only you and your brother can do that. The minute you need me, I'll be there in a flash."

"Are you sure this is what you want?" Alex asked. "You were just telling me you wanted a new adventure—this sounds like you're settling down."

"Merlin *is* my next adventure," she said. "I've never known someone who makes me excited just to wake up in the morning. I don't look at the world and feel useless anymore, because I know I mean the world to him. He's lived as long as I have, made just as many mistakes, and still has all his original teeth—I'm never going to find another man like him! I probably sound like an old loon, but one day you'll understand. When you meet the person you're meant to be with, everything changes—you don't feel like you're fighting the world alone anymore."

Everything she described was exactly how Alex felt about Arthur. Perhaps Alex didn't have to wait until she was older to understand—she would have given anything to have the option of staying. As difficult as it would be to live without her, she could see in Mother Goose's eyes that she had finally found contentment. Any reason Alex had to argue with her decision was purely selfish.

"What about Lester?" Alex asked.

"I want you to take him," Mother Goose said. "I love him like he hatched from an egg I laid myself, but I drive him crazy. I already talked to him and he agrees it's for the best. You'll be good for each other."

"I can't say I'm happy about this," Alex said. "But I *am* happy for *you*."

"Thanks, kiddo," Mother Goose said. "I'm happy, too. *Very happy*."

Alex held her hand and smiled. Merlin entered the cottage and kissed Mother Goose's cheek, but he was alone.

"Good morning, ladies!" he said.

"Where's Arthur?" Alex asked.

Merlin had a seat and let out a heavy sigh. "Arthur has asked me to send you his best wishes, but he won't be joining us this morning. He said saying good-bye would be too difficult."

"Oh...," Alex said quietly. It broke her heart a little knowing she wouldn't get a proper good-bye, but she couldn't blame him. "Well, in that case, I should finish the potion and go home."

Alex placed the potion in the center of the table. She pointed to it and a bright flash of light shot out of the tip of her finger and into the cauldron. The potion bubbled for a few moments and turned blue—the same shade as the bottle her uncle had stolen. The Portal Potion was finally finished.

"Here, put the potion in this," Mother Goose said, and handed Alex the flask she kept in her bonnet. "It'll be something to remember me by."

Alex carefully transferred the potion into the flask. She put the page from *The Wonderful Wizard of Oz* on the floor and poured three drops of the potion on it. The page lit up like a spotlight and a beam of light shined toward the ceiling.

Alex gave Merlin and Mother Goose a hug good-bye. It was difficult letting her go.

"This is it," Alex said. "Oz, here I come."

She edged toward the beam but stopped just before she took a step inside. She was paralyzed.

"What's wrong, Alex?" Mother Goose asked. "Is there something wrong with the potion?"

"No, there's something wrong with *me*," Alex said. "I can't leave without saying good-bye to Arthur. I've got to find him!"

Before Mother Goose or Merlin could respond, Alex dashed out of the cottage and headed into the woods. As if her heart were a magnet being pulled to his, she ran through the trees knowing exactly where to find him. She stepped into the clearing he took her to the day they met and Alex found Arthur sitting by the sword in the stone.

Arthur was shocked to see her; he expected she would be gone by now. His face lit up once he saw her and they stared at each other in silence while Alex caught her breath.

"You're still here," Arthur said.

"Did you really think I would leave without saying good-bye?" Alex said.

Arthur shrugged. "I was hoping if I didn't say it, it wouldn't be true."

"I wish it weren't," Alex said. "Believe me."

Arthur got to his feet and stood as close to her as he could without touching. "Let me go with you," he said desperately.

"Arthur, you know I can't," Alex said. "We both have our separate destinies to live. The people of this country need you. I'm not your future, England is."

"If you believe that, then why did you find me here?" Arthur asked. "Why not just leave and forget about me?"

"I couldn't leave without seeing your face again."

Arthur smiled. "Because you know in your heart we belong together."

"No, because I know in my heart you are meant to be king and I will only distract you," she said. "If you won't say good-bye, then I will. I don't want you spending your life waiting for me to return. You're meant to do great things, and I won't keep you from them."

"I don't think I am," he said quietly. "I'll be worthless without you."

"But you won't be without me," Alex said. "I'll be reading every page of your story and I'll be with you every step of the way. When you pull the sword from the stone, when you establish Camelot, when you create the Round Table, when you search for the Holy Grail—I'll be there and I'll know you're doing it all *for me*."

"But what if we're in *your* story?" Arthur asked. "Perhaps this is all just a chapter in a book about you. Maybe someone is reading it right now in a world far away, and they know you're making a mistake. You said yourself that there are versions of me—so let *this* version be with you. Let another Arthur somewhere else fulfill the legend."

"But I'll always feel like I'm doing something wrong," Alex said. "Maybe after you've completed your story and I've completed mine, we can have a happy ending. But that's several chapters ahead of us. *Good-bye*, Arthur—I'll always treasure our time together."

Alex turned away from him, but he quickly grabbed her hand.

"I know I'm more than just a story to you," Arthur said. "And I have proof—the lock and key I gave you for the potion was from *my* door. It wouldn't work unless you cared about me."

Alex didn't know what to say, so she said nothing. She pulled her hand out of his and left the clearing. As Alex walked away, she realized leaving Arthur was the hardest thing she would ever have to do. It was worse than defeating the Enchantress, battling the Grande Armée, and chasing her uncle through literary dimensions—this time Alex was fighting her heart.

Conner's final days in Nottingham were utterly exhausting. He and the Merry Men, with the help of the Tin Woodman and Peter, searched every corner of Sherwood Forest for someone of magical capability. Their candidates were scarce and very much like the Witch of Papplenick: They all proved to be misunderstood or just total frauds.

After they'd searched for two long weeks, the Portal Potion had soaked up all the moonlight it required. It just needed the one final ingredient to be complete. Everything depended on Conner now. Only *he* could successfully activate the potion by accessing the magic within himself—he just wished he knew how to do it.

Little John and Peter brought the potion down from the treetops and set it in the middle of camp. Conner nervously paced in front of it and bit his nails—he had no idea how he was going to pull it off. All the men gathered around and watched him think it over.

"Well, are you going to do it?" the Tin Woodman asked.

"Does it look like I have a choice?" Conner said.

"How are you going to do it?" Peter asked.

"That's what I'm trying to figure out!" he snapped.

"THE SORCERER IS FRUSTRATED," Robin Hood announced.

"Can you guys all look away for a second?" Conner asked. "I can't concentrate when I'm being watched."

The men did as he requested, but still glanced over their shoulders now and then when he wasn't looking—they didn't want to miss anything.

Conner closed his eyes and tried to find the magic within, but he didn't know where to look. His sister always said magic was in her heart—but girls usually referred to their hearts when they talked about everything. Maybe Conner's magic existed in his head or his stomach? His left knee hurt a little today—was *that* where his magic was?

What was magic supposed to feel like, anyway? Was it a physical or an emotional sensation? Was it like a parasite crawling inside of him, or like the sadness that crept up whenever he saw a dog die in a movie?

Everything always came easily to Alex, and magic was

no exception. He wished it were like telling a joke or writing a story—those were things Conner was good at.

"Wait, maybe that's it," he said to himself. "Maybe magic is different for everyone. Maybe it's what you *want* it to be—I mean, it is *magic* after all."

Conner tried summoning his magic like he summoned his creativity. It started in his *imagination*, not his heart. He visualized magic as an idea for a new story. He let it excite him, inspire him, and flow through his body until it was ready to be expressed.

"Okay, here goes nothing," he said. "I apologize if this ends horribly."

The Merry Men, the Tin Woodman, and Peter all braced themselves as Conner took a deep breath and pointed his finger at the potion. . . .

CHAPTER TWENTY-NINE

ANOTHER MOON,
ANOTHER MIDNIGHT

Another full moon shined on the Dwarf Forests, and at midnight, the witches of the fairy-tale world assembled at Dead Man's Creek on the wreckage of their former headquarters. Gargoylia led the gathering from the tallest pile of debris.

"The gods have smiled upon us, sisters," Gargoylia preached. "When we last met, we feared a witch hunt was in our future—but that fear can now be put to rest. Recently, great forces have descended through the kingdoms, stripping power from the hands of man and the fairies. Those who would have hunted us are now being hunted themselves!"

Rat Mary was among a small group who hadn't heard the news. "What kind of forces do you speak of?"

Witches throughout the crowd were eager to share what they witnessed.

"I *sssaw* a fleet of *sssoldiersss* attack the *Eassstern* Kingdom," Serpentina hissed. "They were tall and *sssquare*—bore *numbersss* and *sssymbolsss* on their armor!"

"The Corner Kingdom was pillaged by a flock of winged monkeys!" Tarantulene said.

"An army of men and women in yellow armor charged into the Charming Kingdom!" Charcoaline announced.

"Crows, wolves, and bees have taken over the Elf Empire," Arboris said. "And I've heard rumors of a flying ship that is holding the Northern Kingdom hostage!"

"Don't you see, sisters, it is the dawning of a new era!" Gargoylia said. "We have nothing to fear anymore—*the age of man and fairy is over!*"

The witches cheered, cackled, growled, and hissed in celebration—but their rejoicing was cut short.

"If you believe that, then you are fools!" said a voice from the forest.

The witches looked around the woods but didn't see who it came from.

"Look! The water is changing!" Rat Mary said, and pointed to the creek.

The creek's current started flowing in the opposite direction and Morina drifted in on a boat magically steering itself. Once the boat was docked, Morina stepped out and joined the gathering.

None of the witches had seen her in a long while and they were instantly intimidated by her presence. The witches parted out of her way as she climbed up the pile of wreckage to where Gargoylia was standing. A large bag containing a small body levitated out of the boat and floated behind her as she went—the witches couldn't tell if the body was unconscious or dead.

"Why are you here, Morina?" Gargoylia said with a scathing look. "You haven't been to a gathering in years."

"I've never been impressed with the leadership," Morina said. "Speaking of which, I think it's time for a change— and I believe I'm the witch for the job."

Gargoylia was outraged. The other witches could tell things were about to get ugly.

"How dare you!" Gargoylia yelled. "I've faithfully led this congregation for years! I will not be asked to step aside—especially by the likes of you!"

"No one *asked* you anything," Morina said.

She raised a hand toward Gargoylia and the witch suddenly went as stiff as a board. Her stone skin cracked and chipped away until Gargoylia crumbled into nothing but a pile of rocks on the ground. The witches screamed and gasped in horror. It was the quickest way for Morina to gain the gathering's attention and respect.

"The enemy of our enemy is not always our friend," Morina told the witches. "These *forces* that have entered our world are led by the Masked Man—the same man you all rejected during your last gathering. Now he has recruited an unstoppable army without your help, and he will not forget the way you discarded him—he is ruthless and can hold a grudge for decades. Once he has wiped the kingdoms clean of the royal families and the fairies, it'll be *our* extermination he calls for next—and none of us will survive it."

The witches looked around nervously at one another. The only thing they were more afraid of than Morina was what she predicted.

"Then what can we do? Go into hiding?" Charcoaline asked.

Morina shook her head. "The answer is not to cower, but to *relocate*. I am tired of being a secondary race, forced to live from shadow to shadow, while others who outnumber us dictate and limit our way of life! It's time to move to a place where we can be the supreme species! It's time for our kind to travel into *the Otherworld!*"

"The Otherworld?" Rat Mary asked. "But that's just a legend."

"No, my sisters," Morina said. "The Otherworld is very real. I have just returned from it and saw it with my own eyes. There are plenty of places for us to prosper, billions of people to rule over, and no one to stop us."

The idea of such a world intrigued the witches—but they had their doubts.

"How do we get to the Otherworld?" Serpentina asked.

"There are portals hidden all over the world left by the late Fairy Godmother," Morina said. "I found one in the woods of the Eastern Kingdom that the Grande Armée entered from, but given the white magic the Fairy Godmother used to create it, the portal weakened and exhausted me; I doubt many of *you* would survive it. But do not fear, for an easier route is coming! I foresaw in my crystal ball that the worlds are about to collide, and when they do, a grand doorway will form that will offer us easy access to the Otherworld."

"But what about the Masked Man?" Arboris asked. "Wouldn't he follow us and conquer the Otherworld for himself?"

"Luckily, I have planned for that," Morina said.

The floating body fell to the ground and she removed the bag from it in one swift pull. It was a sleeping little boy with dark hair, pale skin, and rosy cheeks—*Emmerich Himmelsbach*.

"Behold, *the Masked Man's son*," Morina boasted. "Years ago, this child was hidden from his father before he even knew of the boy's existence. If the Masked Man or his army should ever pose a threat to us, the child will be the perfect leverage to keep him at bay! Our salvation is upon us!"

Before the witches had a chance to question her further, the air was filled with a sudden chill coming from the north and a salty breeze coming from the south. It caught them off guard and they searched the trees for a sign of what was causing it.

The witches watched in amazement as a strong frost traveled down the creek from the north and froze the water as it blew in. From the south, a strong tidal wave of murky ocean water flowed up the creek and flooded the bank. The frost and the wave met directly where the tavern used to stand.

From the north, two enormous polar bears pulled an ice sleigh down the frozen creek. They transported a tall woman with pale frostbitten skin. She wore a large fluffy white coat, a snowflake crown, and a cloth wrapped around her eyes.

From the south, four fins skimmed the creek's surface as a school of sharks swam through the water. An elaborate sled made of several types of coral surfaced behind the sharks. The creature aboard had scaly turquoise skin and seaweed hair. It had six legs and large claws, like the bottom half of the creature was a crustacean.

The legendary Snow Queen and infamous Sea Witch had arrived in style, and the witches were shocked to see them in person.

They stepped out of the creek and walked up the wreckage to where Morina stood. The Snow Queen was blind and used a long icicle to guide her, not caring whom she unintentionally struck with it. The Sea Witch stroked a cuttlefish resting in her arms and glared at the other women around the creek.

Morina may have intimidated the other witches, but they were terrified to be in the presence of the Snow Queen and Sea Witch. They bowed as they passed—even Morina gave a shallow nod.

"Your Excellences, what brings you to the woods tonight?" Morina asked with a quiver in her voice.

"You are not the first witch to see the Otherworld as a potential home, Morina," the Snow Queen growled in her raspy voice. "It has been a passion project of the Sea Witch and me for hundreds of years—but despite the approaching doorway, crossing over will not be as easy as you think."

"You underestimate the Otherworld," the Sea Witch hissed. "It is a world without magic, but a world that possesses technology far beyond your comprehension. They will use it against us the moment we try claiming their home as ours."

Morina didn't appreciate being publicly discredited.

"Have you come out of seclusion just to prove me wrong, or is there a way we can overcome the Otherworld's defenses?" she asked in a spiteful tone that made the other witches nervous.

Snide smiles grew across the Snow Queen's and the Sea Witch's faces.

"We must create a *weapon*," the Snow Queen said.

"Something the Otherworld won't stand a chance against," the Sea Witch hissed.

"What kind of weapon?" Morina asked.

"Not *what*, but *who*," the Snow Queen said. "Years ago,

the Sea Witch and I almost succeeded in creating it. We cursed a very powerful fairy known as Ezmia, the late Fairy Godmother's former apprentice. The curse disturbed her emotions, causing her pain to intensify a thousand times stronger than anything else she felt. Tortured by heartbreak and overwhelmed with despair, she eventually became *the Enchantress* and wreaked havoc on the kingdoms."

"We put the idea of conquering *both* worlds into her head, and she spent the majority of her life attempting to," the Sea Witch hissed. "However, she was defeated by a fairy known as Alex Bailey, the late Fairy Godmother's granddaughter. Interestingly, Alex is a child of both worlds, and therefore has potential to be far more powerful than the Enchantress ever was. So the Snow Queen and I have set our sights on *her*."

"We put the same curse we cast on Ezmia on Alex," the Snow Queen said. "We watched it take hold of her just as it did Ezmia. As the young fairy searched the kingdoms for the Masked Man, she was consumed by anger, and lost control of her powers. We learned we were right—she was much more powerful than Ezmia, perhaps more powerful than any fairy who has ever lived. But with that power comes great strength, and the curse eventually faded."

"If she is too powerful for the curse, then how are we supposed to use her to vanquish the Otherworld?" Morina asked.

The Snow Queen and the Sea Witch turned away from Morina and faced all the witches at the gathering.

"The more witches who participate, the more powerful the curse becomes," the Sea Witch said. "By combining our magic, we can cast a curse on Alex Bailey so powerful, she'll never recover from it!"

"Together, we can transform the young fairy into the ultimate weapon," the Snow Queen said. *"She'll destroy the defenses of her former home, and the Otherworld will be ours!"*

Chapter Thirty

A WORLD AT STAKE

The words from the loose page spun through the air and created the world of *The Wonderful Wizard of Oz* around Alex and Lester. She saw the words *Emerald City* fly into the distance, and before the city was even fully formed, Alex hopped onto Lester's back and they flew into the west, all the while praying her friends would still be at the Wicked Witch's castle.

The words continued to construct the Winkie Country below them as they headed to the Wicked Witch of the West's castle. Alex and Lester circled the castle as it was generated from the ground up. They landed on the balcony just outside the throne room and Alex blasted the glass doors open with a bright flash.

"Goldilocks? Jack? Blubo?" Alex called, but all she heard was the echo of her own voice.

The throne room was completely deserted. Alex's anxiety rose, and she feared the worst. What if her uncle had traveled back through the stories and separated her friends, too? They may never find them. And without a book to travel home through, Alex may be stuck in Oz for a very long time.

A soft breeze blew from the empty room behind her. She turned around and saw a bright golden piece of paper appear out of thin air. The paper landed on the ground and a bright beam of light shined out of it. Seven silhouettes of all shapes and sizes stepped out of the beam.

The silhouettes vibrated like static on a broken television. Like the words of a recently entered story, the figures slowly gained color and texture, until Alex recognized one.

"CONNER!" Alex screamed.

"ALEX!" Conner yelled.

The twins were overjoyed to see each other. Alex ran across the throne room and leaped into his arms. They shared a massive hug until Conner couldn't hold her up any longer.

"I was afraid I would never see you again!" Alex said. She recognized the other silhouettes as they became solid. "Mr. Woodman! Peter! I'm so glad you're all right! Wait— who are *they*?"

Conner was just as surprised to see the Merry Men had traveled into the castle behind him.

"Guys, what are you doing here?" he asked.

"WE COULDN'T LET OUR SORCERER TRAVEL INTO A STRANGE WORLD WITHOUT OUR PROTECTION!" Robin Hood said. "THE MERRY MEN WILL STAND BY YOUR SIDE UNTIL THE END!"

"Whatever." Conner sighed—he didn't have the patience to argue. "Alex, allow me to introduce you to Robin Hood and the Merry Men of Sherwood Forest."

Alex couldn't believe the historic outlaws were standing in front of her. She was a little starstruck.

"*The* Robin Hood?" she asked. "It's so nice to meet you. I've read all about you!"

"THE PLEASURE IS ALL MINE, MY LADY!" Robin Hood said, and kissed her hand. "ANY SISTER OF THE SORCERER IS A SISTER OF MINE!"

"*He's so loud,*" Alex whispered to her brother. "*Why does he call you sorcerer?*"

"It's a long story, but I convinced them I'm a sorcerer," Conner said.

"They aren't the only ones he convinced," the Tin Woodman said with a grin. "You should be very proud of your brother, Alex! He activated the Portal Potion all by himself!"

"You did?" Alex said with an excited smile. "Conner, that's incredible! I've always told you there was magic somewhere inside you!"

Conner shrugged bashfully. "It wasn't that big of a deal. The hardest part was figuring out how to channel it."

Peter animatedly flew into the air. "You should have seen it, Alex! First Conner pointed at the potion and BOOM! *A spark blasted out of his finger!* Then the potion was like WHOOSH! *Ready when you are, Captain!* Then we poured it over the page and it was like BAAM! *Let there be light!*"

Alex was so proud of her brother, she almost burst with pride. "As soon as I found the page I knew you'd find yours and create the potion, too."

"Great minds think alike," Conner said. "Well, I spent two weeks in Nottingham—where did our jerk of an uncle send you guys?"

"He sent us into *King Arthur*!" Alex said. "Conner, I met Merlin and Arthur! They helped me create the Portal Potion!"

"No way!" Conner said, but after his trip he didn't know why he was so surprised. "Where is Mother Goose?"

There was no way Alex could gently break the news to him, so she just came right out and said it. "She's decided to stay with Merlin. They sort of had a *thing*."

Conner looked back and forth between Alex and Lester in disbelief. Lester nodded, confirming it for him.

"Well, I didn't see that one coming," Conner said. "So is she gone for good?"

"I can fill you in on all the details later," Alex said. "Right now we've got to find Goldilocks and Jack—I don't think they're in the castle anymore."

"Alex, we've been gone for two weeks," he said. "I bet they traveled back into the fairy-tale world. Let's find the book."

They searched the throne room and Conner found the copy of *The Wonderful Wizard of Oz* placed neatly on the throne.

"They must have left this here in case we came back," Conner said. "Our uncle would have destroyed it like the books he sent us into."

"There's only one way to find out," Alex said.

The twins opened the book together and a strong beam of light emitted from it. The others gathered around them.

"Be careful, guys," Conner told them. "There's no way of telling what might be waiting on the other side of this."

One by one, the twins, the Merry Men, Lester, the Tin Woodman, and Peter stepped into the beam of light. As they traveled back into the fairy-tale world, Oz was stripped away word by word, description by description. The witch's castle peeled away and a cave was uncovered— the same cave their journey started from.

They heard several voices before they saw anyone. As the cave was revealed, the twins could see it was much more occupied than when they had left.

Jack and Goldilocks were sitting together on one side of the cave with Blubo perched on Jack's shoulder. The Lost Boys played with rocks in the back of the cave, while Red cradled an infant. She looked terrible and stared off into space.

It was late and the twins noticed campfires just outside the entrance of the cave. They saw soldiers from the Northern Kingdom and the Charming Kingdom sitting around them. Sir Grant and Sir Lampton were among them. Each face was longer than the next and they were all badly banged up.

Hagetta tended to the soldiers, setting their injuries ablaze with flames of her healing fire.

The cave was filled with so much despair, it could have been cut with a knife. Everyone looked as if they had been through their own versions of hell.

Finally, the twins and the others became visible to the people in the cave, officially returning from Oz. Everyone was ecstatic to see them, as if they had come back from the dead. Their friends and the soldiers got to their feet and ran to greet them.

"Alex! Conner! Thank God you're alive!" Goldilocks said, and embraced the twins. Her eyes were filled with tears, but Goldilocks wasn't hormonal, she was genuinely relieved.

Upon first glance at the soldiers, the Merry Men's knee-jerk reaction was to reach for their weapons.

"Don't worry, guys," Conner said. "We're all friends in this cave."

"PETER!" The Lost Boys cheered and jumped up and down when they saw him. Peter flew across the cave and let them form a ceremonious dog pile on top of him.

"Wait a second, where's Slightly?" Peter asked.

The Lost Boys pointed to the infant in Red's arms and filled him in on what had happened. Red was the only one who didn't greet the twins. She stayed seated and continued staring off—it was like she was in a trance.

"What happened to Red?" Conner asked.

"She tried rescuing Froggy from Morina and discovered the witch had imprisoned him in a magic mirror," Goldilocks said.

The twins gasped and covered their mouths.

"Unfortunately, that's the least of our worries," Jack said. "Your uncle and the army have arrived."

"That's what we were afraid of," Conner said.

"Jack, tell us everything you know," Alex said.

Jack told the twins how he and Goldilocks returned to the fairy-tale world after a week of waiting for them in the castle. Around the same time, their uncle entered the world and began attacking the kingdoms. From what they knew, the army split up and each kingdom was attacked at the same time.

"We never saw it coming," Sir Grant recalled. "An enormous ship flew down from the clouds in the middle of the night and opened fire on the palace. There was barely anything left after the cannons were stopped. Pirates kidnapped King Chandler and Queen Snow White."

"The Charming Kingdom was stormed by an army of men and women in yellow armor," Sir Lampton said.

"Winkies," the Tin Woodman said fearfully.

"Heaven knows what they did with the royal family,"

Lampton said. "My men and I barely made it out of the kingdom alive. We found Sir Grant and his men in the Dwarf Forests and Jack found us there. We've been hiding out in this cave ever since."

The twins were taking deep breaths so they wouldn't become sick.

"What about the other kingdoms?" Conner asked.

"We assume the same has happened to them, but we haven't made contact," Jack said.

"And the fairies?" Alex asked.

"No one has heard from them, either, but it's possible they were hit first," Goldilocks said. "The first thing your uncle did when he arrived was free the prisoners from Pinocchio Prison—all the soldiers from the Grande Armée and the criminals that aided them are once again under his command."

Alex and Conner exchanged horrified looks—their biggest nightmare had become a reality.

"We need to get to the Fairy Kingdom and find the council," Alex said. "Conner and I will leave straightaway. Everyone needs to stay in the cave until they hear from us."

"You can't leave," Lampton said. "The Masked Man's army is everywhere—even the skies. There's no way you'll go undetected, even if you fly that bird. "

The twins glanced at Lester and he gulped.

"We won't be traveling by land or sky," Alex said. "I'll transport us there magically."

"Are you sure about that?" Conner asked. "Last time I suggested that, you had hesitations."

"We don't have a choice," Alex said. "Come on, let's not waste any more time."

The twins embraced and Alex counted to three. They disappeared from the cave with a bright flash. Alex transported herself and her brother somewhere outside, but they weren't exactly sure where. The air was filled with smoke and the ground was littered in debris.

"Conner, look!" Alex gasped and pointed into the distance. "It's the Fairy Palace!"

The Fairy Palace was almost unrecognizable. Its trademark glow had faded away and most of it had been blown to smithereens. The gardens had been destroyed, too, and were covered in an ashy coat of dust. The statue that had been erected in their grandmother's memory lay in pieces on the ground.

Alex and Conner both became teary-eyed at the sight. There was no sign of life anywhere—they hoped the fairies had fled in time to save themselves. But if the council had been inside the palace during the attack, it wasn't likely.

"The Hall of Dreams . . . Grandma's chambers . . . it's all gone," Alex cried.

"Let's see if we can find anything or anyone inside," Conner said.

They walked across the dusty earth and quietly climbed into the palace ruins. Everything was so damaged, they couldn't tell what anything was anymore. The only room they could identify was the grand hall, and that was just because of its size.

As soon as Conner and Alex entered the hall, seven figures came into view, and the twins quickly dived behind a fallen pillar. The air was still hazy from the attack and they couldn't see who or what the figures were.

"Alex, I don't think they're moving," Conner said.

"You're right, they're not people, they're *statues*," she said. "That's odd, there weren't statues in the grand hall before."

The twins walked deeper into the hall to have a closer look. The statues looked frightened and were awkwardly positioned as if they were trying to run from something. The longer the twins stared at the scared faces of the statues, the more familiar they became.

"Oh my God," Conner said. "Alex, these aren't statues—*it's the council! They've been turned into stone!*"

Emerelda, Xanthous, Skylene, Tangerina, Rosette, Violetta, and Coral were hard to identify now that they were all the same color stone, but Conner was right. It was too much for Alex to bear. She ran to the side of the room and became sick.

"What could have done this?" she asked.

"I don't know," Conner said, and rubbed her back.

"Alex? Conner?" said a little voice somewhere in the palace.

The twins saw something small hovering near a

windowsill on the other side of the hall, and were relieved to see it was only Trix. She was covered in dust and her wings were mangled, making it difficult to fly.

"Trix, I'm so happy to see you!" Alex said.

"What happened here?" Conner asked.

"The palace was attacked by a flying ship," she said.

"What turned the council into stone?" Alex asked.

"A horrible monster!" Trix said, and trembled at the thought of it.

"What kind of monster?" Conner asked.

"I didn't see it," Trix said. "I was so scared, I closed my eyes and hid, but Noodle and Merkle weren't so lucky."

Trix gestured to the windowsill and the twins saw that her friends had been turned to stone, too. Like the council, they also looked terrified and were positioned like it happened while they were trying to escape.

"Trix, what happened to the monster?" Conner asked.

"It left with the pirate ship." Trix sniffled.

"And what happened to all the other fairies?" Alex asked.

"Some hid in the forest, but I'm not sure what happened to the others," she said.

"Trix, I want you to hide in the forest, too," Alex instructed. "Get away from here—find someplace to stay until it's safe again. We're going to figure something out."

Trix nodded and flew off as fast as her wings could carry her.

"Conner, I think our uncle has recruited creatures

beyond the realms of literature," Alex said as she glanced around at the statues. "This looks like something from *mythology*. I don't know how we're going to stop him."

Alex took a seat on the windowsill while Conner paced in front of her. They spent an hour in total silence as they tried to think of ways to save the fairy-tale world. Conner suddenly stopped in his tracks and looked up toward one of the only remaining towers of the palace.

"The south tower survived the attack," he said to himself.

His eyes suddenly lit up and Alex knew an idea was forming in his head.

"What are you thinking?" she asked.

"I know how we can stop him," he said excitedly.

"How?"

"By forming an army of our own," Conner said. "Come on—follow me!"

Before she could question him further, Conner raced through the wrecked palace and found the stairs leading to the south tower. He sprinted up the steps and Alex chased after him. They entered a circular room at the top of the tower. It was covered in dust and cobwebs, and an empty archway stood in the middle of the room.

Conner searched the walls with his hands, feeling around for something.

"How are we supposed to form an army?" Alex asked.

"Exactly how our uncle did it," he said. "We'll travel into stories and recruit characters than can help us—and

I know exactly which ones we'll ask! Do you still have the Portal Potion on you?"

Alex retrieved the flask she had tucked into her waistband. "Yes, but—"

"Great!" Conner said. "We have to make a stop in the Otherworld first. I just need to find the—*oh, I found it!*"

He pulled a lever on the side of the wall and a blue curtain magically appeared in the archway. Alex could see a world of light behind it—the world she saw every time she traveled between the fairy-tale world and the Otherworld.

"Yes!" Conner said. "The portal still works! *Let's go!*"

"I'm confused—why do we have to travel into the Otherworld?" Alex asked.

"Because that's where the stories are," he said.

"Which stories are you talking about?"

Conner paused just as he was about to step through the curtain.

"Mine," he said.

ACKNOWLEDGMENTS

A big thank you to Rob Weisbach, Alla Plotkin, Rachel Karten, Derek Kroeger, Glenn Rigberg, Lorrie Bartlett, Meredith Wechter, Joanne Wiles, Meredith Fine, Christian Hodell, Marcus Colen, Jerry Maybrook, Joseph Roberto, and Heather Manzutto. Everyone at Little, Brown, especially Alvina Ling, Bethany Strout, Melanie Chang, Nikki Garcia, Megan Tingley, and Andrew Smith.

All my friends and family: Will, Ashley, Pam, Jamie, Fortune, June, Jen, Melissa, Babs, Char, Charles, Dot, and Bridgette, Romy and Stephen, Rick and Gale, Frank and Jo, Roberto, Gloria, Jannel, Kelly, Jenny, McCoy, Maureen, Kevin, Tracey, Lexi, Lita, Paris … the list goes on! I couldn't do it without your support!

I'd like to give a very special thanks to the incredible Brandon Dorman for bringing my stories to life. Four books later, your artwork continues to amaze me.

Also, to the main inspiration behind Mother Goose, my dear friend Polly Bergen. Thank you for sharing your stories and your humor, and leaving such an impact on me. I will miss you greatly.

CHAPTER SEVEN

THE CAPTAIN AND HER CREW

I packed you both a turkey sandwich, chips, yogurt, a banana, two bottles of water, and a cookie," Charlotte said. "There's also a sweatshirt, a flashlight, a Swiss army knife, a first-aid kit, matches, and a compass."

The twins' mother handed them both a backpack full of the items she'd packed. Alex and Conner appreciated the gesture, but traveling into a fictitious dimension was very different from going on a camping trip.

"Thanks, Mom," Alex said. "You didn't have to do that."

"Yeah, this isn't our first rodeo," Conner said and looked through his backpack. *"Oh cool, chocolate chip! Thanks!"*

"It's just a few things—I'll feel better knowing you have them," Charlotte said. "So where's your first stop? Any idea how long you'll be gone for?"

Alex turned to Conner and was just as curious as their mother. For the first time in their lives, she was leaving all the planning to her brother. She had offered to help a number of times, but Conner was very set on doing everything himself. Not insisting was a gamble on Alex's part, but he seemed very confident he had everything taken care of.

"First up is my short story 'Starboardia,'" Conner said excitedly. "It's a pirate adventure set in the Caribbean Sea around the early seventeen hundreds. The story's about Captain Auburn Sally and her all-female crew as they search desert islands for buried treasure."

Charlotte hid her concern behind a smile. "Sounds *progressive*," she said.

"Don't worry—we'll be fine," Conner said. "Auburn Sally is based on Goldilocks. We'll find her ship, tell her the situation, and bring her and her crew back to the house. It'll be a piece of cake."

"If you say so," Charlotte said, unconvinced.

"Go get 'em," Bob said and patted him on the back.

Conner had organized his writing neatly in a binder with tabs separating the short stories. He opened the binder to the first page of "Starboardia" and set it on the living room floor.

"Are you sure there isn't anything we need before we go?" Alex asked one final time. "There's nothing you're overlooking or forgetting about?"

"Trust me. I've got everything under control," he said. "If there's one thing I know inside and out, it's my short stories. I've actually been really looking forward to this. I bet my characters will be excited to meet me!"

Traveling into the short stories had been all Conner could think about since he'd first had the idea. Naturally, the circumstances to warrant the trip were terrible, but he still felt like the luckiest author in the world. Who else got to visit the worlds and meet the people that existed only in their imaginations? Conner often fantasized about seeing a film or a play based on his writing one day, but *this* would be much better than that. It wouldn't be *someone else's* interpretation or adaptation of his words; everything would be purely as he'd envisioned it.

Conner removed Mother Goose's flask, which contained the Portal Potion, from his back pocket. He poured a couple of drops on the binder and then stored the flask safely in his backpack. The pages illuminated like a powerful spotlight, shining a bright beam of light toward the ceiling.

"Here we go!" Conner said. "Wish us luck!"

"Good luck!" Bob said. "We'll be here when you get back."

"Make good choices!" Charlotte said. "There's also some sunscreen in your bags if it's sunny out!"

Alex and Conner strapped on their backpacks, stepped into the beam of light, and disappeared from the house.

Just like it had when they traveled into *The Wonderful Wizard of Oz*, *Peter Pan*, and *Alice's Adventures in Wonderland*, the Portal Potion first took them into an endless space with nothing but words. Rather than printed text, words were *written* all around them, as if there were hundreds of invisible pencils moving through the air. Each word was in Conner's messy handwriting.

"Awesome!" Conner said. "It's like we've stepped inside my brain!"

"You've got to work on your penmanship," Alex noted.

The handwritten words stretched into shapes, then gained color and texture, and finally transformed into the objects they described. Conner watched in awe as the world of his first short story came to life around him. Alex was excited, too, until she saw the words *ocean waves* stretching below their feet.

"Hey, Conner?" she said. "Should we be worried about—"

Before she could finish her sentence, the twins fell into an ocean that formed under their feet. Strong waves crashed over them, pushing them farther and farther below the water. The waves were difficult to swim against, but they kicked their way to the surface and spit out mouthfuls of salty water. Conner saw his binder of short stories floating in the water nearby and retrieved it before the waves carried it away.

Alex angrily splashed water in her brother's face. *"Why didn't you say we needed a boat?"* she asked.

"Sorry!" Conner said. "I forgot the first thing I described was the ocean!"

By now the handwritten words had finished forming the world of "Starboardia" around them. They were bobbing up and down in the middle of the Caribbean Sea. The air was so misty they could barely see each other, let alone any land or ships in the distance. Alex snapped her fingers and a small wooden rowboat appeared in front of them.

The twins climbed aboard and caught their breath. Conner put the binder in his backpack, where it would be safe. If anything happened to it, they would have no way back home.

"Well, *that* was a rough start," Alex said. "What's the *second* thing you described?"

"The *Dolly Llama*," Conner said.

"The Dolly Llama?"

"It's the name of Auburn Sally's ship," he said. "Don't judge me, I thought it was a funny name for a ship. We should see it any minute now."

A towering shadow appeared in the mist, and something very large headed their way. The shadow grew larger and darker and formed detail as it got closer. Finally, the twins saw that it was a large pirate ship sailing straight toward their rowboat with no sign of slowing down. It was going to plow right into them!

"Abandon boat!" Conner yelled.

The twins dived into the water just as the ship smashed into their rowboat, crushing it into pieces. Once again, Alex and Conner were caught under the vicious waves. They swam to the surface and were sloshed around the choppy waves as the pirate ship sailed right past them.

"Ahoy!" Conner yelled up at the ship. *"Twins overboard! Help us!"*

A few seconds later, a rope ladder was rolled off the ship, and it landed in the water next to the twins. They grabbed it and climbed aboard. The twins pulled themselves over the ship's railing and collapsed on the lower deck. They were drenched and coughing up seawater.

Alex looked up and saw a large black flag flying above the ship with the skull of a llama on it.

"This must be the *Dolly Llama*," Alex said. She pointed out the flag to Conner, and a giant smile grew on his face. He leaped to his feet and helped his sister to hers. The flag was the first proof he had that they were in his short story.

"We made it!" he exclaimed. "Alex, we're in 'Starboardia'!"

His excitement was cut short when they heard footsteps nearby. A dozen female pirates surrounded Alex and Conner, and they didn't look friendly. The pirates pointed their swords and rifles at the twins and cautiously circled them.

"Well, well, well," said a woman with an eye patch. "Look what we have here."

"What are you two scallywags doing in the middle of the sea?" asked a woman with enormous lips. "Too *young* to be in the navy, too *fair* to be pirates."

Conner almost stepped on a pirate behind him and jumped. Having no legs, the pirate walked on her hands and held a dagger with her teeth.

"My guess is they were *stowaways*!" the legless pirate said. "I'm surprised the sharks didn't find them first!"

Conner couldn't believe his characters were living and breathing before his eyes. The women were just as rough, dirty, and sunburned as he had imagined them. He grinned from ear to ear and jumped up and down.

"I'm so happy to see you guys!" he said.

The pirates tilted their heads at him like confused puppies. No one had ever been *excited* to see them before.

"Guys, it's *me*!" Conner said. "I'm Conner Bailey!"

The pirates raised their eyebrows and scratched their heads—should they know who he was?

"Who?" asked a pirate with a round, flat face.

"Oh, come on." Conner laughed. "I'm the *author*!"

"Author of *what*?" asked a pirate with bare feet.

"Of *this story*," he said. "I created this ocean, I created this ship, and I created all of you. Do you really not recognize me?"

Conner thought for sure it would have clicked by now, but the pirates still stared at him awkwardly, just as perplexed as before.

"He's been marooned for too long—the boy's gone mad," said a pirate with a peg leg, and the other pirates nodded in agreement.

Conner was getting frustrated. "I'm not crazy," he said.

"Look, where is Auburn Sally? Let me talk to her. I'm sure she'll straighten this whole thing out. This is my own fault—I should have written you guys to be smarter."

The pirates stopped looking puzzled and began staring daggers at him. Alex covered her face and let out a sigh—this wasn't going to be as easy as her brother thought.

"*Oooooh, Captain*," the pirate with the eye patch called. "There's someone down here who'd like to have a word with you!"

Suddenly, a woman did a backflip off the upper deck and landed directly in front of the twins. She wore a large black hat, a big brown coat, and tall boots and had a sword and pistol attached to her thick belt. Alex knew this was Auburn Sally from the minute she laid eyes on her. If her acrobatics weren't enough to give it away, the captain looked exactly like Goldilocks. The only difference in their features was the captain's long locks of auburn hair.

"*Sally!*" Conner said like he was seeing an old friend—because, technically, he was. He stepped toward the captain to give her a hug, but Auburn Sally quickly drew her pistol and aimed it at his head.

"Am I supposed to know you, *boy*?" Auburn Sally asked.

Conner was shocked by the treatment he was receiving from his own characters. He had expected a warm and gracious welcome, but instead the heroine of his story was holding a gun to his head. Without him none of them would even exist! He wondered if this was what an underappreciated parent felt like.

He held his hands up and backed away from the pistol. "Okay, time out!" he said. "Everyone just calm down and let me explain! My name is Conner Bailey, and this is my sister, Alex. I know this is hard to believe, but I'm your *creator*! We are living in a short story I wrote for my eighth-grade English class!"

Auburn Sally looked at him with more perplexity than all of her crew added together. "He's got yellow fever," she said. "Prepare the plank! We need to get him off the ship at once!"

"I'm not sick, either!" Conner said. "Fine! If you don't believe me, I'll prove it!"

He walked around the circle of women and pointed at each pirate.

"That's Winking Wendy, Fish Lips Lucy, Somersault Sydney, Pancake-Face Patty, Stinky-Feet Phoebe, and that's Peg Leg Peggy," he said.

"I prefer *Margret*," said the pirate with the peg leg.

"Fine, *Margret*," Conner said and rolled his eyes. "In the back, that's High-Tide Tabitha, Catfish Kate, Too-Much-Rum Ronda, Big-Booty Bertha, Not-So-Jolly Joan, and up in the crow's nest, that's Siren Sue. Your captain is Auburn Sally, this ship is called the *Dolly Llama*, and you're all searching the Caribbean for buried treasure!"

Conner crossed his arms confidently and waited for their apologies. The pirates were startled by how much he knew. They all looked at their captain and waited to see how she would respond.

"There's only one explanation for how a young man we've never seen before could possibly know so much," Auburn Sally said. *"He's a warlock! Tie him and his sister up! We'll burn them at the stake on the next island we find!"*

Before they knew it, the twins' backpacks were yanked off and they were pushed against the main mast. The pirates wrapped ropes around their bodies, confining their torsos to the ship. Conner was so mad he turned bright red.

"Let us go or you'll be sorry!" he yelled. *"Just wait until I get home! I'm going to write a sequel where you all get shipwrecked and have to eat your boots to survive!"*

The pirates laughed at his attempts to scare them. Winking Wendy pulled the ropes even tighter just to spite him.

"Keep it up, Wendy! We'll see who's laughing when I have a seagull peck out your other eye!" Conner warned. "Alex, can you believe this?"

"How did you expect them to react?" she asked. "What would you do if a guy showed up out of nowhere and told us we were characters in *his* story?"

"I would punch him in the face for making everything so damn difficult!" he said. "Alex, you've got to do something! Zap them with a sleeping spell, turn them into sea horses—*anything!*"

"No!" Alex yelled. "I've been asking you for days if you needed any help planning, and you told me you had *everything under control*! Well, so far we almost drowned, we

narrowly missed being crushed by a ship, and now we're being captured by *your* pirates! You and I have different definitions of *under control!*"

"Alex, don't be a child!" Conner said.

"Grow up, Conner!" she said. "This is *your* mess—*you* clean it up!"

"Fine, I will!" he yelled. "I don't need you or your stupid magic! I'll find a way out of this myself!"

Although Alex and Conner were tied up right next to each other, they both pretended the other wasn't there and pouted in silence.

A strong ocean breeze began clearing the mist and uncovered the sun. Soon the ship had a breathtaking view of the ocean surrounding it. There was nothing to see but the bright blue Caribbean Sea for miles around them.

Captain Auburn Sally returned to the upper deck and wrapped her hands around the large helm. She looked out at the open water, and a radiant smile spread across her face. There was nothing keeping her back and no one to stop her; she was surrounded by an abundance of freedom and possibilities. Conner remembered writing about that expression—it was the expression he always wished the real Goldilocks could have more often.

"Once again, it's a beautiful day to be a pirate," Auburn Sally said to her crew. "Ladies, *lower the sales!*"

The twins looked up, expecting the sails above them to come down and fill with the ocean air. Instead, Siren Sue peeked out of the crow's nest with a treasure chest full of scarves, jewelry, hooks, and weapons. The other pirates gathered below her with hands full of gold coins.

"You heard the captain—time to lower the sales!" Siren Sue announced. "For a limited time, everything is half off! Scarves are two coins, earrings are four coins, necklaces are six coins, and the rifles are eight coins! Get your accessories while the sales are low!"

Siren Sue sold off the items to the pirates below until there was nothing left in her chest. The women ogled their new purchases and showed them off to one another. It absolutely baffled Alex, and when she glanced at Conner, he looked just as confused as she did.

"I don't understand what's happening," he said. "I never wrote *that*."

"Did you mean to write *lower the sails*? Like the *normal sails* on a ship?" Alex asked.

"Oops," Conner said. "I must have spelled it wrong."

To his relief, once the *sales* were over, the pirates lowered the *sails*, too. They were made from cream-colored cloth, the exact color of Porridge's coat. They filled with the ocean breeze, and the *Dolly Llama* sailed into the horizon.

Auburn Sally turned the ship's wheel back and forth as she guided her ship through the rough ocean waters. She kept a watchful eye on the entire horizon around them. The longer the ship sailed, the more a familiar expression grew on her face—one that the twins had seen Goldilocks wear many times when they'd first met her. The captain seemed a little sad, like she was hoping something would appear in the distance, but it never came.

Conner recognized this face, too, and suddenly became very worried.

"Oh no," he said. "We're getting close to the part of the story when the navy shows up."

"How can you tell?" Alex asked.

"From the way Auburn Sally is looking out over the ocean longingly," he said. "The pirates are about to get company."

Like clockwork, Siren Sue climbed down from the crow's nest in a panic.

"Captain!" she shouted. "Look, in the east! A ship from the British Navy is approaching!"

Auburn Sally quickly unfolded a long telescope and scanned the eastern horizon. Alex and Conner squinted their eyes and could barely see a small speck moving in the distance. The captain smiled as she spotted the ship—this was what she had been hoping for.

"It looks like Admiral Jacobson has finally caught up with us," Auburn Sally announced to her crew.

"Any orders, Captain?" Winking Wendy asked.

"I'm tired of playing the admiral's game of cat and mouse," the captain said. *"Hoist the sails and prepare for battle!"*

The pirates all saluted her and went to work right away. They loaded the cannons on deck and sharpened their swords. The sails were rolled up and the ship slowed down, allowing the admiral's ship to gain on them. The small speck the twins saw in the distance quickly grew into an enormous ship twice the size of the *Dolly Llama*. Soon they could make out a British flag waving from the tallest mast and the ship's name painted along its side: the *Royal Tantrum*.

While the pirates scurried around the deck preparing for battle, the captain gazed at herself in a compact mirror. Auburn Sally applied lipstick and blush, she brushed her hair to give it extra volume, and she wiped off all the smudges on her clothes. The captain wasn't getting ready for *combat*; she was getting ready for a *date*!

"That's how she prepares for battle?" Alex asked her brother.

Conner nodded bashfully. "Just wait," he said. "In about five minutes it's all going to make perfect sense."

When the *Royal Tantrum* was getting close to the *Dolly Llama*, the pirates dropped the sails and sailed around the navy ship. The twins could see that the *Royal Tantrum*'s lower deck was full of British sailors running amok. They spotted Admiral Jacobson standing on the upper deck.

The admiral was posed regally, with one foot on the railing and a long sword in his hand. He was a very handsome man with broad shoulders and pitch-black hair in a neat ponytail. He wore a big blue coat with several gold buttons and badges. The closer the pirate ship sailed around the navy ship, the more familiar he seemed.

"Conner, is it just me, or does the admiral look exactly like *Jack*?" Alex asked.

She glanced back and forth between the captain and the admiral. Just like her brother said, it all finally made sense.

"Oooooh," Alex said. "I get it now. Auburn Sally is based on *Goldilocks*, and the Admiral is based on *Jack*. 'Starboardia' is a love story! That's so sweet!"

Conner grunted like his sister had just insinuated something very crude.

"Excuse me," he said defensively. "'Starboardia' is a *pirate adventure*! It might have *elements* of love, but it is absolutely *not* a love story!"

Alex raised an eyebrow at him. "*Sure*," she said mockingly.

By now, the *Dolly Llama* was sailing around the *Royal Tantrum* with gusto. The British sailors ran back and forth across the deck to watch the pirates circling them. Winking Wendy took the wheel and Auburn Sally went to the railing to see the admiral. She mimicked his pose on the railing of her own ship, and the two commanders locked eyes. If Alex hadn't known there was something between them before, she definitely knew it now.

"Good afternoon, Admiral," Auburn Sally said. "What brings you to this part of the Caribbean today?"

"You're a wanted woman, Auburn Sally," the admiral said.

"You mean, by more than just you?" the captain said playfully. "Honestly, Admiral, you're so persistent, I'm starting to think you have a little crush on me."

The pirates roared with laughter. Even the navy soldiers were amused and covered their mouths to hide their chuckles. The whole scene felt like it should have happened in a high school hallway instead of the Caribbean Sea.

"The entire British Navy is just *smitten* with you, Captain," the admiral said. "They've asked me to personally escort you back to land. Come willingly and I won't sink your ship."

"Admiral, may I remind you I am *literally* sailing circles around you," she said. "It's *your* ship I'm worried about. I'd hate to destroy it and embarrass you in front of all your men. By the way, *nice tights, gentlemen!*"

"So it's going to be the hard way, is it?" Admiral Jacobson said with a grin.

Auburn Sally laughed. "Oh, Admiral," she said, "haven't you learned by now I'm the kind of girl who likes—"

"PLAYING HARD TO GET!" Conner yelled, finishing her sentence.

The captain and her crew quickly turned to him, wondering how on earth he knew exactly what she had been planning to say.

"I told you this is my story," Conner reminded them. "I wrote the cheesy dialogue coming out of your mouths! Would you quit the innuendos and just get to the battle already?"

Auburn Sally glared at him suspiciously for a moment, then turned to face the admiral again.

"I agree with the warlock," she said. *"Ladies, open fire!"*

As the *Dolly Llama* circled the *Royal Tantrum*, it was like the ships were joined together in a dangerous waltz and the pirates were taking the lead. They lit their cannons and fired them at the navy sailors, blasting large holes in the British ship. The admiral's sailors retaliated, but the pirate ship was much smaller and moving fast, making it a much harder target.

The few times the pirates were hit, the entire ship would rattle and sway in the water. But the damage the navy was inflicting was nothing compared to the mark the pirates were leaving. The sailors looked to the admiral for guidance, but he seldom gave them orders. It was almost like he *wanted* to lose.

Cannonballs and chunks of wood flew through the air. Parts of the navy ship were set ablaze and the sky filled with smoke. Conner had written the entire battle, but writing it was nothing like living it. Even though he knew exactly what was going to happen, it was still terrifying to see it come to life.

"This is the most dangerous flirting I've ever seen!" Alex said.

"Don't worry, the pirates win!" Conner said, then looked up at the captain. "Sally, would you hurry up and tell your pirates to aim for the navy's cannons already? I don't want to get splinters in my eyes!"

The thought had come into the captain's head just a moment before Conner suggested it. "How did you know I was—"

"JUST DO IT!" he yelled.

"Aim for their cannons, girls!" Auburn Sally ordered.

The pirates followed their captain's orders and aimed their cannons at the navy's. They blasted them off the ship, leaving the *Royal Tantrum* virtually defenseless. The pirates cheered and shook their swords at the sailors.

Winking Wendy jerked the wheel, and the *Dolly Llama* slammed into the *Royal Tantrum*, bringing the pirate ship alongside it.

"Now let's take their ship!" Auburn Sally ordered.

The pirates each grabbed a rope and swung aboard the navy ship. The battle continued with hand-to-hand combat on the decks of the *Royal Tantrum*. The sailors were barely trained for sailing and were no match for the pirates attacking them.

Winking Wendy flashed her empty eye socket at the sailors, scaring them and causing them to trip over themselves. Stinky-Feet Phoebe held her bare feet against their noses, and the fumes made the men temporarily lose consciousness. Having no legs made it easy for Somersault Sydney to tumble into the sailors and knock them down like bowling pins. Pancake-Face Patty seemed to enjoy head-butting the men, which explained the odd shape of her skull. Big-Booty Bertha simply turned her backside to any of the sailors charging toward her, and they bounced backward onto the deck.

Some of the pirates weren't as efficient fighters. Siren Sue sang high notes to hurt the sailors' ears. Fish Lips

Lucy irritated them with slobbery kisses. Too-Much-Rum Ronda drunkenly argued with the sailors about religion and politics. Not-So-Jolly Joan simply cried onto their shoulders. These pirates offered perfect distractions for Peg Leg Peggy (or "Margret") to sneak up behind the sailors and trip them with her wooden leg.

On the upper deck, Captain Auburn Sally and Admiral Jacobson walked around each other with their swords raised. They were so lost in each other's eyes that they almost forgot they had to fight each other to keep up appearances. When the two eventually started dueling, it resembled more of a passionate tango than an actual sword fight.

"This is the most nonviolent violence I've ever witnessed," Alex said.

"I kept it tame in case I had young readers," Conner said.

"That explains why the antagonists are so simple," she noted. "To be honest, I was really worried about what kind of villains your imagination would come up with. I'm glad they're just men in tights."

"The navy sailors aren't the bad guys in this story," he said. "The bad guys are *way* scarier. They're based on people I've seen in nightmares. But we'll be long gone before they show up . . . *I hope*."

Eventually, the sailors surrendered and the pirates rounded them up in the center of the *Royal Tantrum*'s lower deck. Auburn Sally pushed Admiral Jacobson off the upper deck, and his men caught him. The pirates raised their weapons in celebration—they had won the battle!

"You've lost, Admiral," Auburn Sally said. "The British Navy is going to be so disappointed."

"Sometimes a man fails in order to win," the admiral said with a smirk.

The navy sailors were stripped of their weapons, and their hands were tied behind their backs. The pirates placed a plank between ships and forced the sailors to cross it and board the *Dolly Llama*. Once everyone aboard the *Royal Tantrum* had been taken prisoner, the pirates blasted the navy ship with cannonballs until it sank.

"Put the prisoners in the cells belowdecks," Auburn Sally ordered and glanced at the twins. "And I mean *all* the prisoners."

The pirates sliced the ropes that tied the twins to the mast and pushed them along with the sailors.

"Oh no," Conner said. "The bad guys are going to show up soon! I've got to convince Auburn Sally I'm the author of this story before they get here!"

"I'm willing to help you if it speeds things up," Alex said with a sigh.

"Well, I'm not willing to accept your help yet," he said. "I told you I can take care of this on my own!"

Conner managed to push past the pirates manhandling him and his sister. He dashed across the deck, but just before he was a couple of feet away from Auburn Sally, he was tripped by Somersault Sydney and tackled by Catfish Kate and High-Tide Tabitha.

"Captain, don't lock us up!" he pleaded from underneath the pirates. "I'm warning you! Something really bad is about to happen, but you can avoid it if you just listen to me!"

Auburn Sally laughed at his warning. "Take him away," she said and turned her back on him.

The pirates forced Conner to his feet and dragged him away, but he wasn't ready to give up.

"I know what you stole from SMOKY SAILS SAM!" Conner yelled.

The entire ship suddenly froze as if he'd shouted something obscene. Alex could tell that all the pirates and sailors knew who her brother was talking about. Just the mention of the name Smoky Sails Sam sent a collective chill down their spines.

Auburn Sally turned back to Conner with large, fearful eyes. He continued his warning, desperate for her to listen to him.

"He knows what you stole from him, too—he knows about everything that happened on the island!" Conner said. "Smoky Sails Sam is looking for you and your crew right now! He's going to see the smoke from this battle and be here before sunrise!"

Conner knew that if anything would get through to her, this would be it. The captain looked him up and down but didn't say a word.

"Your orders, Captain?" Catfish Kate asked.

Auburn Sally put on a brave face for her crew. "Throw this boy and his sister in the cells with the others," she said. "If he has tall tales to tell, he can share them with the other prisoners."

Auburn Sally turned around and faced the ocean. Conner struggled against the pirates, but it was no use. They were too strong to break free from—that's how he had written them. Conner and Alex were pushed down the steps to the cells belowdecks with the sailors.

"Well, that *totally* worked," Alex said. "Are you sure you don't want my help?"

"Give it a minute," Conner said. "She'll come around—she'll have to."

The captain looked down at the burning wreckage of the *Royal Tantrum*, and her eyes followed the trails of smoke ascending into the sky. Once all the sailors and the twins were belowdecks and there were no pirates around to bear witness, she pulled out a necklace she kept hidden in her shirt. Dangling from a golden chain was a bloodred ruby the size of a human heart.

While she refused to believe everything Conner had said, she couldn't deny that he possessed extraordinary knowledge of her ship and crew. If what he said about Smoky Sails Sam was even remotely accurate, then the captain's greatest nightmare was about to come true....